First Edition March 2021

Copyright© 2021 Sarah Swan

Follow me on Twitter: @SarahSwanAuthor
Follow me on Facebook: @SarahSwanAuthor
Follow me on Instagram: @SarahSwanAuthor

Like the Down of a Thistle is a work of fiction. The Highland Clearances and Jacobite Rebellion, however, were very real. For the purpose of the story, I have made references to these and other historical events, but this has been done with artistic license and are used fictitiously. Other names, characters, places and events are products of the author's imagination, and any resemblance to actual events, places or persons, living or dead, is entirely coincidental.

LIKE THE DOWN OF A THISTLE

SARAH SWAN

Contents

Chapter One

ANNA

The rain lashed down across the grassy expanse of the Glenkeld Valley, warm enough not to be sleet but cold enough to penetrate to the bone. Having never left the Highlands, Florie, my seven-year-old daughter, seemed not to notice. She ran down the hill from our cottage in her bare feet, her dark blonde hair matted and plastered to her face. "I'll get them, Mam!" she called out, her voice barely audible over a loud crack of thunder which echoed off the side of the mountains.

I stood in the doorway of the longhouse and called out to her to return, but the child was already halfway down the hill and headed into the valley.

Berating her under my breath, I flung my cloak over my shoulders and pulled the hood down low before stepping into the storm. I hurriedly followed my daughter down into the valley, my flimsy leather shoes almost instantly filling with cold water as I squelched through the grass.

Even though I hurried, it took a good few minutes to catch up to the little girl. The sky lit up with a flash, which was immediately followed by another loud crack when Florie came into view again. Through the sideways rain, I could see her holding a stick and trying to persuade our flock of fourteen sodden sheep to venture back up the hill. She was struggling, and I regretted not moving the sheep into the barn before the weather had turned. Something about storms seemed to make the creatures more stupid and stubborn than they usually were. They were skittish - bleating and darting about aimlessly along the muddy bank of the river. Though if it wasn't for the river which carved its way through the valley, the sheep may have ventured much farther from home. I bent down to pick up a stick. It was a bit short, but it would have to do. Then I approached the flock from the opposite side to Florie and stretched my arms wide.

The river Domhainn had swollen and burst its banks, and the stupid creatures were sinking into the mud, dangerously close to the rushing water.

In the summer the valley was a beautiful, serene place where the river meandered peacefully the full six miles to Loch Drumfell. An image of myself, Florie, and my husband Robert all sitting in the sunshine briefly flashed through my mind, and my throat constricted as I considered how different life was now.

"They won't go back up, Mam," Florie shouted as I approached.

"We'll come at them from two sides," I shouted back. "You stay there. I'll stay on this side, and we'll force them back towards the house. When I say go, understand?"

She nodded vigorously.

Just then, the whinny of a horse sounded from upstream. On the track which ran alongside the river, I turned to see Artur approaching. He was a heavyset man I didn't know very well, in his late fifties with an impressive grey beard. I assumed he was headed back to the village from the lowland town, and he pulled his mount to a stop and called out to me.

"You alright there?" he said, squinting through the pelting rain.

"Ay, we're alright, thank you," I shouted back, hoping he would go on his way and leave us alone. My cloak was now saturated, and the cold was starting to numb my fingers.

"Would you like some help getting the sheep back up to the barn?" he said, preparing to dismount from his horse.

I knew he meant well, but he'd probably just get in the way and I was loath to put myself in a position where I might be indebted to him, even in the smallest way.

"No, honestly, we have it sorted, thank you. You can be on your way," I called back.

The man looked incredulously from me to Florie, then shook his head and rode on, muttering something under his breath.

Glad to be rid of him, I turned back to my daughter. "All right, let's get them back up," I said, swishing my stick. At the same time, Florie started waving her arms, trying to shoo the animals away from the river.

Another bolt of lightning and deafening crash, and three of the sheep next to Florie panicked and bolted, knocking her and sending her staggering backwards into the deeper mud. She managed to retain her upright position, using her stick to steady herself as she sunk down to her knees into the clay-like sludge. The three sheep that had broken from the flock were now labouring to free themselves from the shallow water of the riverbank, their legs sinking into the silt beneath. Their struggles were only leading them deeper into the water, and I screamed at Florie to stop as she turned and waded deeper into the swell, clutching onto the nearest one. The animal was still struggling, still trying to jump free, and was now dragging her further down the bank.

"Let it go!" I screamed at Florie, shoving the rest of the flock out of my way as I desperately scrambled to get to my daughter.

The water was swelling around Florie's skinny waist as she pulled at the sheep, trying to drag it back up the bank. A look of panic spread across her face as she struggled to pull her feet from the suction of the mud beneath her and the water rose to her chest. She let go of the sheep and splashed desperately with her arms as she tried to claw her way through the water, back up the slippery bank. The current was pulling at her now, and she struggled to fight against it.

"Help me, Mammy!" she called out.

The three renegade sheep were now bleating pitifully, their eyes wide, as they were sucked towards the middle of the river, but all I could focus on was reaching the small hands which now stretched out helplessly towards me.

Please dear God, not my child! Not her too!

I felt an instant surge of dread as I saw Florie's head disappear under the surface, just as I threw myself into the water after her.

The icy torrent stung every inch of my body as it swept me along, and I gasped, trying to keep my head above the surface and see across the chop. The rain still lashed down, making it difficult to see anything, and though both Florie and I could swim, we had never done so at this time of the year when the current was so powerful.

A few feet ahead, I caught a momentary glimpse of Florie's pale face and the waving of her arms as the child fought the surge. The heavy wool of my cloak and dress dragged me down and made my progress sluggish as I fiercely kicked my way towards Florie. I shouted my daughter's name, stretching out for her as she reached back. She was so close, our fingers brushed together, but then she went under again. I screamed her name and kicked harder, urging myself forwards as I swept my arms back and forth in front of me, feeling for the outstretched hands I knew were there.

Then I felt them. The little fingers gripped the sleeve of my dress and I felt for the tiny wrists, then pulled with all my might, drawing the child against me and sinking under the water myself as I tried to elevate Florie's head.

During the summer months, there was a game Robert always insisted we play. One of us would swim to the middle of the river and pretend to be in distress, then another would swim out to save them. It was just a game, but I knew Robert always liked to play it, in case an instance such as this ever came about. Whoever was doing the saving would have to float the victim on their back and use one hand to support their head and the other to swim to safety. I did this now with Florie, gripping her chin with my hand and paddling backwards.

"Florie, do like Daddy always showed us," I gasped, hoping the child would remember.

She did. Florie gripped my hand under her chin and kicked her legs, helping me as much as she could.

We were heading towards a bend in the river and I reached out for the muddy reeds as we were swept along. Most of the long grass slid through or came away in my hands, but I repeated the attempt until I had slowed us both to a stop and the swell of the water washed around us. My daughter had now swung around in front of me and I brought my hand down around Florie's chest so she wouldn't be swept away again, but I struggled to pull us up the bank. My feet found the bottom, but it was just as muddy and it served as no help for purchase or grounding. I began to panic, wondering how I would get both of us out of the river, when a length of fabric flopped into the water next to me.

"Grab hold!" a voice called out.

I was unable to see who had thrown the lifeline, but I grabbed the material and held on as it was pulled back up the bank.

Once Florie and I were back over the edge of the embankment and in the shallows where the river had overflowed, we both crawled through the thick mud, through the reeds and up onto the grass. Panting and gasping, I wrapped my arms around my daughter, squeezing her close.

After a few moments, I sat up and looked to see who had helped us. The rain had lightened a little but still drizzled around the soaking figure who stood next to her horse, now wringing out a dark woollen shawl.

I recognised her instantly as Katherine Scarth, the young woman who had recently married Ailig, who lived on the croft right next to mine. She slung the wet shawl over her horse and stepped forward, crouching down and holding out her hand to Florie.

"Are you two alright?" she asked, her green eyes wide with concern.

Florie took her hand, then stood up and nodded. Still somewhat out of breath and shaken from the ordeal, I got up and stood behind my daughter, putting a hand protectively on her shoulder.

"We are," I said. Then added, "Thank you for helping us."

I took Florie's hand, intending to walk back to our cottage.

"Can I take you home? We can all fit on Ailbeart," Katherine said, patting the neck of the stocky, brown Clydesdale.

My first instinct was to decline the offer, but feeling Florie's freezing fingers squeeze mine, I thought better of it. The child needed to be inside and in front of a fire as soon as possible.

"Thank you, that's very kind," I said.

The young woman smiled and helped me hoist Florie up onto the horse. The weight of my own sodden cloak and dress made it an effort to climb up behind her, but I felt the heel of Katherine's hand push up under my foot to help me, then she climbed up herself and trotted Ailbeart back up the valley to our longhouse.

Chapter Two

I carried Florie into the cottage and put her down on the woven mat in front of the hearth in the centre of the room. She was shivering uncontrollably, but I breathed a sigh of relief as soon as I saw the embers were still going strong. At least the fire wouldn't need to be re-lit. Katherine was hovering by the door, looking uncertain about whether or not to come in. I would have preferred her to just leave, since I could handle things on my own now, but I felt it would come across as ungrateful if I told her to go right after she'd dragged us out of the river and then delivered us home.

"You can put Ailbeart in the barn with Sim if you like," I said to her.

She smiled gratefully and went back outside to tend to her animal.

I deftly threw an extra chunk of peat onto the glowing embers and began stripping the saturated clothes from my daughter.

"Hands up," I said, a stiffness to my voice as I fought back the chatter of my teeth.

She did as I asked, and I pulled the soaking dress over her head. There was a blue tinge around her lips and eyes, and her chin quivered as she drew her arms around herself. When I got to the ties which secured the back of her petticoat, my stiff and shaking fingers struggled to undo the knots. I cursed silently before a gentle hand touched my arm and moved me to the side. I sat back, surprised, and watched as Katherine bent down and quickly untied the knots.

When she was done, she stepped away again. Then I pulled off Florie's undergarments. I moved her as close to the fire as I could, then hurried around the wicker partition at the back of the room to the little wooden bed and took the folded woollen blanket which lay upon it. It had been unused for months since Florie rarely slept in her own bed any more.

Not since November.

I unfolded it and wrapped it around her, rubbing her hair and drying it as much as I could.

"Let me do that," Katherine said. "You need to get yourself dry too." She nudged me to the side and took over drying Florie's hair.

Katherine was young, but I imagined she must have had younger siblings growing up, because she didn't seem to shy away from taking charge. If I hadn't been so cold and uncomfortable, I probably would have been irritated by her approach. Instead, I nodded gratefully, my teeth still chattering too hard to verbally respond. I began to shed my own clothes, which flopped heavily onto the woven mat which covered the packed dirt floor. But once I was down to my last undergarment, my white, muslin chemise, I hesitated, reluctant to bare myself in front of her. I edged up to the fire and held my shaking hands in front of the flames, which were now crackling away nicely again.

Katherine wrapped the blanket around Florie, then walked over to my bed and pulled off the top blanket which covered it. She brought it over, then held it open in front of me. I went to grab it, but she stepped back.

"You should take off all your wet clothes."

I hesitated, fixing her with a frown.

"You can't get dry unless you do," she added. "Being too cold for too long is a serious thing, trust me. I won't look."

As she said this, she modestly turned her head away, looking at something on the opposite wall.

Too cold to argue, I quickly pulled the chemise over my head and dropped it on the floor, then took the blanket from her outstretched arms and wrapped it around myself as I crouched in front of the fire with Florie.

"Thank you," I muttered.

"It's nothing," she said, looking back at me and smiling. "Neighbours should take care of each other."

I didn't acknowledge the comment. People were better off taking care of themselves. Help, kindness, favours; it all came at a cost. There was always something which was expected back in return, even if people didn't ask for it straight away.

Katherine walked around the room, picking up the wet clothes.

"You don't have to do that," I said. "You've done enough."

There was no reason for her to stay any longer, and I'd hoped she'd just leave now that Florie and I were warming up.

"It's no trouble," Katherine said cheerfully.

She took the clothes to the door and rung them outside, before bringing them back in, then pulled one of the three wooden chairs from next to the small table in the corner of the room and placed it next to me, in front of the fire. She laid my dress over the back of it, then brought over the other two chairs and did the same with Florie's clothes and our undergarments.

I felt obligated to get up to help her, but my joints were so stiff and I was still so cold I could do nothing except get my body as close to the flames as possible without setting fire to my blanket.

"There," Katherine said. "If you keep the fire going for the rest of the day and tonight, you might have dry clothes in the morning."

"Thank you," I repeated. Then, trying to sound a little friendlier, I added, "Those clothes were all in need of a wash, anyway."

Even Florie managed to crack a little smile as she sat huddled in her blanket, and it relieved me to see the blue was fading from around her lips. Katherine grinned too, then leaned over the fire and peered inside the cauldron, which was hooked on a long chain that hung down from the centre beam of the roof. It was never left empty and there was a small amount of water in the bottom which was steaming away.

"Do you have any tea?" she asked.

"There are some Centaury leaves in a bowl on the shelf there," I said, nodding her in the direction.

She bent down and scanned the little shelving unit until she found the bowl. Then she selected a few of the leaves, rubbed them together in her hands and then dropped them into the cauldron. She picked up the long wooden ladle which lay across the top of the cauldron and stirred the liquid in the bottom for a minute or two.

"I'm so sorry," she said, suddenly breaking the silence. "I've lived on the next croft over for four months now and I still don't know your name."

"It's Anna," I said. "Cumnock. And this is Florie. But don't apologise, we don't really leave the croft much these days."

She smiled uncomfortably, and I wondered if her husband had already told her about Robert. The only reason I knew Katherine's name was because Alis, my brother-in-law's wife, stopped in to check on us periodically. Whenever she did, she'd share brief updates about whatever was going on in the township.

"Well, I'm delighted to meet you both," she said, smiling.

She walked over to the bench at the end of the room and picked up two small mugs which were stacked at the back against the stone wall, then brought them back over to the cauldron. She ladled some tea into each and then passed one to Florie and the other to me.

"This should help warm you both up, but it doesn't have much medicinal value. Do you have any remedies?" She said, sitting down on the floor next to us.

I stared at the mug she'd handed me, noticing she'd picked up Robert's and given me that one.

"What?" I said.

"If you don't, I can bring some from my cottage. I have a herbal mixture my mother taught me to make. She was sort of a medicine woman in my village back home. It's very good for staving off fever. I could bring some for you. You mix it with warm mead and—"

"Thank you, but that isn't necessary," I said quickly, then took a sip of the hot, bitter liquid.

"Are you sure? It's no trouble. It might help your little one—"

"No really, we'll be fine," I insisted.

Katherine nodded and stared into the flames for a short while.

Then she got up and said, "I'll be right back," and she walked outside, closing the door behind her.

I sighed and shuffled myself closer to Florie before putting an arm around her.

"Are you alright?" I asked her.

She nodded back at me with her thin little face, gripping the mug of tea Katherine had given her with both hands.

"I'm alright, Mam. Don't worry yourself."

"Do you feel a fever starting? Because I can go and get some remedies. I don't mind."

"Really, Mam. I'm warming up and I feel alright."

I sighed again and squeezed her closer.

The reality of what nearly happened was sinking in and my chest constricted as I ran over in my mind what could have been; what nearly happened. Then my thoughts went to the sheep which were still in the valley. The storm had abated to a mild drizzle and the thunder had stopped, but I worried for the flock. I knew we had lost at least three. They would be swept all the way to Lock Drumfell and would drown long before they reached it. But I pushed that thought to the back of my mind and concentrated on the fact that it could have been far worse. My daughter was alive, I was alive, and those were the most important considerations. The sheep would be a problem for later. Now I just held my daughter close and thanked God he had taken the animals instead.

Florie rested her head on my shoulder, breathing calmly.

"That was nice of Katherine to help us like that, wasn't it, Mam?"

"It was," I said. Then, wanting to reassure my daughter, I added, "Even if she hadn't shown up, I still would have got you out of the river, you know. I would never let anything happen to you."

Florie nodded. "I know, Mam," she said. "But I still think that Katherine is very kind. I like her."

I looked at my daughter, and my heart swelled. I loved her so much. She was still so innocent and trusting. I wanted to tell her what the world was really like; that kindness doesn't come for free. The only person one can rely on is themselves. But then she'd been through enough trials already for her young age and somehow she hadn't let it change her. I tried to recall if I'd been like that once. Maybe I'd had too many knocks and now bore too many fractures and sharp edges. Florie wasn't like that yet and I didn't want to change her, but I also worried that the world would be cruel to her if she didn't harden up a bit.

I said none of this and instead just responded by saying, "I agree. She is very kind. But we still would have managed if she hadn't been there."

Florie sat and chewed her lip for a few seconds. "I just think..." then she trailed off.

"What do you think, sweetheart?" I said.

She hesitated a moment longer. "I just think we should have let Artur help us with the sheep."

She stiffened slightly as she said it, as if expecting me to get angry at the comment. Instead, though, I squeezed her again and rested my cheek on top of her head.

I was starting to wonder if Katherine had gone off to get the remedies she was talking about; she was gone so long. It annoyed me because I didn't have the money to pay for them and I was already indebted to her enough. Then the door opened and she came inside again, her red hair hanging damply on both sides of her face.

She smiled and breathed a cheerful sigh. "Phew. Well, I rounded up your sheep and got the ones I could find into the barn, just in case the weather turns bad again. So you don't have to go into the valley anymore today. You can stay warm until your clothes dry."

I got up stiffly from the floor and tucked a long chestnut strand of hair behind my ear. My hair usually didn't hang as low, but the water had temporarily extended the length, weighing down my loose locks.

"You've done too much already," I said, pulling the blanket tighter around my body. My bare leg was exposed for a second as I stood, and I didn't want to make her uncomfortable.

"Oh, it was nothing," she said. "I used the horse. It was quick. I counted eleven of them. Did I miss any?"

"It's the best I could have hoped for," I said. "Three were lost in the river. That's how we fell in."

Her brow furrowed in concern. "I'm so sorry," she said. "If you like, I can ride down river and see if—"

"No, you've already gone too far out of your way," I interjected. "They're gone. The current was too strong."

She nodded slowly, looking solemn. "Well, I better be going. Ailig will think I've got lost. He's waiting for some supplies I was collecting from the brewery."

Florie got to her feet and padded over to say goodbye. She still had her blanket wrapped around her and draped over her hair, and she peeked out, grinning at Katherine.

"Thank you for helping us today," I said.

She smiled again. It was a warm and attractive expression which I suddenly realised I liked, even if she was a bit bossy.

"It was my pleasure," she replied. "Like I said, we neighbours have to look after each other." After another moment, she added, "You know the menfolk are going away in a week. Raids on the McLean Clan and probably a battle. They're expected to be gone for two or three months this time, so we women will need to stick together."

She looked at Florie and winked, and Florie grinned back.

I returned a brief smile before she headed out, then I walked back to the fire and sat down again.

I knew it. Now she'll expect us to help her with her farm chores after her husband leaves. As if I don't have enough work already.

Chapter Three

O ver the next couple of days, I kept a close eye on Florie, and every little cough or sneeze brought me hurrying over to the child to check her forehead for the telltale warmth. My daughter is usually a patient child, but by the end of the first afternoon of my constant fussing over her health, she started to lose her patience. Pushing my hand from her head, she said, "I'm fine, Mam! I don't have the fever."

"Sorry, love. I just worry," I said.

We were outside, taking advantage of a short break in the rain, and I had fitted Sim with the harness and plough. Being April, it was a little early for tilling, but since we were a set of hands short this year, I made the decision to get a head start.

"Lead him on," I called to Florie, who held the reins.

I gripped the heavy plough handles with both hands and guided it as the large, black Clydesdale started forward. The field spread out before us, down the hill and into the valley, almost up to the track which ran parallel to the river. It was muddy, messy work, and we had tilled three rows up and down when Florie stopped the horse and I looked up to see the reason for the intermission.

I caught sight of the figure turn off the river track and ride slowly up the hill towards us, and even though my mind instantly knew who it was, my heart was always a little slower to tell the difference.

The jet black beard, the broad chest, the perfect riding posture. I could not stop the inevitable pounding of my heart, then the terrible sinking disappointment. It happened every time, and there was nothing in my power to stop it. I hoped that, with time, the effect would dissipate.

Faolan stopped his horse in front of us.

"Hello, Anna, Florie," he said, smiling cautiously.

His thick calves were bare and rested on either side of his steed under his dark green kilt, and I had to look away for a moment and swallow. He was the spitting image of his brother. He knew it too, and I was fairly certain it was one of the reasons he rarely came around anymore.

"What do you need, Faolan?" I asked, not looking at him.

"Do you think we might talk inside?" he said.

I would not look at his face, but pictured an expression I knew well. I could hear it in the tone of his voice; he was concerned about something. Whatever he came to talk to me about wasn't good.

Faolan sat down at the small table in the cottage, and after bidding Florie to go outside and play, I turned to look at him. His piercing blue eyes were wrought with worry and he clasped his hands together on the table in front of him. Another mannerism he shared with his brother.

"Anna, I wanted to come and talk to you about something I overheard at the tavern this morning." He cleared his throat, clearly trying to think of a way to lighten whatever blow was about to come.

I sat and resisted the urge to tell him to just get it over with and spit it out.

"Ailig Scarth was there, your neighbour, you know how he always starts early... Well, he was going on as he always does and usually most of us just ignore him, but today he was talking about you, so I listened. Sorry." He apologised and then continued. "He was ranting about you having his new wife running around after your sheep and he also said you drowned three of them."

I clenched my jaw but tried not to show any reaction.

He went on. "Frang was there too, and Ualan, and they were talking to Ailig about it. I did go over and I sat with them. I thought I could put in a good word, you know? No matter what had happened, I thought it would help if you had a representative in the conversation."

I was getting impatient now. "Where is this going, Faolan? Just tell me."

He rubbed his thumbs together uncomfortably. "Frang wanted to know more about the sheep, and Ailig said that you fell into the river trying to rescue some of them, but you ended up losing three. Frang then complained to Ualan. He said you can't manage now that you don't have..." He trailed off for a few moments and I took a slow breath in and waited for him to continue. "He said you can't run the farm on your own and it's too much for you. I spoke for you. I told them if any woman in the clan could manage, it was you, but Frang leaned hard on Ualan. He said if you have lost three sheep then you will fall short on your wool quota this year and that affects the prosperity of the township."

I was finding it difficult to control my anger now. Frang and his family produced the textiles for the clan. Some of the fabric they produced was used to fashion clothes for trade within the clan, but the majority of it was traded in the lowland town for things the clan needed; things we couldn't produce on our own. The iron for the ploughs, dyes, horses sometimes, blacksmith tools, and this year we were going to get a batch of new vegetables which we were going to start propagating. They called them 'potatoes.'

Faolan continued hesitantly. "Frang asked Ualan to transfer your lease to him."

"What?" I snapped, no longer able to keep quiet.

"He asked Ualan if he could take over your lease and join your croft to his. He said you and Florie could help his wife and daughters run the looms, keep house, and help with his younger grandchildren. And in return he will have his sons take over your crops and livestock. He said he will replace the three sheep you lost as part of your compensation."

I slammed my fists down on the table and stood up with such force my chair fell backwards and clattered on the ground.

"Oh, will he now? How damned considerate of him!"

"I spoke for you, Anna," Faolan said, also rising to his feet. "Ualan was going to agree, but I told him it wasn't fair to do that to you without giving you the chance to prove him wrong."

I was seething, but Faolan continued.

"I asked Ualan to at least give you until the autumn. That you should be allowed to keep your croft until it is proven fairly that you can't manage on your own."

I was breathing heavily now, fighting back the tears. How could they do this to me? To Florie? I'd worked this farm my entire married life and Robert had worked it since he was a boy. He was barely cold in his grave and Frang was using the first possible excuse to try and take it from my family. I didn't know what to say. I clenched my fists and shook my head, trying to calm my fury.

"You know we're leaving in a few days. We may not be back until the summer. Frang will be here, of course, but I got Ualan to agree to my suggestion. If you meet the usual quotas for wool and turnips, then you can continue to run the croft as you have been. Ualan agreed that ending your lease wouldn't be what Robert would have wanted for you and—"

"Don't you dare talk to me about Robert!" I suddenly shouted at him. "Ever!" The words were out before I could stop myself, but even as he stepped back, looking shocked and hurt, I felt my anger rising. Tears streamed down my face, but I stared hard at Faolan. I pierced him with a look brimming with all the anger and blame I could muster, because this new problem was his fault, too.

Faolan swallowed and shook his head slowly. "Anna, I—"

"Just don't," I cut him off again.

He stared at me pleadingly for a few more seconds, then sighed and walked to the door.

He opened it, then spoke again. "I'm riding to battle in a few days with the rest of the men, but my youngest son will be here if you need any help with anything. I really do hope you will ask if things get difficult. We're always here for you, Anna."

I sat back down and stared between my hands, refusing to answer him.

"I truly hope one day you will forgive me," he said.

I looked up at him again, through the blur of my tears. "I'll forgive you the day Robert walks back through that door," I said.

The hurt in his eyes was evident, but he nodded slowly, then left.

Chapter Four

After Faolan's visit, I no longer felt in the mood to till the farm; that job would have to wait. My mind was preoccupied with what I had learned. I hated Frang, who was a self-serving, greedy bastard, and I hated Ailig and his giant, drunken mouth, and I was angry with Katherine for telling him about what had happened. If she'd kept her mouth shut, I wouldn't be in this situation right now. Maybe. I sighed and ran my hands through my loose curls, racking my brain.

I now had eleven sheep. Some would be lambing soon, but lambs don't produce a full fleece in their first year, so that wouldn't help me this summer. Usually I would hope for three to six lambs and trade them for other supplies, but now we would have to keep them in order to replenish the flock. To make matters worse, when I'd let the flock out of the barn in the morning, I'd checked them and discovered that two of the ones we lost were ewes, one of which I was quite sure was pregnant. That was terrible luck as well. With three sheep gone, Florie and I were facing a deficit of three full fleeces, and at this point, I was at a loss as to how to fix that. I could leave the flock a few weeks longer, so their fleeces would be heavier. If I sheared them in late July or early August, instead of June, I would get eleven slightly heavier fleeces, which would count for something, but I would also risk the health of the animals who could overheat if the summer days got too hot. I would still be short, though, by a long way, and there was no guarantee that Ualan would allow the eleven larger fleeces to offset one or even half of a missing fleece. I also had no doubt that if I were even an ounce short, Frang would use it as an excuse to make trouble. The best possible fix was to find a way to get my hands on three sheep with their fleeces, or just the three fleeces on their own. It wouldn't be easy, and I had only one idea about how to achieve that. It wasn't ideal, but it would have to be done, and it might as well be done today.

With a heavy heart, I gathered what I needed and went outside to find Florie and prep the horse.

"Do you fancy a ride to the tavern?" I asked Florie.

She grinned and nodded enthusiastically. We only went into the village now if it was absolutely essential. I preferred to avoid the other clan folk who were mostly well meaning, but I'd grown tired of being asked how I was getting on without Robert.

With Florie holding onto my waist, we trotted down the hill from our cottage to the river track, which was still thick with mud from the night before, but at least the Domhainn wasn't overflowing anymore.

It was a forty-five minute ride along the track to the village of Glenbeag, which was about three miles from our croft. I would have preferred to go at a faster pace, but the mud was so thick, anything quicker than a walk would have caused bits to be kicked up and we would have been filthy by the time we arrived.

Florie was quiet as we travelled, but I could sense her excitement, even as she sat behind me. We hadn't done this in quite some time, and I could feel her shuffling as she strained to look for the village in the distance and kept peering around at the passing countryside. She seemed particularly alert while we were riding past Katherine's croft, and though she didn't say anything, I knew she was looking up towards her longhouse to try and spot her.

The Domhainn was just to our left, still wide and deep at this time of year, and to the north, on the other side of it, the barren, craggy Dombeinn mountain range, still topped with snow. There were crofts and longhouses on either side of the river, but the nearest crossing was next to the village at the Glenbeag bridge.

As we rode, I couldn't help looking along the banks of the river and thinking about my lost sheep. I'd been toying with the idea of riding back downstream to see if they had washed up anywhere, but had eventually decided against it. They almost certainly would have been carried all the way to the loch and even if I did find them, and even if I got the bodies home, it would be unlikely that the fleeces would still be in a condition good enough to sell or submit as part of my quota. I tried not to think about it anymore and turned my head in the other direction, looking up the other side of the valley to the south, the side our croft was on. This was definitely the better, more sought after side of the river, and the crofts on the south side of the valley were considered much more desirable. The main reason for this was because the range of hills behind us were not as high and served as better pasture for the sheep to graze on. Back when the run rig system was still in place, it was normal for families to have to swap between farming the fields on either side of the Domhainn every two or three years, and when the long-term leases of the crofts were finally introduced, there was a lot of bad feeling and quarrels over who should get which parcels of land.

As we gained elevation and got closer to the village, our croft and Katherine's croft had shrunk in the distance behind us. Glenbeag appeared ahead and was situated on the south side of the river. The village was a collection of small cottages and a handful of other buildings from which local businesses were run. There was a blacksmith, a mill, a trading post which wasn't usually active at this time of the year, a tavern and a wheelwright. The village lacked a church, and the cottages were occupied by folk who were employed in industries other than farming, such as weavers, fishermen, and mill workers. The chief didn't live in this village and was situated further upriver in a nearby township within the McGowen Clan territory, but his son, Ualan, lived not far from our croft and oversaw the running of the Glenbeag township.

We finally approached the tavern, which lay at the edge of the village and was by far the biggest building in Glenbeag, as well as the busiest. There were a couple of horses hitched to the post outside, and after dismounting and lifting Florie down, I slung Sim's rein over it and left him with the other animals. Then I took Florie's hand, and we entered the building through the small wooden door at the front.

The tavern was large, open, and warm. There were several hearths spaced throughout the centre of the massive room, with two fires burning and the sound of laughter, chatter and drinking filled the space. Men and women sat around on benches at the many tables and a few children played on the floor, which was spread with fresh hay. Florie ran off instantly to join in with one of the groups and I was pleased she would be distracted while I conducted my business.

There was a cauldron simmering over each of the two fires and the smell of mutton brought back memories of occasions where we took our meals here with Robert. Florie and I hadn't had any meat in several months now, our diet currently consisting mostly of eggs and broses. The bland diet of barley and oats made me very tempted to order a bowl of the meaty stew, but that wasn't why I'd come. I looked around the room for the man I wanted to see, hoping he would be here.

It was then that I noticed Katherine, sitting at a table with her husband Ailig and another man. I had half a mind to march over and confront both of them about the trouble they had caused, but something stopped me. Katherine looked quite different from a couple of days ago when I'd last seen her. Nothing like the cheerful, bossy, young woman I was familiar with; she sat hunched over at the table, staring blankly at a mug in front of her. Her red hair was untidy and hung down over the sides of her face, but did little to cover the dark purple bruise across her right cheek, or the puffy split in her bottom lip. My anger towards her ebbed a little, and I glared at Ailig. I knew he was a drunk, but he'd barely been married five months and if he'd started on Katherine this soon, it didn't bode well for her. His last wife had died a little under a year ago, and while the clan chalked up the death to a tooth infection, I had always believed the unrelenting beatings Ailig used to give out were a major contributor to her early demise. It made me angry that Ualan would interfere with the running of my croft, but when it came to protecting the vulnerable members of the clan, he and his father did nothing.

I continued to rove around the room until I spotted the man I wanted to see. He was seated at the other end of the room by the wall and, fortunately, was drinking alone.

I strode over to his table.

"Can I sit?" I asked.

He frowned at me, but nodded.

I sat down across from him with my back to the room and tried to speak as quietly as I could while still allowing myself to be heard over the thrum of noise.

"I would like to do some business with you," I said. Then I pulled an object wrapped in a scrap of cloth from my pocket and placed it in the centre of the table.

Daniel sat up straighter and looked at it curiously. I folded back the cloth and revealed a beautiful, silver, annular brooch. It had been handed down through my family from my great grandmother and was a treasured possession. All around the ring were delicate engravings of thistles, and I knew it was quite valuable. I had always planned on giving it to Florie one day, and it strained my heart to lay it on the table now as a bartering chip.

Daniel picked it up in his big hands and looked it over. "What do you want for it?" he said gruffly.

"I don't want to trade it," I said. "I just want to use it as collateral for a loan."

He looked at me but kept his face neutral, so I couldn't tell if he was open to the idea or not.

"I need four sheep," I went on. "With their fleeces."

He cracked a huge grin under his wispy, greying beard, then bellowed in laughter. "Hah, you have to be joking. Four sheep?"

I sat resolutely, not impressed by his outburst.

When he had finished and looked at my face, he quickly became more serious. "Sorry, lass. The brooch is nice, but it's not worth four sheep. It's not even worth four fleeces."

"What is it worth then?" I asked.

"Well, I could give you one ram for it, with the fleece on. Or possibly two small fleeces, but not the animals."

The fact that he had offered a less valuable ram for the loan did not escape my notice. "That brooch has been in my family for generations," I said. "It's silver. It has to be worth more than that."

"Sentimental value is not tradable," he said, leaning back and picking up his mug of mead. "One ram is all I can offer you for it and that's me being generous because I'm aware of your situation."

More like taking advantage because he knows my situation, I thought.

I ran through the options in my head for a few moments.

"One sheep," I said. "Then you will return the brooch when I replace the sheep next season?"

"You're forgetting about interest," he said. "One sheep and one large fleece next year."

"That's outrageous!" I said, raising my voice.

"It's business," he said, giving me a hard stare from under his bushy eyebrows.

"I thought you said you were going to be generous?" I said.

He shrugged, then slowly leaned forwards. He looked straight at me as he stretched his arm out over the surface of the table, then ran a rough finger across the back of my hand. "Well, there are other things you could barter which I'm partial to."

I pulled my hand back quickly and stood up. "One sheep for the brooch," I hissed. "One sheep and one fleece next year to buy it back."

He leaned back in his chair again, pursed his lips and then nodded. "I'll have my son bring the sheep down to your croft tomorrow morning," he said, picking up the brooch.

It took everything I had not to grab his mug of mead and throw it in his face. I turned away, feeling sick, then almost bumped into Katherine, who had been standing right behind me.

"Sorry, Anna," she said as I recoiled.

Close up, her face looked even worse. It was the only thing which stopped me from accosting her over her loose tongue.

"I couldn't help overhearing," she said.

"No, I suppose not when you stand right over me like that," I snapped.

She looked down for a moment, as if embarrassed.

I felt a twinge of guilt for speaking so harshly and then said, "Sorry, it's been a difficult day."

"I know," she said, looking up again. Her big green eyes were tired and sad, and the cut on her lip distorted the face that had been so beautiful less than three days ago. She stood slightly hunched and clutched her abdomen as she spoke.

"I'm so sorry. That's partly my fault. I really didn't mean to—"

"It's done," I said shortly. "It doesn't matter."

"It does to me. I feel terrible. It's costing you so much." Her eyes trailed behind me to the table where Daniel was still turning the brooch over in his fingers.

"Don't let it worry you," I said, walking past her and heading for Florie.

As soon as the child looked up and saw Katherine behind me, she broke into a wide smile, then leapt up and ran forward to say hello. Then she noticed Katherine's face and stopped short, her smile instantly replaced by a look of innocent concern.

"What happened to your face?" she asked.

Katherine walked up behind me and stooped a little to address Florie. "Oh, I was so silly," she said, smiling. It looked like it hurt her lip to do it. "I wasn't very careful when I was stacking some logs and a few of them fell on top of me."

Florie gasped and reached out to take Katherine's hand. "Did it hurt?" she asked.

"A little bit," Katherine said, taking Florie's hand and squeezing it. "But I'm alright. It's getting better."

"We need to go home now, Florie," I said gently, and put a hand on her shoulder.

I wanted to be cross with Katherine, but the longer I looked at her face, the harder that was getting. Katherine stood up straight again and gave me another apologetic smile. I lifted the corner of my mouth in an attempt to return the gesture, then turned and led Florie back outside to the horse.

I let Sim take us home at his own pace, and he plodded along as I stared blankly ahead. My mind was busy running back through the day. I tried to push thoughts of Katherine to the back of my mind and focus on the problems that lay before me. I now had twelve sheep, but I needed at least two more good sized fleeces and I had no idea how I was going to manage that before the autumn.

Chapter Five

After a couple of days, I still hadn't come up with a solution to my problem. I tossed a bucket of slops into the trough in the pigpen and headed back around the side of the building to the barn which formed the north gable end of our longhouse. After mucking out Sim's stall, I pushed the wooden wheelbarrow back outside and was about to go around the back of the barn to check the roosting boxes for fresh eggs, when my eyes were drawn to Florie. She was standing next to the sheep shelter, a hundred yards across from the house, chatting animatedly to another figure.

As I quickly hurried over, I realised it was Katherine, who waved at me as I approached. The bruising on her face had lightened somewhat to a yellowish-green colour, and her eyes had more life in them.

"Look, Mammy, Katherine's here," Florie piped delightedly.

"Good morning, Anna," Katherine said, smiling.

"Hello," I replied as I reached them. I looked questioningly at Katherine.

"Err, I just came over to say hello to Florie and to ask if you needed any help with your chores this morning?"

"No, thank you," I said. "We can manage."

"Oh, I know," she said quickly. "I just thought it would be nice to have a bit of company. Ailig's at the tavern and I'm ahead on my chores, so maybe I could be of some use here? I also had some ideas I wanted to talk to you about, Anna."

I couldn't fail to notice that some of the cheerful bossiness had returned to Katherine's demeanour and wondered if it had anything to do with the fact that Ailig would be leaving very soon.

Florie looked from Katherine to me with a hopeful expression.

"Aren't you supposed to be taking water to the barn?" I said to Florie.

"But, Mam, I was just—"

"Now, please," I said, adding an edge of sternness to my voice.

The little girl huffed, then scampered off, clearly determined to finish the chore as fast as possible so she could get back to Katherine.

"She's such a bonnie lass," Katherine said, smiling as she watched Florie go. But as soon as the child was out of earshot, she immediately turned back to me with an enthusiastic grin. She seemed intent on me hearing what she had to say, whether I wanted to or not.

"I had an idea about how we could meet that quota," she said, still beaming.

"We?" I said. "There is no 'we.' This is not your problem."

Katherine looked at me, her expression changing from excited to pleading. "Please, I feel responsible. If I hadn't said anything, then this wouldn't have happened."

"You're right," I replied gruffly.

"I didn't mean to cause you trouble. I thought Ailig might be able to do something to help. He knows Ualan and—"

"It sounds like you don't know your husband very well," I sniffed curtly.

Katherine looked like she was about to say something, but then stopped and looked down.

I instantly regretted my words. I knew she hadn't intended to cause harm, but I also thought she was far too naïve. She would need to harden up quickly or she wouldn't survive with Ailig for very long.

"Look," I said, attempting to make my words more gentle. "I know you want to help, but there really isn't anything you can do. I'll sort something out; I always do. This isn't your problem and I have no doubt you have enough of your own to deal with."

I couldn't help looking at her bruised cheek and split lip as I said the last part.

She lifted her chin higher, defiantly. "I think you should stop being so stubborn and hear me out," she said.

I sighed and folded my arms, resigning myself to at least pretend to give her idea some consideration.

"I think we should combine our crofts—"

I made to cut in, but she held up her hands, wanting me to wait until she finished.

"—just for this season," she said. "We can combine our livestock and care for them together. Larger flocks do better anyway, and it will be easier to keep an eye on them if they graze together. I have extra turnip seeds which I brought with me from my father's bumper crop last year. If we combine our seeds and plant one big crop across our crofts, then we can tend to it together. It will be more efficient and we'll get more produce. When we harvest in September, we'll split the produce fifty-fifty."

"And how will Ailig feel about you sharing the produce of your extra seeds with me?" I asked, feeling silly for even listening to this plan which already was exhibiting significant flaws as far as I could see.

"He doesn't have to know," Katherine said. "He didn't really pay attention when my father told him about the seeds. He was drunk and he won't be here when they are sewn, so he won't know that we had more than you."

"And what do you get out of this, then?" I asked. "Why would you give me those seeds?"

"Well, I thought it might be a way I could help make things up to you," she said. Then when she saw me starting to shake my head she quickly added, "We'll call it a trade."

I scoffed. There was no way I was going to go ahead with this plan of hers. "I have nothing I can trade you for them," I said impatiently.

"You have the horse-drawn plough," she said.

I was about to laugh at her and tell her there was no way I was going to trade that for a few seeds when she cut in again before I could speak.

"I just want to share it this season, that's all."

I looked at her suspiciously, but she continued.

"If we plant one big crop, as I suggested, then we can plough and till it together, using your plough. All I have is the caschron, the hand plough, and it takes a lot of effort and a great deal of time to get anything done with that. If we use your horse plough to do all of it, that helps me immensely. Really, I'd be getting the better deal," she added, grinning. "Also, I've calculated that if we can increase the yield by fifteen percent, which we should be able to with the extra seeds, you'll have enough surplus turnips that you can trade for a full fleece, and if you're short, I'll make up the extra."

She was grinning widely now, seemingly sure she was going to convince me.

"Ailig also put an order in for a bag of those new vegetables. The potatoes. Apparently they are easy to grow and propagate, so we can see what we can do with those as well."

I was in a mild state of shock. Why had she put so much thought into this?

"Why would you help me so much?" I asked.

"I told you, it helps me. I do not want to plough my entire croft with the caschron by myself. If we use the horse plough, it will save me a huge amount of time."

"You know as well as I do, you can hire a plough from a number of people in the village and it would cost you less than what you're offering me right now," I said, still not believing her.

"But I don't want to hire one from someone else. I want to hire yours," she said. "I also think it would benefit both of us if we worked together. It can get lonely, working by one's self all day. I know you have Florie, but I'd be so grateful for the company."

I stood in silence, mulling it over in my head. I hated being indebted to anyone, and any deal I made with Katherine would also be with Ailig, and that wasn't attractive to me.

"You would be helping me too," she said quietly, as if she knew what I was thinking. "I've never run a farm by myself before, and if I don't do a satisfactory job, Ailig will be angry when he gets back. I really think we could help each other."

My thoughts were cut short by Florie, who came skipping back to us.

"I did it, Mam!" she announced, cheerfully.

"You put a full bucket in the water trough?" I asked.

She nodded gleefully.

"You didn't spill half of it on the way?"

She shook her head. "Can I show Katherine my chickens now?" she asked.

I nodded, then glanced at Katherine, who still had an anxious look on her face.

"I'll think about it," I said to her as I turned to fetch the wheelbarrow.

Chapter Six

I hadn't known Katherine very long, but since my first real interaction with her less than a week ago, I now decided I had her sussed. She had a good heart; she was kind, and she clearly loved children. But the biggest trait which stood out to me now and which I wasn't sure if I liked or not, was her unrelenting persistence. Katherine didn't know how to give up. When I wouldn't give her an answer two days ago, she came over again the following day and then again today. She didn't bring up her proposal any more and, in fact, mostly ignored me, insisting the purpose of her visits were to see Florie, who in turn was not shy about showing her delight. This morning she was met with a huge hug from my daughter, who after a few moments, came running over to me squealing excitedly. She was waving a small doll over her head, made from wool and straw. Two large wooden buttons had been sewn into the head as eyes, and the little face seemed to stare at me imploringly as Florie waved it in front of my face.

"Look Mammy! Look what Katherine made for me," she enthused.

"That's lovely, Sweetheart," I said. I could see Katherine hanging back, smiling and shrugging her shoulders.

"Wasn't that kind of Katherine?" Florie said, her voice still high with excitement.

"It was, it was very kind of her," I agreed, pushing the doll down from in front of my nose. "Did you thank her?"

Florie nodded, then skipped off back to Katherine and gave her another hug.

The young woman never stayed very long. She just seemed to stop by in the morning, then hurry away after twenty minutes or so. I expected she needed to get back to her husband, who might not appreciate her leaving her own farm every day to come and spend time on ours. I had plans this morning but took my time prepping Sim and let Florie enjoy her visit with her new best friend. I knew Florie would have loved a brother or a sister and one of my biggest regrets was not being able to give her one. When I gave birth to her, it was very touch and go for both of us. The birth was incredibly difficult and neither of us were expected to live at first. Florie was so small and I lost a great deal of blood. I always believed something inside me was damaged after that, because I was never able to conceive again. Katherine looked like she was only about eighteen or nineteen, probably about the same age as I was when I had Florie, so if she wanted to play big sister to my daughter, I wasn't going to interfere.

After Katherine said goodbye to Florie, I called the child over, lifted her onto Sim and set off along the track towards the village.

Ualan lived about two miles away, his croft being closer to Glenbeag and about triple the size of everyone else's. There were a handful of people in the village who he employed as labourers on his land and because he lived so close, he was frequently in the village conducting some business or other.

If he wasn't at home, I would have to continue on to the tavern and try to find him there. I didn't like the idea of venturing into the village twice in one week, but it was times like this when I was especially grateful for having Sim. Owning a horse was certainly not the norm, and many of the people in the township had to get by without one. They were valuable assets, and Robert had brought Sim back from a raid nearly four years ago. I had known better than to ask him about the details of the acquisition. Robert never enjoyed the raids and after returning from the only two I'd known him to go on, he was quiet and suffered from nightmares for weeks after. Sim was his pride and joy, however, and he spent a lot of time with the horse when he was alive.

When we neared the outskirts of the village, I steered Sim off the main river track, down a smaller road which ran for about three quarters of a mile to a large longhouse which sat surrounded by multiple large pastures and tilled fields. Smoke billowed from two chimneys and a mouthwatering smell emanated from the building. I dismounted, then got Florie to jump down to me before tethering the horse to the post next to the water trough.

Then, taking my daughter's hand, I approached the front door and banged on it with my fist.

After a few seconds, the door was opened by a tall woman with dark hair, a thin face and high cheekbones, who was wiping her hands on her apron.

A look of surprise crossed her face when she saw me, then she said, "Anna? I haven't seen you in a long while. What can I do for you?"

"Good morning, Agatha," I said, forcing a smile. "I came to see Ualan. Does he have a few minutes to speak with me?"

Agatha seemed less surprised by my statement. She smiled and nodded. "Of course."

She opened the door wide and stepped back to let me enter.

I stepped into the house, pulling Florie alongside me, then waited for Agatha to close the door. Like all longhouses, the inside of the building was very open, with the hearth featuring at the centre. A very large cauldron hung above the roaring fire, suspended by an impressively thick chain which was fixed to a beam in the roof, and a hearty stew, responsible for the smell I'd got whiff of outside, was bubbling away inside it. There were several large wicker partitions set up along the sides of the room, cordoning off other sections of the building as private sleeping rooms for different members of the family. I would have loved to see what was hidden behind them, but I figured even if I did, it would lead to unnecessary envy and I was better off remaining ignorant. Since there was only one fire which I could see in the main room, I assumed there had to be another hearth in one of the bedrooms as well, and almost the entire floor was covered in intricate woven mats, making the place feel very cosy. The shutters on the windows were professionally carved with beautiful designs, and there were several sets of cupboards and shelves lining the back wall.

I could see Ualan sitting at a large table at the other end of the room with his two young sons. Agatha went over to him and spoke softly in his ear, while I waited by the door with Florie clutching my hand. Ualan nodded, then turned to me and waved me over.

Agatha tapped the two boys on their shoulders and gestured for them to follow her, then she stopped in front of Florie. "Come. You can play with my boys," she said. Florie hesitantly let go of my hand and followed them to a corner of the room in front of one of the partitions where there were several soft sheepskins on the floor and a number of small wooden toys scattered about.

I walked over to the table where Ualan was now sitting alone, and after he indicated towards a chair, I sat down to face him. The chair had a soft, straw-filled cushion on the seat, which was far more comfortable than the hard surfaces I was used to, and as I settled into it I looked up at the tacksman.

Ualan had dark hair which was cut shorter than was typical and greying at the temples. He was about Robert's age, with dark eyes, in his early thirties, clean shaven, and tall like his wife.

"Hello, Anna," he said. "I have to admit, I was expecting a visit from you."

"Then you must know why I've come," I said, keeping my voice low so Florie wouldn't hear the conversation.

"Your lease," he said. It wasn't a question.

I nodded. "I want you to rescind what you said to Frang," I said. "It's wholly unfair. This is my first year without Robert, and I stand to lose the lease over a few fleeces. You could show some compassion."

I realised I was coming across rather aggressively and made a mental note to try and tone it down the next time I spoke.

"Anna, I have shown compassion by giving you until the autumn to prove you can run the croft on your own," he said. "I was under a lot of pressure to transfer the lease now to avoid the potential of a poor yield."

Forgetting what I had just told myself, I balled my hands into fists and leaned forwards, hissing, "Well, I am truly humbled that you were benevolent enough to at least give me the chance to fail miserably."

He sighed and looked away for a moment. "I'm sorry, my hands are tied, Anna. We are all under pressure lately. There's the stress of this raid looming. If it isn't successful, we all stand to lose a great deal. There's mounting pressure from my father, who himself is at the mercy of the crown. Every year, it seems another of our allies or neighbouring clans are cleared out to the coast. If the township isn't productive enough, we will all end up farming kelp, and no one wants that. I therefore can't be lenient on anyone. Every single crofter in this community must be productive and meet the minimum quota. I can't give you special treatment, Anna. I'm sorry."

He leaned back in his chair and rubbed his eyes. He looked stressed and tired.

"But why Frang? Why him? He's been after my husband's lease for years - you're well aware of that."

"What difference does it make, Anna? Would it make you happier if someone else took over your croft?"

"If I had to lose it, then yes, actually," I said, stubbornly.

"Frang has a large extended family living with him and his croft is on the other side of yours. It makes sense that it be him."

"What about Ailig?" I asked, thinking about Katherine. I silently chided myself and pushed her out of my thoughts.

"Anna, you know as well as I do that Ailig is a good soldier, but he's a useless crofter. He barely meets quota every year, and to be honest, I have more faith that you will do a better job than him as far as production."

"You flatter me," I said dryly.

"I will not be giving him an extra croft, let's put it that way," he said. "In fact Ailig himself is in danger of losing his lease this year if he doesn't shape up."

This comment surprised me. Ailig was a lazy, drunken sod, but I had no idea he was struggling with his farm.

"Maybe his new wife will help matters," Ualan added. "She's young and strong and the extra pair of hands this year might be what he needs."

Among other things, I thought.

"So that's it then?" I asked. "If I'm short on the wool, then I lose my farm and my seven-year-old daughter and I are out on the street?"

Ualan frowned and leaned forward again, shaking his head. "No, Anna. Of course not. Frang has offered to let you stay in your cottage. I thought you knew that. All you and Florie have to do is work in the textiles with his wife and daughters. You would be looked after."

"By Frang?" I scoffed. "I can already picture what our lives would be like under him. I'd rather go to the kelp farms."

Ualan shook his head wearily. "There's nothing else I can say, Anna. It's been decided. Meet your quota of wool and turnips and you can maintain your lease. Otherwise, Frang takes over in October."

❧❧❧❧❧ ❧❧❧❧❧

I left Ualan's house feeling discouraged, but not defeated. I didn't agree with his decision, but I could understand why he felt he needed to make it. The highland clearances were an ongoing stress to all the clans and weighed heavily on the chiefs and tacksmen. More and more townships across the land were being completely uprooted to make space for larger flocks of sheep. I'd heard that many of the farmers and their families were migrating to the lowland cities, and some were even sailing abroad to start again in new lands.

The kelp industry on the coast always had employment, and there were even villages built specifically for the highlanders who worked there, but it was spoken about with disdain. No one wanted to leave the lives we had here, and I felt as strongly about that as anyone else.

The thought of Florie and I being under Frang's control for the rest of our lives, however, felt worse to me. He would revel in the power he had over us, of that I had no doubt. He was older, fifty-five, and he had a hobbled leg, so he couldn't go to battle with the other men, so his presence in the village was constant.

Frang had been after Robert's croft for years. Robert had once told me that Frang had even had a duel with his father over it. At the time, the run rig system was being substituted for the crofts. When Robert's father Tiobaid was a boy, the land which each family farmed would swap after every year or two, and a lottery system would determine which families were assigned which plots for the term. That system was later replaced by the fixed tenancy crofts and both Tiobaid and Frang had wanted the same plot of land. An agreement could not be reached, and it ended in a duel to determine who would take the lease. Robert had been a baby at the time, but he said his father had won the duel and Frang had hated Tiobaid ever since.

That hatred had passed down to Robert, and Frang never had anything friendly to say to me or Florie, so I assumed he harboured the same distaste towards us too. Still, I couldn't rule out the chance he could be reasoned with until I spoke to him directly, so that's what I decided to do.

After leaving Ualan's house, I didn't want to waste any time. Once Florie and I were back on the horse, I pushed Sim into a fast walk back in the direction of home.

After we passed Katherine's croft, then ours, we continued further down the river track and towards the loch, in the direction of Frang's house, which was half a mile from ours. Frang was technically our neighbour, but fortunately there was a much bigger gap between us and him than there was between us and Katherine, with a large pasture separating our properties.

The sky was heavy with grey clouds and a light drizzle had started up since we left Ualan's. As we turned off the river track onto Frang's property, we could see our longhouse in the distance to the left. I realised this conversation might not be as civil as the one I'd just shared with Ualan and abruptly pulled the horse to a stop before we got to the cottage where Frang lived. I told Florie she could just run across the pasture and go home by herself, which she seemed quite eager to do.

"Go straight home, alright? Nowhere else!" I called to her as she scampered off.

She yelled something back which I didn't catch but hoped was an acknowledgement of my instructions. She was headed directly for our cottage, so I tried not to worry as I walked the horse on again to the central courtyard of Frang's residence.

There were multiple buildings on Frang's property. Some were dwellings for his extended family, and I knew he had at least two sons who lived here with their own families and children. There was also the warehouse with looms for the textiles, two storage sheds, and two large shelters for the sheep, as well as various smaller buildings such as wood sheds, a covered well, and a tool shed for his farming equipment.

I had no doubt part of the reason why Frang wanted my croft so badly was so he could spread his family out a bit and reclaim some space back. Even if he meant what he said about letting us keep our cottage, I could just imagine another longhouse or two being built right next to us for another set of his in-laws or grandchildren to move into. We would have no space to call our own anymore.

Frang's flock of sheep was at least three times the size of mine and were currently scattered across the pasture at the base of the hills to the south. Overall, his family was probably the most wealthy in the township after Ualan, though that wealth was clearly spread between a large number of them.

I dismounted and hitched Sim to a long post, which stood next to the biggest longhouse I knew was Frang's.

Before I could get to the door, it opened, and Frang stepped outside. He was dressed in a loose white shirt which exposed the grey hairs on his chest and a long great kilt displaying his family tartan. It was certainly not legal attire, but then Frang didn't seem to care much about the new laws.

Our clan had not been involved in the Jacobite Rebellion, which had happened a few years ago, and at the time, the clan chief had called a big meeting to discuss whether or not our clan should support Charles Stuart and join in with the movement. Had it been up to Frang, we would have. He was very vocal about joining in at the time, something which didn't go down well with some other men who were angered by the fact that Frang himself would not be fighting because of his leg. When the rebellion was later crushed and the clans who were involved lost many of their men, Frang made himself less popular by blaming certain members of the township for being cowards and not fighting. Unfortunately, even though he wasn't liked much within the clan, his family had a monopoly on one of the biggest industries of the surrounding area and he could get away with a lot.

Frang didn't invite me in out of the rain and instead limped over to confront me in the courtyard.

He had a polished wooden staff which he leant heavily on and I couldn't help being slightly pleased that he appeared to be in pain. I expected his leg was getting stiffer in his advancing age.

He stopped a few feet in front of me and twisted his stick into the mud and leaned on it.

He scratched his scruffy white beard and said, "What do you want, Anna? I don't suppose you've come here because you've come to your senses?"

"I wanted to speak with you about my lease," I said.

His lips curled into a smug grin and he twisted his hands over the top of his staff again. "I don't think there is anything to talk about," he said. "Did Faolan not pass on what Ualan said?"

"He did," I said. "I just wanted to see if you and I could come to an agreement between ourselves."

He gave a short chuckle but said nothing.

"I thought, perhaps, you might agree to loan me two fleeces this year and I could repay it next year with three."

As I finished my sentence, I knew I was wasting my time. If anything, I was just feeding his sense of victory.

"Anna, if you can't make the quota this year, why do you think you will be able to next year?"

"I lost three sheep last week. It was a very unlucky, unforeseen event. I plan to keep all the new lambs this season so I will have a full flock again next year. You don't have to worry about that."

"Unless, of course, another unlucky, unforeseen event happens between now and then," he smirked.

"Please, can you not just be reasonable? That farm is our home, Frang. Whatever your grievances were with Robert and his father, don't let that spill onto me and Florie. My daughter is an innocent child who—"

"Who has the blood of that bastard running through her veins, and she bears his name," he growled. "That croft should have been mine years ago and it would have been if Tiobaid had fought with honour. I've waited patiently for thirty years to claim it and now that it's within my grasp, what makes you think I would do anything to hinder that victory?"

"And what about us?" I said, getting angry. "Florie and I have done you no wrong."

He took a few long breaths, and his lips curled into a hateful leer. "I would have preferred to inflict some form of revenge on Tiobaid himself, but like his son, he put himself in an early grave, and I never found the chance." He spoke quietly and now looked down at his bad knee. "This leg has been a curse in many ways, but I do believe the limitations it forced on me have prolonged my life. And now I'm thankful it has allowed me to live long enough to see at least one of Tiobaid's descendants pay for what he did."

I gritted my teeth and glared back at him. I'd always thought of Frang as a miserable grump who didn't get along with many people, but I'd never considered that he might be truly wicked. It wasn't until this moment that I realised how strong the grudge he held against my family was, or how much he looked forward not only to taking the croft but seeing what was left of Robert's family suffer. It seemed both events promised equal gratification to him.

"Hear this, Frang," I said. "I will find a way to make the quota, one way or another; of that you can be certain. The croft will never be yours as long as I'm breathing, and I can't wait to watch as the victory you think you've won, flitters away with the autumn wind, leaving nothing but a bitter defeat and another chip on your shoulder."

Now he lifted his staff and stepped towards me, pointing the top of it at my face. I knew he wanted to hit me, but I stood my ground and met his stare with equal force.

"You are a foolish wench," he snarled. "You will regret your words. In October, when you lose your farm, and mark my words, you will lose it, I will have no mercy on you or your little brat. I would have let you stay in your cottage and given you employment in my business, but now you will be given no quarter. I'll burn your house down myself and you can watch me do it before you are both packed off to a stinking kelp farm on the coast."

He lowered his staff again but stood in front of me, breathing deeply, leering at me with unadulterated hate. I held my ground but said nothing to antagonise him further.

"Now get off my property, and don't set foot on it again," he said. Then he turned and limped back to his house, slamming the door behind him.

As I led Sim over the fields towards my own cottage, I tried to calm my burning anger. Matters were no better, and I had to concede that the plan to talk to Frang had not been a good one. I shouldn't have provoked him, but then I'd always hated the idea of working for him, and now knowing how much he wanted to see us suffer, I decided that option would have been disastrous, anyway. The one thing I could take away from that exchange was the new knowledge that Frang wanted to hurt us, and if he got our lease, he'd find a way to do it one way or another. Whether he let us stay in our cottage, had us move onto his property, or kicked us out completely, he had plans to make our lives miserable, and now that I knew that, it reinforced my determination not to let him win.

Chapter Seven

T he following day Katherine showed up as usual, and Florie, who had been clutching her doll and waiting for her by the stone wall at the edge of our field, ran over to greet her.

Katherine seemed even more buoyant and cheerful than the previous few days, and Ailig's departure clearly had a lot to do with that. The men had left early this morning and Florie and I had watched a long line of them marching along the river track, past our croft, towards the lock. They would be turning off before they reached it and joining up with other allied units as they made their way south, and it would probably be at least a month before they made it to their destination. Our clan didn't participate in a great number of raids, but every few years it seemed the majority of the men grew restless and another was planned.

Long-standing enemy clans were usually targeted, and for as long as I was aware, our clan had always come off well. Raids were a way for the chief and the clan to replenish wealth and riches, but it came at the cost of the devastation of other towns and villages across the land. In an effort to reduce the chances of being attacked ourselves, our clan was always careful to travel far afield for our raids. This avoided upsetting the neighbouring clans, who would be more likely to join forces and retaliate against us, and the strategy seemed to have worked well over the last few generations. Our clan had been widely successful and had grown prosperous because of it, but the tradition never sat comfortably with me. For Katherine, however, it would be a time when she could look forward to a long break from Ailig.

For the rest of the day, I watched as Florie dragged Katherine around the farm, showing off her favourite animals and demonstrating how she did her chores. Katherine didn't leave after the first twenty minutes like she usually did and I guessed it was because she now didn't have anyone to get back to. I didn't blame her as I could imagine how lonely it would get in the cottage on her own, especially if she was used to living with her family before she married Ailig. Though, given the choice between living alone or living with him, I was fairly sure I knew what Katherine would have preferred.

Over the course of the day, I couldn't help but smile a little and admire Katherine's patience. Even when the rain started, she stayed outside and showed Florie how to mend the little dry stone wall that partitioned our yard from the turnip field. As on the previous two days, Katherine did not attempt to approach me or talk to me, and as the afternoon wore on, I began to feel a bit lonely myself. Usually Florie would stick near to me and help me with my tasks in between completing her own chores, and this was the first time I could remember spending most of the day working in silence, other than the one or two occasions when Florie called over to me and gleefully announced that she and Katherine had finished a particular job in record time.

When it came time to eat, I called Florie inside.

"Florie, it's time for supper. Come on," I called out.

I looked on as Florie gave Katherine a hug, and Katherine bent down to say something to her. Then Florie came skipping across the grass towards the house and Katherine walked towards the barn to retrieve Ailbeart.

After a moment's hesitation, I called out to Katherine. "You can join us if you like."

She stopped and looked back at me, then walked over.

"I don't want to impose," she said.

"You've just spent the entire day working on our croft. It's the least I can do," I said, opening the cottage door and gesturing for her to come in. "Besides," I added, "there was something I wanted to talk to you about."

The smile on Katherine's face was instant, and she hurried inside without waiting for further invitation.

I divided up the broses into three wooden bowls, swallowing a lump in my throat as I wiped away the thick layer of dust which had accumulated on the third. I put it in front of Katherine, who ran a delicate finger over the carvings around the edge.

"It's beautiful," she said.

"Yes. Robert had a lot of talents," I said, putting Florie's bowl in front of her. Then I sat down at the table with my own.

Katherine stirred the porridge uncomfortably before lifting the spoon to her lips and taking a mouthful.

I made to break the silence. "Thank you for today," I said, slowly.

"It was nothing," Katherine said. "I wish I could do more."

I knew she meant it, and I let another moment of silence pass before I spoke.

"What you said to me the other day, is that definitely what you want?"

"It's what I need, Anna," she said. "I don't want to spend the season struggling on my own. I'm not as strong as you."

Something told me Katherine was strong enough to handle almost anything, but I just nodded in response. "Well, I guess we'll see you here tomorrow, then," I said, taking a spoonful of my food.

I wasn't able to get it past my lips before Katherine reached forwards, grabbed my other hand and squeezed it between both of hers. "Thank you, thank you, Anna. You won't be sorry, I promise. We'll make this work together. All of us," she added, reaching out for Florie's hand as well.

Chapter Eight

The late April rain drizzled down lightly as Katherine and I stood with our backs to the river and looked up towards our homesteads. My croft was a long, narrow strip which ran from behind my house to the edge of the river track where we were now standing. Katherine's was wider but didn't run back as far, and her house sat slightly further down the valley.

Our strips were side by side, which made it easy to plant one large field of turnips, but because Katherine's croft was wider, it meant more than half of the crop would have to be planted on her side. The potatoes were to be planted on Katherine's side too, in a small plot we planned to till, just where the turnip field ended.

Florie walked along the river bank, ripping up bits of long grass and throwing them in the water as Katherine laid out her plans for me.

"So, I've placed a pile of big stones on that side of the field as a marker," Katherine said, pointing to a small mound in the distance. "And the same on that side," she said, pointing again. "If we make the plot this wide and then all the way up to the markers up the hill, I think that should be big enough."

I held Sim's reins in one hand as I surveyed the proposed plot for our joint turnip crop.

"Are you sure we'll have enough seeds to sew a field this size?" I asked, a little dubiously.

"I told you, I have extra from last year," she said. "I've also marked out a smaller plot on the other side of my cottage for the oats, and then in the walled garden we can plant the beans, peas, onions and cabbages. I know you have your own patches at your cottage for those, but I'm happy to help there too."

"There's no need," I said. "We can manage our own oats and vegetable patch."

Katherine nodded, then smiled. Florie took my free hand and the three of us started walking back up the hill towards my cottage.

"I stopped at the village earlier today," Katherine said. "I got a mutton head, so we can have some stew later if you want."

Florie squeezed my hand and suddenly started bouncing on her toes excitedly.

I sighed. "You really don't have to feed us."

"I got it with you and Florie in mind," she said.

I hesitated. I didn't want this thing we were doing to become more than a temporary business arrangement. I wasn't interested in becoming best friends, or spending every other evening at each other's cottages, but the sound of mutton stew, and Florie's less than subtle gestures of excitement, forced my hand on this occasion.

"Alright, thank you," I said. "But this can't be a frequent occurrence. I don't feel right taking your food. You're helping us enough already."

The rest of the morning was spent with Katherine enthusiastically explaining how we should arrange the fields, when each crop should be planted and laying out a schedule of tasks which would need to be done to achieve the most effective results. As we walked back up the hill to my cottage, she started talking about the possibility of penning our pigs together in the hopes that they might breed. That conversation quickly became humorous when we realised both of our pigs were female, and Katherine had a lot to say on that subject, it seemed.

"Well, they might like to live together, anyway. We can always rent a boar for a month or two and then send him back after he's done his job. Personally, I think that's how it should be with people. Women should live together and just bring in a man as and when necessary."

I had to laugh, but I could understand where she was coming from. "Not all men are like Ailig, you know," I said, as we got back to the yard outside my cottage.

"I know that. But I still think women are more fun and they get along better together. They help each other, don't go off to the tavern every night, they take turns with the cooking and this year you'll see we don't even need a man to pull in a great harvest, either."

I smiled again. "I definitely see the logic in what you're saying. In fact, in some ways, I agree. I certainly couldn't see myself living with another man again. Not after Robert."

She looked at me quizzically. "Really? Why's that? How old are you?"

"I'm twenty-six," I said. "But, I don't know. When Robert and I were first married, I didn't love him. It was an arrangement between our families. He was always a good man, but I wasn't happy with the union at all and I didn't want to be married. Eventually, though, I did fall in love with him and he gave me Florie, so I have no regrets at all."

"So what will you do once Florie gets married herself and leaves?"

The very thought of it made my stomach twist into a knot. "I don't know," I said. "I guess I haven't really thought that far ahead."

"It would be lonely by yourself and there are far more widows available for companionship than widowers."

"I suppose you're right," I said. "I guess I just imagined it would always just be Florie and me. Seems silly now."

"Well, sometimes when the future is scary or uncertain, it's easier to just not think about it," Katherine said matter-of-factly

"Dangerous though," I said. "I'm afraid I find myself constantly thinking about what it would mean for us if we lost our croft."

She smiled. "You don't have to worry about that. You'll see. We'll make sure you meet your quota. And who knows?" she said, playfully nudging my shoulder with hers. "Maybe Ailig will get maimed or killed in this raid and the two of us can keep each other company and run our crofts together for the rest of our days."

She said it jokingly, but I knew some part of her really did wish it would happen. At least the part about Ailig.

Katherine didn't let the problem of the two female pigs deter her and soon became serious again and went on to contemplate how we might get a male pig, which we could share for breeding purposes.

"You're very organised and ambitious," I said, once I could get a word in edgeways again. "If I didn't know better, I'd think you'd been planning this all winter."

Katherine laughed. "My father used to do something similar with our neighbour. I have firsthand experience with this system and it always yielded great results."

"Huh," I said, surprised. "Why didn't you tell me that before?"

She shrugged. "I guess I didn't think it would make a difference. You come across as a bit, you know, standoffish, and I thought the main reason you didn't want to work together was because you wanted to be left alone."

"Hmph," I sniffed. I suppose it was an accurate hypothesis. "I'm surprised you didn't mention the idea to Ailig." I almost went on to mention how he had been struggling with his farm, but thought better of it.

"Oh, that would be a complete waste of time," she said.

I had taken Sim's bridle off and pushed him back into the pasture. We were now walking through the bee skeps towards Katherine's croft.

"When I first left my home to come here and be Ailig's wife, he made it very clear that things would be completely different to what I was used to. He's so stubborn, he would never agree to the idea of me implementing a strategy which came from my clan, even if it was a good one. So I kept quiet about it. But perhaps when he gets back and see's for himself how well it works, he'll be more open to the idea," she said. Though there wasn't much conviction in her tone.

"What a pig. Why on Earth did you marry him?" I asked.

"He wasn't my first choice, believe me," she said. "My father had some debts and Ailig offered a reasonable dowry. I wasn't really given a say."

"I'm sorry,"

She shrugged. "That's life. It could have been worse."

Now that we had marked out where the turnips would be planted, we planned to start ploughing the field the following day, ready for sowing. As Katherine had suggested, I agreed to combine our flock of sheep. We left them to graze on the hillside together and agreed to encourage them all to sleep under the shelter on my croft when needed, rather than try to separate them again every night.

"I think this is going to work out really well," Katherine said cheerily, as we swept out Ailbeart's stable together. "It's too bad we both only have the one stable," she added. "Otherwise, we could have brought the horses together. It would have made for just one building to muck out every day and it would have been company for Ailbeart too, isn't that right Ailbeart?" she said, reaching over and stroking his nose.

"Mmm," I mumbled. I was starting to think Katherine was becoming a bit too comfortable with our arrangement and all this talk about moving our pigs and horses in together felt like it was pushing the boundaries a little. But then, she did have a point. It was a pain to muck out two stables every day, even if the job was done faster with two of us. I picked up the shovel and began putting the manure into the wheelbarrow when Katherine started talking again.

"I was thinking," she said, resting on her broom for a minute. "I'll give you one of our lambs when it's born. As long as it's weaned before Ailig returns. He can't know."

This took me aback. "You can't do that," I said, stopping shovelling. "You're helping me enough as it is. I'm not taking one of your lambs."

"Ailig's lambs," she said, winking. "And you will take one. His plans for our lambs are to trade them for gin from the brewery near the lowland town. Fewer lambs means less gin, and I'm sure I don't have to tell you how I'd feel about that." She smiled. "Think of it as doing me another favour."

"You have some strange ideas about what constitutes a favour," I said.

She picked up her broom and started sweeping again. "Well, if you think about it, Ailig is responsible for your predicament. It would be a good way for him to make it up to you."

"He probably knows how many lambs your flock is expecting and he'd kill you if he found out. I wouldn't bet on my own chances either," I said.

"He won't know," she insisted. "If he says anything, I'll tell him one of them didn't survive."

She stopped sweeping for a second. "It happens. Sometimes babies die." Then she looked back at me and gave a feeble smile.

I sighed. "Alright, but only if it can be done without him knowing and as long as you can afford it."

"Good, that settles it then," she said, looking bright again.

I decided this definitely had to be the last thing I accepted from Katherine. It was only the first full day I had spent working with her and she had already got me to tell her several intimate details about myself and I'd agreed to share a meal with her for the second time in forty-eight hours. As much as I didn't want another person in my life who I'd inevitably have to worry about, she was rapidly growing on me. I had never been one for making lots of friends, and most of the acquaintances I did have, I'd shut out after Robert died. It hadn't bothered me to lose those contacts, and I'd never been good at making new ones, but Katherine was different. She had a spirit I couldn't help but admire and I had a feeling she'd set her heart on us being friends.

Chapter Nine

O ver the following four weeks, up to the last week of May, Katherine, Florie, and I worked together every day.

Using the horse-drawn plough, we were able to get the entire double field ploughed and sown with the turnip seeds within ten days, and I had to admit, the work went much faster with Katherine helping. It would have taken me just as long, if not longer, to plant my own single crop if it had just been me and Florie. Katherine and I took turns leading the horse and guiding the plough, and when the person on the plough tired, it was just a matter of switching places. I could see why Katherine was so anxious to have someone to work with.

In addition, it was nice to have another adult to talk to during the day. Since Robert died, I'd got used to being reclusive, and I'd forgotten how refreshing it was to have someone besides a seven-year-old to talk to. There were frequent jobs which Katherine and I did separately. Sometimes Florie would help Katherine, sometimes she would help me, and sometimes all three of us focused on our individual jobs, but even with one extra person to communicate with every day, there was a sense of community which I realised I had been missing for many months.

As much as I had first wanted to keep the arrangement purely professional and maintain an emotional distance to Katherine, it had now become routine for the three of us to take our meals together. At first it was just suppers we shared. After the first day when Katherine shared her muttonhead stew, I had felt obliged to return the gesture the following night, and we had broses at my cottage. Then Katherine brought over a rabbit she had snared the following day, and from there the precedent was set. Lately, at Florie's insistence, we had also started sharing breakfast, and I was now so used to having Katherine around, I looked forward to her arrival each day.

The sheep took very fondly to being combined into one large flock, and it occurred to me that even after harvest, it may be difficult to keep them separated in the future. I had a feeling they would seek each other out and flock together, given the chance, but that would have to be dealt with when the time came. There had already been four lambs born in the last couple of weeks, two from my flock of twelve and two from Katherine's flock of fifteen. This delighted Florie, who looked forward to lambing every year, but so far all of the births had happened when we were asleep or not around. Florie was a little disappointed. The process fascinated her, and she desperately wanted to watch them be born.

"Can't we keep one of the ewes who haven't given birth yet in the barn?" she asked one day. "Then I could keep checking on it and I might get to watch."

"That wouldn't be very fair on the mother," I replied. "Sheep like to be together and they like to be outside. Locking up the mother for possibly weeks on end would put stress on her and we can't afford to have anything go wrong with the births. Not to mention feeding and mucking her out. We don't have the time to babysit one sheep."

She sighed, but accepted my explanation.

"Anyway, there are still three ewes in our flock who are pregnant and four more in Katherine's flock, so the chances are good that you'll get to see at least one of them give birth," I said, trying to encourage her.

The potatoes were next to be planted. They arrived in the village in mid-May and Katherine went to the tavern to pick up the sack which Ailig had reserved. I should have arranged for my own sack and regretted not having done so, but at the time the orders were taken, Robert had just died, and many of the things I should have done were neglected. When Katherine returned with the large sack, she opened it excitedly.

"Look at these," she said, pulling one out and holding it up for me to see.

I took it from her and turned it over in my hand. "I wonder what they taste like," I said, sniffing it, then running my fingers over the little tendrils sprouting from around it. It smelled earthy, similar to a turnip, but not as strong.

She took it back from me and examined the yellowish-brown tuba herself. "I don't know. This is the first time I've seen one. Apparently you can eat them like this, though I was told not to eat any green parts. If we eat any of these, though, we'll have less to plant, so we should probably be patient and wait for the first harvest. We'll never need to trade for these again, you know. One potato can be put in the ground and more will grow from it, so we should have more and more each year."

I smiled. Katherine was always so enthusiastic about everything and it was reassuring to hear her talk about the future like she did. She always seemed so sure that things would work out. Often, I thought she was leaving herself far too open to disappointment, but sometimes, like today, I was grateful for her unrelenting positivity, which was energising.

It took us two days to plough the potato patch and then plant them. Katherine acted as foreman, telling me and Florie that potatoes had to be grown in a particular way, but not to worry because she would teach both of us exactly what she had been told. The oats were planted separately, one crop on my croft and Katherine's on hers, as were the vegetable patches. The planting was all completed so quickly, we had more time to devote to other chores. The fence around the pigpen, which was falling into disrepair, was mended, and three more roosting boxes were built for the chickens. As June began, I felt this planting season had gone better than any I could ever remember. There was more time for rest, more time for meals, and gradually the stress of the looming autumn faded as I realised I would be able to make quota and potentially have some surplus as well.

It was the first day of June and we sat together around the table, eating the pease stew after a long day. Katherine had gone into the village earlier and come back with news from the raids. The men had reached the borders of the McLean Clan lands and the armies of several allied clans were in the process of assembling. So far, there had been no casualties, and the news was good. Though, when Katherine recounted it, she didn't seem particularly thrilled to inform us that Ailig was alive and healthy. She was specific in telling me that Faolan and his two elder sons were also fit and well, but I gave a bland response. Sensing my discomfort at the topic of my brother-in-law, she quickly moved on.

"Well, I think tomorrow I should go and see Mary about borrowing a boar for a month," she said. She had brought her own bowl from home, which now stayed at our cottage, and she now scooped a spoonful of pea slop into it. "I'm sure she wouldn't mind lending him out for a few weeks in return for a few of the piglets when they're born."

"That's a good idea," I said. "It needs to be done soon, though. I don't want to end up with the sow and a pile of piglets in my barn at the end of the autumn if they're born too late."

"Understood," she said, grinning. "I'll go tomorrow and see what I can do."

"Do you need me to come with you when you go?" I asked.

"No, no, that's alright. It's just a dumb boar and I've dealt with enough pigs in my life to know how to manage one on my own."

She grinned at the double entendre, and I couldn't stifle a small chuckle. Now that her face was completely healed, and I got to see her up close every day, I began to appreciate how attractive she really was. I couldn't decide if it was her deep green eyes, or her vibrant red hair which was her most striking feature, but overall I wondered how a man like Ailig had managed to find himself such an attractive wife. Moreover, I wondered why he didn't appreciate what he had and why he kept hitting her. It would make sense for any man to want to preserve a face so lovely, as it was a symbol of status to have a beautiful wife. But then, Ailig never struck me as the sort of man to make sensible choices. Since he'd been gone, though, a new life shone from Katherine, and I had to push the thoughts of his return to the back of my mind and remind myself that my time, and possibly friendship with Katherine, could only be temporary.

Later that night, I lay in bed with Florie, cuddling her.

"Katherine is clever, isn't she, Mammy?" she said, softly.

"She is," I said, running my fingers through her hair. "She has lots of good ideas."

We lay in silence for a while. The room was still quite light, the daylight hours now stretching much longer into the evenings. Sometimes it made it harder to fall asleep.

"I'm glad I fell in the river," she went on. "Even if we lost those sheep."

I knew why she felt that way, but I humoured her and asked anyway. "Why is that, my love?"

"Because if I didn't fall in the river, then we might not have made friends with Katherine," she said.

"Ay, that's true," I said. "Katherine is kind, and she's helped us a lot. She's helping us to keep our farm."

"And that makes you happy?" she said.

"Of course. Doesn't it make you happy? You don't want to leave our home, do you?"

"No. I'm happy here," she said, squeezing my hand. "But you weren't happy before and now you are."

"Well, I'm happy because we'll be able to get enough wool to satisfy the quota and we might even have extra turnips too."

Florie was quiet for a few seconds. "I think Katherine makes you happy," she whispered.

I wasn't quite sure how to respond to this. "Well, yes, that too," I said. "She's a good friend."

"You were sad before. Even before the sheep fell in the river."

"I was sad because I miss Daddy," I said.

"Do you still miss him?" she asked.

"Of course I do. I'll always miss him."

"Me too," she sighed. "But I don't think Daddy would mind," she added, yawning.

"What wouldn't Daddy mind?" I asked.

"That you're happy again," she said. And still holding my hand, she closed her eyes and turned over.

Chapter Ten

Katherine was late arriving the following day. She missed breakfast, much to Florie's disappointment, and I was behind the cottage collecting eggs when I finally caught sight of her approaching. She held a long tether in her hand and was making slow progress, coaxing along a large boar which didn't seem keen on the long walk.

I waved to signal that I'd seen her, and she waved back before pulling on the tether again, trying to drag the reluctant creature forwards. I grabbed the last of the eggs and carried them into the cottage in my apron, before running across the pasture to help her.

"You got the boar," I gasped, a little out of breath.

"Ay," she grunted, heaving on the tether. "He's ours until July. Though he won't be much good unless we can get his lazy rear end into the pen!" She pulled again, and the animal took a single lazy step forward.

I couldn't help but giggle. "Are you sure he's up for it? I mean, if he can't find the energy to walk a couple of miles, I wouldn't hold out much hope for his stamina in the pen."

She huffed and let slack into the tether, putting her hands on her hips. "It's not funny," she said. "I've been up since the early hours and it's taken me all morning to get him this far. Just getting him over the bridge was a nightmare!"

I sniggered again. "What was it you said yesterday about being able to handle one dumb pig by yourself?"

She narrowed her eyes at me, clearly not appreciating the humour in the situation anymore. "Well, this is a particularly stubborn one," she said, yanking on the tether again.

"Oh, those are the worst kind," I said in mock sympathy.

"I'm sure, once he has proper motivation, he'll perform just fine," she puffed, heaving repeatedly on the tether as she spoke. She managed to move the pig another two feet forward before it grunted and stopped again. "Mary says he was lent just three months ago to Caitlin and her sow is due any day." She dropped the tether again and crouched down, trying to catch her breath.

"Hmm, well maybe we just need to find the right motivation to get him to walk faster," I suggested.

"I'm open to all ideas," she sighed, wiping her arm across her brow.

Five minutes later and I had run back to the cottage and grabbed a turnip from the pit larder. Florie came running up as I grappled with the fence of the pigpen.

"What are you doing, Mam?" she asked.

"Katherine has got a boar, but we're having some trouble getting him to the pen. We thought if he sees the sow, he might get a move on," I said.

"Oh, can I help?" she asked.

"No, lass, you stay here. The pigs are big and we don't know how they'll act when they're brought together, so it's better if you're out of the way, just to be safe."

She grumbled at this and walked around to the other side of the cottage. I assumed she wanted to watch the action, even if she couldn't be part of it.

I eased open the gate of the pen, held out the turnip and made cooing noises to try and tempt the sow. My feet squelched in the thick mud and I stopped, just two paces in, not wanting to go any further if I could avoid it. The sow had been lying at the back of the pen, looking disinterested, but now stood up and lumbered towards me. I rarely ever took her out, and it was usually Robert who dealt with her in the past, but she had never been too difficult to manage as far as I could remember.

I held onto the turnip and backed up, letting her follow me out, then turned and walked slowly between the bee skeps, towards the pasture where Katherine was still trying to shift the boar. The turnip was working, and she was following and keeping up. If the male walked this quickly, then we'd have them both in the pen in no time. The sow continued to snort and follow me as I made my way back towards Katherine, and when we were about a hundred yards away, there was a sudden change in the boar's temperament, which was clear even from a distance. He started to move forward and Katherine grinned and began leading him once more. Once they were properly under way, I stopped and walked around in a circle to come behind the sow, coaxing her to turn around and head back towards the pen. I could see the male getting closer. He'd picked up his pace and was now moving with purpose, and Katherine was briskly walking next to him, looking very pleased.

"Come on, come on," I said, urging the sow to hurry up. Ideally, I wanted her back in the pen before the boar caught up to us. The fastest route was to cut between the skeps again, the way we'd come, so I held out the turnip and walked backwards, calling to the sow. However, she was taking her time now and clearly catching on that the food was a tease. She was also distracted by the male who she was watching approach. Now, rather than pulling the boar to make him hurry up, Katherine was pulling against the tether to slow him down, but he yanked her along like she was a mere annoyance and was set on his goal.

They were now only twenty feet away, and in a desperate move to get the sow to go back to the pen, I threw the turnip on the ground ahead of her, ran behind her and pushed against her rear, trying to guide her back.

She walked as far as the turnip, but then stopped in between the skeps and started munching on it. The boar came up behind, still towing a red faced Katherine, and I jumped out of the way as he snorted and nuzzled the sow's backside.

"No, no, that way!" I shouted, trying to herd both of them towards the pen.

Florie ran towards us, calling out, "Do you need help, Mam?"

"No! Stay back, Florie!" I shouted.

Both Katherine and I were pushing the pigs, both of which took little notice. The boar was now sniffing along the sow's side and she didn't appear to be impressed by his curiosity. She grunted and stepped away from him, but the male was persistent. He grunted and followed her, still nuzzling along the length of her body.

"Go round the other side of her," I told Katherine. "We need to push them towards the pen."

Katherine ran between the skeps and stretched her arms out, trying to block the path of the female who was heading off in the wrong direction. It seemed she was getting frustrated with the male's attention and turned herself around to face him, knocking one of the skeps in the process. A loud buzzing sound erupted from the skep as the bees began to vacate.

In another desperate effort, I bent over and shoved the full weight of my body behind the sow, pushing her a few steps in the right direction, towards her pen. The boar came back around and brushed up against her again, nuzzling at her face, and she grunted and pushed back at him. She pushed forward to get past him, but as he turned himself to follow her, he knocked against the stand of another skep, this time with enough force to knock it down.

I cursed, and both Katherine and I ran forward at the same time to pick it up and place it back on the stand.

Too late.

The hum grew louder all around us as the swarm erupted from the small opening at the bottom of the skep and the angry residents surrounded us. The buzz served as the necessary motivation for both pigs and the sow trotted back towards her pen, closely followed by the unrelenting boar.

I felt the first sting on the back of my arm as I shouted to Katherine. "Come on! Get inside, quick. Florie, get in the house now!"

Katherine slapped at the side of her face and swatted at the air and I felt another sharp pain on the back of my neck and then more on the backs of my hands. I waved my arms around wildly as I ducked my head and made for the cottage. Another burning sting on my face and several more on my arms, and I ran full tilt around the side of the longhouse and reached the door moments after Florie. The three of us clambered inside and I slammed the door behind us, while Florie ran to the open windows and pulled the shutters closed. Katherine was still crying out and slapping at her hair and face, and I continued to pat my hands over my various body parts to make sure no more of the insects were on my person.

The burn was excruciating and there were so many stings I couldn't decipher where the pain from one ended and the next began. Katherine flopped into one of the chairs, whimpering and bending over in agony, as Florie nervously scuttled between us, afraid to touch us but asking what she could do to help.

I staggered over to the corner of the room and picked up the bucket we kept in the corner. I heaved and vomited into it, before flopping down on my bed and panting. Katherine was also retching and gripping the table with both hands.

"Florie," she croaked when she was able to get a handle on herself.

The child immediately ran up to her.

"Can you please run to my cottage? There's a cabinet next to the back wall, behind the hearth. If you open it, you'll find a leather bag with a tie around it. Can you bring it straight away? It has medicine," she wheezed.

"Put on my cloak and the bee hat before you go," I added.

Florie nodded and quickly donned the protective gear, then dashed out to get the supplies.

I pulled myself into a sitting position on the bed and examined the backs of my hands. The white dots surrounded by the angry red swelling told me I had been stung two times on one hand and three on the other. I used my fingernails to tease out the tiny barbed stingers that remained. Several areas of my face stung and burned, and when I looked at Katherine, I saw what my own face probably looked like.

Katherine's face was red, one of her eyes was half closed with the swelling, and tears streamed down her cheeks.

"Well, that could have gone better," she croaked.

I gave a weak laugh and nodded. "Stupid pigs," I said. "I knew there was a good reason why I always let Robert deal with them."

She gave a small smile, then lowered her head slowly onto her arms and shut her eyes.

Within ten minutes, Florie had returned with the medicine bag. With instructions from Katherine, who still hadn't risen from her chair, Florie found the medicine Katherine needed and was now crushing the herbs and powders with a pestle in a bowl.

"So this is one of your remedies?" I whispered, my throat now very dry.

"My mother's," she said. "She's the best healer in our clan. She's very good. I haven't seen a sickness yet that she hasn't been able to help. I was learning from her before I left. The one I'm showing Florie to make is very potent. My mother used to use it when setting bones and draining tooth abscesses. It's very effective at dampening the pain and it can be used for other things as well."

"I'm sold," I said. "What do you take it with? Shall I get some mead?"

She laughed. "No, no. We have to take this one with water. Mixing it with mead will make the effects too intense. It can lead to... interesting behaviour from those who drink it that way."

"Really?" I asked, interested.

She nodded. "Ay, it can make you feel very drunk. Invincible actually, and you forget a lot after you take it, or so I'm told. It's not meant to be taken often, and I've never personally tried it before, even with water. But I've heard of one or two people using it too often and it making them very sick when they run out. It contains laudanum, among some other things, so needs to be treated with caution. I think we need it today though."

"Well, I hope it's as good as you say it is," I said, closing my eyes. I felt nauseous with the pain.

"You can tell me when you try it," she replied.

After following Katherine's instructions for another ten minutes, the powder was finally mixed into a bowl of water which Katherine then pulled towards her. She asked Florie to pass her medicine bag again, then she opened it and felt around inside carefully before pulling out a little bottle with a cork in the top. She held it between her thumb and forefinger and even from the bed I could see it was made from a dark brown coloured glass with a label on the front. I was too far away to see it clearly, but even if I were closer, I still couldn't have read it. I wondered if Katherine was able to.

"What's that?" I asked, curious.

Katherine carefully twisted the cork loose but still held it against the top of the bottle. Her hands were visibly shaking and her forehead glistened with perspiration, but she carefully tilted it, allowing several small drops of a reddish-brown liquid to fall into the bowl.

"This is the laudanum," Katherine said, not taking her eyes off her task. When she seemed happy with the amount she had dispensed into the bowl, she twisted the cork back into the little neck of the bottle, put it back into her bag and looked at me. "The secret ingredient," she added, winking. She used her finger to mix the contents of the bowl, then picked it up and drank half.

Florie then carried the rest over to me. "Can I try some?" she asked.

"Absolutely not," I said, taking the bowl from her and drinking the rest. It tasted bitter but there were some other flavourings in there too which took the edge off.

"How long before it works?" I asked.

"Usually one would see the effects start to kick in after ten minutes," Katherine said, resting her head back on her hands again.

Florie came and sat next to me on the bed as I closed my eyes and tried to forget about the agonising stinging across my hands, arms, chest, face, and neck.

As Katherine had said, after a few minutes I felt the pain start to ebb, and within twenty I felt well enough to stand up and walk over to Katherine. I felt a bit dizzy on my feet, but I wasn't sure if that was because of the medicine or the stings.

She looked up at me from the table and smiled. "Feeling better?" she asked.

"Much," I said. "That medicine is incredible."

"Yes, and you'll sleep well tonight," she promised. "Try not to do anything too strenuous for the rest of the day, though. You might feel a little light-headed."

"I don't think either of us will be fit for much else today," I said. I ran my fingers gingerly over my chest and neck, finding a couple more of the little stingers still embedded in my flesh.

Katherine got up and picked up her medicine bag again. "If you boil some water, I'll prepare a remedy which we can apply to the stings. The medicine takes away the pain for now, but the paste I'm going to make will help to bring down the swelling and neutralise the poison. It will make it less uncomfortable tomorrow."

For the next thirty minutes, Katherine made the paste, assisted by a fascinated Florie. The resulting mixture was a thick, chalky white substance which had a gritty texture.

"There," she said as she finished mixing it. "We need to spread this on all the stings and let it dry, and don't wash it off until tomorrow."

She put the bowl down in the centre of the table, then turned her back to me and lifted her red locks away from her neck.

"Can you help me with my dress?" she said. "The paste is difficult to wash out of clothes, so I'd rather do this with just my undergarments on."

I nodded and stepped forward, gripping the ties which held her bodice together at the back. I briefly wondered why she didn't just loosen it from the front, a job she could have done without my help, but my attention was quickly distracted by the red lump on the back of her slender neck. The stinger still protruded from the white centre, and after hesitating for a second I said, "Hold still for a moment."

Using my nails, I delicately gripped the tiny thorn and pulled it free of her skin. I was surprised that she didn't move or flinch, and I flicked it away and ran my finger lightly over the lump to make sure nothing had been left behind. I slowly loosened the ribbon on the back of her bodice and pulled the garment apart at the back, revealing the stay she wore underneath. Then I released the lower ties which held her skirt in place. When the ribbons were undone, I stepped back as she turned again to face me.

"Thank you," she said, giving me another smile.

I nodded, then watched as she slid her bodice off over her stay, then untied the front ribbons of her skirt and let it fall to the floor.

She now stood in just her chemise and stay, and though I had seen plenty of women in this state of undress and never given it a second thought, in this instance, I felt my cheeks start to burn. I quickly looked away and focused on my own fastenings, wondering what had just come over me.

We were soon standing together in our undergarments, applying the chalky white paste to the welts across our bodies. Neither of us had sustained any injuries to our legs or feet, but we both had plenty on our arms, faces, chest and necks. Florie delightedly smeared the substance over the stings on our faces, giggling and laughing as she used more of the paste than was necessary and made elaborate patterns resembling different animals.

"You look like a rabbit, Katherine," she giggled. "And you are a horse, Mammy."

"Thank you, darling, that's very flattering," I said, sharing a grin with Katherine. "Why am I the horse and not the rabbit?"

"What's wrong with a horse?" smirked Katherine. "Horses are noble creatures."

"Yes, and they work hard," added Florie.

"Mmm, well, I suppose that's fitting," I grumbled playfully.

Looking quite ridiculous covered in chalky white patches, I got up and hung the pot of stew on the chain over the fire to warm up. Meanwhile, with the paste that was left, Katherine and Florie were giggling away as Katherine now decorated Florie's face. The child soon skipped up to me with a wide grin.

"Look, Mammy, Katherine made me into a princess."

I looked down at her and laughed. Katherine had smeared the white paste on her cheeks, around her lips and above her eyes.

"Your rouge is a little on the pale side," I said, "But I think it looks lovely. And you are always my princess, even without that lovely face paint."

Florie grinned and hugged me, then skipped back over to Katherine as I dished out the broses.

Over supper, we laughed about the disastrous day.

"At least we got the pig over here, though," Katherine said. "I'll count that as a win."

She lifted her cup to her mouth and sipped her water. Usually, we would be drinking mead, but Katherine insisted we stick to water until the morning when the full effects of the remedy would have worn off. I had been a little dubious about whether Katherine's remedy would be as effective as she'd claimed, but I now thought if anything, she had undersold its potency.

"Well, your mam must be a heck of a good medicine woman," I said, pushing my empty bowl off to the side and drumming my fingers on the tabletop. "I expected to be in agonising pain for hours with that many stings, but I have to admit, I can hardly feel a thing now."

This was true, and in fact, even the tips of my fingers felt a little numb and distant as they tapped against the wood.

Katherine smiled, looking pleased. "She was very knowledgeable. But what you're feeling is mainly down to the laudanum, not any real skill on my part."

"I think you're being overly modest," I said. "But how do you make laudanum, then? I think every household should have it on hand. It's miraculous."

Katherine gave a slight shrug. "Well, like I said before, it's very helpful when it's really needed, but my mother always insisted it could be dangerous, too. It will kill you if you take too much at once."

"But that goes for many things," I said. "How is this stuff not more popular?"

"Well, as a matter of fact, I've heard it is getting quite popular in the lowlands and in England. But it's expensive here," Katherine said. "My mother always got it from the traveling traders who come up from London once or twice a year, but they'll rarely barter for it and usually want coin. You need special equipment and ingredients to make it, so it has to be bought. My mother gave me this bottle, but she told me to be careful about how I use it. Not everyone agreed with her, but she always insisted that it never be used too frequently and only ever when really necessary." She shrugged again. "When she first discovered the drug, she used it to treat all kinds of things, but she said it led to problems. People who she'd given it to repeatedly, starting asking for it more often, paying her to treat them when they had nothing to treat, then getting sick when she stopped giving it to them. She even had one patient come to her and threaten to hurt her if she didn't give him her total supply. After that she changed how she used it and became a lot more particular about when she administered it and how much."

"Well, that's helpful to know," I said. "But I'm glad you had it on hand for this."

She grinned. "I agree. And we only had a very weak dose so you don't have to worry."

"Oh, I'm not. I trust you. I think your mam taught you well."

"I really enjoyed learning the trade, and she taught me a lot. I'd wanted to take over from her one day and become the healer for my clan, but then my father decided differently." She stared off into the distance for a few moments. "Anyway, I think I learned enough before I left to be helpful in times like these," she said, running a finger over a welt on the back of her hand.

"I can't argue with that," I said, giving her a broad smile.

It wasn't until we were clearing away the bowls and spoons from dinner that I remembered the pigs.

"Oh, crumbs," I said. "I don't even know if the pigs went back into the pen. I should probably go out and check."

I cringed at the idea of battling with the stubborn animals once again, but they couldn't wonder about on the farm all day.

"Oh sorry, I forgot to tell you," Florie piped up. "When I got back from getting the medicine, they were both in the pen, so I closed the gate."

"You are a little flower," said Katherine, patting her on the back.

Florie looked very pleased with herself.

"Good," I said. "One less thing to worry about. Well done, sweetheart." I wiped the surface of the table down with a small cloth, then added, "Hopefully they get on with things quick, though I really haven't been paying attention to the sow. I have no idea when her time will be right. Did the two pigs seem to like each other, Florie?"

"Um, I don't know," she said. "The boy pig was sitting by himself on one side of the pen and our pig was in her usual place sleeping."

"Huh," I said. "That doesn't sound promising."

"Oh, I wouldn't worry about it," Katherine said. "The boar will know when the time is right."

"What about your sow?" I asked her.

She rubbed her jaw and sighed. "Yes, that. I think we'll have to move the boar every three days between the two pens so he can service both of them."

"What? I do not want to do that every three days!" I said.

"Well, we could move all three pigs into one pen," Katherine suggested.

"Is the pen big enough?"

"It should be, for a month. We could always let the pigs out in the day so they're not on top of each other too much."

"Ugh, they'll eat the crops," I said.

"Then we expand the pen," Katherine said. "My pen is a bit bigger and there's some extra fencing poles in my barn. We could probably extend the fence in a day or two."

"I suppose that's the best plan," I consented, examining a chalky lump on the back of my hand. The swelling was already going down, so the remedy was working. "We better get two good litters out of this."

Katherine smiled. "We will, don't fret." Then she said, "I also didn't mention to Mary that I was sharing the pig with you. The deal was, I give her a percentage of my litter. Nothing was said about yours so you can keep all your piglets."

I looked up at her, and she looked back, still smiling.

"That isn't right," I said. "We should both contribute to the payment, not just you."

"I knew you'd say that," she said. "But think of it this way. I rented the boar for a month for a price I felt was fair and a price Mary agreed to. Neither of us are guaranteed to get a litter out of it, but we will both be feeding that boar for the time we have him. If I want to let you put your pig in my pen, that's my choice, and if you get a litter of piglets out of it, then they're yours. If you have enough by winter to be comfortable, then you can give a piglet or two to Mary if your conscience tells you to, but don't worry about me. It costs me nothing to share the boar I rented."

"Except time and resources to extend your pen," I said.

"Well, I was going to do that anyway," she said, waving her hand in a brush-off motion. "I wanted to keep one of the females from the next litter, rather than sell them all, so I would eventually need a bigger pen, anyway. I've just found a way to rope you into helping me." She winked and grinned again.

"How devious of you." I smiled and got up to tell Florie it was time for bed.

Katherine stood and picked up her dress, ready to put it on.

"You don't have to leave yet, if you don't want to," I said. I felt slightly sheepish making the offer, but I was still somewhat lightheaded from the remedy and I was sure Katherine must have felt the same. I didn't like the idea of her walking home alone while it was still in effect. "You can stay tonight, if you want," I added. "Florie rarely sleeps in her own bed anymore, so you are welcome to it tonight. Your cottage has been empty all day; it's getting late and it'll be cold."

Katherine held her dress and hesitated for a few moments.

"Please, Katherine, don't go," Florie pleaded.

"Are you sure? I don't want to impose," Katherine said.

"Don't be daft, it's no imposition," I said, walking over and taking her dress. I laid it over the back of the chair.

Katherine smiled and sat back down. "Thank you," she said.

I helped Florie out of her dress and put her linen nightgown on before tucking her into my bed. I bent over and kissed her goodnight, and she wrapped her arms around my neck and hugged me.

"I love you, Mammy," she whispered.

"I love you too, lass," I whispered back, then walked back to the table and sat down next to Katherine.

"Goodnight, Katherine," Florie said, turning over and closing her eyes.

"Goodnight, Florie," Katherine said, quietly. She watched Florie for a few seconds, then turned back to me. "She's a good child," she said, her smile fading slowly.

"She is," I replied.

"She's lucky to have you for a mam."

"Sometimes I'm not so sure," I said.

"She is," Katherine insisted. "It's clear to anyone how much you care for her. And she loves you to bits."

"I just wish I could do better for her," I said.

"It's not easy times, for anyone. You do your best."

"Sometimes I feel like I can't protect her. I nearly lost her that day at the river. I've lost Robert. I nearly lost our home. I might lose it still. I don't think I've been the best mother," I said, quietly.

Katherine gave a gentle smile and shook her head. "You can't blame yourself for those things. That is not—"

"Artur offered to help that night with the sheep," I cut in before she could start making excuses for me. "He passed by right before it happened and he asked if I wanted help getting the sheep back to the shelter. I turned him down. If you hadn't been there, I don't know what would have happened."

"If I hadn't been there, you would have saved her yourself," she said.

"I thought so at the time, but now I'm not so sure."

"You're strong, Anna, you would have," she said.

I sighed but said nothing.

Katherine looked down at her hands, which were clasped together on the table in front of her. "You've been so strong for Florie. I admire you so much for that. She's a kind, beautiful child and that's because of you."

"You'll be the same, Katherine, if not better. You'll be a good mother one day," I said.

She shook her head. "No, I'm not strong like you, Anna."

I reached out and gripped her hand. She looked up at me quickly, her green eyes wide and sad.

"Of course you will," I said, determinedly. "Look how you are with Florie. Don't doubt yourself."

She looked down again. "I've already failed my first child. I wasn't strong enough to save him."

I sat back slowly. I really didn't think I wanted to hear what was about to come.

"Not two months after I married Ailig, I found myself with child," she said, in almost a whisper.

I listened intently. I had a strong feeling what she was telling me was something she hadn't shared before.

"I was so happy," she continued. "Even Ailig was pleased, but then one night he became angry. I can't even remember what it was about, or what triggered it. But when he gets angry he...." she trailed off.

I sat in silence, holding my breath, waiting for her to continue when she was ready.

"The baby came later that night," she said, her voice cracking. "I did everything I could to stop it, but my body failed and he came."

I shook my head slowly. "Oh, Katherine," I said, leaning forward and reaching out for her hand again. She took it slowly, and I squeezed. A single tear spilled from her right eye and ran down her patchy cheek, leaving a trail through the dried white paste as she continued.

"He was so tiny, smaller than the palm of my hand, but he was perfect. I wanted to take him to the burial site and have a private ceremony, but Ailig refused. He said he hadn't been baptised, he was too small, that he wasn't a person, just a lump of flesh and I should let him go. He made me bury my son in the garden."

Her voice was choked and barely a whisper, and she stared at the top of the table as she spoke. My own eyes were brimming as I tried to think of something comforting to say to her.

"I wrapped him in a cloth and put him under a patch of thistles, down the hill from my cottage. Ailig wouldn't let me mark the grave, so the thistles are my reminder."

She quickly lifted her hand and wiped away the moisture in her eyes before any more tears could fall, then tilted her head down, letting her red hair form a curtain around the sides of her face.

I tried to speak, but my own voice had locked up and my words caught in the back of my throat. I'd never liked Ailig, but now I hated him with a passion.

"So you see," she whispered, "I can't protect my own children. Not my son, who now lies under the thistles, and when Ailig comes back, I fear so terribly for this one."

She let go of my hand and placed her palm over her abdomen and my blood ran cold as I realised what she had just told me.

As I lay in bed that night, cuddling my child close, I had great trouble falling asleep, in spite of the medicine I'd taken earlier. The light snores coming from Florie's bed, behind the partition, told me Katherine had already drifted off. My heart broke for her as I thought about the beatings she had sustained barely six weeks ago. Ailig had already cost Katherine one baby and still he continued to hit her. Katherine could not be very far along in her pregnancy and she would still be so vulnerable when Ailig returned. This was the reason I hadn't wanted to get close to her in the first place. I hadn't wanted to have to worry about her when Ailig returned, and now there was a child to consider as well. Tonight was the first time I'd seen Katherine upset or afraid. She was usually so positive and resilient; I had started to imagine her as having no vulnerabilities. But the conversation had been a stark reminder that, like me, she was facing real dangers of her own. Without even being asked, Katherine had gone to extreme measures to help me overcome my problems, and what really bothered me now was that I couldn't think of anything I could do to help her with hers.

Chapter Eleven

"Not too many," I called to Florie. "And be careful with that blade!"

"Yeees!" she called back. She was hunched down in the dirt, holding her basket and using a knife to cut leaves from the rows of little plants stretched out before her.

"She's doing fine, Anna," said Katherine, grinning and nudging me. "Leave her be."

The three of us were outside in the turnip field together, and the turnips had sprouted their first tender green leaves. We were harvesting a few from each plant in the first few rows, which we planned to enjoy for lunch outside on the grass later.

We'd been treated to an unusually warm day for mid-June and intended to make the most of it. Five more lambs had been born, none of which Florie had managed to watch, much to her dismay, and the pigs were all in together in the expanded pen next to Katherine's cottage. The boar and Katherine's pig had been getting very friendly, so we were optimistic about that, and there was still hope for my sow, even if she was a grump. Getting the pigs over to the other pen, once it had been enlarged, turned out to be much easier than the first time we undertook the challenge. This time I agreed to let Florie help, and we found that with Florie and Katherine holding fresh turnip leaves and feeding the pigs one or two every thirty seconds, and me following behind swishing a long stick, we were able to motivate them to keep walking. We also decided it might be better to lead the pigs around the bee skeps instead of in-between them and that decision was enthusiastically and unanimously agreed on by all parties involved.

The potatoes appeared to be doing well, but since none of us had any prior experience growing them, we were all a little unsure about whether to declare that crop a success or not. The vegetable patches were flourishing, as were the oats, and the three of us were in good humour when we sat down on the grass with our cheese, bannocks and turnip leaves. Katherine had ground up some oats earlier in the morning and baked some bannock, which we now broke up and shared out. I still felt Katherine was too generous with her food, considering she provided at least half of the meals and there was only one of her, but I had given up arguing with her about it and now took my chunk and bit into it hungrily.

"How is it?" she asked, taking a bite out of her own piece.

"Horrible," I mumbled, my mouth still full. "You should give me yours and I'll save you the trouble of having to eat it."

She grinned back at me as she chewed, then addressed Florie. "How about you? Do you like my mam's recipe?"

Florie said nothing but nodded enthusiastically, her mouth so full she could barely chew.

"Slow down, Florie," I said. "No one's taking it away from you."

The sound of the river was pleasant as we enjoyed the warmth of the sun's rays and the tasty food. I was thankful as I watched the gentle current sweep by, that things were as they were. I couldn't help thinking what I would have been doing right now if things had happened differently right in this very spot, two short months ago. I reached over and rubbed Florie's foot affectionately, then smiled at Katherine. I struggled to remember the last time we'd had such an afternoon. Certainly not since we'd lost Robert.

My thoughts were interrupted when Florie pointed behind me and said, "Look."

I swallowed the last bit of my cheese and turned around to see Frang riding along the river track towards us.

"Ugh," I said, not hiding my disdain. "It's Frang."

I hadn't seen him since our argument several weeks ago and I had no wish to today. He continued his approach, making no effort to adjust his direction and avoid us, then stopped a few feet away and looked down at us all.

"Playing happy families, are we?" he said, smugly. His eyes roved between all three of us, then up over the field towards our crofts. The little green shoots popping up from the turnips looked smart in their neat rows and he leered disapprovingly at the sight.

"A joint crop, I see," he said.

"It's not your business, Frang," Katherine snapped. "Be on your way."

Frang sneered and lifted his chin, looking down upon her as he might towards an unsightly cowpat on the ground.

"I don't recall Ailig saying anything about combining your crofts," he said.

Katherine stood up, her hands clenched into fists at her sides.

"Does he know about this?" Frang added in a low voice, his lips curling into a cruel smile as he spoke.

"As she just told you Frang, what Katherine does with her farm is her business, not yours. Now piss off before something regrettable happens," I said, also standing up to face him.

He continued to sit atop his horse, holding the reins lazily in one hand as he leaned back in his saddle.

"Well, your manners have gone downhill since last we met," he said. "I didn't think that was possible. But then what can one expect when you spend every day consorting with trash from the Carnegie Clan."

Katherine lurched forward at Frang's horse and I reached out to pull her back. Frang laughed, then spat on the ground in front of us.

"You see? Nothing but a little savage. I thought Ailig would have put you in your place by now and taught you some respect, but then he has been gone for a while. I'm sure he'll work on the problem when he gets back."

"You've seen nothing yet," I said, pulling up a long switch from the edge of the water. I pointed it at him and pulled Florie behind me. "Leave now or you really will see some savage behaviour."

Frang sat still and watched me for a few moments as I continued to point the switch at him, my hand now shaking slightly.

He gave another scornful smile. "Tsk, tsk," he tutted, shaking his head slowly and licking his lips. "What would Robert think?" he said. "Replacing him so quickly with a little bitch from the south?"

Visibly shaking now, I stepped forward, still pointing the switch at Frang.

He laughed again. "What are you going to do? Swat me with that piece of straw?"

"No," I whispered. Then I leapt at his horse's head and brought down the switch over the creature's face. I screamed at the same time, repeatedly striking the stiff reed around its neck and face. I knew the switch wouldn't injure the animal, but that was not my intention. The horse reared in fright, neighing loudly, and Frang, who had not been ready for the reaction, toppled over backwards, rolling off his horse and landed with a thud on the ground behind the frightened animal. I continued to yell, waving my switch and distressing it further until it bolted.

Breathing hard, I watched in satisfaction as the horse galloped away, back towards Frang's croft. With Florie still behind me and Katherine looking at me with her mouth hanging open, I pointed the switch, which was now bent and floppy, at Frang again.

He struggled to his feet, grunting and swearing, and Katherine stepped beside me and gripped my arm. He stood but remained hunched over, clutching the knee of his bad leg, and spittle gathered on his wispy white beard as he limped one step towards us.

"You foolish cunt," he spat, wheezing heavily. "You will pay for that, mark my words."

Then he spat at my feet and turned away, limping slowly towards his croft. I continued to point the switch at him until there was a good twenty feet between us, while Katherine clutched my arm and Florie hid behind my skirts.

"Anna," Katherine gasped, once he was far enough away. "That was amazing!"

My heart was still hammering in my chest as I slowly lowered my arm and dropped the tattered weapon.

Florie crept out from behind my back, still clinging to me, and Katherine beamed, watching the shrinking figure of Frang as he slowly limped further into the distance.

"Are you alright, Mammy?" Florie said, wrapping her small arms around my waist.

I put my hand on her head, stroking her hair before crouching down to hug her. "Ay, darling, I'm fine," I said.

"You were so brave," Florie said, her words slightly muffled as she buried her head into my shoulder. I hugged her and swallowed hard, my nerves still shaken.

"I'm not sure if it was brave or foolish," I said slowly.

"Florie's right," Katherine said, "It was brave. You had to stand up to him, Anna, and you gave him fair warning."

"I just fear what he may do now in retaliation," I said quietly.

Katherine gave me a smile and took my hand in hers, squeezing me encouragingly. "Try not to fret," she said. "He's already doing the worst he can. He's trying to take your croft and we're stopping him. He can see that and that's why he's angry. He can't do more to you than he already is."

I smiled back and nodded. I wanted to believe Katherine. I wanted to dismiss Frang's words as empty threats, but I could not shake the heavy feeling in my gut that I had just invited an altogether new danger into all of our lives.

A few days passed and the feeling of foreboding I had started to dispel. Nothing had come of Frang's threats and I began to rest easier, thinking Katherine was probably right and Frang really couldn't do more than he already was. The men were still at the battlefront and the latest messenger had once again delivered good news. The clan had suffered very little losses; no one Katherine or I knew had died, and the spoils were projected to be good.

It was a rainy day with more than a drizzle coming down, so we all sat inside Katherine's cottage, knitting, while we waited for the weather to clear enough to resume our usual chores. The fire crackled pleasantly, and the pot hung above the flames, giving off delicious smells of tasty hare stew.

"My string fell off my stick again," grumbled Florie, thrusting her needles under my nose.

"Yarn," I said, taking the needles from her. A scraggly, lumpy mess hung from them and I decided I really would have to sit down and teach the child how to knit properly one of these days. I patiently picked up the dropped stitches and handed the project back to her, making a mental note to unravel the work later and re-knit it after she'd gone to bed.

"That looks lovely, Florie. Remind me again what it's going to be?" Katherine said, diplomatically.

"It's a dress for the doll you made me." Florie grinned, holding it up for Katherine to see. "See, there's the bottom of the skirt and here is one of the sleeves." She pointed to a particularly lumpy part of the project and Katherine tilted her head to the side, peering hard, clearly struggling to see the same vision Florie did.

"Oh, of course," she said exuberantly. "It's gorgeous. I wish I had a dress like that."

I grinned as I focused on my own work, a thick pair of socks for next winter.

"Thank you," said Florie. "I can make you one after I finish dolly's."

"Oh, that's so kind of you," Katherine responded, grinning. Then she turned to me.

"You too, Anna. I can't believe you've nearly finished that first sock already. You're so fast."

"Practise," I said. "I can't count how many of these things I've made over the years. I used to knit a new pair every winter for Robert, he always asked for them." The smile faded from my lips and Katherine cleared her throat and looked back at her own work.

"I'm sorry," she said.

"For what?" I said, quietly. "You're not to blame."

"That's right, it's uncle Faolan's fault," Florie added flatly, focusing on her knitting.

My throat constricted as Katherine looked up quickly at Florie, then looked to me for confirmation. I shook my head in disbelief, shocked that Florie would say that. I knew I had blamed Faolan, but I thought I had always been careful not to say it outright, or influence Florie's opinion of him.

I cleared my throat and swallowed uncomfortably. "No, Florie, don't say that about your uncle. It isn't true."

She stopped knitting and looked up at me. "You told Uncle Faolan that Daddy would still be alive if it wasn't for him. So it's his fault."

An awful silence filled the room as I tried to think how to respond to that.

I took a shaky breath, then spoke quietly. "I said Daddy might be alive if it wasn't for him, and I'm sorry Florie, it was a bad thing to say. It wasn't Uncle Faolan's fault. I said that because I was hurting."

I felt a surge of guilt wash over me and I fought to keep my voice steady. Katherine kept her eyes down and slowly worked on her knitting, but the tension had made the room feel stale. Florie just stared at her hands and I wondered if she was processing what I had said. I looked back at Katherine, who sensed my eyes on her and looked up slowly. Her expression was a mix of sadness and understanding.

I breathed a heavy sigh. "In November last year, Faolan, Robert's brother, came to us very excited. He said his eldest son had spotted a large stag in the next valley over. He said it was magnificent, the biggest he'd ever seen, with a rack wider than he could stretch his arms. Foalan wanted Robert to go with him to hunt it. Robert was excited, too. He wanted the trophy and the meat would have been enough to see us through the winter, even after splitting it with Foalan.

"Both Robert and Faolan had lost their pistols when the Act of Proscription came into effect. Robert felt the risk was too great to keep them, so both men only had their bows, which are poor weapons to take down such a large creature. I asked them both not to go, but Faolan insisted it wouldn't be difficult between the three of them. So they went. Robert and Faolan and Cormag, Robert's nephew.

"When Faolan arrived back at my house later that night, I knew. Something inside me knew Robert was gone. Faolan told me they had found the stag and shot it twice, but it didn't go down. They chased it all the way along the valley and into the glen, but Faloan's horse stumbled in a rabbit hole and he was thrown. He injured his ribs and was unable to ride with speed or draw his bow, so Robert decided to go after the stag alone, leaving Cormag to watch over his father. Robert tracked the stag through the glen on foot, but when he caught up to him, the creature fought back. It attacked Robert and mauled him to near death."

Both Katherine and Florie had stopped knitting and were watching me intently now.

"He was able to make his way back to the edge of the glen where Faolan was waiting, but Faolan had already sent his son home to fetch help. There was no one there who could ride Robert home quickly, and he bled to death in the valley."

I felt the tears run down my cheeks as I finished the recount of my husband's death. Katherine, who had not taken her eyes off me during the story, slowly rested her knitting on her knee and shook her head.

"Anna, I'm so very sorry," she said gently.

"I was so angry at Faolan," I whispered. "I blamed him for Robert's death because it was his idea to hunt the stag and he let Robert go after the animal alone."

Florie put her knitting down and ran over to me, putting her arms around my neck and giving me a big hug. Tears brimmed out of her eyes too, as I hugged her back.

"I know it wasn't Faolan's fault. Robert made his own choices, but I still couldn't help hating him, wishing it was him who had died and not Robert."

Katherine got up and came over to me. She crouched in front of me and put her hand on my knee.

"I still can't look at him," I went on. "I see Robert every time I look at his face. I want to forgive him, but I can't. I know I shouldn't, but I blame him for taking away my chance at seeing Robert one last time before he died. Maybe if Cormag had stayed, he could have brought Robert home in time for me to do something, or at least see him before he... I know it's wrong, but I can't help but think it."

Silence filled the room again as neither Katherine or Florie spoke.

"Anyway," I said, wiping my eyes. "What are you making, Katherine? It's lovely."

She moved the square of knitting around in her hands, absently. "I don't know," she said. I've never been very good at knitting. I only seem to be able to manage things like scarves and squares. I guess this could be a kitchen hand towel."

"If you made it a little bigger, it could be a baby blanket," I said, trying to smile.

She held it out and inspected it.

"You're right," she said, smiling back. "That's what it will be."

Chapter Twelve

KATHERINE

It was the last week of June, and Anna, Florie, and I had spent the afternoon contemplating how to care for the new potato crop. When I had first picked up the sack of vegetables from the village, I'd asked the man who'd delivered them how to plant and care for them. He'd given me specific instructions, but now that I stood and regarded the little plants which protruded from the soil, I felt unsure about exactly what to do.

"I think," I said, "that we're supposed to pile the earth up around the stalks now."

"What? Bury the plants?" Anna asked, looking at me with a raised eyebrow. She didn't believe me and I didn't want to disappoint her by wrecking the crop.

"Not bury them all of the way," I said. "Only about this high up the stalks." I gestured with my hands.

Anna looked incredulous, but shrugged. "Alright," she said. "I trust you."

Her words made my heart swell for a moment and I smiled hesitantly, hoping desperately that I remembered correctly.

"We better get it done quick," Anna added. "There's a storm coming, and it looks like a big one."

We spent the next hour hilling the potato plants as the sky darkened and the clouds started closing in.

When the first few raindrops started to splash down, I said, "Anna, why don't you take Florie and go inside. I'll get the sheep into the barn."

Anna shook her head. "You can't do that on your own. I'll come with you."

"Me too," Florie said.

"No," Anna turned to her. "You go on into the cottage. Light the fire for supper and we'll be back in a little while."

The child looked disappointed and crinkled her freckled nose, but she nodded and walked back towards the cottage.

"She looks just like you when she's irritated," I said to Anna.

"Really?" Anna said, grinning. "I would have hoped I looked a little more menacing when I got cross."

"I'm afraid not. I think it's the freckles. Makes you both look too adorable."

"Let's go," Anna laughed. She quickly turned away from me to walk towards the pasture, but she wasn't fast enough to hide the pink flush which had spread across her cheeks.

Together we made our way to the base of the hills to the south, the spot the flock had been favouring for the last few days. Without much trouble, we were able to shepherd them back across the pasture and towards the barn. The sheep seemed to know where they were supposed to go, and very little supervision was necessary to guide them to safety.

Once we were close, I said to Anna, "Why don't you go and see to Florie? I can see the sheep into the barn from here."

"Are you sure?"

"Of course, they know where they're going and the rain is picking up. Go ahead, I'll be two minutes behind you."

She nodded and jogged back towards the cottage as I followed the sheep back to the barn. I opened the door wide and let all twenty-six sheep and nine lambs file in. The last one was Anna's ewe, which had still not given birth, and she waddled in a little slower than the others, bleating testily.

"Poor thing," I said. "You look uncomfortable. I'm sure I'll know what that's like before too long." I put my hand over my slightly distended belly and smiled. The ewe was unusually late for lambing and was the only sheep left in the flock who still needed to give birth. From the way she was behaving, however, I was sure it could easily happen tonight. I shut the door and ran around the side of the longhouse to the cottage. By the time I made it inside, I was quite wet.

"Well," I said, as I tried to brush the water from my clothes. "That was none too soon."

"Did they all make it inside alright?" Anna said as she stirred the pot over the fire.

"Every one," I said. "Florie, the pregnant ewe looks like she could give birth any time. You might get to watch it in the barn after all."

Florie's face broke into a huge grin and she jumped up and down on her toes.

"Oh, I hope so, I hope so. Can I go and check later, Mammy? In case it starts?"

"It depends how bad the storm gets," Anna said, rolling her eyes at me.

The thunder and lightning soon followed the rain, and the three of us sat inside and chatted. Anna pulled out a backgammon set which Robert had made. It was beautiful, the triangular markers on the slab of wood having been neatly chiselled out, and the little counters that came with it were stained, circular chips.

"The dice are a little weighted," Anna said, smiling. "Robert never could get them perfect. This one rolls a lot of threes and this one rolls a lot of fives. It's fair, though, because we both use them."

I laughed. "Oh, I'd love to learn! I've never played backgammon before."

"A merchant came from London one year, peddling all sorts of interesting things. He had a nice backgammon set and taught quite a few of the men in the tavern, Robert among them. He was trying to sell it, but Robert just remembered the rules and pieces and he came home and made his own."

"Clever," I said.

"He was," Anna sighed.

I didn't show it, but my heart ached a little every time I listened to Anna talk about Robert. I wished so much to have someone love me the way she clearly loved him. Robert was dead and Anna still loved him more than Ailig would ever care for me. It was ridiculous to be envious of a dead man, but it seemed the more I was around Anna, the more I had feelings which I found myself having to hide. I struggled to identify exactly what they were. It was like an intangible longing for something beyond my ken. I cleared my throat and brushed the thoughts aside.

Trying to lighten the mood, I teased, "Well, come on and teach me then. I'm looking forward to beating you."

Anna grinned back at me. "That's fightin' talk," she said. "And I hate to disappoint you, but I happen to be a master at this game. I may have considered letting you win because you're new to it, but after your cheek, I don't think I'll be so kind."

We laughed, and Anna went about explaining the game.

After a few hours, the thunder started to subside and after having been beaten no less than five consecutive times at backgammon, I pushed the board away and got up.

"Agh, I think you're cheating," I said.

"Now, now," Anna said with a cheeky grin. "Learning to lose with dignity is as important as learning to play. Especially when you play with me," she added.

Florie, who had been hovering by the window and incessantly peeping between the shutters, now skipped over to both of us.

"It's not raining as much now," she said. "Can I go to the barn and check on the sheep?"

Anna sighed, "I suppose. But run and come straight back."

Florie grinned and raced to the door, disappearing into the light rain. I turned to Anna, who was now packing away the backgammon board. "I really hope she gets to see that lamb being born," I said.

"Well, it's going to stay locked in the barn for the night, so she may get her wish," Anna said.

The door crashed open, and Florie ran back in looking distressed.

"The door to the barn is wide open and the sheep are gone!" she shouted.

"What?" said Anna, running over to Florie. "The door was open when you got there?" The child nodded and Anna turned to me. "Did you not latch the door?" she said, striding quickly over to the hook to grab her cloak.

"I thought I did," I said, wracking my brain and trying to remember. "I'm sure I did. I know I closed it."

I could see Anna's jaw clench and she said, "Well, if they got out then it couldn't have been latched." Her voice had a hard edge to it, a tone I had not heard directed at me before.

"Anna, I'm sorry," I said. "I really thought I latched it." She pulled the hood over her head and hurried over to the door, ignoring my comment. "Come on, we need to find them and get them back into the barn. Florie, get your cloak now."

I grabbed my cloak too and followed Anna outside. I looked along the side of the longhouse towards the barn at the end, and as Florie had said, the door swung in the wind on its hinges. Though it was around seven in the evening, the sun still shone somewhere above the heavy clouds, and the visibility was not affected by the lack of light but more so by the pouring rain, which was still accompanied by the occasional clap of thunder. Anna stood next to me and put her hands above her eyes, shielding her face from the rain as she peered down into the valley towards the river.

"I don't see them down there," she said. "We should check the hillside."

Then she took off, heading south again, towards the hills, closely followed by Florie. I trudged along behind, leaving a little distance between us as I silently cursed myself for being so careless. I knew how important those sheep were to Anna, and I should have double checked the door.

The three of us ran to the base of the hills, where the sheep had been earlier, and scanned the expanse of the land in either direction.

"There!" Anna pointed. Halfway up hill to the west was the flock of sheep, trotting around together aimlessly. "Come on, we need to get them back in the barn!" she shouted.

We all scurried up the face and circled round behind the flock, whistling, waving our arms and clapping to herd them back down towards the longhouse. The flock bounded back down the hill, in the direction we wanted them to go and we ran along beside them, urging them on. Other than one or two individuals who tried to break ranks, the flock generally headed in the right direction and we soon had them all filing back into the barn.

Florie held the door open as they trotted in and I wiped the water out of my face as I said, "That was lucky, I'm glad they didn't go too far."

Anna shook her head slowly. "Sometimes I really don't understand these stupid animals. Even if the door was unlatched, what would possess them to wander out into the storm like that?"

"I'm so sorry, Anna," I apologised again. "I really did think I'd latched it. I'll be more careful next time."

She looked at me and gave me a weak smile. "Well, no harm was done," she said. "We got them back and they're alright."

"No!" shouted Florie. "Where's the one that's still pregnant?"

My stomach tightened as I looked around frantically for the ewe. With a sinking feeling, I realised Florie was right. The ewe which was due to give birth was missing. I counted the adult animals quickly, then counted them again to be sure. "Twenty-five sheep," I said.

"And nine lambs," Anna added. "She's right, we're one short."

My stomach knotted tighter. Of course, it had to be one of Anna's sheep which was missing, and the pregnant one at that. I'd die if she lost another two sheep.

"We have to go and find her," Florie said, opening the door to leave the barn.

"No," Anna snapped, sternly.

"But we have to, Mammy!" Florie cried.

"No, we don't. She's probably in labour, which is why she broke off from the others. She'll come back after the lamb has been born. The storm has nearly passed and she'll be alright."

"But the baby lamb?" Florie said.

"The baby will be safe with its mother," Anna said. "Go back to the cottage, Florie."

With tears welling in her eyes, Florie ran back to the cottage, slamming the door behind her.

"Anna, let me go and find the ewe," I said. "Even if it's just to reassure Florie that she's alright."

Anna shook her head. "There's nothing you can do even if she isn't," Anna said, her voice hollow. "You can't carry a labouring sheep back to the barn. Two of us together couldn't do it. We'll just have to leave her and hope for the best."

Anna walked back to her cottage door. "I'll see you in the morning," she said, before opening it.

I nodded. "Alright. Goodnight, Anna."

She returned a single nod and went inside.

I slowly trudged back to my own cottage, feeling flat. I wanted to kick myself. Things had been going so well. I'd found a friend in Anna that I never thought I'd have, and Florie and I were getting closer every day. Then, in one careless moment, I let them both down and compromised my new friendships. If something happened to Anna's ewe or lamb, or God forbid, both, I would not forgive myself. Anna wouldn't trust my ideas ever again. Florie had been desperate all spring to see at least one lamb born, and I had spoiled her last chance to do so. As I reached my cottage, I was feeling thoroughly miserable. I tried to think of something I could do to help.

Go and find the sheep by myself? Anna was right. If the mother was in labour, which was the most likely reason she broke off from the flock, then there would be nothing I could do.

Find her and assist with the birth? It was unlikely she'd need help, but if the ewe did get into difficulty and I was with her, then her chances would be better. It wasn't much of a gesture, but I couldn't just go to bed and do nothing, so I went to my barn to get Ailbeart. It would be faster on horseback and I could cover much more ground.

My mind wandered as I put Ailbeart's bridle on. I often wouldn't bother with the saddle, but since I had no idea how long it would take me to find the ewe, and because I had more reason now to avoid falling off, I heaved it up onto Ailbeart's back and fastened it on. When I finally had Ailbeart ready, I led him out of the barn and mounted him. I tried to think of the most logical place to start looking and what I would do when I found her. If she was alright, should I go and tell Anna? Or wait with the ewe for as long as it took for the lamb to be born, then try to herd them both home? That could take all night, assuming I was able to find her in the first place.

A surge of helpless indecision washed over me as I came to terms with how unlikely this endeavour was to improve the situation. All I wanted was to make things right again; do something meaningful. Going after a wandering sheep suddenly felt very weak.

I sat on the horse, letting him toss his head up and down and meander around the cottage as I battled over what to do. Then a thought occurred to me. Maybe going after the sheep was a waste of time, but there was something else which could be done. Something that really would make a difference to Anna and earn her forgiveness for my stupid mistake. I made up my mind and spurred Ailbeart down the valley and onto the river track.

It was three hours before I made it home again. My endeavour was as successful as I could have hoped for and it was as dark as it was going to get by the time I got back to the cottage. While it wasn't raining anymore, it was still overcast and the sun, which hid just below the horizon to the north, illuminated the sky in a dark purple glow. The mountains beyond the river were silhouetted against a beautiful, dark pink backdrop and I admired the view as I dismounted and took the riding tackle off Ailbeart. I had always loved the summer, when the nights never got completely dark and the twilight beauty of the world around persisted for hours each night.

The day had been all around exhausting and I yawned widely as I went back into my cottage. There was no heat inside, since the fire hadn't been lit all day, but I was still warm from the ride. I took off my cloak and flopped down on my bed, still fully clothed, and closed my eyes. I may not be right with Anna and Florie tomorrow, or the next day, but I hoped that by the end of the week, I would have achieved something to make up for my stupid blunder today. I had also decided I would get up early and go looking for the sheep anyway, just in case she did need some help getting back home.

It felt like I had only been asleep for a few minutes when a banging on my door jerked me awake and I staggered over to lift the latch. I rubbed my blurry eyes as I pulled the door open and squinted when I saw Anna, looking stricken.

"Anna, what's wrong?" My heart rate instantly spiked.

"It's Florie," Anna said, her voice quaking in panic. "She's gone! I reckon she's gone after that stupid sheep." Her voice cracked and I could tell she was fighting back the tears.

I immediately grabbed my cloak, which was still damp, and pulled it over my shoulders. "Don't worry Anna, we'll find her," I said, trying to sound confident. "Come on."

As we set out into the twilight, I said, "Have you any idea how long she's been gone?"

A light drizzle had started up again, and I worried about Florie getting wet and cold.

"No," Anna said. "I put her to bed right after the sheep were put back in the barn and I went to bed with her soon after that. I woke up about twenty minutes ago and she was gone, and when I checked the latch on the door, it was open. Her cloak and the lantern are missing too."

"Well, that's something," I said. "If she has the lantern, she'll be easier to see."

Anna didn't say anything as we kept walking, but even in the dim light, I could see the panic in her face.

"Do you think she would have gone into the hills?" I asked.

"That would be the most likely place she would look first," she said.

Her voice was slightly calmer now, and I felt that actively doing something to find Florie had helped give Anna something to focus on. I felt a strong urge to apologise again, tell Anna how sorry I was and that I knew it was my fault this had happened. But at the same time, I knew it wouldn't help, and it was better to just stay focused on the task at hand, rather than invite more anger and disappointment from Anna. When we reached the bottom of the hills, we stopped and peered up, scanning the hillsides for a point of light or movement which might reveal Florie's location. The rain still sprinkled down lightly, which didn't help the visibility, and neither of us could see anything.

I shouted up towards the hills, "Florie!" But my calls were dampened by the rain and lost in the barren landscape. Anna called out as well, but there was still no response.

We decided to climb into the hills and head in the direction where we had found the sheep. Every thirty seconds, one of us would call out to Florie. Thankfully, the rain was lightening up again and had now dissipated to a fine mist, the tiny droplets dancing in front of us as we climbed higher.

"Let's go right to the top," I suggested to Anna, panting from the exertion of the climb. "We might get a better view from up there, and you never know, the ewe might have gone down the other side."

Anna was breathing heavily too and just nodded. The incline wasn't exceptionally steep, but the grass and heather was muddy and slippery. It was difficult to see exactly where I was putting my feet and once or twice my foot slid back under me and I went down on my hands and knees. It would help matters if we had more light, and I was hopeful that dawn wasn't more than a couple of hours away. Even in the hour before dawn, as the sun rose closer to the horizon, we would have better light to see by which would make the search much easier. But it bothered me to think that Florie might have been out here by herself for an hour or two already. I looked over at Anna, who seemed to be thinking the same thing. Though her face was still shrouded in darkness, she appeared to have found a second wind. She picked up her pace, staring straight ahead, and clambered to the top of the hill with urgent determination. I staggered up after her, breathing hard and licking the moisture from around my mouth, which had settled there from the rain. Anna reached the top before I did and stood tall, scanning in every direction as she tried to catch her breath. When I caught up, I stood beside her and peered down into the next valley and along the side of the next rise in the distance, but I couldn't see anything. It was still too dark, and I knew it was foolish to think we might see the flicker of one tiny candle, even if she was somewhere down there.

"I can hardly see anything," Anna choked.

"It will be getting a bit lighter soon," I said. I reached out to lay my hand on her shoulder, but on second thought, pulled it back before she saw.

"Florie!" Anna shouted, cupping her hands around her mouth. "Florie, where are you?" She shouted again. She shook her head and sank to her knees. "I don't even know which direction to look," she said.

"We could split up," I suggested, gently. "You could walk west along the top of the hills and I can go east, and if we keep calling out to her, she might hear us. Once it starts to get a bit lighter, it will be easier too, but we will find her, Anna, I promise."

She looked at me and the dim, purple sky cast enough light across her face to reveal the sudden anger in her features.

"You cannot promise that," she shot at me. "You don't know any more than I do where she is, or if she's hurt or lost. You act like you know so much, but you don't. You can't even be trusted to latch a bloody barn door. We wouldn't be here now if you hadn't been so careless, and if anything happens to Florie, I'll never forgive you."

I wanted to turn away so I wouldn't have to see the way she was looking at me, but my body was stiff. I wanted to say something, but the words caught in my throat, and what could I say, anyway? I had no words because what she said was true. It was my fault, there was no excuse, and I had lost her trust now, so no matter what promises I made her, it wouldn't alter her opinion of me. I had endangered the most precious thing she had, the last person she had, so how could I expect her to forgive me, no matter what the outcome of tonight was.

She turned away from me and stood back up, putting her hands on her hips as she looked down into the next valley again. She was shaking her head slightly and swallowing hard, and it was an excruciating few seconds as she stood silently debating. I didn't dare say anything else but just took a deep shuddering breath and stood next to her in silence.

"Alright, let's split up," Anna said eventually, not looking at me. Her voice was calmer, but still trembled. "I'm going that way," she said, "and you go that way." She pointed in the opposite direction, along the top of the hill. "We'll meet back at the cottage in two hours, whether we find her or not, just in case she goes home."

I nodded again and turned to walk in the direction she instructed. Right before I turned, she looked like she was about to say something more, but my heart was hurting enough and I didn't wait for the words. I walked slowly along the top of the hill, looking down both sides. There was a small stream running through the trough of the valley between this hill and the next. As I walked, I scanned my eyes along the stream below and over the face of the next rise. I was slightly tempted to walk down into the small valley and climb the next range of hills on the other side, but then the chances of the ewe wandering that far away while in labour were small. I decided to keep walking in the direction I was going, for at least another mile.

For forty-five minutes I walked, calling out the child's name every two minutes. I'd had to start leaving longer gaps between my shouts, as my voice was starting to go hoarse. The twilight had taken on a brighter hue now and I knew the dawn could not be far off, though the more time that passed without finding Florie, the more my concern deepened. She was just a seven-year-old child, and I started to seriously question whether she'd have come this far by herself. I kept telling myself that if I hadn't found her yet, then Anna probably had and after all, what was likely to happen which might hurt her? There were no dangerous animals in these parts, no cliffs or steep ravines she could fall down. Still, plenty of grown men had broken their legs by falling into rabbit holes, and if she had suffered even a mild injury which inhibited her from walking, then that could be dangerous. It wasn't freezing at night anymore, but it had rained and that might be enough to make her dangerously cold if she had got too wet.

I was just in the process of deciding that if neither I nor Anna had found Florie by dawn, then a search party would need to be arranged, when my eyes were drawn to a patch of bracken halfway down the hill, towards the little stream. I quickened my pace to get closer, and there, next to the bracken, was a patch of white, and crouched next to it was the figure of a small child. My heart raced, and I broke into a run, staggering down the side of the hill.

"Florie!" I called.

Florie looked up, then waved me over frantically. As I got closer, I could see she had taken off her woollen cloak and draped it over the ewe's belly. She looked damp and her pale face had an expression of deep concern, but she appeared to be alright and my heart hammered with relief. She had her lantern on the ground beside her, but the candle had burned down to nothing more than a pool of wax in the bottom. It had clearly long since gone out and she hunched over, stroking the ewe who was sprawled out on her side, bleating weakly. As I got close, I bent down next to Florie and hugged her tightly.

"Florie, we've been so worried about you! Your mother is going out of her mind. You need to come home, now." I took her hand and started to try to pull her up. It worried me to feel how cold her fingers were. "And why did you take your cloak off? You're freezing!"

"I can't," Florie said, pleadingly. "I can't leave her like this, she's having trouble."

I took a closer look at the sheep, who appeared to be exhausted. She lifted her head to look at me through frightened eyes, then lay her head back down again.

"How long has she been like this? Have you been out here all night?" I asked, pulling the cloak off the ewe and pressing my hands on her swollen belly.

"I found her a few hours ago. I thought the lamb would be born, and I wanted to watch. Her water bag broke and I can sort of see the lamb there, but for the last hour he hasn't come any further. All she's done is lie here and cry," Florie said, breaking into a sob herself. "I think something's wrong, she's getting too tired."

"Let me see," I said, gently moving Florie to the side.

I positioned myself behind the ewe's back legs and examined her vulva, from which the tiny dark nose of the lamb had started to protrude. I'd never helped a sheep give birth before, but I had seen it done and was aware of the possible complications which could occur during the process.

I turned to Florie. "I think she's going to need help getting the lamb out," I said, gently. "Don't worry, it'll be alright." I looked at the ewe again. "I think," I said, "that one of the lamb's legs is stuck. Both feet should be forward, but since the lamb isn't moving, that probably means either one or both of the legs are pointing backwards. We have to get both legs up under his chin."

She nodded, wiping the tears away from her eyes.

"Florie, my hands are bigger than yours, so it will be a little easier for the ewe if you help her. Come closer and I'll show you what to do."

Florie shuffled closer, and I moved along so she could sit right in front of where the lamb was coming.

"You need to slide your hand inside the mother, under the lamb, and feel around for his front legs. When you find them, pull them gently, one at a time, so they come out under the baby's chin. Alright? Are your hands clean?" I took Florie's hand in mine and rubbed it, then rolled the sleeve of her dress up high. I was glad to feel her arms were a little warmer than her fingers were.

Once her arm was clear, I guided her hand under the lamb's nose, then let go and put my hand on her shoulder reassuringly.

"You can do this," I said. "Slide your hand inside, slowly and carefully. Everything will feel wet and strange, but you need to feel around and find where his legs are."

Florie slowly inserted her hand. After her wrist disappeared, she stopped and looked at me with a worried expression, but I patted her shoulder.

"It's alright, Florie, you're doing so well. Use your fingers, feel around for the legs."

She nodded and pushed her arm in further, looking across the horizon as she concentrated on her task.

Then she took a quick breath. "I think I feel one," she said.

"Good, good," I said, quickly. "Is it forward or pushed back under him?"

"It feels like it's forward," she said.

"Alright, can you find the other one?"

She shifted her arm again, feeling around, then slid in deeper. "I feel it," she said, grinning. "It's pointing backwards."

"Now see if you can grip his foot. You will have to pull a bit, but you need to get his leg out from under him and stretch it out so it's pointing towards us. It's his leg which is stopping him from getting out. Once it's straightened out, he'll be able to come out quickly and we will have a lovely baby lamb." I squeezed her shoulder again, and she nodded.

She frowned as her arm worked and she pulled gently.

"If it won't come forward, then we might need to push him back inside a little more so he has more room to move his leg," I said.

"I think it's coming," she said. Her arm started to re-emerge from inside the sheep and as her hand came out, the little hoof followed with it and the nose edged forwards.

"Well done!" I breathed, patting her on the back.

The ewe gave another bleat, and the nose protruded a little further out.

"She may be too tired to push properly now," I said. "If you want to help her the rest of the way, then you can use your hands to pull the head carefully and get him out."

Florie nodded and reached inside around the lamb's face. She pulled, slowly increasing the pressure, and gradually, the lamb's head and legs emerged. Finally, the head popped free, and the lamb slid out onto the ground in front of Florie.

"Well done, Florie," I said, reaching forwards and rubbing the lamb, which twitched slightly. I grabbed the lamb's back legs and slid him around to his mother's head. The ewe immediately started licking her infant, and the baby shook its head, trying to clear the mucus from its face.

Florie stood up and came around to see, looking incredibly pleased with herself.

I looked up at her and grinned. "You saved this lamb, Florie," I said. "You were amazing."

The ewe continued to lick the baby but made no attempt to stand, and I could see her abdomen still stiffening.

"Florie," I said. "Come back around here."

We both crouched behind the ewe again.

"Is there another?" Florie asked excitedly.

I nodded. "I think there might be. You can put your arm back in and check. If you find another, you can pull his head or his front legs and help him too."

Florie beamed and slid her hand back inside the ewe. She immediately looked back at me excitedly.

"I feel him! I have him under his legs!"

"Alright, pull him slowly," I said.

She worked her arm and slid it back slowly. Another little nose protruded and as Florie pulled, more and more of the head emerged, along with two more little hooves. With a final pull, the second lamb was born. This time she did as she had seen me do and pulled the lamb to the other side of the ewe for it to be licked clean.

"Two lambs," I said delightedly.

Florie stood up next to me and gave me a hug. "Thank you, Katherine."

"For what?" I said. "You did all the work."

She smiled. "I wouldn't have known what to do if you weren't here."

"We make a good team, don't we?" I said, smiling back down at her.

She nodded, then said, "Don't feel bad about the sheep getting out."

My smile faded.

"It wasn't your fault. I know Mam is cross about it, but she'll be happy again once we get the ewe back and she'll be thrilled when she sees we've got two lambs."

"Thank you, Florie, that's very kind of you to say," I said. "It was my fault though, I was careless and your mam is so worried about losing your farm. She has every right to be cross with me."

The ewe suddenly got to her feet and both of us smiled as the lambs tried to copy her, standing on shaky legs and nuzzling to find her teats.

Florie sighed. "Mam is hard on lots of people. She didn't used to be, but she changed after Daddy died."

"I know that must have been so hard for both of you," I said. "He sounds like he was a wonderful daddy and good to you both."

"He was," Florie said. "I miss him very much. But you're kind too, Katherine, and Mammy's been much better since you've been around. She might not notice it, but I can tell."

She reached out and took my hand and I felt a lump rise in my throat. I squeezed her hand to let her know her words meant a lot to me, but I didn't trust myself to verbally answer. We stood and watched the lambs take their first feed, before the two of them settled down together on the grass. It was almost fully light now, as the first rays of dawn began to shine over the tops of the mountains in the north.

"We really need to go now," I said. "Your mother is worried sick about you. Do you think you can manage a lamb?"

She grinned and nodded, then stooped down and lifted one of the little animals. I lifted the second, and we started back up the hill away from the stream. The ewe followed us without hesitation as we carried her babies back to the croft. We had to stop a few times, as Florie struggled to carry her lamb back up the hill, and once we reached the top, I carried both back down the other side. When we were out of the hills, it took the better part of an hour to get back to the cottage, where we saw Anna waiting anxiously outside.

As soon as she saw us, her face relaxed into a huge expression of relief and she raced forward with her arms outstretched. Florie put her lamb down on the ground and ran towards her mother as I stopped to wait with the ewe. I lowered the other baby onto the ground next to her and watched the joyful reunion. Florie and Anna shared a deep embrace, and while I couldn't hear what was said between them, from Florie's body language it was clear Anna was being given a hasty recount of the morning's events. Florie then pulled her mother by the hand, back towards me.

"You see?" came Florie's high-pitched voice as they got nearer. "Two lambs! And I delivered them both. Katherine showed me how." The child beamed up at me and Anna knelt down to look at the lambs.

"That's incredible, Florie," she said. "Well done."

The lambs were nursing from their mother again, and I took a couple of steps back. Anna's longhouse was only a few hundred yards away now, and the rest of the flock were in the barn. I knew Anna would be letting them out now that it was morning, and the storm had passed.

"Well, that was quite a night," I said, quietly. "Florie, you should be so proud of yourself. I'm going to go back to my cottage now, for a sleep, but I'll see you later on in the morning alright?"

"I think we all could use some sleep," Anna said, offering a conciliatory smile. "Come on Florie, we'll get the lambs to the barn and then it's back to bed for you."

Florie didn't argue, but ran back to me and gave me a hug. "Thank you, Katherine," she said, then picked up one of the lambs as Anna picked up the other and the two of them made their way back towards their barn.

Chapter Thirteen

ANNA

It was the early afternoon when I went back into the cottage to check on Florie. As I popped my head around the door, I could see her still lying in bed, dead to the world. I decided to let her sleep for another half an hour, but if she wasn't awake by then, I'd have to get her up. She wouldn't sleep at her usual bedtime tonight, otherwise.

I walked back outside and resumed my usual chores. I had let the flock out of the barn to go back to pasture, but kept back the ewe and her two lambs. I thought it best to keep the three of them in there for a day or two to give the mother time to rest and recover. According to Florie, she'd had a hard time of it.

I smiled when I thought about Florie delivering the babies. She would have loved that, and I was sorry I wasn't there to see her do it. Thank goodness Katherine had got there in time, or we may have lost all three sheep. Thank goodness for Katherine; I ran the thought over in my mind, feeling guilty. I wondered what she was doing right now. She hadn't come back today yet, and I had a heavy feeling in my gut that it wasn't because she was still sleeping. I knew I had been unfair on her and I regretted what I'd said. I had no doubt she felt terrible about her mistake yesterday, so why did I insist on rubbing salt in the wound and hurting her more? And blaming her for Florie? Why did I say that? After me, I didn't believe there was anyone who loved Florie more, so why did I throw that in her face?

I was partially glad Katherine hadn't come over yet because I really had no idea what to say to her. If I said nothing, then things would be awkward, but I'd never been very good at apologising or admitting I was wrong, and I never thought I would have to do that with Katherine. Evidently, there was no one safe from my wrath or my cutting words. Katherine had been nothing but kind to me and Florie. She had gone out of her way to help us, and the first time she made a mistake, I'd crucified her for it. What was wrong with me?

I breathed a heavy sigh and went about the rest of the afternoon as usual. I woke Florie up after a short while and she immediately asked about Katherine, as I knew she would.

"Did Katherine come back?" she asked me, stretching.

"No, she was tired, and she wanted to sleep," I lied.

Florie wasn't completely convinced. "Did you see her?" she asked.

"No, I haven't seen her come out of her cottage today," I said. Though to be honest, I had made a point of not going near her croft or looking in that general direction.

"Are the lambs alright?"

Happy to have a question I could answer truthfully, I brightened and said, "Yes, I'm going to keep them in the barn for a day or two with the mother. Do you want to go and see them? They've dried out now and they're very cute, just like the others."

Florie nodded, then jumped out of bed and ran out the door to the barn in her nightgown.

For the rest of the afternoon, Florie helped me with my chores and I was wracked with guilt every time she asked if we could go and wake Katherine up and I told her no.

"Katherine will get up when she's ready," I kept telling her. As the early evening rolled around and we still hadn't seen her emerge, Florie insisted on going to her croft to feed the pigs.

"If she's still asleep, then the pigs won't have been fed," she said.

This did make sense, so I agreed to walk over with Florie to take a pail of slops to them.

"That's under the condition that you don't wake Katherine if she's not outside," I said. "You're not to go banging on her door, understand?"

Florie nodded.

In actual fact, I was curious to go over to her croft, just to see if she was up and about. A few minutes later, pail in hand, Florie and I started walking over the pasture towards Katherine's cottage. When we were about halfway there, Florie pointed.

"Look, there she is. She is up!"

Sure enough, Katherine was outside her barn, climbing up onto Ailbeart.

"Where is she going?" Florie asked me.

I shook my head, clueless.

Florie started to call out and wave to Katherine, but I shushed her, and either Katherine didn't hear or pretended not to, because she spurred her horse and cantered down the path to the river, then turned onto the track that led into the village. She had soon disappeared, leaving both of us perplexed.

"Did she not see us?" Florie asked me.

"I don't think so," I said. "Come on, let's get this to the pigs."

The pigs did well that day because when we got there we saw Katherine had already fed them.

"Both of you better be eating for two now," I grumbled as I poured more slops into the trough. "Or on second thought, ten."

The boar would have to be returned in just over a week and I hadn't actually seen any activity happening between my sow and him. I hoped I had just missed it, since most of the time Katherine was at our cottage, rather than us being at hers.

Neither Florie or myself saw anything of Katherine that day. Neither of us saw when she returned, and whenever that happened to be, she didn't come over to our cottage afterwards. Florie kept hypothesising reasons for why that might be, and I cringed as she seemed to be more aware of the truth than I would have liked.

"I think you made Katherine feel bad about the barn," Florie said cautiously, as we ate our broses. "I think she thinks you're mad at her."

"Well, I suppose I was a bit mad about it," I said, slowly.

"Are you still mad?" Florie asked.

"I don't think so," I said. "No, I'm not still mad. The sheep are alright, you are alright, so I'm not mad."

"If something had happened to the sheep, would you still be mad?" Florie asked.

I thought about this for a minute. "I don't know," I said. "I would have been upset. We can't afford to lose any more sheep. We're a hair's breadth from losing the croft— Or we were." I added, after a short pause.

"Before Katherine helped us," Florie said.

"Yes."

We ate for a while longer in silence.

"It's not been the same without her today," Florie said.

I said nothing, but I knew she was right. Katherine always brought with her a sense of cheer and fun. She made every task seem less daunting, and there seemed to be no challenge which was too big. I had spent the day feeling miserable, and I'd blamed it on a lack of sleep and the guilt I felt for what I'd said to Katherine. But now that I thought about it, that was only half the reason. The entire day had felt bleak, despite the two new lambs and my pride in Florie's achievements. There was an underlying feeling that something was not right, and it slowly dawned on me that most of my anguish was not caused by my conscience, but by the absence of something I missed and the fear that I may not have it again. I'd missed Katherine. She'd only been gone one day, and I really missed her.

I stirred my broses slowly in my bowl, my appetite gone, as I came to terms with this realisation. Something in my face must have changed, because Florie put her spoon down and reached over the table to take my hand. I wrapped my fingers around hers and looked at her with a heavy sigh.

"You're right, Florie, as always," I said. "I did make Katherine feel bad and I shouldn't have done that. If she doesn't come over in the morning, then I'll go over and see her."

"Can I come?" she asked.

I shook my head. "I need to tell her some things and I'm not sure how to go about it."

"Just tell her you were wrong and you're sorry."

I smiled at her. "Who's the mammy here?" I said, shaking her hand gently.

She smiled back at me, then went back to her food.

I slept a little better that night. Partially because I was still exhausted from the previous day, but mostly because I think it helped having a plan in mind to make things right with Katherine. In the morning, once again, Katherine did not show up for breakfast.

Florie and I finished our oats and then went out onto the croft to start on the morning's chores. I told Florie I would go to see Katherine as soon as those were done. Together we collected the eggs, let Sim out of the stable so he could graze and mucked out his stall, checked on the mother ewe and the lambs, refilled the water troughs and made a pass through the bee skeps. The colony we had offended a couple of weeks ago seemed to be fine and flourishing, much to my relief. We swept inside and outside the cottage, inspected the vegetable patches and disposed of a handful of pesky invaders, then took a pail and little stool each and headed to the pasture to milk the ewes.

As we walked back with our pails full, I was about to suggest getting started on making the cheese as another procrastinatory measure, when I noticed Katherine out in the turnip field.

Florie looked up at me expectantly and I sighed and said, "Yes, I'm going to talk with her. We'll just get the milk inside and you can start warming it."

Once I had Florie going with the milk and she had answered my questions, satisfying me that she knew what she was doing, I walked back out of the cottage and made my way towards Katherine. She was hunched down in a section of the field on her own croft, pulling weeds, but she stood up and brushed her hands off as I approached. I tried to walk in a friendly, non-threatening manner, but she still looked worried.

I was finally standing in front of her and managed a weak smile, but she just looked back with an anxious, slightly sad expression. I let my smile go and looked down for a moment, trying to think of what to say.

"Katherine, I—" I paused as I tried to think of the right words. "I just came over to say sorry to you." I looked up at her again.

She shook her head. "You don't have to say sorry," she said. "You were right to be angry."

"No," I said. "I shouldn't have said what I did to you, Katherine. It was wrong and cruel and I didn't mean it."

She stood in silence, chewing the inside of her cheek nervously, looking from my face, then back down to the ground again. "I just keep thinking you were right," she said. "If something had happened to Florie—"

"It didn't," I cut in, "and you didn't make her go off after the sheep and you didn't sleep through her leaving the cottage and you don't know her like I do. I should have expected it. You never intended to hurt either of us and you haven't hurt us. I'm ashamed to say I can't say the same for myself, so I should be asking for your forgiveness. I'm so sorry, Katherine."

Katherine's eyes glazed over with moisture, and she nodded slowly.

"Can we go back to how things were before?" I asked, quietly. "Florie misses you so much." After a moment I lowered my voice further and said, "I miss you."

Katherine swallowed and blinked a few times, then nodded again and looked down.

I wasn't sure what to say next. I didn't know if my apology had truly been accepted or how she'd taken my admission that I'd missed her, but I did know my strongest instinct at that moment was to touch her. I stepped forward and wrapped my arms around her, pulling her into a hug. She stiffened for a second, surprised by my sudden show of affection, but then I felt her relax and her arms slowly wrap around my back. She rested her head on my shoulder, her face turned outwards and her soft red locks brushed against my cheek. I'd never been close enough to become acquainted with her smell before, but now, as I breathed in, the scent of her hair enveloped my senses. It smelled fresh, like a field still covered in early morning dew, but there was a warmth there too. Not a bodily warmth, but more of a radiant heat, like one would feel on a windy summer's day. For a brief moment, I was lost in the new sensation, then I realised my eyes had closed and I snapped myself out of it and released her.

She looked at me and smiled warmly, but for some reason my pulse was racing and I couldn't think of a single thing to say or do. In that moment, I ascribed my physical reaction to a sense of relief that I had saved our friendship, but that explanation still felt off, like a puzzle piece which didn't fit well.

She looked at me for a few more seconds and I feared she might question me about my sudden impulsive gesture, but she just said, "I think I should go and say hello to Florie now. I've missed her too."

Then she walked across the field towards my cottage, and I followed her slowly. I knew I was reading too much into it, but I couldn't help wondering if she meant she missed Florie too, because I'd said Florie had missed her, or if she meant she missed Florie too, in the sense of as well as me. I shook my head. What was wrong with me? First, I find myself clinging on to her and sniffing her hair, and now I'm working myself up wondering if she missed me when she was gone.

Still running circles in my own head, I walked into the cottage where Florie and Katherine were parting from a hug, then Florie picked up the wooden paddle and continued to stir the milk over the fire.

"How's it coming?" I asked, walking over and dipping my finger in the cauldron.

"It's nearly there, I think," Florie said.

"It's there," I said. "Let's take it off quick before it overheats."

The milk was only lukewarm, so I was able to lift the cauldron off the chain with my bare hands and set it on the floor. I took the bottle of rennet from the cupboard and poured in a few drops.

"There, you can stir that in," I told Florie.

Florie brought the paddle over and began to stir the mixture. "Where did you go last night?" Florie asked Katherine.

"What?" Katherine asked. There was a trace of anxiety in her voice, as though she'd hoped we hadn't seen her.

"We came over to feed the pigs and we saw you leaving on Ailbeart," Florie said.

"Oh, um, I just went for a ride," Katherine said. "I thought Ailbeart could use some exercise."

I could see Florie was about to question Katherine further, so I quickly said, "What a good idea. We should all go for a ride together later today. You and me on Sim, and Katherine on Ailbeart. The weather looks like it will be nice and we could go along to the glen."

"Could I ride on Ailbeart with Katherine?" Florie asked.

"Of course you can. As long as your mother says it's alright," Katherine said, clearly pleased to have had the subject changed.

The next few days passed and as July came upon us, we were blessed with excellent weather and a lot of warm days.

"It's a blessing and a curse," I said one morning. "I was hoping to push the shearing until the end of the month, but if these hot days persist, we will have to do that sooner rather than later."

We were down by the river and we had brought a picnic lunch of cheese, bannock, mead, and honeycomb. The previous day, I had started a new barrel of mead and had kept aside some of the comb as a treat. It sat in a bowl covered by a piece of cheesecloth, and the honey had pooled in the bottom. Florie had stripped down to her linen chemise and was paddling in the bank of the river. The current flowed lazily along and I leaned back on my hands, enjoying the warmth of the sun.

"Come in and swim, Katherine," Florie called.

Katherine had been sitting watching Florie play while nibbling on a piece of bannock.

"Can you swim?" I asked Katherine.

"Of course," she said. "Back home, we used to swim in the loch every summer."

"Well, it's a bit of a ride to Loch Drumfell from here, but we could always go one of these days if you wanted to," I said. "But the river is nice, too. It's safe to swim in at this time of the year."

"Well, it must be nice," she said with a cheeky grin. "I've even seen people swimming in it during April storms."

"Sounds to me like some crazy people," I muttered, grinning back.

"Oh, definitely completely insane. But lovable," she winked.

I felt my face flush with warmth and was happy when Florie called out and drew Katherine's attention away from me.

"Come on Katherine, come on Mammy!" she called out, this time splashing water towards us.

I sighed, stood up and stretched, then started to shed my clothing. I removed everything except my chemise, then waded into the water, bracing myself against the cold. Katherine followed suit and dropped her things on the ground before walking to the edge and dipping her toes in.

"It's better if you just get it over with quickly," I suggested.

Without her stay and dress on, I noticed the small bump that had begun to form on her abdomen and I wondered if anyone else in the village was aware of the pregnancy. If Ailig didn't know, he would soon find out when he got back, unless he was blind. There had been no recent news regarding the men who were away, but it was believed by most of the village that if anything disastrous had happened, word would have arrived.

The three of us swam about in the water and, as expected, a game of 'get everyone else as wet as possible' soon erupted, with Florie doing the majority of the splashing. We played the rescue game and Florie showed Katherine how to save someone from drowning, just as her father had taught her, then insisted that we all practise saving each other. When it was my turn to be the drowning victim, I swam to the deepest part of the river, then splashed about, feigning distress.

Katherine swam over to me and played along. She looked at me with mock concern and said, "Don't panic, I'm here to save you. Float on your back and I'll swim you to safety."

"Oh, my hero!" I gasped in my most pitiful, damsel-in-distress voice.

I lay back in the water, pointing my face towards the sky and felt Katherine swim behind me. Her cool fingers slid under my chin and the water swelled under my body as she kicked herself backwards, bringing us towards the shore. I was aware of the back of my head grazing against her chest as she pulled me closer to her own body, and I focused on my chin and the bottom of my face, where her hand was in direct contact with my skin. Her long, wet hair trailed along at the sides of my face and I couldn't stop myself from bringing my hand up and gripping her wrist where she held me.

When we got back to the bank, Katherine let go, and I sat up in the water. Florie's cheers were muffled while the water drained from my ears and whatever she said, I missed, as Katherine's eyes momentarily met mine. The look was fleeting, her jovial expression replaced by one unfamiliar to me, and for that instant the game seemed forgotten.

"Yey! Katherine, you saved my mammy!" Florie shouted, jumping up and down, clapping. "You're a hero!"

Katherine's eyes tore from mine as she looked back to Florie. She lifted her fists in the air in a gesture of victory and waded out of the water and back onto the grass. I slowly followed and sat down next to them both.

I cleared my throat, attempting to shift the lump which had somehow got stuck there and said, "Who's for bannock and honey?"

The rest of the day lazed by and we let a few chores fall by the wayside, all of us deciding we had earned an afternoon off. After lunch, we swam a little more and then I sent Florie back to the cottage to fetch the backgammon set.

"This has been really nice," Katherine said, leaning back on her hands. Her chemise was still quite wet and the thin fabric clung to her figure in a manner which had me on the verge of blushing again.

"We do this every summer when we get the chance," I said. "It was a tradition of Robert's from when he was a boy."

"Well, it's a tradition well worth keeping up," Katherine said, wringing out her wet hair and then letting it fall in a clump over the front of her shoulder.

I smiled. I'd never really thought about it like that before, but it was a fine way to honour Robert's memory.

"Do you think Ailig will still let you come for swims with us when he gets back?" I asked, then instantly regretted mentioning his name.

Katherine's face darkened, and she frowned.

"He would be welcome to come too," I added quickly. Though in all reality, I thought having Ailig present for one of these afternoons would entirely detract from the fun of it. I don't know why I said it, because the image of the scenario was actually quite ridiculous.

Katherine must have thought the same because she laughed suddenly. "Ailig can't swim. He's terrified of water."

"Really? I never knew that," I said.

"Well, I suppose he doesn't go around advertising the fact. It would detract from his manly image and all. But when he was a boy, there was an incident, and he nearly drowned. He's been frightened ever since."

"Did he tell you that?" I asked, thinking how unlike Ailig it would be to admit to such a thing. But then maybe when they first got married he was more tender with her.

"He told my father after our wedding," she said. "He sort of had to. He made a real cock up of the ceremony."

I gave Katherine a perplexed look, struggling to understand how the two points fit together.

"Back in my clan, there's a specific ritual which is followed in every wedding ceremony. Marriages are always conducted at a sacred location right at the edge of the loch. The clan chief oversees each one, and after the vows are exchanged, the marriage is blessed in the water. It involves being submerged together briefly and signifies the couple being reborn again as a single entity. The couple goes in separately, the man first, then the woman, and they go under for a few seconds and then re-emerge together. That solidifies the union."

"Sounds very romantic," I said.

She grinned. "Depends on the time of the year you get married, I guess. I'm sure I don't have to tell you that summer weddings are the most popular in my clan. Though people also say couples who get married in the winter have stronger unions because it takes more courage to go through with the ceremony at that time."

"I can imagine," I said, grinning back. "So I take it the ceremony didn't go down well with Ailig, then?"

She gave a wry laugh. "It was disastrous. After the vows, the chief told him to go into the water and he only went in as far as his ankles. When he was told to keep going until he was up to his chest, he started making excuses that he didn't want to wet his best kilt. Obviously this didn't go down well with the chief and there was an argument, and then Ailig stormed off. I honestly thought at that point the wedding was going to fall through, which I wasn't sad about, of course. But in the end there was a meeting and I guess Ailig must have told the chief and my father about his problem because later the same day, I had to go back to the loch with Ailig and the chief announced that a slight alteration was being made for this particular ceremony. We ended up getting a bowl of water tipped over both of us at the same time, while we stood just at the edge of the loch. Other than my mother and father, none of my family or friends or anyone else was allowed to attend. It really was a joke."

I snorted. "I'm sorry," I said. "I shouldn't be disrespectful about your marriage."

She shrugged. "Be as disrespectful as you like. I have no respect for it. Even if he hadn't turned the ceremony into a farce, I wouldn't consider it a proper marriage. Marriage to me is about two people who love each other and want to spend the rest of their lives making each other happy. I don't know if I believe in love at first sight, or soulmates, or any of that other romantic nonsense that some people like to talk about, but I do believe in committing to a partnership that benefits both parties equally. To me, love is about being there for your partner, trying to predict what they need before they know it themselves, enjoying every moment you're with them and missing them every moment you're not. Drawing courage from each other and being able to face anything together and even if you fail, it doesn't feel like losing because you still have that other person and you know they'll still love you, no matter how badly you cock up."

She stopped for a moment and gazed off into space before adding, "And that doesn't come close to defining my marriage with Ailig."

I let out a long breath. I always thought my marriage with Robert was one of the very best I could have hoped for. Robert had been a good man and a good husband and I'd loved him, but not with the passion that Katherine had just described. I felt a heaviness descend upon me as I realised how totally unjust the world was to allow someone with a view of marriage like hers to end up with someone like Ailig. He really didn't deserve her.

"Wow," I said, slowly. She was staring down now at her outstretched feet, with a look of sadness which I suddenly found painful. I tried to think of something to say to lighten the mood.

"Well, in spite of my experience, I now feel like between the two of us, you understand marriage better. If Ailig kicks the bucket in this raid, maybe you and I should give it a try." I tried to add humour to my voice as I said it, but it came out instead with a wistful smile and lacking the joking tone I was aiming for. She looked up at me quickly and I couldn't read her expression at all, but she certainly didn't laugh at the joke.

I felt my cheeks go hot and was overwhelmingly relieved to hear Florie come scampering down the hill behind us, carrying the basket with the game in it. I turned away from Katherine and made a fuss of Florie, congratulating her for being so quick.

The awkward moment had seemingly passed as Katherine rubbed her hands together and said, "I have a good feeling about today. It's time you were knocked down from your pedestal. I'm not going to go easy on you this time, so prepare to fall hard."

"Hah! We'll see about that," I retorted, but after I'd beaten her twice, I let her win the last game.

By the time the early evening had set in, we had dried off and re-dressed. Katherine came over to our cottage for dinner, and to finish the day off, we had rabbit stew. Since the weather was so nice, we decided to eat it outside and sat on a couple of benches and looked down the valley towards the river as we ate.

"What a lovely day it's been," I said.

"We should do this every day," Florie piped up.

"I'm afraid we'd have a pretty poor harvest if that were the case," I smiled. "But we could certainly afford to do it more often if things continue as they are."

As things stood, all of the crops were doing remarkably well. We were set to have a bumper crop of turnips and even split in half, it looked like there'd be enough for me to trade for the extra fleeces I needed. We got more lambs than we expected so by this time next year my flock would be bigger than it was before, and besides being able to keep my croft, the next best thing was that we'd achieved it without having to put in extra hours of work. On the contrary, I couldn't remember a year where I'd had so much free time.

After Katherine finished her stew, she stood up. "Well, I'd better get going."

"No, stay. Please," Florie pleaded.

Since the night after the barn door incident, nearly a week ago, Katherine had taken to riding off on Ailbeart every night at about the same time. She said it was to give him exercise, but I guessed she just enjoyed a little time outside to herself. Maybe she really did want to exercise the horse, but when Florie had asked if she could go with her, or even if me and her could ride along with her on Sim, Katherine had said no. She was very vague about where she went riding, and I had to tell Florie she needed to accept that Katherine was entitled to do some things by herself and was not expected to spend every waking minute with us. Florie was disappointed, but accepted what I told her, though it didn't stop her from pleading with Katherine not to leave so early every night.

Her rides were quite long, and she usually didn't get back for at least a couple of hours. Or at least, that was how long she was gone on the days I witnessed her return. I didn't press her about it though, as I didn't want to come across as nosy. After all, Katherine was a grown woman and owed us no explanation at all.

Katherine smiled at Florie and squeezed her arm. "Don't worry. I won't be long and you'll see me in the morning."

Florie sighed and nodded.

"How about tomorrow I won't go for my ride? I think Ailbeart will need a rest anyway after this week, I've worked him hard."

This seemed to cheer Florie up a bit, and she gave Katherine a hug before heading back into the cottage to get ready for bed.

"If you want to come over after your ride, you can." I said. "Florie will be in bed, but I'll be up knitting, so you're welcome to join me. You really need to get a move on with that blanket if you want it to be bigger than a tea towel by the time baby gets here."

Katherine smiled at me.

"Perhaps I'll do that," she said, then turned to walk back to her croft.

After Katherine left, I went inside my cottage, cleaned the bowls and spoons, and put Florie to bed. I told her a story I made up about a man who sailed all around Loch Ness, looking for the fabled monster. Then I picked up my knitting and decided to work on a blanket for Katherine's baby, just in case she didn't manage to finish her own in time.

After a couple of hours, there came a light knock at the door. I put my knitting down and went to answer it, pleased that Katherine had taken me up on my offer. I opened it, grinning when I saw Katherine holding her kitting in her hands and smiling back at me. She looked tired, but happy.

"You look exhausted," I said. "These nightly rides seem to knock seven bells out of you." I stood back from the door to let her in, then added, "I'm glad you're taking a day off tomorrow, but I really think in future you should keep those rides down to just an hour or less. You're getting further along in the pregnancy and it can't be good for the baby."

She stepped inside and walked over to the table and sat down heavily, sighing. "You're right," she said, closing her eyes. "I don't think I'll go on with them anymore. This was the last time."

I nodded. "I think that's a wise decision."

I walked to the table and sat down next to her. She really did look tired. She continued to sit in the chair with her head tilted back and her eyes closed, breathing softly.

"You know, if you just want to go to sleep, please don't feel like you have to be here." I reached out and rested my hand on her arm. "The knitting can wait. I was just kidding about your baby blanket. We'll make sure it gets done in time."

She opened her eyes and smiled again.

"I'm not worried about that," she said. "And don't fret about me, I'm fine."

"Are you sure?" I asked, pulling my hand back slowly.

She nodded, then placed her knitting on the table. "The knitting can probably wait. I really came because I have something I wanted to give to you."

I sat back, curious.

"What?" I said.

She smiled, then reached down into her pocket and withdrew a leather pouch about the size of the palm of her hand. She placed it down on the table, then slid it over to me. I looked at her before picking it up. It was heavy and my heart raced as I loosened the drawstrings and opened the pouch. Then I slid out the brooch and placed it on the table in front of me. I took a deep breath, then put my hand to my mouth and bit down, trying to convince myself I wasn't dreaming.

"My mother's brooch," I whispered. I looked at her again, but she simply sat there, faintly smiling.

"How did you get it back?" I asked. "You had nothing to trade."

Her smile remained, but grew tense. "A woman always has something to trade, Anna."

As her words sunk in, I rested my elbows on the table and buried my face in my hands, feeling sick to my stomach.

"No," I whispered. "Why? Why would you?"

"I thought that would be obvious by now," she said quietly. Her voice sounded hollow. "And why not, Anna? What does it matter? I've already been forced a thousand times by a man I hate. What's a few nights with another man I can't stand to touch me?"

I felt the tears well up in my eyes as I shook my head behind my hands. I wanted to un-hear what I'd heard, un-know what I knew. The thought of Katherine's delicate body being used by Daniel sent a sickening chill to my very core. Daniel had returned the brooch, but it felt as though he had taken something else in its place, something just as valuable. I knew it was silly. She said it herself. What was a few more nights with one more man? But what Ailig did to her was out of my control and had nothing to do with me. Daniel though; that was directly because of me and I hated that thought.

I stood up and walked to the other side of the room, keeping my back to her, unable to face her. I couldn't stand to see the dark circles under her eyes, or the pain in her face that she was trying so hard to hide.

I breathed heavily, and trying to keep my voice steady, I said, "I need some fresh air." Then I opened the door and stepped outside.

I walked a few paces away from the cottage, gripping the hair at the back of my head with my hands. My mind raced with a multitude of thoughts. Why would she do so much for me, after everything she'd already done? Every time I thought I couldn't possibly sink further into her debt, she proved me wrong.

I heard the door squeak open behind me, but I still refused to turn around. I kept my back to her, even as I heard her walk up and stand inches behind me.

"I understand if you feel completely disgusted at me," Katherine said quietly. "I'm so sorry, Anna. I just knew how much that brooch meant to you, and the day you had to trade it to Daniel has replayed in my mind so many times. After the barn, I was so afraid you would lose that sheep. It was the only thing I could think of to help at that time. If you want me to leave; if you don't want to see me anymore after this, I won't hold it against you. I—"

"Stop," I choked, still not turning to look at her. "Don't, Katherine. Please. I can't. I can't stand here and listen to you apologise to me. Not for this."

There was a long silence, and I struggled to keep my shoulders rising and falling steadily.

"Alright," she whispered. "I'll go."

I heard her take a step back. "Please don't think too badly of me, Anna. I don't know how I would cope if I thought you couldn't look at me again."

"Think badly of you?" I whispered, unsure if she could even hear me. Then I spun around to look at her. Her chest rose and fell heavily, her cheeks were streaked with tears, and her eyes were wrought with pain.

"I could never think badly of you again," I said. Then I grabbed the front of her dress, pulled her towards me, and pressed my lips against hers.

I kissed her for what felt like an age. I closed my eyes, and I felt her arms move up and a soft hand rest on the back of my neck as she kissed me back, pulling my lips deeper into hers. I could taste her salty tears and the softness of her mouth seemed to draw me away from reality. Her other hand rose to find my cheek, and her fingertips grazed behind my ear, sending tingles down my spine. I wanted to freeze that moment; keep it for longer. I didn't want it to pass in case I opened my eyes to find I was dreaming.

Then I felt her slowly pull away, and I opened my eyes. Her thumb now caressed the side of my cheek as she smiled. A beautiful smile which sent the same tingles through my core once again. I had no words, but she didn't seem to need them.

"I'll see you tomorrow," she said, withdrawing her hands slowly. Then she turned and walked back to her cottage.

Chapter Fourteen

KATHERINE

I opened my eyes and turned my head to look out of the window next to my bed. It was such a warm day yesterday that I hadn't closed the shutters last night, and now the daylight shone across my face. I couldn't see the sun, which was high in the sky, and that meant I had slept much longer than I'd intended. For the first time in a long time, I had slept through the night, content and happy, despite the last several days which had been tiring and stressful.

I'd had to visit Daniel every day for a full week and he'd made the most of every last minute we had agreed to. It had been worrying me all week that he might back out and not give me the payment he promised. It was a lot of work on my part, and he'd made many requests I struggled to comply with, but thankfully, he was a man of his word and he did hand the item over in the end.

I had always regarded prostitution as an abhorrent profession, but now I felt guilty for my previous judgments and deeply pitied the women who had to make it a lifetime career. However, when all was said and done, it had been less depressing to lend my body to someone for payment, even with his disgusting preferences, than it was to be forced by Ailig for nothing. Not only did Ailig refuse to give me even a small measure of love in return for the satisfaction he derived from my body, but he'd taken from me the only good thing which came from his unwanted attention; my baby.

I thought back to last night and smiled to myself as my heart gave a sudden flutter. How different it was, kissing Anna. I replayed the moment in my head as I had already done countless times last night before I finally fell asleep. She had kissed me. And it had been so unexpected. When I followed her outside, I was overcome by a sense of loss and sadness. I was sure she was disgusted at me, that she wouldn't want to be in my presence ever again. My heart was breaking, and then she kissed me. I touched my fingers to my lips, trying to recreate the feeling again. I sat for a while on the edge of my bed, reliving the moment.

Until last night, I had never felt the way Anna made me feel when her lips met mine. I never knew the touch of another person could have such a strong effect on my body and mind, or at least, not in a good way. Even the memory of it was enough to send that warm rush through my core once again. I grinned to myself, standing up and enjoying the halo of happiness which seemed to surround me.

I went outside to find Anna and saw her and Florie at the back of their cottage, collecting the eggs from the roosting boxes.

"Good morning," I said as I approached them.

"Good morning, Katherine," Florie said cheerfully. She had half a dozen eggs held in her apron and she showed them to me proudly.

"Those are big ones," I said enthusiastically. "Maybe when you've put those inside, you can come to my croft and check the boxes there too."

She grinned and nodded, then skipped off around the front of the longhouse to unload the eggs.

Anna smiled warmly at me, setting off another spate of tingles which travelled from my chest, down to my feet.

"You slept late," she said.

I noticed she was wearing her mother's brooch, and the silver glinted beautifully in the sunlight. She had secured it to a light shawl, which she wore around her shoulders. The day felt a bit warm for it to be necessary, but I was pleased she was so happy to have it back that she was creating excuses to wear it.

"I know. Sorry about that. I didn't mean to," I said.

"Don't be silly. You clearly needed it." She looked down at my stomach, but my small bump was hardly noticeable through my dress. "You really have to start taking things a little easier now, for both of your sakes."

"I will," I said.

She smiled again and held my gaze for a few moments, before Florie came running back.

"I'm ready!" she said, looking up at me cheerfully, then she grabbed my hand and started pulling me back towards my croft.

"Alright, alright, I'm coming," I said, then shouted back to Anna. "The boar needs to go back to Mary today. I think we should get that chore over with sooner rather than later."

Anna nodded, and I turned to follow Florie to the roosting boxes next to my cottage.

The rest of the day was busy, and it took a good two hours to get the boar back to his owner. He wasn't much easier to move than the first time, but we had slightly less far to go because he was now in my pen

Having learned from the last couple of times we'd moved him, we all stocked up on turnip leaves and a few turnips in order to coax him when he felt less motivated. Florie followed behind him with a switch, giving him a gentle tap when necessary, and Anna and I walked on either side of him. They both hung back when I knocked on Mary's door to inform her the boar was back in his pen, then we all walked back to my croft together.

It was another warm day, and the sky was mostly clear, so we spent the afternoon weeding the turnip field, checking on the health of the crop, and then tending to the vegetable patches. Since it hadn't rained in several days, we decided to give the potatoes, vegetables and oats some water, so spent a good while filling buckets from the wells on both properties and pouring the water where we felt it was needed.

"I'm glad we're doing this," Anna said as we trudged back to her vegetable patch with two more full buckets. "I know it's a pain, but the soil is quite dry."

"Ay, it's been warm," I said. "I know you wanted to wait a couple more weeks, but I think we really need to consider shearing the sheep in the next day or so."

"You're right," Anna said, sighing. "At least we managed to push it a bit longer than normal. We may get slightly bigger fleeces out of it."

When the early evening came around, I suggested having supper at my cottage. Anna's sow was still penned up with mine, but after the long trek earlier in the day with the boar, we felt she could wait until tomorrow before going home herself. Anna and I got started on preparing the dinner while Florie played with her doll on the floor. It was now wearing the little woollen dress she had made for it, but I had a strong suspicion Anna had 'helped' with the project while Florie was sleeping. It had turned out very nice and the little doll looked very cute in it.

"I should probably start working on my baby blanket again," I said. Then I remembered it was still over at Anna's where I'd left it last night. "I'm just going to run back to your cottage to fetch my knitting," I said. "Is there anything else you want me to bring?"

"You can bring my knitting too if you want," Anna said. "And the backgammon board if you fancy being thrashed again later."

"Oh, I don't know if I'll be able to carry it," I said in mock disappointment. "I'll have my arms full with all that heavy knitting."

"Sounds like a poor excuse to avoid being beaten again," she grinned.

I chuckled and then headed out the door.

I jogged across the pasture between Anna's croft and mine, past the empty pigpen at the end of her longhouse, then came around the corner to the front door. I pushed it open and went inside, then looked around for my pitiful lump of knitting which I found on top of the shelf at the back of the room. Anna's knitting was right next to it, so I picked that up too, and smiling, I also grabbed the wicker basket which had the backgammon board in it. While I remembered, I also picked up Anna and Florie's bowls and spoons, and with the pile in my arms, I went back outside.

I made a subconscious decision to go back around the longhouse via the barn side, and as I did, I could hear Sim inside. He was whinnying and nickering softly, and I could hear the thud of his hooves on the ground as he stamped anxiously. Something was agitating him. I placed my bundle of items on the ground and opened the large barn door slowly to peek inside.

I was instantly aware of the smell of burning and looked around for where it was coming from. I could see in the back corner of the barn a small coil of smoke rising from one of the hay bales. There were several small flames at the base which were gradually growing and I instantly panicked over what to do. Trying not to concentrate at this moment on what might have ignited the flames, I turned and raced to the well to get a bucket of water. I pulled the pail up as fast as I could, then hurried back towards the barn, trying not to spill it as I went. It was my intention to douse the flames, then try to get the panicked horse out safely. If I could put the flames out, then I might go back to get Anna to help me with Sim. The last thing I needed was to get kicked or trampled in an attempt to get him out.

I was about twenty feet from the barn door when Frang limped around the side of the longhouse and stood in front of it, blocking me. He held his staff suspended off the ground, gripping it as if it were a weapon and my blood froze as I realised he must have deliberately set the fire.

I walked as close to him as I felt was safe and said, "Get out of the way, Frang!"

He sneered at me and didn't move. "You're not going in there," he said. Then he looked at the pail of water in my hands. "Not with that bucket, anyway."

"Move!" I shouted again. My heart was now hammering and I could hear the horse whinnying louder. "There's still time to put it out!" I screamed, now striding forward and trying to force my way past him.

He slammed his hand down on the bucket, knocking it roughly out of my arms, and it fell to the ground, cascading the water in a large puddle around my feet. Then he moved his staff into both hands and used it to shove me backwards, away from the door.

I staggered back and toppled over onto my bum. Then he reached behind him and closed the barn door, dropping the latch. He limped towards me, kicking the bucket off to the side, and his lips curled into a malignant sneer. His leg was damaged, and he wasn't young anymore, but he was strong nonetheless. Stronger than me.

I looked beyond him at the barn and noticed a considerable amount of smoke rising from the roof at the back of the building. The bastard had lit more than one fire. The last week had been so warm and dry, the roof would go up like tinder, and sure enough, the yellow flames started to become visible under the smoke as the fire spread. I couldn't sit here and watch as Anna's house burned.

"You bastard!" I screamed.

I got to my feet and ran towards him to pick up the bucket, which was lying near his feet. As I bent down to get it, I felt a pair of powerful arms wrap around my chest. I struggled and kicked, dropping the bucket again and tried to release myself, but I gasped as he grabbed a fistful of hair and yanked my head back with an agonising tug. His other arm came around my neck and he locked me in the vice of his elbow and squeezed until I saw stars and stopped struggling.

He yanked me around so I was facing the building. "Now you can watch as that savage little whore's house burns to the ground," he rasped into my ear. His breath reeked of whiskey and I raked at his arm, trying to loosen his grip.

"Please," I gasped, struggling to breathe. "The horse; let him out of the barn."

I could hear the terrified creature inside, neighing pitifully, and my vision blurred as my eyes streamed with tears. Smoke was now starting to creep out of the windows and the crackling sound of the flames on the roof were getting louder.

"Don't worry, it'll be quick. The smoke will get him before the flames do. You'll see."

I gasped and struggled, but the more I did, the tighter he squeezed his arm around my neck.

"Please," I begged again. I could hear the banging as Sim repeatedly kicked against the door of his stall, still whinnying in panic, and the flames were now spreading along the roof to the cottage.

"Let's see that whore keep her croft now," he said.

"You won't get away with this," I croaked.

"Really?" he said. "Are you going to tell?" he squeezed harder again, and I choked and slapped my hands against his arm. "Because if you tell, I'll tell," he whispered. He loosened his grip slightly so I could breathe again and went on. "What do you think Ailig will do to you if he thinks that brat inside you isn't his?" he snarled, and the hand that had been gripping my hair let go and swept around the front of my belly. He rubbed my bump through my dress softly as he continued to whisper in my ear. "I wouldn't think much of that child's chances, or yours, if I were to tell him about your nightly visits to town." His hand slid down and cupped me between my legs, then he squeezed my crotch hard, making me wince and cry out. "I never took you for a whore, but then I suppose every woman is for the right price." He squeezed again, causing me to jerk back in pain. "And let's not forget about that moving moment between you and your whore last night." He must have felt my whole body stiffen because he went on. "Oh yes, I saw that. You're lucky. I was there last night, and I was going to burn down the house with all of you inside. But then you both came out, and well, what can I say? I was moved by your... exchange. But can you imagine what Ailig would do to Anna if I told him about that? And what would happen to her little brat? I'm sure you'll agree Anna doesn't need any more enemies in this town."

The smoke now billowed up from the house. The barn had gone quiet, other than the crackle of the flames, and I sobbed, the tears running uncontrollably down my face.

It wouldn't be long before people started to come running to find out what was on fire. He seemed to be aware of this too because he started dragging me backwards, away from the cottage.

"So we have an understanding then, yes? You say nothing about seeing me here and I'll keep my secrets to myself too."

Then he released me, shoving me away from him, before picking up his staff and limping away, back to his own croft.

I stood doubled over for a few moments, coughing and trying to catch my breath. Through the blur of my tears, I looked up to see the entire roof of the longhouse engulfed in flames. The stone walls were not burning, but the barn door had gone up, along with the shutters on that part of the building, and over the cottage, flaming parts of the thatched roof were dropping down and burning on the ground next to the door.

I raced to the well and pulled a pail of water as fast as I could, then ran back to the longhouse. The roof of the cottage was ablaze, and the inside was dark with smoke, but there was no fire in the interior yet. I removed my apron and dipped it into the bucket of water, threw the wet cover over my head and took a deep breath. Then I ran inside.

I had been in Anna's cottage enough times to know where she kept most of her more valuable belongings. I grabbed the blankets from her and Florie's beds, the large wooden spoon which was used in the cauldron, Robert's bowl and his carving knife from the shelf. I dashed outside with the items and dropped them on the ground several meters away from the building, then I ran back in and pulled out the three chairs she kept around her table, as well as both her and Florie's cloaks. There was a sack of oats next to the door, which I also dragged out, but the cottage was becoming too smoky to keep going back in, so I dropped my wet apron and ran back to the well to get more water. As I did, I saw Anna and Florie running across the pasture towards the burning building, and when I glanced at the track down by the river, I could see several people on horseback hurrying to our aid.

I ran with the bucket back to the cottage and threw the water against the door to try to protect it from the flames, then turned around to refill it. As I raced back to the well again, Florie and Anna came running up, both staring in disbelief at the sight.

"What happened?" cried Anna. Her face was white with shock, but I saw a bucket in her hand, so she had at least had the sense to bring mine from my cottage.

"The roof of the barn was on fire when I got here," I said. I grabbed her empty bucket and handed her the full one I'd just pulled from the well. "Here, throw this on the shutters and doors of your cottage. The roof will be lost, but we might be able to save the rest of the house if we can get it wet enough."

Anna stood for a moment, staring at her burning home, while Florie clung to her skirts, sobbing. I grabbed Florie and had her stand next to the well, then bent down to her. Her eyes were red and her lip quivered as I spoke.

"Florie, you need to stay here where it's safe. More people will be here to help in a minute. Keep drawing water up from the well. Your mammy can run back and forth and swap buckets with you. It will save time, alright?"

She nodded, still crying.

"Anna, go!" I shouted.

Anna seemed to snap out of her frozen state and ran across the garden to the cottage, where she threw the water at the window shutters. Thick grey smoke continued to billow up from the thatch roof and she ran back to refill her bucket. I had filled my own bucket and also ran back and forth, throwing the contents into the house, on the door, windows, and walls.

Within another minute, several people had arrived on horseback, most of them with buckets. There were five women I knew from the village, and a handful of boys too young to go to battle, but old enough to help. One of the women ran over to Anna and there was a hurried exchange, then there was a lot of shouting and directing, but there soon formed a relatively organised bucket brigade.

Florie was relieved of duty and one of the bigger boys began pulling water at a much faster pace, and bucket loads of water began to be thrown steadily onto the roof. Everyone worked frantically and after another fifteen minutes, a further twenty or so people had shown up to help, most of them having run over from the village or the surrounding crofts. After nearly an hour, the fire had been doused to a smoulder and the beams above the cottage were charred and bare, most of the thatch having burned away. The inside of the house was trashed with embers, bits of blackened thatch, puddles, and soot. Everything the fire hadn't taken was blackened with smoke damage and the barn was even worse. Most people had focused on trying to save the cottage, so the barn and stable inside had almost completely burned. The stone walls still stood, but the wooden beams of the roof were destroyed and the bits that were left looked like an open ribcage with mottled black bones. The stall where Sim was kept was mostly gone, and the body of the massive clydesdale lay still on the floor, his once shiny coat barely recognisable under the black layer of soot which covered him.

As Anna walked around her property, I held Florie back with me to save her from the sight in the barn. What remained of the thatch on the roof still smoked, but it would likely take hours, if not days, for that to stop unless we had rain tonight. I looked up at the sky and hoped the clouds in the distance would bring some. The people who had come to help slowly filed away, many of them speaking to Anna first and offering gestures of sympathy.

"You're her neighbour, aren't you?" came a voice from beside me.

I looked up to see an elderly woman speaking to me. Her name was Mujre, I think.

"Yes," I said.

"I take it your husband is away right now?" she said.

I nodded.

"Once the men get back, there will be a meeting and we can discuss how we can help Anna. For now, though, would you be willing to let them stay with you?"

"Of course," I said. I would have been thrilled with the idea under any other circumstances.

"Good," she said, patting me on my shoulder. "Did you see how it started?" she said, looking back at the smouldering roof.

I gritted my teeth but shook my head.

She sighed. "Sometimes all it takes is a spark from the fire, and it's been so dry lately. I know you're quite new here, but a few years ago we had a bad one nearer to the village. The McDoogal family. It was an absolute tragedy, they lost two of their sons to that fire." She sighed again, shaking her head. "At least this time no one was hurt."

I didn't answer and just looked over at the barn where Sim lay lifeless.

Chapter Fifteen

"It was Frang! I know it was him!" Anna said in a choked voice.

We were picking up the few items which I had saved from the fire. The knitting, backgammon board and bowls which I had originally gone to pick up, and the chairs, blankets, cloaks, oats and carving knife I had gone back for. The ground all around the house was soaked and full of mud, soot, and bits of burned straw from the roof. As much as we had tried to save the doors and shutters of the cottage, they were charred and damaged and everything inside was wet or burned or both. It was impossible to tell which objects might be salvageable under the layer of ash which covered everything.

"It couldn't have been anyone else!" Anna said, wiping away her tears and smudging clear patches across her sooty face.

Florie sat on the ground further away from the house, clutching her doll, not saying anything.

"Of course it was," I said. "But you can't go around saying that without proof."

"Which we'll never get," she said, choking back another sob. She turned her back to her home and walked a few paces away to a patch of grass which was dry. "He burned down our home and killed Sim, and the bastard will get away with it scot-free!"

I didn't know what to say to this. I couldn't tell her I'd seen him doing it without endangering her, and I struggled to think of any words which would bring comfort.

"How can we possibly come back from this?" she said, slumping down onto the grass, next to a patch of thistles. The beautiful purple flowers had been just far enough away from the cottage to have avoided the trampling feet of all those who were frantically running back and forth between the burning building and the well. Staring at them now with my back to the devastation, I could almost pretend for a second that the last few hours hadn't really happened. But when my eyes shifted to Anna's stricken, sooty face and filthy clothes, it was a stark reminder of the reality we were facing.

I walked over and sat down beside her on the other side of the little flower patch. "Mujre said the men would have a meeting when they returned," I said quietly, trying to make her feel better. "I'm sure they'll think of some way to help, and in the meantime you can both stay with me. It's going to be alright."

"How can they help?" she said. "They can't replace Sim. He was worth more than the cottage. They're not going to build a new home for us. We'll end up losing the croft."

"You won't Anna, we won't let him win," I said, firmly. I couldn't let her fall apart like this.

She shook her head, then pulled her knees up to her chin and buried her face. "There are some things that can't be fixed, Katherine, and you're naïve if you think anything else."

I reached over and put a hand gently on her back. "Anna, you lost a house and a horse. It's a lot to lose; I'm not saying it isn't, but you're strong enough to survive this."

"How do you know how strong I am or what I can survive?" she said, sitting up suddenly and looking at me. Her eyes were red and puffy and her chest rose and fell with each laboured breath. A fresh set of tears welled up in her eyes as she continued. "I don't feel strong and I don't feel like I'm surviving, and every time I think things are getting better, something comes along and knocks me down again." She took another shuddering breath before she continued, but her words were strained and stifled. "Sim was part of our family, he was more than just a tool on the farm and more than just a mount. He was Robert's pride and joy. Sim was with Robert when he died and I know it's silly, but it feels like another piece of Robert has been taken from me. I-I can't explain it." She was sobbing again now and looked down at the ground beside us. Her eyes lingered on the thorny plants for a few moments, then she went on. "It's like the down of a thistle. In one instant, everything you love and care about can be stripped away from you, and you have to watch as the pieces scatter to the wind and disappear, and all you're left with is an ugly, naked, raw patch, atop a mass of thorny spines. That's how I feel, Katherine. Naked and raw."

I nodded slowly and let her catch her breath and settle down before I replied.

"I understand, Anna. There are some losses that can't be replaced. You're right, some things can't be fixed. No one can bring back Sim or Robert. We've all lost things. Life is full of hurt and sadness and loss. But there's also love and happiness, if you're open to it. You didn't lose everything. You have a beautiful daughter who loves you immensely. You have me, and I—- care for you deeply. We still have the crops, the pigs and the sheep. Don't let the anger and hurt you feel make you blind to what you have sitting right in front of you."

She turned away from the flowers and stared intently straight ahead, still silently sobbing.

I reached over and carefully picked one of the spiny, beautiful flowers from the patch next to us, then held it out to her. She turned to look slowly, her eyes still glistening, then she reached out and took it from my fingers.

"Do you know what I love about thistles, Anna?" I said.

She had been looking at the flower she held, but now lifted her eyes back to mine.

"Given time, thistles bloom again. Even if you chop down the whole plant, eventually it grows back stronger. The colours return and that plant has the chance to be whole and beautiful once more."

Anna looked back at the flower again and closed her eyes, sending a fresh stream of tears down both cheeks. Then I lowered my voice and said gently, "This will not be your undoing, Anna. And I'll help you in any way I can, but you can't give up." Then I stood and went to pick up a handful of the items I'd saved before walking back to my own cottage, carrying the few possessions she had left in my arms.

Before the last of the people who had come to help left, it was agreed that a few of the older boys would return in the morning to help dig a grave for Sim.

The sky had darkened and heavy clouds loomed overhead, making me hopeful that the rain would come soon and douse the remaining smouldering patches on the roof.

Fortunately, Anna's sow was still penned up with my pig, and though the pigpen at the end of Anna's cottage was mostly unscathed, it now made sense to keep both pigs where they were while Anna and Florie were staying with me. The sheep still had the shelter, and the chickens had steered clear of the building while it was burning, so they were all unharmed.

I suggested to Anna that we take Florie back to my cottage for something to eat and come back to her house tomorrow to check for anything we could salvage. She nodded absently in agreement and followed me as I took Florie by the hand and led her back across the pasture. The stew had been cooking over the stove and was ready, so I dished up three bowls and brought them to the table. Florie took hers gratefully and began to eat, but Anna sat on her chair and stared vacantly at the wall.

"I want him to pay for what he did," she said quietly. Her eyes had dried, but were still red and there was now a hardness to them. A look of hate.

"I want him to suffer. I want to go over to his house and set it ablaze."

I shook my head and reached out to take her hand. "We'll think of something," I said gently. "We won't let him get away with it, but we have to be patient and you mustn't do anything rash. He has children, grandchildren and a wife. And you're not wicked like him."

As I said this, I recalled what Frang had told me earlier in the evening. He'd come the night before, planning to set fire to the place while we were in it, and the only thing which stopped him was that Anna and I had come outside before he could do it. He had locked the barn deliberately to make sure the horse wouldn't get out. Would he have gone as far as to block the door of the cottage last night while we were in it? I wanted to think not, but I would never know for sure and the thought sent cold shudders through my body.

"I feel wicked," Anna replied in a hollow voice.

She was still filthy, and I imagined I didn't look much better. Anna hardly touched her food, and I decided the best thing to do would be to fill the bathtub so she could get clean and mix her something to help her relax.

I went out to my barn and brought in the large tin tub, which had not seen much use over the summer. In fact, I couldn't remember an occasion where I'd seen Ailig use it. I dragged it inside, wiped the dust out of it with my apron, and then went back and forth to the well for what seemed like the thousandth time that day. It took me about fifteen minutes to fill the tub about one third of the way up. I emptied the remainder of the stew into a large wooden bowl, then carried the cauldron outside to the well. After rinsing it out, I filled it with as much water as I thought I could carry and brought it back to the cottage, then hung it over the fire to heat. While I waited for it to boil, I took out my medicine bag and mixed a few herbs and powders together in a cup of mead, before pushing it into Anna's hands.

"Drink this," I said. "It will make you feel calmer."

Anna continued to stare ahead at nothing, but obediently lifted the cup to her lips and began to sip the contents.

When the water in the cauldron was near to boiling, I dipped the pail inside and filled it with hot water, which I poured into the tub, then repeated the process until the water in the tub was warm. I dipped my hand in to check the temperature, then went back to Anna, who had drank about half of the liquid in the cup.

"I've drawn you a bath," I said. "Come on."

I pulled her arm to get her to stand up, then started to undo the ties of her skirt. She still said nothing, but her bloodshot eyes, which had been vacant and expressionless, now looked straight at me as I worked, exploring my face with intensity. Then she reached out and put her hand on my cheek.

"Why are you always so kind to me, Katherine?" she said.

I paused from undoing her ties, and tilted my face further into her hand, closing my eyes. "Because it's the right thing to do," I said quietly.

It wasn't exactly the whole truth, but it wasn't a lie either. I went back to the fastenings, and once her skirt was loosened I let it fall around her feet. Next, I removed the brooch and shawl she still had on, placing the items on the table, then I loosened the ribbons on her bodice and pulled it over her head. I undid the ties at the front of her stay and removed that too, but hesitated when it came to the last layer, the thin white chemise.

Last time I'd needed her to strip off, the day I pulled her and Florie out of the river, she'd been reluctant to do so in front of me. Working with my mother, I'd got used to seeing both men and women in various states of undress and the prospect hadn't bothered me in a long time. But even though Anna currently seemed so lost in her own thoughts I doubted she would have noticed or even cared if I stripped her now, I felt it would be wrong not to respect what she would have preferred in any normal situation.

"Take the rest off and get in," I said to Anna, who had gone back to staring into space. "I'm going to the well for more water to heat, but I'll be right back. The soap is in that cupboard there," I pointed, then picked up both pails and headed back outside.

I walked slowly to give her enough time to get undressed the rest of the way and get into the bath, and by the time I got back inside, she was sitting hunched in the tub with her arms wrapped around her knees. Her eyes were closed and her face was still filthy, her light brown curls framing her grimy cheeks.

Florie had sat herself on my bed and was leaning back against the headboard, cuddling her doll.

I poured the next batch of water into the cauldron to heat up, added more peat to the fire, and then picked up the soap and grabbed a small cloth from the cupboard. Then I walked slowly to the edge of the bath and crouched down next to Anna. I did my best to respect her modesty and avoided looking down as I dipped the cloth into the water and then rubbed it with soap. She watched me in silence as I carefully wiped her face clean, revealing more and more of her smooth, pale skin and the light smattering of freckles on her nose.

When her face was clean, I dipped the cloth in the water again to rinse it, then, because she was still hunched over with her arms around her knees, I repositioned myself behind her and rubbed the cloth slowly down the back of her neck. The water from the cloth trickled in tiny rivers down her back and along her spine, which protruded slightly due to the position she sat in. The little trails of water met no obstacles. Her skin was smooth and perfectly blemish-free and I had a sudden urge to touch her, just to find out if she was as soft as she looked.

I gave myself a mental shake, then applied more soap to the cloth, before rubbing it over her shoulders and then up and down her back, being careful not to stray too low. I could feel each individual vertebrae bump under the cloth as I moved it up and down her centre. Soapy suds gathered in little clusters as I washed her and I found the ritual therapeutic, even for myself. My mind wondered for a moment and the cloth slipped out of my hand and splattered in the water below. I paused for a moment, deciding whether or not to retrieve it. Hesitating, I looked down at my hands. In one, I still held the soap, so I rubbed the bar between both palms, building up a few suds, then placed the soap on the floor next to me. Cautiously, I placed both of my hands directly on Anna's back and waited for her reaction. She gave a small sigh, her back rising then falling ever so slightly under my fingers, but she gave me no indication that she wasn't alright with me touching her.

I swept my hands over her back, gliding my fingers slowly up and down over her soapy skin. I wasn't sure if it was because of the soap, but her skin was smoother and softer than I had even imagined. While I had the chance, I set out to touch every last square inch of her back that I had access to, while being careful never to run my hands too low, or far around her sides. She sat all but motionless, breathing softly as my hands trailed up over her neck, across her shoulders and down to just above the base of her spine. I could have sat there all night, but I was aware the water in the tub was getting cold and the water in the cauldron had started to bubble vigorously. I withdrew my hands and then reached down to grab the cloth. I was careful not to touch her as I did it, but she lifted her head slightly and gave a deep sigh, as if coming out of a daze.

I wrung out the cloth and wiped my face as thoroughly as I could, then stood up and walked over to the table. I passed the cup of medicated mead back to Anna and told her to drink the rest, then rinsed the cloth once more and took it over to Florie. Having stayed back from the fire, she was not as filthy as we were, but I wiped her face nonetheless, and she seemed to enjoy the lukewarm cloth on her skin.

"After your mammy's done, you can go in the bath next if you like," I said. "I've got more hot water ready so it will be lovely and warm for you."

This cheered her up, and she nodded happily.

After Anna had finished her remedy, I took the cup back and gave her the cloth so she could finish cleaning the rest of her body. Then I took a blanket from the shelves and handed it to her so she could get dry and brought her my linen nightgown to wear. All of our clothes were filthy, but washing them would have to wait for another day. I hung Anna's dress over the back of a chair and put it next to the open window in hopes it might air out a bit.

After pouring the next batch of boiling water into the tub and waiting a minute for it to disperse evenly, Florie got in the bath next, and this seemed to bring Anna out of her daze further. She sat next to Florie and rubbed her down with the soap and cloth.

While she was busy with that, I went outside to my barn and grabbed an armful of hay, which was stocked in there for Ailbeart. I brought it back to the house, and I spread it thinly on the floor before taking the blanket from my bed and covering it. I then put one of the rescued blankets on top of this and the other on top of my bed.

Then I went over to Anna and said, "You and Florie can take my bed. I'll sleep there."

Anna looked to where I had pointed and shook her head. "No, you can't do that. We'll sleep there. We're not taking your bed."

"You are. There's two of you and you're my guests. Don't bother arguing, it won't do you any good."

After her bath, Florie was dried off and redressed in her petticoat, then tucked into my bed where she fell asleep quickly.

Anna and I sat at the table for a while. She seemed to be a little better and more alert, though the cocktail I gave her would knock her out fairly soon.

"I didn't thank you for saving my belongings," she said quietly.

"It's alright, it was nothing," I said.

"It's something to me," she said. "Those things are all I had left of Robert. It meant a lot that you saved them."

I smiled, "You would have done the same for me."

She clasped her hands together slowly and looked down at the table. Her loose brown curls were damp and her grey-blue eyes were tired, but there was more life in them now than there had been for the last couple of hours.

"I don't know how I could ever repay you for everything you've done for us," she said.

I reached out and took her hand softly. "You don't have to repay me," I said, and I meant it. "I do it because you're my friends and I love you both."

Anna looked up at me again, her eyes darting back and forth between mine. "I've done nothing to deserve that kind of loyalty."

"You've been friends to me, you and Florie," I said. "I know I act invincible, but sometimes..." I wasn't sure exactly what I wanted to say. "I don't know where I'd be now, Anna, if I didn't have you or Florie in my life. I don't think you realise how much strength I draw from you." I gave her hand a squeeze.

"Nothing ever seems to frighten you, Katherine," she whispered back. "You're always so positive and strong, even in the worst of times. I wish I had your fortitude."

I let go of her hand and slowly sat back in my seat. "You give me too much credit, Anna. Until I came to live with Ailig, my life was good. My dad isn't the best, but both of my parents were loving when I was a child. I have two sisters, we always had enough to eat, I had a strong foundation. I've had a lifetime of finding things relatively easy and my outlook on life mostly stems from that. Since being with Ailig, life has been so much harder, but I made up my mind that I wouldn't let him break me."

Anna listened, but shifted uncomfortably when I mentioned Ailig.

"He nearly did, though. When I lost my son, it felt like the end of the world. I had no one to turn to or talk to about it; no one grieved for that baby except for me, and I had to hide that from Ailig. Yes, I made it through, but I don't know if I could a second time. You have no idea how much these last couple of months have meant to me, and when Ailig gets back, my life will be different to how it is now. I know that and I'm as prepared for it as I can be, but I also know I'll survive longer if I have you and Florie, and I hope, no matter what happens, that we'll always be friends."

Anna continued to stare at me across the table. I hadn't noticed it happen, but something in her expression had changed. It was so subtle I couldn't put my finger on it, but where before I was looking into a face wrought with despair, now she looked back at me with pity and something else. It was not what I wanted. I didn't want her to feel sorry for me. I just wanted her to know that she had given me as much as I'd given her, because she didn't seem to be aware of it.

"Katherine, I'm so sorry," she whispered. "I wish there was something I could have done to help you. I wish I would have known you then so you would have had someone to talk to."

"Don't be, Anna. You had your own grief to deal with," I said.

Anna tilted her head forward and rubbed her eyes. The remedy would be starting to take effect now.

"Come on, you need to lie down," I said, standing up and taking her elbow gently.

She rose and followed me towards the bed where Florie lay, but then she stopped. My hand tugged on her elbow behind me and I turned to see what was the matter.

"She's sleeping so soundly," Anna said. "I don't want to disturb her. Can I just lie there for a while?" She nodded her head towards the makeshift bed I had created on the floor. The fire was dying down now, casting a warm glow across her face and it crackled occasionally as the embers slowly began to collapse in on themselves.

"Of course," I said, then led her over to the bed and pulled back the top blanket so she could get in.

She positioned herself under it and rested her head back as I crouched next to her and smoothed out the top blanket. She turned her head to look at me, her eyes heavy, then she reached out for my hand. I took it in mine and pressed it between my other palm.

She squeezed my hand and whispered, "Please don't go."

"I'm not going anywhere," I said. But she pulled on my hand, drawing me towards her.

"Come next to me," she whispered. Her soft brown curls were spread out from her head and the shadow cast by the glowing embers behind us fell over her face. Her tired eyes glistened as she looked up at me pleadingly and she continued to pull gently on my hand.

I pulled the blanket back again and undressed down to my chemise before sliding into the bed next to her. I lay on my side facing her, and she turned her own body to face me. The thin, white nightgown I'd lent her draped loosely, low on her chest, leaving her shoulders and clavicle exposed. She was so beautiful. I had the urge to reach out and touch her. I wanted to kiss her again, but I resisted, instead just enjoying being so close. I explored her face with my eyes and rested them for a while on her lips, remembering how they had felt just one night ago.

I faintly regretted giving Anna the tonic, as I could now see her struggling to stay awake. She was blinking back the sleep, trying to keep her eyes open and look at me. Then she reached out under the covers and found my hand again, which she gripped in hers.

"It's been a terrible day," she said quietly. "But I want you to know that I'm happy to be here with you right now."

My heart gave a swift flutter as she said the words, then she turned herself over to face away from me, drawing my arm over her body. She clutched my hand tightly to her chest, and the smell of her hair next to my face was intoxicating. There was the strong smell of smoke, but it didn't completely mask her natural scent, which was sweet and pure. My arm rose and fell on her ribs as her breathing became deeper in slumber, and the warmth of her body radiated against me.

Her steady breathing and the slackening of her hold on my hand told me she would not hear the words, but if I thought she could, then I probably wouldn't have said them.

"It may hurt me one day, but I think I'm falling in love with you, Anna Cumnock."

Chapter Sixteen

ANNA

The day after the fire was tough.

True to their word, a handful of the older boys from the village and the surrounding crofts showed up with some shovels and helped to dig a grave for Sim. I ended up choosing a spot in the valley, down by the river, and Florie said this way we could visit him whenever we went down for a picnic or a swim. With so many helping hands, the grave was dug within a couple of hours, but getting the horse to the site was a challenge.

I didn't want them to simply drag his body, and he was a massive creature, which made things more tricky. In the end, Katherine suggested I leave her to organise it while I tended to the potato crop. I knew she'd suggested that to get me far out of the way, but as upset as I was, I realised there was no delicate method in which five adolescent boys could get a two thousand pound horse down into the valley.

I agreed with her and left the vicinity so I wouldn't have to watch. Katherine collected Ailbeart from her pasture, and I assumed they were going to use him to help shift the body.

I stuck around Katherine's croft with Florie, tending to the chores which needed doing there and avoided looking across the pasture towards what was left of my longhouse. After another couple of hours, Katherine came back to find me and said there were only a few shovelfuls of earth left to throw on the grave and did I want to finish burying him myself. I said I would and followed her back down to the valley with Florie.

The boys had all gone, and I was disappointed I hadn't been able to thank them, but Katherine insisted she already had on my behalf.

"I gave them two rabbits I caught in my snares this morning, so they were happy with that," she said.

There was a large patch of dark, loose earth with a smaller amount next to it, which had been scraped up into a neat pile, ready for me. As I scooped up the last three shovel loads and sprinkled the earth on the grave, also giving Florie a turn to do the same, I could not stop the silent tears from flowing again.

"Sorry," I said, as I wiped them away. I hated constantly crying in front of Katherine. She didn't exactly have an easy life herself, and I'd yet to see her lose control the way I kept doing.

"Don't be," she said. "It's alright to grieve."

I wanted to mark the grave, but considering Katherine hadn't been permitted to do that for her own son, I felt it would be inconsiderate to suggest it. Sensing what I was thinking, Katherine walked over to an overgrown patch where several different plants and flowers were growing.

"Thistles or Dwarf Cornel?" she asked, leaning on the shovel.

"I think it has to be thistles," I said.

She nodded and started digging up a patch of them. When she brought them over, she gently rested them in the middle of the grave, then covered the roots with the loose earth. Then she dipped the shovel into the river and poured a trickle of water around the base of the plant. She repeated this until the soil was dark with moisture.

"Did you want to say anything?" she asked, standing next to me, still holding the shovel.

I shook my head. "No."

We went back up the valley to my croft, and the next job involved picking through the cottage to find anything worth saving. It had rained through the night as we'd hoped, and the smouldering in the roof appeared to be completely gone.

"I'm glad we didn't wash our clothes this morning," I said, sighing. "We're going to be filthy again by the end of the day." My hands were already black from picking up charred lumps of wood and thatch, and the front of my dress was going the same way.

"We can worry about that tomorrow," said Katherine. "Anyway, I've cancelled the party, so there's no one we have to impress."

I knew she was trying to cheer me up, and rather than disappoint her, I returned a single-sided smile and rolled my eyes. "Very funny," I said.

We spent the rest of the day clearing out the cottage. We dragged out the scorched woven mats and threw them on the rubbish pile, which would be burned at a later time, then scooped out the blackened hay from the bed boxes. The bed boxes themselves were in reasonable condition, so we left them, but they would have to be cleaned thoroughly before they could be used again. The table was severely damaged and would have to be re-made, but we found the chain and cauldron sitting in the hearth. The chain had fallen from the roof beam after it burned and had mostly fallen inside the cauldron itself, and though both were filthy, they were not damaged. My set of shelves would have to be replaced, as would the cupboard, but amazingly, the items inside the cupboard; some wicker baskets, the tinderbox, the bottle of rennet, my kitchen cloths, coin pouch, soap, spoons, small brush and two wooden pails had been untouched. I was happiest about a table covering my mother had woven years ago. I rarely got it out for fear of spoiling it, but when I pulled it out of the cupboard and unfolded it, it was pristine, though smelled as smoky as everything else in the house.

The barn was far worse hit. There was virtually nothing left of Sim's stall, or his tackle. Not that it mattered, since we no longer had a horse and would likely never be able to afford another. The hay we'd kept in there was almost all burned, along with the water trough, the long-handled broom and the wheelbarrow. The scythe and shovel blades were salvageable, though the handles would have to be replaced, the plough was almost completely destroyed, and all in all, the damage was catastrophic. An entirely new roof would need to be built; beams, thatching and all, and much of the equipment which was lost, I relied on to do chores around the farm. The loss of the wheelbarrow and plough were both huge blows, and though Katherine insisted we could get by with just hers, I didn't think Ailig would be so generous about loaning out his equipment when he got back.

As Katherine kept reminding me, though, it could have been worse, and we did have the livestock and the crops, and of course, we all had each other. This didn't stop me from plotting over and over in my mind a hundred excruciating ways to make Frang pay, and though most of them went far beyond what I could probably bring myself to do, it still helped me to feel a little better.

As the first two weeks of July passed, Florie and I continued to sleep and take our meals at Katherine's cottage. After the first night when I shared the floor with Katherine, I had slept like a rock, but woke up in the morning stiff. I had then insisted that a new rota system be introduced. I refused to agree to Katherine's idea that she take the floor and Florie and I sleep on the bed and instead demanded that we reach a compromise. So it was decided that each night we would take turns in the bed. One night Katherine would sleep in it, and the next, I would, but an unfortunate backlash of this plan was that it took away the opportunity to sleep next to Katherine again. Either she was on the floor and I was in the bed with Florie, or I was on the floor and she was in the bed, often with Florie who suddenly and frequently seemed to value comfort over cuddles with me.

On the occasions where Florie asked to sleep in the bed with Katherine, (and Katherine never told her no), I had faintly hoped that Katherine might come down next to me. I didn't remember much from the first night at Katherine's cottage, I was so tired and groggy, but the feeling of her body against mine, and her arm wrapped around me, was still vivid in my mind, and I longed for that feeling again. I repeatedly told myself it was the physical contact of a friend I yearned for; a closeness I had missed since Robert had been gone. But if that was the case, why did I constantly keep having to remind myself that's all it was? If it was that simple, why did I keep thinking about it? Why did I keep thinking about that kiss? I loved Robert, and I had kissed him thousands of times, but there was never a single kiss I'd shared with him that kept replaying in my mind the way the one I shared with Katherine did. I spent half of every day hoping to experience that moment again. I kept trying to create circumstances where the two of us were alone together, sending Florie off to fetch things, asking her to do chores on other parts of the croft. I wanted, needed, to find out if I had made more of that event than it really was, or if I was making more of it than Katherine meant it to be. I hoped I was. I hoped that's all it was. Because if it wasn't, then what? I couldn't even identify what it was I felt for Katherine, so how could I possibly know what to do if those feelings became stronger? I was afraid of defining what I felt for Katherine, because only one definition kept springing to mind and I didn't want to accept or acknowledge it. The only description which so far seemed to fit what I felt for Katherine was... love. But that couldn't be. How could I feel love for a woman that was meant for a man, especially when I felt it more intensely? It had to be something else, and for my own sanity, I needed to find out what it was.

With the fire causing a significant amount of extra work to be done, the sheep shearing had been delayed by a fortnight, so it was mid-July when we finally set aside a couple of days to do it. My shears had also survived the fire in the barn, but were in desperate need of sharpening, so Katherine, Florie and I sat on the grass outside her cottage with a bucket of water and a small whetstone each. As we both sharpened our blades, Katherine was cheerfully talking about her upcoming plans.

"With twenty-six sheep and two of us shearing, we should definitely be able to finish this job in two days or less. Then we can take the fleeces and deposit them with Agatha. Once they're inspected, we'll know for sure how much you're short and we can tackle the problem of making up the deficit. I would give you one of my fleeces, but Ailig has already acquired a lot of things on credit. We already owe all fourteen fleeces to Ualan."

"That's alright, I couldn't accept it anyway, but I appreciate the thought," I said. Then added gloomily, "We'll have to make more than one trip, though. We can't fit them all on Ailbeart in one go."

I couldn't help but think about Sim and how much faster it would have been to load the fleeces between two horses.

"Don't worry," said Katherine, ever the optimist. "We'll make it work."

The sheep were sheared over the next two days and the fleeces were all a good size and a decent weight. The extra few weeks had made a bit of a difference, and the fleeces all felt thicker and heavier to me, though maybe I was just being hopeful.

We had to make two separate trips to Ualan's croft to drop off the fleeces which Agatha received and inspected. She came out to look at the stock, carrying a slate in her hand, which she used to make marks on.

Katherine brought her fleeces first and Agatha asked us to unload the cargo, one fleece at a time. She closely inspected each one, measured the thickness with her fingers and poked around and ran her hands through the wool. The fleeces would be washed in bulk elsewhere, so they were not very clean, but Agatha didn't seem to find any problems with the lot. She made a few marks on her slate and told Katherine she had brought enough to balance the books and Ailig's debt was cleared.

Later the same day, when I brought my fleeces, a smaller stack than Katherine's had been, Agatha eyed the pile on Ailbeart's back with little enthusiasm. She ran through the same ritual as she had with Katherine's stock and when she was done, she made a few more marks on her slate.

I held my breath as I waited for the verdict.

Agatha sighed and looked up at me. "You have eleven large fleeces, so you're short, my dear."

"My quota was a minimum of thirteen medium fleeces. Does eleven large not cover it?" I asked, trying to keep the desperation in my voice under control.

Then Katherine cut in. "Her home just burned down, and she lost her horse. Can you not make a small concession?"

Agatha sighed again and tapped her slate with the chalk. "I'm sorry. Ualan left very strict instructions. I'll count your eleven large as twelve medium, but that's the best I can do. It still leaves you short by one. I'm very sorry, Anna."

I nodded, disappointed but not surprised.

"She has until the autumn," Katherine interjected again. "We'll be back before then with the last fleece, don't worry."

Then she turned Ailbeart around and I followed her back down the track, trying to ignore the tight knot in my stomach.

"Don't fret, Anna, we planned for this," Katherine said, reassuringly.

Florie, who I still refused to leave at the croft on her own, and probably wouldn't now until she was twenty, was sat atop the horse, and Katherine and I walked alongside.

"The turnip crop is doing really well. There will be enough surplus for us to trade for another fleece, easily. And there's also the potatoes, don't forget."

I tried to adopt Katherine's positive attitude, but finding that extra fleece had now become one problem among many. If I got it, it would solve the immediate problem of keeping the farm, but I still had no idea what to do about the longhouse. It needed a new roof, and other than the stone walls, the barn had to be completely rebuilt. If I used the surplus crops, or the piglets which I may or may not get, to trade for the fleece, then I was still stuck with the problem of replacing all the equipment I'd lost and making our cottage habitable again. Much of what I'd lost had taken my family years to acquire. The plough had been passed down to me from my father. The metal parts were alright, but it would take more expense and resources that I had to get it back into working order and I no longer had a horse to pull it. Katherine did, but I had no guarantee that Ailig would be as willing to work cooperatively as her.

Katherine must have noticed my strained face when we arrived back at the farm because she pulled me to the side, out of Florie's earshot.

"Hey, you mustn't go all doom and gloom on me again," she said. "We'll think of something. I know it's stressful but this too shall pass, alright?"

I managed a weak smile and nodded. I didn't want her to worry about me. We still had heard nothing about the battle in over a month, and the men could arrive home at any time. I had no doubt this played heavily on Katherine's mind and I didn't want to add to her worries. Her bump was still small and neat, but it was getting bigger by the week and the safety of her child had to have been a constant worry for her.

"You know, we've all worked so hard these last few days and things have been very stressful. I think tomorrow we should take an afternoon off," Katherine said.

Later that night, Katherine suggested a game of backgammon. I wasn't really in the mood, having a lot on my mind, but I knew that's why Katherine had suggested it.

"Come on," she said. "You don't even have to let me win this time."

I gave her a tired but playful smile. "Alright, but let me put Florie to bed first."

It was supposed to be Katherine's turn in the proper bed, but since Florie now seemed as comfortable sharing a bed with Katherine as she did with me, she had taken to sleeping in that bed every night, no matter whose turn it was. I tucked her up with her doll and kissed her goodnight. Then Katherine came over and did the same. I took the backgammon board from its temporary home on Katherine's shelves and we sat down to play.

My game was terrible, and Katherine easily beat me in the first round.

"You're playing horribly," she said as she reset the board. "Worse than me, and that's saying something. One might think your mind was elsewhere."

I gave a short laugh, "I suppose it is."

"You really need to stop worrying about things you have no control over right now," Katherine said sympathetically.

"It's not easy to turn off," I said. "And it's more than just the fleece I'm worried about."

"I know, but when the men get back, I'm sure the township will pull together to help with the roof."

I sighed, unconvinced. "I doubt Ualan will prioritise it during harvest time, and why would he when I'm still short on my quota? Why re-build a home that has no one to live in it? He already thinks of me as a burden on his township now that Robert's gone."

"You can't think that way. If that happens, then we'll deal with it at that time, but it does no good worrying about it now," Katherine said.

"It's not just that," I said.

Katherine looked at me, concern written all over her face. "Then what else?"

"I just—- worry about you too."

Katherine scoffed and sat back in her chair. "That should be the least of your concerns. I'll be fine."

"Will you, though? You didn't look fine before Ailig left and I'm afraid of how he'll treat you when he gets back."

"Let me worry about that."

"And how much will you see us then?"

"Whenever I can, Anna. I'm not going to just cut you and Florie off once Ailig gets back. Yes, it will be different. We won't be working together as closely, but we'll still be friends. We'll still see each other."

She reached out to take my hand and gave it a comforting squeeze. But I didn't feel comforted, and I didn't think this new scenario she was talking about sounded as dandy as she was trying to make it out to be. I didn't know how I felt about just seeing her occasionally. Even as I looked at her now, there was a stirring inside me, and the thought of losing her to Ailig in a few weeks caused my chest to tighten.

I wanted to ask her outright about the kiss we'd shared. Neither of us had mentioned it, and I had no idea if she regretted it, or thought about it like I did, or if it meant so little to her that she'd simply pushed it out of her mind or even forgotten it. The way she was talking now, she acted as if she wasn't really bothered about the changes which were going to come, and as much as I knew I had no right to feel that way, I was annoyed about this. Did I mean so little to her that the thought of hardly seeing me anymore didn't upset her? I stared down at the game board and frowned.

"Anna, please don't worry about me. I promise I'll be alright. We have an amazing crop this year, better than I can remember. Even from back home. Ailig will come back from the raids with spoils, he will have raped and pillaged to his heart's content. The surplus we have will please him. The baby will please him. He'll have no reason to be angry or cruel, so you can rest easy."

"I don't recall Ailig ever needing a reason to be cruel or get drunk," I muttered flatly.

Her talk of how great things would be with Ailig when he got back had hit a nerve and my mood darkened. I didn't look up at her, but there was now a poignant silence across the table.

I clenched my jaw, not wanting to say anything else I'd regret, but something inside me made me want to tell her what I really felt. "If you think just because you did an amazing job with the croft, that Ailig is going to come back a changed man, then you are far more naïve than I pegged you for, and it borders on idiocy. His last wife was a good woman who worked like a horse, yet he still constantly beat the living daylights out of her until it killed her. But if you want to pull the wool over your eyes and act like everything is going to be fine and you and Ailig are going to have your happy ever after, then go ahead. Far be it from me to get in your way, or take up your time once the hero comes home."

My voice, which had started off low, had risen to a level which now caused Florie to grunt and turn over in the bed. I took in a breath and held it, partially thankful that I was stopped from saying anything else, though I was certain I had already gone too far. If she had lost interest in me before, I had certainly sealed it now, and I couldn't stop the tears from welling up in my eyes.

"I need some fresh air," I said, my voice cracking, then I strode to the door and left.

I could not stop the tears from sliding down my cheeks the moment I was outside in the cool evening air. The sun was nowhere near set and so blighted my plans of storming off into the darkness so I could sit and wallow in misery on my own. I considered just sitting outside by the vegetable patch. After what I'd just said to her, I felt the likelihood of Katherine coming out after me was next to none. I'd be surprised if she ever spoke to me again.

I hadn't looked at her face as I ranted at her and I didn't look before I left the cottage, so I had no idea what her reaction might have been. Half of me was glad of that. I didn't want her expression of anger or hurt to be burned into my memory, but it also left me wondering how she was feeling now.

I didn't want to stray too far from Florie and since I had nowhere to go, I couldn't just collect her and leave. At any rate, I was definitely not going back into that cottage again tonight and I couldn't stand the thought of facing Katherine, so I'd have to find somewhere else to sleep. It didn't look like it was going to rain, but the idea of sleeping on the ground outside didn't appeal to me at all. I would be damp from the dew by the morning and I had no extra clothes.

I walked to the end of Katherine's longhouse to the barn. It would be no less comfortable sleeping on the hay in there than it would on the floor in the cottage. As I let myself in, Ailbeart gave a soft nicker, and I walked over to stroke his velvety nose.

"Is it alright if I sleep in here with you tonight?" I asked him.

He threw his head up and down against my hand and shook his mane and then gave another nicker.

"I'll take that as a yes," I whispered, stroking him again.

Then I turned around and walked the few paces to the end of the barn where the hay was stacked. There was a bale which had already been untied, so I grabbed a few handfuls and scattered it on the floor, then grabbed another handful and scrunched it together to make a pillow at one end. I lay myself down on my new 'bed,' glad it was a mild night. There was a horse blanket folded in the corner, but I decided I didn't want to use that unless it was absolutely necessary.

I had lain there for about ten minutes when the door of the barn slowly opened and a set of pale, slender fingers appeared along the inside edge. I sat up suddenly, leaning back on my arms, my heart suddenly going a mile a minute. Katherine pushed the door the rest of the way open, then stepped inside and closed it behind her. Her eyes were sad and her face was pale in the evening light. The orange tint of the fading sun shone through the barn window, painting a glow across the red locks that cascaded over her shoulders. She stared at me with her piercing green eyes and stepped forward. Her face was not angry but had a look of such deep and sorrowful apprehension, I felt anger would have been preferable.

She walked up to the end of my bed and knelt down to my level, locking her eyes on mine.

"Anna, I think there are some things I should say to you," she said, her voice barely a whisper.

The look on her face broke my heart. It was worse than I could have imagined. I had hurt her deeply and, yet again, wrongly. What I had said to her was unfair, and she had done nothing but be kind to me and Florie. I had no right to be angry at her, or jealous— the word made me stop mid-thought. I had just labelled my feelings, and that was the organic word. Jealous. I couldn't remember the last time I had felt jealous, but even if I'd never felt it before in my life, I would still know exactly what it was now. Just as it dawned on me that there would never be another word to describe my feelings for Katherine besides the one that constantly kept inching its way into my head.

Love. I loved Katherine. More than a friend, and heaven help me, more than I had loved Robert.

A well of longing rose within me as the realisation of something that was so obvious for so long suddenly hit me, and in almost the same instant, a sickening heaviness settled in the pit of my stomach because she wasn't mine to keep and she never would be. I shook my head. More tears were threatening to spill over. Why had I done this to her?

"I'm the one who needs to say something, Katherine," I said.

She continued to kneel in front of me, piercing me with that same look.

I took a deep breath. The words stuck in my throat, but I needed to say them.

"I'm so, so sorry, Katherine. I didn't mean to— I don't know why I keep doing these things, attacking you when you've done nothing wrong. I just —" I was cut off by a soft pair of fingers which had come to rest against my lips.

"I do," she whispered.

Tingles seemed to arc through the tips of her fingers and strike me through my very core.

"You do it for the same reason I pretend that everything will be alright when Ailig gets home. Because that's the only way we both know how to cope with reality."

I reached up and took the fingers which still rested against my lips. "What reality?" I whispered.

She furrowed her brow and glanced down for a moment, as if struggling to say the words, but I so desperately needed to hear them.

"The reality that you and I— even though we..." She trailed off, but looked at me again and ran her fingers down the side of my cheek.

"Even though we what?" I whispered again.

She hesitated.

"Please, Katherine. I need to hear you say it," I pressed, my voice barely audible now.

She swallowed. "I love you, Anna."

I closed my eyes, emptying the new well of tears which had risen, and took her hand in both of mine. I pressed the backs of her fingers against my wet face and kissed them. As I did, I felt her other hand rest gently on the back of my head and her fingers slide down through my hair with the lightest touch. I lifted my face and looked at her again. She no longer appeared tormented, but there was still a sadness behind her green eyes.

"I love you, Katherine," I said. "And I'm so sorry it took me so long to work that out."

She smiled. "That's alright, Anna. I think I've known it for a while." She brought the hand I was not clinging to back up to my cheek and cupped the side of my face. "I'm sorry if I made you feel like I didn't care. I just didn't know what else to say."

I stared back at her, into those beautiful eyes. There were so many unknowns in the future, so many uncertainties, and for the first time I was able to let them all fade away and bury them somewhere deep. I would dig them up later, but for now, all I wanted was to focus on this moment.

I let go of her hand and, using one arm to brace myself as I leaned forward, I took her face and leaned in towards her. Her eyes remained fixed on mine as I drew in, only breaking contact when our lips were so close we could no longer focus.

Still, I kept my eyes open as her lips met mine and I felt her perfect softness press against me. Other than Katherine, I had never kissed someone without a beard in this way, and the smoothness of her skin was an exquisite sensation. I traced my hands to the back of her neck and felt an urgency rising from the pit of my stomach, but I resisted kissing her harder or faster. I didn't want this moment to end, and I intended to make it last as long as possible. Perhaps Katherine felt the same, because she was equally as delicate, and I marvelled at how someone who had been so badly abused could naturally know how to be so tender.

I kissed her over and over, softly and slowly, tilting my head one way and then another, wanting to feel her lips at every angle. Her hands dropped from my face, lightly tracing down my neck and sending more tingles rippling through my body. I didn't know how far this would go, how far it could go, but I did know I didn't want her to stop.

I didn't want to stop.

Her fingers crept down to the front of my chest where my bodice laced up and she pulled away, her eyes roving up and down my body with intensity, before she took the end of the ribbon which held my bodice together and pulled slowly. The small bow fell apart. Then she hooked her fingers over the criss-cross ribbon in the front and pulled again, slowly slackening the garment. When mine was loose, she untied the ribbon of her own bodice and then slowly pulled the garment over her head.

I was mesmerised for a few moments before I had the wherewithal to pull my own off.

Once it was over my head and on the floor next to me, I was able to gaze at her again and enjoy this next state of undress. I had seen her in her stay before, but the corset had an altogether new effect on me now. I stared adoringly at the swell of her breasts, admiring their fullness, which seemed to be more conspicuous than the last time I'd seen her like this. I'd never enjoyed wearing stays, considering them to be the invention of some man to force a woman's body into a shape they found more pleasing, but now, as I gazed at Katherine with intent, I suddenly found myself very agreeable to the idea that all women should wear them.

She looked me up and down again, a smile creeping its way onto her lips. Then she pulled her long, red locks around to the front, exposing her neck and back, then turned herself slightly, presenting the fastenings of her stay to me while grinning at me over her shoulder.

I couldn't resist the invitation, and I reached up between her shoulder blades and gripped the ribbon which bound it. I noticed Katherine had already left a little slack in the side fastenings to accommodate the slight swell in her abdomen. I slowly loosened the bow, then pulled on each side of the corset, splaying it outwards and allowing the ribbon to flow through the ringlets all down the back as the garment came apart. She held her arms up above her head and I slid it off her body.

She stood up, now wearing only her skirt and linen chemise, and began to untie the ribbons which held the skirt in place. She let it fall to the floor and kicked it aside, making my stomach do a quick somersault when I considered there was now only one thin layer of fabric between her skin and my eyes.

She bent down and took my hand, gesturing for me to stand, before beginning to loosen the ribbon on the front of my stay. I felt the release of the pressure around my ribs and back as the garment slackened off and she used both of her hands to pull the front panels away from each other.

As she had done, I lifted my arms and allowed her to pull it over my head and discard it. All I could do was stare into her face as her hand moved down and I felt my skirt slacken and drop to the floor around my feet. My chest rose and fell with deep breaths as I looked into her eyes, then she pushed me backwards slowly until I was up against the closed barn door. She put her hands against the wood on either side of my face, then leaned in to kiss me again, her perfect, full lips pressing into mine, her breasts rubbing against me through the thin linen.

I gave a stifled sigh as she tilted her head and traced her lips over my cheek to just behind my ear. She kissed me softly, trailing the kisses down my neck until she reached my exposed shoulder. The feeling of her teeth brushing over my bare flesh made my knees buckle. Every touch was exquisite torture, so light, but so potent. I was aware of one hand lift away from the door then slide down to my shoulder. Her finger crept under the loose neckline of my chemise, then traced along the edge to the centre of my chest. She unhooked her finger but trailed her hand a little lower, then brushed it over my left breast. It was no more than a brush to start with, but enough to draw another sudden intake of breath.

My reaction seemed to embolden her, because now she pressed the palm of her hand right over me, gripping me gently, caressing me through the muslin. Her hand on my breast, even through the fabric, sent dizzying waves through my body and she continued to plant soft kisses on my shoulder.

I pushed against her, moving myself away from the barn door and walking her backwards to the hay bales at the back of the barn. I was vaguely aware of Ailbeart softly nickering again as she backed up, staring at me, trusting me to guide her. I pressed her up against the stack of hay and bent my head to kiss her neck and chest. She tilted her head back, giving me full exposure, and I ran my lips over the soft, smooth skin under her chin. My hands found their way to her breasts, and I took my time exploring her through the thin fabric.

I could feel her nipples, fully erect, the fullness and firmness of her bosom. Then I traced my hand lower, feeling her stomach, the small bump low on her abdomen, and she drew in a sharp breath as my fingers made their way further south. Through the chemise, I felt the soft padding of her curls and as I reached lower still, Katherine uttered a soft moan. I pressed my body against her, with my arm in between us, and my fingers reached under her. I felt the warmth of her and a dampness through the material. Even without directly touching her, I could feel the softness of her. I could feel her desire, and I pressed my fingers more firmly against her. She uttered another moan, gripped the neck of my chemise and threw her head forward, resting her forehead against my shoulder.

"Oh, Anna," she whispered. "Please."

I wasn't sure precisely what she meant, but since she hadn't told me to stop, I guessed she liked what I was doing. Touching her this way was glorious, and sensing she wanted more, I pressed my fingers against her more firmly. I moved them back and forth slowly, pushing the palm of my hand against the tiny swell above where I knew from my own experience, so much pleasure could be drawn from. She gasped and threw her head back again, pulling harder on my chemise. I leaned into her neck again and kissed her as I worked my fingers rhythmically, feeling the contours of her womanhood, my hand becoming damp from her desire. I pressed my own groin against my arm, wanting to be as close to her as possible when she finally let herself go.

Her breaths quickened, and she pressed her forehead onto my shoulder again. I was aware of her whole body stiffening and she squeezed her thighs against my hand, locking my fingers in place, and her knuckles went white as she gripped my chemise and moaned softly into my shoulder.

"Oh Anna, you're an angel," she gasped. Then I felt her relax. She lifted her head, which glistened with a light layer of perspiration, and she leaned against the hay bales, before sliding slowly to the floor. I lowered myself down next to her and took hold of her hand, kissing it. As she leant against me, still breathing deeply, she closed her eyes, sending a single tear down one cheek.

"I didn't hurt you, did I?" I asked hesitantly.

She shook her head, then opened her eyes again and turned to look at me. "I just never knew it could feel that way," she whispered.

Chapter Seventeen

I woke up in the early morning, in the cottage, next to Katherine. We had gone back the previous night, feeling it might raise questions if Florie woke up to find us both gone, and we had slept together on the floor bed. I had spent the night with my arms wrapped around Katherine, holding her close, and even this morning I did not begrudge the stiffness in my back from the hard surface. I'd slept soundly and now smiled warmly at Katherine as she turned herself over to face me. She smiled back, pushing a lock of hair out of my face, then gently leaned in and placed a soft, light kiss on my lips.

"Good morning," I whispered, not wanting to cause Florie to wake just yet.

"Good morning," she said.

I lay there for a while, staring at the person I now felt to be the most beautiful woman in the world. No matter what happened, I would treasure last night for the rest of my life, and I hoped the memory of it would be enough to keep me going once Ailig returned. The thought made my stomach knot up, and I reached out to take her hand, squeezing it possessively. I hated that she was under the control of a man who had no appreciation for her whatsoever. He would never recognise how perfect she was, never appreciate her hard work or kindness, never love her the way she deserved to be loved. It was so unfair and it made me so angry.

There was a shuffling from the other bed as Florie started to awaken, and I slowly and reluctantly released Katherine's hand.

It was quite early in the morning, but the day looked like it would be a nice one and the open window showed a clear, bright sky.

"How about I go and get some eggs for breakfast?" I said. "I can make some bannock too."

"Yum," said Katherine. "That sounds like a very good idea."

Grinning, I got up off the floor. I had brought my clothes back to the cottage with me last night, but since it was early morning and I was just going to the roosting boxes behind the house, I decided I didn't need to bother getting dressed just yet.

I flitted to the door, feeling light, and carefree, then went out into the garden.

There was a slight cool breeze, which I found refreshing as my feet padded over the soft grass. I said a quick hello to the pigs as I walked past, and then got to the roosting boxes which were already vacated by the chickens who were now roaming about in the grass, pecking at the bountiful summer insects.

I grabbed the hem of my chemise at the front and used it as a hammock to carry the still warm eggs which I collected. There were seven today and there would be more in the boxes at my cottage, but I couldn't be bothered to walk all the way over the pasture to go and get those. These would be more than enough for breakfast, so I walked back to the front of the cottage, treading carefully so as not to knock the eggs together.

It wasn't until I was almost back to the front door and I looked down the valley that I noticed a patchy, long line of men walking along the track towards the village. My heart sank so fast I nearly dropped the eggs, and a sickening feeling lodged itself in the pit of my stomach. They were still quite far away, but it was clear who they were. The men had returned from the raids.

As I stood and squinted down at the procession, it was clear the clan had been successful. About a third of the men who had left as infantry were now on horseback. All the horses were loaded heavily with bundles and packs, some so much they didn't have a rider, but instead were led along slowly by their new owners. A handful of horses pulled wagons, and some riders towed along second horses behind them. It didn't look as if the clan had taken too hard of a hit, at least not this township, as the number of men coming home appeared similar to the number that had left over two months ago. I couldn't count them, but there looked to be well over one hundred of them. If I were closer, I'd be able to see how many looked maimed or injured, but that wasn't my priority at the moment. Somewhere in that long line of men and horses was Ailig, and he'd soon be breaking from the group to head up the valley towards the cottage. I opened the cottage door and stepped inside quickly.

"Florie, get dressed," I said. "We have to leave."

Katherine's face contorted into a look of concern as I dashed up to the table and unloaded the eggs, then ran to my pile of clothes and started pulling them on hurriedly.

"What's the matter, Anna? What happened?" she said, walking over to me quickly.

"The men have returned. The whole battalion is coming up the river track and Ailig will be back any minute."

I pulled my stay over my head and pulled the ribbon tight, cinching the garment around my torso, before tying it off with a swift bow. Then I hurriedly adorned my skirt and bodice. I felt a little relieved, even though the bodice hadn't been laced together at the back yet. The last thing I wanted was for Ailig to come in and see me in my undergarments.

"I didn't expect them back so soon," Katherine said as she picked up her own clothes and started to get dressed.

I got Florie to tighten and tie the fastenings on the back of my bodice. "Neither did I," I said.

I turned to Katherine, and she looked back at me sorrowfully as I helped her to straighten her bodice and I drew the ribbons tighter across her chest. I deftly tied off the ribbon at the top, then put my hands on her shoulders and looked into her lovely face.

"Where will you go?" she whispered, reaching up to hold my wrists.

I shook my head. "I don't know. Back to our croft, I guess."

"Maybe Ailig will let you stay," she whispered again. "We can ask him, he might..."

I wanted so badly to kiss her and tell her it would be alright, but I resisted the urge, feeling Florie's eyes on us both.

I squeezed her shoulders. "We'll manage," I said, forcing a smile. "Don't worry about us, just focus on taking care of yourself."

After a moment, I stepped back from Katherine and instructed Florie to gather up the rest of her things. I picked up and folded our blankets and started piling our other possessions on top of those. Then the door to the cottage banged open, revealing Ailig standing behind it.

Both Katherine and I jumped, and we turned to face him. The grin which had rested on his face beneath his short brown beard fell away as his eyes darted between me and Florie. He had a large sack slung over his back and another dangling from his hand, so big the bottom bulged out where it rested on the ground. It looked as if he'd done very well for himself.

"What are you two doing here?" he said gruffly.

Katherine immediately put on a smile and walked over to him quickly, throwing her arms around his neck and planting a kiss on his cheek. I clenched my jaw but kept my face neutral.

"Welcome home, my darling," she said. "I'm so happy to see you back in one piece."

I was sure that was a lie.

Ignoring me and Florie for the moment, he grinned down at her and let go of the bag in his hand. Whatever was inside clunked and clattered as the bag settled the rest of the way onto the ground. He wrapped his massive arm around her waist and pulled her roughly against him, then pressed a hard kiss on her lips. I would have considered him a handsome man had he not marred my opinion with his awful personality. He was not particularly tall, but he was strong and well built. He had dark brown hair, a strong jaw, and his light eyes stood out through his thick, dark eyelashes.

"Ay," he said, once he released her. "Your man's back now and I come laden with a bounty you'll not believe."

He lifted the bag off the ground again and shook it for her to hear.

I didn't know if it was because Katherine came from further abroad than I or Ailig did, but his accent was much thicker than hers. Maybe it was the masculine timbre of his voice which amplified the effect, but he sounded downright abrasive to me when compared to Katherine's dulcet tones. I wondered if I sounded as coarse to her as Ailig did to me, and tentatively hoped that was not the case.

Pushing Katherine aside, he strode into the cottage, bashing the doorframe on both sides with the sacks he was carrying, and Florie ran and ducked behind my skirts. Ailig seemed to have forgotten we were here, however, or decided he didn't care for the moment, because he simply tossed both sacks on the floor next to the table, then turned and leaned against it, looking pleased with himself.

Katherine approached him cautiously. "How were the raids?" she asked.

Ailig placed his hands on the edge of the table on either side of him and sniffed.

"Very prosperous," he said, waving a hand towards the two large sacks. "There's a few more things still loaded on the horse, too." He gave another grin and Katherine looked momentarily perplexed.

"Horse?" she said.

"Ay, a beautiful filly for my Ailbeart. I took her from a McLean bastard who gave me this," he said, lifting his elbow and pulling the sleeve of his shirt up as far as it would go. This revealed a jagged, bright pink scar that ran from his elbow all the way up to just under his armpit. "Then I took his wife, then his daughters, and then his life." He let out a single wheezing laugh. "The bastard had nothing by the time I finished with him." He slapped his thigh, amused by his own joke, then noticed the cluster of eggs lying on the table behind him. He picked one up and cracked it directly into his mouth with one hand, then chucked the slimy shell back onto the tabletop.

"You're so brave, darling," Katherine cooed as she picked up the shell and placed it in the rubbish pail.

I rolled my eyes. I understood perfectly well that Katherine was acting the way she was out of sheer and desperate self-preservation, but I still couldn't help being quietly irritated that he should keep having his ego stroked at every opportunity.

Ailig's eyes fastened on mine, catching my expression.

"So, what are you doing here? I noticed your longhouse has had a bit of a mishap." He glanced down at the floor where Katherine's blanket still lay over the makeshift bed. "You needn't think you're going to just make yourself comfortable in my house," he said. "You can start by cleaning that mess up off the floor, then take your crap and your brat and get back to your own croft. That's while it's still yours," he added, sneering at me.

"Please, Ailig," Katherine put a hand tenderly on his bulging bicep. "Can they not at least stay in the barn?"

"No, they bloody well cannot," he snapped. "We have two horses now, and even if there was room, we are not running a charity. I'm not having my barn filled with a couple of mangy squatters."

"It's just, Anna has helped so much with the crops and the sheep."

"What the hell are you on about, Woman?" he snapped again, pulling his arm away from her.

"We— we combined our turnips into one field and have been tending to them together. It's done very well, we'll have a surplus this year."

"That's bloody marvellous, but it changes nothing," he said. "I don't care what you said to this woman, or how you managed the crops, but now that I'm back, we'll be doing things my way. There'll be no more of this cooperative work going on. You will harvest our croft, she will harvest her own."

"But, part of her crop is on our croft. We agreed to split the crop down the middle, it's—"

"You agreed, not I," he cut her off. "And since when do you make the decisions as to what happens with my bloody croft? We are not sharing anything. What grows on my land is mine."

I felt bile rise to the back of my throat as he said this. Well over sixty-five percent of the crop was planted on Ailig's croft, which was wider than mine. If he claimed everything which had been grown on that side, there would be no way I'd have enough to trade for the last fleece. I would barely have enough to make my turnip quota, let alone stockpile for our own consumption over winter.

"That isn't right!" I said, "We worked that whole field together."

He jumped off the table and stomped over to me, puffing his chest out, then pointed a thick, dirty finger directly at my face.

"My wife doesn't make the decisions around here. That's my privilege and I'll hear no more about it! Now take your things and get out of my house right this second."

I stepped back, feeling the blood drain from my face. "Come on, Florie," I said quickly, trying to conceal the shake in my voice. "Get your things."

Florie was already holding her doll, but she now gathered a few more of the items we had already assembled on the floor, and I quickly wrapped everything else up in one of our blankets, then hoisted the sack-like bundle over my shoulder. Ailig stood and watched me, a satisfied sneer on his face, as the two of us edged past him to the door. I took one moment to look back and caught sight of Katherine's anguished expression before the door was slammed in my face.

Chapter Eighteen

F lorie followed me, clutching her doll as we trudged back over the pasture to our own croft. When we were about halfway there, she ran up beside me and took hold of my skirt. "Where are we going to sleep, Mammy?" she asked.

I took a quick look down at her and sighed. She stared back up at me with wide eyes, trusting that I would know exactly what to do. I really didn't, but I couldn't let her know that.

"Well, we're going to take these blankets and lay them out under the sheep shelter after we sweep it out, and put down some hay—" I cut myself off. We had no hay. It had burned in the barn. "Grass." I corrected myself.

There was some grass under the shelter already, but even though the sheep had not congregated under it for two or three weeks, it was still very patchy, dirty, and sparse. I wanted a fresh layer to cover where we would sleep, since I didn't like the idea of bedding down where twenty-six sheep had previously defecated and urinated, even if we did have a blanket to lie on.

We spent the rest of the morning cleaning up the floor of the shelter as much as we could. Since the long handled broom had burned in the barn, this took a long time. We used the short brush which had been salvaged from the cupboard in the kitchen, but it was backbreaking work. I made a mental note to stop the sheep from coming inside for the rest of the summer, if this was where we would have to sleep now. If there was a bad storm, they would have to be directed to the shelter on Katherine's croft.

The building had three walls and was open at the front, so it provided a fair bit of protection from the wind and elements, especially if we slept at the back. Once it was properly swept out, I took Florie down to the river and together we pulled up bunches of long reeds and grass from the river bank. We laid them out in the sun to dry as we gathered a sufficient amount, then, after a couple of hours of back-and-forthing, we managed to cover a small patch of the floor, in the back corner of the shelter, which we spread a blanket over.

I lay down on it and smiled up at Florie, quite surprised.

"This is actually quite comfortable," I said, silently thinking I should have done something similar in Katherine's cottage. The long reeds were thickly laid and the ground underneath was far softer than the compacted dirt floor of the cottage. Florie lay down on the bed beside me and I put my arm around her, cuddling her close.

"I'm so sorry it has come to this," I whispered to her.

"It's not your fault, Mammy. Ailig is mean," she said.

"He is that," I sighed.

"I feel sorry for Katherine," Florie said. "I'd rather sleep here like this than live in that cottage with him."

I said nothing, but I imagined Katherine probably felt the same.

I thought about everything I'd need to get done that afternoon and regarded all of it with dread. My sow would have to be moved back to her own pen, but I decided to do that when Ailig was at the tavern, so I wouldn't have to talk to him again. A hearth would need to be built under the shelter and the cauldron hung over it so we could cook. I would need to go and see Ualan because something had to be done about the roof of the longhouse and I would eventually need some replacement equipment. As far as the harvest; I could pull the turnips up with my bare hands, but it would take a long time and it would be a nightmare moving the vegetables around without the wheelbarrow. We would have to make do with the wicker baskets, but that would also be painfully slow. I would eventually need a working plough to till the soil after all the vegetables were harvested, and I still had no idea how I was going to meet the wool quota either. I sighed, thinking it would probably be best to get the worst of the tasks over with first.

"Do you feel like going on a walk to Ualan's croft?" I asked Florie.

"Will he help us?" she said.

"I don't know. But he definitely won't if we don't ask."

I didn't think Ualan would appreciate me turning up at his door the very afternoon of the day he got back, but our situation was dire and it was an urgent matter. It was just under two miles to Ualan's cottage and it was well into the afternoon by the time we arrived. I didn't have to bang on the door, since Ualan was already outside with two of his older sons. They appeared to be sorting through some of the booty they'd brought home and Agatha was also there with her hands on her hips, admiring the items her husband and sons were showing off to her. They all looked in very cheerful spirits and this gave me hope that Ualan might be feeling in a more compassionate mood today.

One of his sons spotted me approaching and nodded his head, causing Ualan to turn around. I gave him a quick wave as I walked, and his smile faded slightly as he waved back.

"Hello, Anna," he said, when I was close enough to start a dialogue.

"Good afternoon, Ualan," I replied. "It looks like the raid was a success."

"A resounding success," he said, looking at the items around him. There were a few large piles of clothes, some fine-looking shoes, various stacks of plates and bowls, a few candlesticks, blankets, and I noticed a couple of nice brooches glinting on the stump of a tree behind him. Then there were other smaller items, such as ink pots, cooking utensils, blades, and a large pile of assorted weapons, which seemed to include everything from slings to swords to crossbows. It certainly looked like Ualan had secured himself a lion's share of the spoils.

Florie, who held my hand tightly, gaped in wonder at the assortment of treasures. I could feel she desperately wanted to wander around and have a closer look, so I let go of her hand so she could explore for a bit. One of his sons, who was sat close by, held up something which glinted, inviting her over to have a look. I could see it was a thick, silver bracelet which looked like it had several purple stones set into it. It looked valuable, and I wondered what Ualan planned to do with so many beautiful treasures. Seeing how much wealth he had acquired gave me hope that he might feel more inclined to be generous with Florie and I.

"I wanted to speak to you, if I could," I said.

"About your house?" he said.

"That and some other things, yes."

"Frang has already informed me that your home burned down and is no longer habitable," he said, tucking his thumbs into the top of his breeches.

"He didn't waste a second, did he?" I said, stiffly. "It needs a new roof, that's all. The rest I can probably manage on my own."

Ualan sighed. "Putting a new roof on a house isn't a small job, Anna."

"It's a smaller job if more people pitch in and help," I said. "Surely if a dozen of the men were to come for just one day, we could—"

"Harvest time is approaching, Anna. The men have just arrived back today, the ones who made it back. Many of them are still nursing wounds, they are all tired."

"Yes, I can imagine sorting through all these riches would be taxing," I snapped, unable to mask my anger.

He frowned, clearly not impressed by my comment, but I didn't care. How dare he stand around being merry with his family, organising the piles of booty he didn't even need, while my daughter and I were homeless and sleeping in an animal shelter.

"I understand your frustration, Anna," he said. "But you do have options. Frang told me this morning he would be willing to house both of you if you turn the lease over to him now. Or there's your brother-in-law. I'm sure he would help you if you asked. He did well for himself, as did his son. I have no doubt he would make room for you."

I gritted my teeth hard, trying to control my rage. "I am not giving up my croft," I said. "Frang can go to hell. He's the one who set fire to my house. He's the reason I'm in this situation, and as for Faolan, I didn't see him finding the time to stop by on his way home to check in on us."

Ualan's eyebrows raised, and a look of surprise crossed his face when I mentioned Frang. "Frang burned your house down?" he said.

"I know it was him," I said, my voice rising. "He threatened me and my daughter and he—"

"Did you see him do it?" Ualan said, his expression now obstinate.

I took two long, deep breaths. "No," I said.

"Did anyone else see him doing it?" Ualan pressed.

Again I paused, trying maintain control of my emotions before I answered. "No," I said again. "But I know it was him. Who else would have the motivation to do that?"

"Fires start for all kinds of reasons, Anna. I'm afraid without a witness, there's nothing I can do. I can't punish him for something you just think he did, whether he had motivation to or not."

"So that's it? Frang gets away with burning down my house and you are happy to leave me and Florie homeless? We are to get no help?"

"I'm afraid not before the harvest," he said.

My chest heaved. I wanted to slap him. "Don't think what you're doing has gone over my head," I growled, pointing at him. "You're hoping I won't make the quota, and my croft will be handed over to Frang. Then no one will have to bother helping me with the roof."

Ualan stepped forward suddenly, his eyes burning into me angrily. "You will change your tone immediately," he thundered.

Florie, his sons, and Agatha all turned to look.

"Don't forget who you're talking to. I could take your lease at any moment if I wanted to. I could hand your croft over to Frang today and be done with it. I've given you the chance to keep your head above water on your own and you're well on your way to proving you cannot do it. After the way you've just spoken to me and the nerve of your ridiculous demands, that's exactly what I ought to do." He lowered his voice and took a deep breath. "But because I'm a man of my word, I'll still give you until the autumn to prove everyone wrong."

I stared back at him hard, willing myself not to say anything which would antagonise him further.

"What about Ailig?" I growled quietly through gritted teeth.

"What about him? What has Ailig done that you don't like?" Ualan snapped, impatiently.

"Katherine and I worked together over the spring and the early summer. We agreed to combine our crop and plant one field across our crofts to make it easier for us both. Because of the shape of my croft, more of the turnips got planted on her side, but we tended to it all as one field. We both did equal work, contributed equal seeds, and now Ailig's back, he says he's keeping everything on his own land."

The last part about the equal seeds wasn't true, but Ualan and Ailig didn't know that and they were Katherine's to give, so I felt it to be a fair comment.

Ualan closed his eyes wearily and sighed. I was getting the impression that clan politics were not his strong point.

"Did Ailig agree to the arrangement before he left?"

I knew where this was going and the fire in my belly burned hotter, but I made my best effort to control my temper this time. "No, it was an idea Katherine had after he left. She used to do it back home, and she said it usually resulted in a better harvest and was a more efficient way to work. She was right, we will have a surplus."

All of this seemed to be completely inconsequential to Ualan, who had started shaking his head the moment I had said the word 'no.' I wondered if he had even heard the rest.

"I'm sorry, Anna, but if she didn't ask Ailig for his permission to do that, then he has every right to keep the produce on his own property."

"If she'd asked him, he would have said no!" I complained.

"And that's his prerogative!" Ualan snapped back. "Get it through your head, Anna. Ailig is in charge of that croft. Katherine is a woman; his wife. It's not up to her to make the decisions on how it's run."

"That croft has been run better this year than it ever has since Ailig was in charge," I said, tears now welling in my eyes. "You said it yourself. Ailig was in danger of losing his croft because it was managed so poorly. He goes away for a couple of months and now he has a surplus, so what does that tell you?"

"I don't have to answer to you, Anna," Ualan growled. "You've made your point, but the fact remains that Ailig is head of his household and his croft. I can't possibly go and override his word in favour of what two women think is fair, and I think you know that. Ailig picked a good wife to run his croft while he was away, and that reflects well on him. There is nothing I can do about your problem and your full quota of turnips is due on the usual date. If you couldn't get that on your own without relying on Ailig's wife to help you, then that doesn't bode well for next year either and you should be letting the lease go, instead of fighting a losing battle."

He turned away from me and went back to his family as I stood there fuming and trying to hold back the sobs which bobbed at the bottom of my throat. I called Florie back to me, then took her hand to leave. Before I walked away, I called back to Ualan.

"You've just come back from a very successful raid and we don't have so much as a spade for the harvest. I came here hoping you might be willing to help us, even if it was in a small way. I'm sorry to have taken time from your busy day." My voice cracked as I said it, but Ualan kept his back to me. Agatha met my eyes with a sympathetic glance but did not say anything, so I gripped Florie's hand harder and headed back down the track towards home.

As we walked, my mind wandered back to Katherine. I had tried not to think about her all day, but unless I was actively engaged in something which required my full attention, my thoughts constantly came back to her. Was she alright? Had Ailig hurt her? What was she doing now? Was she worrying about us? I sorely wanted to see her. I told myself it was to make sure she was alright, just to put my mind at ease, but in reality, I had so many other reasons. It had been less than a day, but her absence was already painful, and the new reality we were facing had yet to fully sink in.

I still had to retrieve my pig before the bastard could claim her as his own as well, though realistically I knew he'd have a hard time getting away with that. Still, I'd feel better about it if she was back on my property. Then there were the sheep. They were all tagged with markings so there could be no argument as to whose was whose and the lambs all stuck to their own mothers. I wondered if Ailig had found out yet that we had put the flocks together. Well, if he had, it wouldn't matter. I didn't think he would get away with claiming my sheep either and doubted even he would be stupid enough to try that. I sighed, realising there was no chance I would be getting the lamb Katherine had promised me, but then I had told her at the beginning I didn't want to take it. That was before my house burned down, though. Right now, any extra resources would help me dig us out of this pit of despair. And the fleece. How would I get that now? I had my mother's brooch back, but I didn't want to trade it away again after the sacrifices Katherine made to get it back for me. If the sow was pregnant, there were the piglets, but they would be born too late. There were the lambs. I had five of them, thanks to the twins, but it would take at least three of them to get a fully grown sheep, though I'd be surprised if there was anyone left in the township who hadn't sheared theirs yet. I would have to trade for a fleece, or try to offer Ualan three lambs in place of the deficit wool. Hardly a fair trade, but it might be the last resort. Though, I half figured he wouldn't accept the lambs as a substitute, if only to be difficult. There was no doubt in my mind he wanted to see my croft in Frang's possession, just to save himself any future hassle, and if I gave him even the smallest justification for doing that, he would use it.

Fortunately, the firewood and peat had survived, being stored in a separate shelter across from the pigpen, so we still had fuel for cooking. I got Florie to help me bring the stones which had outlined the hearth in the cottage, into the shelter, and we placed them in a circle just a few feet inside the entrance. I would have preferred the fire to be closer to where we were sleeping, but the smoke needed to vent and I wasn't prepared to start trying to put a hole in the roof for that, so by setting up the fire next to the entrance, most of the smoke would drift out.

Getting the chain suspended was the next challenge. The roof of the shelter wasn't particularly high, but even with Florie on my shoulders, she struggled to get the heavy chain over the rafter and secure it. Each time she was able to throw the end of the chain over, the weight of the rest of it dragged it back over the beam and it came back down heavily on the floor. After this happened several times and both of us had been painfully hit by the heavy chain as it fell, we decided to bring a few roosting boxes inside and use them as steps to gain enough elevation to get the chain secured where it needed to be. With the chain and cauldron hung, the hearth set up, and our bed and possessions all neatly arranged at the back, the place looked quite homey.

I considered lighting the fire and getting some stew on the go, but I'd forgotten the sack of oats at Katherine's house. I would have to retrieve that fairly soon, too. Last season's stock of turnips and salted meat was still available in the pit larder, in the cottage, though I kicked myself for not preparing more of it while we had the chance. We'd moved the table over the top of the pit to keep the rain off it, and the wooden planks which covered it kept the rodents away, but I considered that we should probably use the stock we had in there first, before it got too damp and went to waste. At the very least, we weren't in immediate danger of starving.

"I have to go over to Katherine's croft to get our pig back," I said to Florie as we tended to our vegetable patch together. We were plucking a few leaves of kale along with some cabbage, peas, and beans, which would be added to the stew later.

"Can I come?" She asked, no subtlety in her hopeful tone.

"I don't think that's a good idea," I said gently.

"Please, I can help," she said. "And I want to see Katherine."

"I'm not going to see Katherine. I think we need to stay out of her way for a while, in case Ailig gets mad. I'm just going to get the sow and bring her straight back here." As I said this, I grabbed a few extra bits of kale. The pig would need to be fed later and I would need something to lure her back again. I stripped some of the more limp leaves from the beans and peas while I was at it and shoved them into my pockets too.

When we had enough, we went back to our roofless cottage and moved the boards which covered the pit larder, then pulled out a handful of turnips. We chopped a few up on the charred kitchen table, keeping some aside for the sow, then shoved them into the bucket Florie was carrying the kale, peas and beans in.

When we got back to the shelter, Florie tipped the vegetables into the cauldron and I bent down to get started on the fire. I chose some small sticks of kindling, which I broke apart and spread across a little mound of dried grass.

"We need some water in that cauldron," I said to Florie, not looking up.

"If you're not going to see Katherine or Ailig, then why does it matter if I come?" she whined, unwilling to let the matter drop.

"Because Ailig might come out and accost me anyway, and I don't want you to be present for that," I said, wearily. "Now please go and get the water so we can get the dinner started."

She gave a loud, exaggerated huff and stomped off outside as I brushed off my hands. I got the tinderbox from the back of the room behind the bed, silently thanking the Good Lord that it had survived, then lit the kindling. The little bits of dried grass and slivers of wood crackled as the flames took hold, and I bent down lower to blow more life into them. After a few minutes of tending to it, the flames took off and Florie stomped back in, carrying a bucket of water. I thanked her and told her to empty it into the cauldron, then added more peat to the fire.

"You can stay here and look after the dinner if you want, or..." I tried to think of what else there was to do. With the losses we had incurred and because we only had our own croft to see to now, a good number of the daily chores we usually did were no longer necessary. There was no barn to clean, no horse manure to spread, no horse to let out to pasture or wrangle back in, and the sheep were looking after themselves. They could be milked but that wasn't a job Florie could manage easily on her own. The chickens needed almost no oversight, the pig would be fed later. We had no broom to sweep up with, there was no point in even trying to do any repair work on the house at this stage. Florie stood there with an eyebrow raised, waiting for me to finish my sentence, clearing thinking the same thing. She was growing up far too fast.

"Err, well, you know. Find something useful to do," I finished weakly.

"Right," she said. There was a definite hint of sarcasm in her voice, and I gave her a warning look as I headed out of the entrance.

It was the late afternoon, and I hoped that Ailig would be off at the tavern. I knew the chances were low, but my heart beat faster as I got closer to the longhouse, hoping that Katherine would be at home on her own and maybe she'd see me and come outside. So far, I couldn't see anyone out and about and my heart dropped a little as I thought perhaps both of them were down in the village.

I headed directly for the pigpen and could see that my sow was fortunately nearer to the gate than Katherine's was. I was grateful for that small stroke of luck, as I didn't want both pigs to be trying to get out at the same time, or lure Katherine's sow out instead of mine. It was still too early to tell if she was pregnant, but my hopes were high, and I dug my hand into my pocket and gripped a turnip, ready to entice her.

Just then, a shape caught the corner of my eye and I looked up to see Katherine come around the side of the cottage. She looked up at me in surprise, then hurried over.

"Anna," she said, looking around, worried.

"I'm just collecting my sow," I said quickly, my heart going ten to the dozen. "I'll be gone in a jiffy."

Katherine's eyes anxiously darted around behind me for a few moments, then she stepped forward and grabbed my hands in hers. "I'm so, so sorry," she whispered. "This is my fault. I should never have suggested we plant the field that way. I never thought Ailig would steal—"

"It's not your fault, Katherine," I said, squeezing her hand. "I know you were trying to help and who could have known he would be so unreasonable."

"I tried to talk to him, but he won't hear anything more about it, and I'm worried if I push it he might..." Her hand crept across her abdomen, protectively.

"Don't push him on it, Katherine. You can't afford to antagonise him, it's not worth the risk. I'll think of something. I might be able to get credit for the litter of piglets. I'm going to see Faolan tomorrow to see if he can help. We'll be alright."

"What about your roof and tools and things?" she said. "Did you talk to Ualan about that?"

I shook my head. "Don't worry about that, it will be sorted eventually." I stepped closer up to her, still holding her hands so that my face was only inches from hers. "You need to look after yourself now, Katherine. Please promise me you won't do anything stupid for my sake which would endanger you. We'll find a way through this, alright? You just need to stay safe."

She smiled, her bright green eyes staring straight into mine. "Look at you," she said. "This is a bit of a role reversal, isn't it?" She leaned forward and lightly kissed my lips, then she said. "I can't stand it, Anna. He's such an egocentric, braggart. He's spent the entire morning showing me the new horse, the things he stole, his battle scars, and telling me all about the disgusting atrocities he's taken part in. And I have to act as if I'm impressed by it all. I thought he was bad to me, but he's evil to his core, Anna." She shook her head and scrunched her eyes closed, as if trying to stop an image from coming to mind. "You wouldn't believe what he's done on that raid; to other women, children, even. Just people like you and me and Florie. I can't stand listening, and he goes on and on about it."

She looked so distressed, and I didn't even want to imagine what Ailig had made her listen to. I thought about the sacks he'd brought home and the horse. Those were all taken from a family somewhere who were not much different to us. How many people had died for all the treasures Ualan had at his cottage? And for all the other men who came home laden with goods? The one good thing about Robert not being here meant he had not taken part in those horrors, but then he had participated in more than one raid over his lifetime and come home with the bounty. I had always got by, by not thinking about where it all came from or how Robert came to possess his spoils, but then that was easy because Robert never talked about any of the details.

I never believed he enjoyed the raids, either. He was bound by the clan chief to participate in them, but he never once gave me the impression he liked it. I'd always figured the same would go for the other men, but clearly it was not so for Ailig.

I shook my head, not knowing what to say to Katherine. Then I heard the door to the cottage slam. Katherine jumped and stepped back, then went to hurry around the corner, but too late. Ailig had already emerged and seen me.

"I thought I told you to stay off my property," he growled at me.

"I've just come to collect my sow," I said firmly. "She was housed in your pen after the fire. I helped Katherine to extend it so it would accommodate both of them."

One side of his top lip curled up as he eyed up the pen. I knew he was dying to tell me to leave the pig and go away, but I had no doubt he knew he wouldn't get away with that. He turned quickly to Katherine. "Why are you just standing there?" he snapped. "Don't you have work to be getting on with? Piss off."

Katherine hesitated for the briefest second, then scampered around the corner of the longhouse and disappeared from sight.

Ailig turned back to me. "Take your pig and get the hell out," he snarled. "And if I see you back here one more time, there will be trouble. Do you understand?"

I gave a slow nod as I opened the gate of the pen. He turned to go, but before he rounded the corner of the building, he stopped and turned back to me.

"What I said goes for Katherine too," he snarled. "Stay away from her." Then he stepped out of sight, leaving me adrenaline charged and angry. How dare he. He didn't own Katherine, and it wasn't for him to say who she could talk to. As I opened the gate and teased the pig out, I tried to convince myself that Ailig couldn't have been serious. Katherine and I were neighbours and surely he couldn't expect us to never talk to one another. Eventually, he would have to settle down. One of us would need to relent and it wouldn't be me because there was no chance I could cope with not being able to see or talk to Katherine anymore.

I found it fairly straightforward getting the sow back to her pen. It seemed as though she was happy to get back to her own space, as once it came into view, she trotted ahead of me, went in and lay down in her usual spot.

"Welcome home," I muttered, dropping the latch on the gate.

Our first night under the shelter wasn't as bad as I might have imagined. Fortunately, it was a mild night, and we were warm under our blankets. The bed I had fashioned was indeed far more comfortable than the floor-bed in Katherine's cottage, and sleeping in the open air had an adventurous feel to it. Florie snuggled close to me and held my hand in hers. She seemed to me to have grown up so much over the last few months, and I was so proud of how strong and brave she'd been. She hadn't complained about the situation once and seemed to take every challenge in her stride. It killed me that I couldn't give her better.

"I'm sorry for this, Florie," I said, stroking her hair.

"For what?" she said, turning her face to look at me.

"Everything. Not being able to give you a proper home, losing Katherine, your daddy, us having to sleep here in the sheep shelter."

She was quiet for a minute. "None of those things are your fault, Mam. Anyway, this bed is comfy, and it's fun sleeping outside."

I gave a light laugh and hugged her closer. "You always manage to stay cheerful, don't you?" I said, then dropped my smile. It was on the tip of my tongue to say 'just like Katherine,' but that made me think about what she might be doing at this moment, and I didn't want to go to sleep with that on my mind. "Things are tough right now, but they will get better," I said. "I'll find a way for us to keep the croft and tomorrow I'll ask Uncle Faolan if he has any tools he can lend us to help with the harvest. He might have an idea as to what we can do about the roof, too."

Florie nodded. "I know you will, Mam. But you know, even if we do lose the croft one day, I'll be happy as long as I'm with you."

My heart melted, and I kissed her forehead. "Thank you, sweetheart. And you're right; there are some things which are more important than the croft."

"Like family," Florie said.

"That's right. Love and family are the most important things."

Florie was quiet for a few more moments. "I wish Katherine was part of our family," she said.

"So do I," I said quietly.

"But we still love her, don't we?" she asked.

"Very much." I sighed and gave Florie a final goodnight kiss, then turned over and closed my eyes. The last thing that ran through my head before I drifted off to sleep, was to wonder how Katherine was surviving her first night back with Ailig.

Chapter Nineteen

KATHERINE

Ailig sat across from me, eating his stew noisily. It was late for supper. Usually I preferred to be in bed by now, but Ailig had always been one to stay up late, often because he was drinking. He was already onto his sixth horn of mead and he took another several swigs now, finishing it off, before banging his fist which held the empty vessel, back down on the table.

"Beautiful, isn't it?" he said, turning it in his hand. It was one of the many treasures he had brought back with him from the raid, and it displayed some beautiful Celtic carvings with a high polish finish.

"It's lovely," I said, with as much enthusiasm as I could muster. It apparently wasn't enough.

He snorted and leaned back in his chair, giving me a disparaging look. "Of course, coming from where you do, I wouldn't expect you to appreciate finery such as this."

I said nothing and just looked down at my hands. I could feel his eyes burning into me as he drummed his fingers over the top of the table.

"The man I took it from put up a good fight. Said it was a family heirloom and begged me not to take it." Then he gave a snigger. "He fought harder for this than he did for his wife!" I took a deep breath and closed my eyes as he went on. "Though I can't fault him for that. His wife was bloody ugly and easily replaceable, but this," he held it up in front of him and turned it as he inspected it again. "This is a masterpiece."

There followed a silence, and I knew he was waiting for my reaction.

"Have you nothing to say? Do you not wish to hear about my victory? One day our son will inherit this fine horn, and he will want to know the story of how it came to be mine."

My stomach twisted into a knot at the mention of 'our son.' I hadn't yet told him about the pregnancy, and since I still wore my clothes, he hadn't noticed the small bump. "Maybe you could tell me about it tomorrow," I said quietly. "I'm quite weary tonight. I'd like to go to bed." I knew it wasn't the answer he wanted, and I glanced up to see how he'd taken it. He was staring at me with a stony expression.

"I don't know why you should be weary. You've done nothing all day."

I shook my head. "I'm sorry."

He looked down at the floor where the temporary bed had been. There were still a few stray bits of hay lying on the woven mat. "Perhaps you're not used to working the croft on your own anymore. Is that it?" The tone of his voice was dangerous. I didn't dare answer. "Or perhaps you miss that wench?" There was another drawn out silence before he continued. "Yes, I think that's what it is," he said.

"It's not. I don't miss her. I just used her to help me with my work when you were gone. You're the one I missed." I reached across the table and put my hand on the back of his, but he sat stiffly and didn't acknowledge my gesture.

"I don't think you're being very honest with me, Woman. You haven't seen me in months, and ever since I've been back, you've been moping around sulking. Don't think I haven't noticed. You don't seem excited to see me, you don't want to hear about my victories, and now, on my first night home, you just want to go to bed." He pulled his hand away from me. "Too weary to be a decent wife, is that it?"

"I didn't mean I wouldn't— I'm not—" I stammered, trying to think of what I could say to settle him.

He pushed his chair back suddenly and stood. "Clearly you've forgotten what a hard day is, so tomorrow I will remind you, and weary or not, you will find the energy you need to perform your conjugal duty tonight."

He put the horn down on the edge of the table, then began to unbutton his shirt and walk towards me. I shrunk in my chair. One hand automatically went to my belly and the other stretched out towards him defensively, in a futile effort to ward him off.

"Please, Ailig, can you just be gentle. I—"

"Remove your clothes, or I will," he said, now pulling his shirt off.

There were several new marks and scars on his torso. Most were healed, or near healed. One or two looked pinker and more recent. I nodded and stood up shakily, then reached between my breasts to begin loosening the ribbon on my bodice. He stood watching me in just his kilt with an expression of utter contempt as my fingers fumbled with the bow. I finally loosened it and began teasing the front of the bodice loose so it would be slack enough to pull off over my head.

Impatiently, he shoved my chair out of the way, stepped up to me and yanked on it with both of his hands, then pulled it off me roughly. He grabbed my arm and turned me to face away from him, then he loosened the ribbon on my stay and yanked that off, too.

I turned back to face him in my chemise, then folded my arms over my chest and looked at the floor.

He stood over me, breathing deeply, and the stink of alcohol which washed across my face was enough to bring on a bout of nausea. I wanted to take a step back, but the table was directly behind me, blocking my retreat.

"Take it off," he growled, then grabbed the front of the garment and yanked me towards him.

I reached up and gripped his wrists. "Wait, please!" I gasped. I needed to tell him about the pregnancy, to be careful, but the look in his eyes had now become one I knew well. A feverish, intractable lust that he needed to satisfy immediately.

A feeling of nausea had risen right to the back of my throat, and I swallowed, desperately willing myself not to vomit. I felt a coldness filter down my face and a clammy sweat erupt on my forehead as he roughly pulled at the top of my chemise again. He was breathing heavily and grunting as he yanked at the material.

Still hanging onto his wrists, I pleaded with him again. "Please, Ailig. Let me just—" But he was in a frenzy now.

I pulled away from him, staggering back into the table, which jolted behind me. There was a clatter and then a light thud as the horn, which had rested on the edge at the other side, rolled off onto the chair, then onto the dirt floor. Ailig snapped his head towards the sound and, upon realising what had happened, his face darkened with fury.

He snarled at me, "You clumsy bitch!" Then his fist came down over my face and the room went black for a few moments. My body had become limp, and bright lights and stars danced in front of my vision. I felt him throw me down on the table and pull my legs to the edge, towards him. Then he stood over me and did what he had done so many times before.

I closed my eyes and bit down on my lip and tried to go somewhere else in my mind. I knew better than to fight him during this stage. Nothing would make him stop. He pushed my chemise up high, bunching it around my neck and exposing my breasts and torso. My skin felt cold and my ears were still ringing, so I tried to concentrate on that sound, rather than his grunts and heavy breathing. He lifted his kilt up out of the way, and I counted down in my head, waiting for it to be over. It usually didn't take too long.

When he finished, he stepped back and wiped the sweat from his brow with the back of his arm. "Well, well, well," came his voice between heavy breaths. "Maybe you did have a good reason to be weary after all. It looks like you've been growing more than turnips while I've been gone." He stared down at me, then ran the tips of his fingers over my little bump and I cringed inwardly. I hated him touching me or having his hands anywhere near the precious cargo I was carrying. He sneered down at me. "When were you planning on telling me about this?" he asked in a low voice.

"I was trying to tell you," I said shakily. "I wanted you to be careful, that's all."

He curled his lips. "And so I was," he said. "I didn't hit the baby, did I?" Then he tilted his head to the side and cracked his neck, before walking to the other side of the table and picking up the horn. He held it above him, inspecting it closely and brushing the dust off it. "You're lucky this wasn't damaged," he said, looking back at me. I had started to sit myself up again and was smoothing my chemise back down over my body. "It would have been bad for you if you'd broken it. You may have had two babies you were responsible for losing."

The nausea returned, and I had to sit forward and lean over my knees. Ailig went to the jug on the bench against the wall and refilled his horn. "This jug needs more mead," he said, sliding it along the table towards me.

I nodded silently and carefully slid myself off the table and onto my feet. As the shock wore away, the familiar pain began to creep in, and the left side of my face began to ache and throb. I was aware my eye had closed a little, but I thought he had struck me low enough to land most of the force against my cheekbone. If I was lucky, my eye wouldn't close altogether. I obediently picked up the jug, then staggered towards the door to refill it from the barrel outside.

When I returned, Ailing had drawn a chair up to the fire and was sitting in front of it, swigging from his horn. I approached cautiously and topped it up again from the jug as he lazily held it out. Still feeling sick and dizzy, I put the jug back down on the table, then went over to the bed and sat down. A headache had started, and I knew the pounding would keep me up for much of the night, but Ailig behaved like we'd done no more than just finished a pleasant meal together when he spoke.

"A new shelter will have to be built for the filly," he said, staring into the fire. I nodded. Ailbeart had been moved out of his stable in the barn in order to shelter the young female horse, who was a little more skittish. He would be spending the night tethered to the hitching post outside, which wasn't a problem currently because the weather was fair. However, both horses would eventually need decent shelter. "I'm going into the village tomorrow to see about getting some timber and thatch. Brian has some stock, I think, so we might even be able to get started on it tomorrow. While I'm gone, you can start preparing the foundation. If we build the new shelter at the end of the longhouse, up against the barn, then that's one less wall we need to build. I'll see about arranging for some stone as well. I know we have a pile at the back of the house, but it's probably not enough."

I nodded again. "Good thinking," I mumbled.

I had spent much of the day thinking about how Anna and Florie were doing. I had seen them bringing reeds and grass up from the valley this morning, and I had not seen them leave their croft in the evening. After my brief encounter with Anna by the pigpen, Ailig had warned me to stay away from her, but I had made a point of frequently looking over the pasture towards the remains of her longhouse to see if I could spot her. The sheep shelter was on the other side of the building, so it was impossible to tell if they were inside it from here, but I assumed that's where they were bedding down. It was the only place on her property which now had a roof, other than the shelter used for storing the firewood and peat.

I tried not to let Ailig's unreasonable attitude about Anna get me down. He had only just arrived back and was still flexing his muscles and asserting his authority, but once things settled down again, I hoped he'd be more easygoing and we could visit each other again. So far, he hadn't seemed to have noticed our sheep were flocking together. They'd been favouring the pastures along the hillside recently and since it was only ever me who went off to milk them, I figured it might take him a while to catch on. I hoped he might not care too much about it, as it really didn't make a difference, but then Ailig's strengths did not lie in his ability to reason sensibly. Despite that, it was my hope that eventually Anna and I could milk the sheep together and use that time for a visit each day, but I didn't dare try it yet and risk Ailig getting angry.

There was a thud as Ailig chucked another lump of wood on the fire and it seemed clear he wasn't planning on sleeping anytime soon. My head was throbbing painfully now, so I got up and went to the cupboard to retrieve my medicine bag. Ailig had his back to me and didn't bother to ask what I was doing, so I quietly mixed a remedy which was good for pain and inducing sleep. I stirred it into a cup of mead, which I filled from the jug on the table, then stowed away the bag before sitting back on the bed, sipping the slightly bitter liquid.

Once I'd finished, I lay back and listened to the crackle of the fire as I waited for the remedy to take effect. I let my mind wander back to Anna and hoped she and Florie were alright. I thought back to our night in the barn and how different that was compared with tonight.

Before joining this clan, I had heard plenty of women whisper about their men and their abilities as lovers, or occasionally, their lack thereof. In my childhood, I knew plenty of girls who experimented with boys, some even with young men, and they spoke about their experiences. Sex was out in the open and all children were exposed to it from an early age. Everyone knew what was expected on a wedding night and it was no secret among families. As children grew up in the tight confines of the longhouses, nightly activities between the adults could not be concealed, nor were there attempts made to do so. Whether hearing or seeing their own parents at it, witnessing the farm animals, or hearing other people speak about it, children knew what it was and how it was done from an early age.

Children were frequently present during the births of new babies, both of their own siblings and the animals they helped to tend. One of the boys in my village had even touched me as a child. Curious, I had let him in return for a closer look at his equipment. It had given me no stirrings, though I'd found it amusing when his willy had stood up by itself, and other than some light exploring, it hadn't gone anywhere. Growing up, I had always avoided situations where I may be pressured into engaging in the act before marriage and I liked to tell myself it was because I was being chased and it was the expected thing to do. Deep down, however, I knew it was because I had no urge to do it. I had imagined the act many times, but never could understand why some of the girls and women in my village would talk about it with such excitement, and sometimes longing; like they looked forward to it.

I'd heard plenty of women swap tips on how to encourage their men to initiate the act, and even my mother had a remedy she would sell to ladies who would quietly drop by when their men were having trouble with their stamina, as they discreetly put it. She had taught me the quantities and herbs to use prior to my departure, in case I should ever need it. I had to give a dry laugh at the irony of it; if only…

Before I met Ailig, I used to anxiously think about the day I would find out what it was like to feel that pleasure they spoke of. I wanted to believe that after partaking in the act, something magical would happen, and thereafter I'd be like all those other women who found it exciting and enjoyable. Mostly, I was nervous, but a small part of me was curious and I went into my marriage with Ailig with an open mind. It took just one night with him for me to discover I would never experience pleasure from sex with Ailig. He wasn't violent my first time, but there was an utter lack of tenderness and he took me like an animal, with no care or concern for my feelings or comfort. He didn't take his time; he wasn't gentle, and I'd hated every moment of it, and every moment since.

It wasn't until last night in the barn with Anna that I'd ever experienced the sort of feelings I'd heard talk about. That rush of overwhelming pleasure, which I'd believed would always be beyond my grasp, had come so easily, so naturally last night, and I loved Anna all the more for it. I knew I would never have that with Ailig, and I hated the idea of spending the rest of my life with a person I couldn't stand. A person who may well kill me one day. I feared for my baby, who I didn't know how Ailig would treat once he or she was born, and I hated the thought of not being allowed to see Anna or Florie anymore.

I fought back the tears and did my best to clear my mind as the pounding in my head started to dampen, and the remedy took effect. Ailig would come to bed drunk in a while and snore loudly all night, but at least I knew I wouldn't hear him.

Chapter Twenty

ANNA

I woke up to the early morning crows of the cockerel, and Florie shuffled beside me as she too started to rouse.

I yawned and stretched, feeling rotten. I hadn't slept very well at all, though it was not because of the sleeping arrangements. The bed was relatively comfy, and we were warm enough. The main issue which kept me awake was the concern I felt for Katherine. I desperately needed to know if she was alright and if she had survived the first night with Ailig. I missed her very much and the more I thought about what Ailig had said about staying away from her, the more I convinced myself he couldn't be serious. Even if he was, he couldn't possibly expect to stop us from ever seeing each other; we lived next to each other for heaven's sake. She would need help when it came time for her to give birth. Our sheep shared the same pastures. I'd made up my mind that even if I had to trade the sow, I would do it to keep the croft, and therefore Katherine and I would be neighbours for the rest of our foreseeable lives. I simply couldn't imagine a reality where Katherine was not part of my daily life, and since Ailig couldn't enforce this new regime forever, it made me feel a little better. I had already decided that once he left for the village this morning, I was going to go and check on Katherine.

Feeling more motivated now I had a mission, I encouraged Florie to get up so we could get started on the chores; the ones we were still able to do. The first thing we did was set out to the hillside pasture with two pails and the stools we kept in the yard, and we milked the ewes. We no longer had the cheese cloth which got destroyed in the fire, so making cheese was not on the plans today, but we could still drink the milk which was very rich and nutritious.

After we'd filled both pails half way, and Florie had spent a few minutes playing with the lambs, we headed back down to the 'ruins' as I now referred to my longhouse. We collected some eggs, then we went back to our shelter, and I lit the fire. We cooked some beans together with the eggs and washed it down with the milk.

I couldn't see Katherine's house from the inside of the shelter, but while we'd been out and about, I'd kept careful watch as I waited for Ailig to depart. I sincerely hoped he wasn't going to break the habit of going to the village in the mornings, and common sense told me he wouldn't make Katherine go with him or nothing would get done on the croft. I just needed to be patient.

After breakfast, Florie and I set about the rest of the jobs which needed doing. We fed the sow the leftover breakfast, refilled the water troughs for her and the chickens, did some weeding in the vegetable patch, and walked up and down the turnip field to inspect the plants. They all seemed to be doing very well, which was fortunate, and as midmorning approached, I spotted Ailig getting onto his new horse and then heading out to town.

As he rode down the track, I was aware of him looking over towards us, so I crouched down and pretended to be busy with a weed until he had his back to us and was on the road to the village. Once he'd gone, I told Florie to stay where she was and dashed over the pasture to Katherine's croft. I ran up to her cottage door and banged on it.

There was a shuffling inside, and the door opened. I gasped, drawing my hand to my mouth when I saw her.

"What did he do to you?" I cried.

She looked surprised to see me, then worried as she leaned her head out of the doorway and glanced down the track towards the river.

"What are you doing here?" she said in a hushed tone. "If Ailig sees you here, he'll kill us both."

"Your face? What happened?" I asked again, ignoring her question.

She took another quick glance out of the door, then stepped back, gesturing for me to come in quickly. Florie suddenly appeared behind me.

"Florie, didn't I tell you to wait in the field?" I said, impatiently.

"I wanted to see Katherine," she said, then looked up at Katherine and her jaw dropped. "Katherine, what happened to you?"

"Good Lord," Katherine whispered, exasperated. "Come in, quick, both of you."

We scuttled in and she closed the door quickly behind us. No sooner had Katherine dropped the latch when Florie ran to her and threw her arms around Katherine's waist, hugging her tightly. "We've missed you," she said, her face buried in Katherine's dress and her voice muffled.

Katherine sighed and stroked the back of Florie's hair. "I've missed you too," she said.

I could not stop staring at her. Her beautiful face was dark blue and purple down one side, and her left eye was almost shut with the swelling. There was a small graze on her cheekbone where the skin had been partially broken and I felt my blood boil. "What happened?" I whispered.

She just shrugged her shoulders and shook her head.

Florie let go of her and looked back up again. "That looks really sore," she said sympathetically.

Katherine managed a lopsided smile. "I've taken some medicine which helps," she said. "It looks worse than it is."

"How would you know?" I said, the anger still rising in my core. "You can't see it."

She shook her head, giving me a pleading look. "Please, Anna, don't. It won't help. It doesn't matter."

"It does matter," I snapped. "He's back less than twenty-four hours and-and, well, look at you!"

Katherine glanced down at Florie, who stared back at her, her face still full of concern and sympathy. Then Katherine looked back to me again.

"And that's just the part of you I can see," I added.

"He didn't hit me anywhere else," Katherine said quickly, as if that made it better.

"This time," I said. "What about next time? He shouldn't be hitting you at all! One of these days, he's going to kill you. This simply can't go on, Katherine!"

"And what do you want me to do about it, Anna?" she said, her eyes tearing up. "Don't you think I worry about that? Don't you think I wish it were different?"

Seeing her upset sent a lance through my heart. I stepped closer to her and took her hands. "You need to leave him," I said, my voice gentler.

"And where would I go? What would I do? Become a single mother? Work on the kelp farms?"

"Can't you contact your family? Wouldn't they help you?"

"Ailig paid a dowry for me. We haven't even been married a year. He would want the money back and I can guarantee my father won't have it."

I felt utterly helpless and tried desperately to think of something comforting I could say. I couldn't stand the thought of having to see Katherine like this all the time. Or waiting for the day I'd hear she'd been killed. "There has to be something we can do," I said, refusing to accept that the situation was hopeless.

"He knows I'm carrying his baby," she said quietly. "He wouldn't let me go for that reason alone."

"What about going to Ualan? What Ailig is doing is wrong, surely other clan members would step in if they knew—"

"Of course they know," she said, before I could finish. "Ualan doesn't care. He won't interfere with another man's family life or tell Ailig how he should or should not treat me."

Of course, I knew she was right. I thought back to Ailig's previous wife who'd died because of her 'teeth,' they'd said. No one acknowledged that the poor woman had half her teeth smashed out by Ailig, and any resulting infection she got was because of him. She was barely thirty and the attitude of the village was 'these things happen.' I'd despised Ualan even then for letting Ailig get away with it, and I couldn't imagine watching Katherine suffer the way that woman had suffered.

"You might be married to Ailig, but he doesn't own you," I said, still trying to think of a solution. "Come and stay with us. We could make it work together, I know we could." I knew I sounded ridiculous and desperate, and I wasn't surprised at Katherine's reaction.

She gave a short laugh and looked at me. The desperation in my eyes must have been evident, because she let the smile fade away and gave me a compassionate look instead. "I wish that were possible," she said. "But if I came over to you and stayed with you and Florie, Ailig would be humiliated. He would be so angry. I don't know how he'd react, and if anything happened to either of you as a result, I would never forgive myself."

"And what about me? Do you think I can just stand by and do nothing as he slowly beats the life out of you?" I said.

"That's exactly what you'll have to do," she replied. "But he'll never beat the life out of me, Anna. Please believe me. I'm strong and I won't let him destroy me."

I wanted to believe her, but I didn't. I'd seen more than a few women in my life who'd been abused by their husbands. It was the same with horses. No matter how fiery they started off, they were all eventually broken, and the harder they were to break, the more the owners were determined to do it.

Ailig would regard Katherine's spirit as a challenge, something for him to stamp out, and he would gauge his manhood by his ability to dominate and control her. He was already doing it. My coming to her door was already enough to scare her. I knew that it might take a while, years perhaps, because Katherine was strong, but eventually her determination to fight would wither and the bright spark in her eyes would fade and she would give up. Even the strongest cliffs are eventually eroded by the relentless sea. I didn't say this to her. There would be no point in upsetting her further, but I decided I wasn't willing to leave things as they were. Something needed to be done and I would find a way to do it.

"I hear what you're saying, Katherine, but you can't ask me to just give up trying to help you. You didn't do that when Florie and I needed help," I said.

"Yes, and look where it got you," she whispered.

I stared hard at her for a few moments before answering. "Ailig might have taken a portion of our turnips, but the truth remains we are no worse off because of you Katherine. We're better off, in more ways than just having crops, or the sheep. You saved my daughter's life, probably both of our lives, because I would have died trying to save Florie. You've given me strength I lacked before. You've taught me to see that nothing is impossible, and now you need to bear those consequences because I refuse to just sit back and let this happen to you, Katherine. I'm going to see Faolan today, and I'm going to ask him for help."

Katherine looked back at me, her eyes brimming, then she stepped forward and wrapped her arms around me, embracing me tightly. Florie then joined in, wrapping her skinny arms around both of us, and we all stood there like that for several seconds.

"You're impossible, sometimes, Anna," Katherine whispered.

Just then, the sound of hooves clattered outside as someone rode past the front door to the hitching post next to the barn. Katherine jerked back, terror on her face.

"It's Ailig!" she whispered. "He shouldn't be back so soon."

I felt my hand suddenly gripped by Florie's small fingers and her panicked face looked up at me. I started pulling her to the door, but Katherine grabbed my arm and pulled me back.

"He'll see you!" she whispered. "He probably just forgot something. You need to hide. Now!" She turned around and pulled open the small cupboard by the wall, then dragged the contents out onto the floor. There was a large bucket, a pile of cloths, a couple of long wooden spoons, and a short-handled broom. She held the door open wide and said, "In here, quickly!"

I ran over and scrambled inside. I had to hunch right over, and the cupboard was only just deep enough to fit the width of my body. Then Florie climbed in next to me. She sat facing me, with her knees also drawn up against her, though it was a far less tight fit for her than it was for me. The cupboard door was closed, allowing only a thin crack of light to enter along the seam of the door, then there was the sound of Katherine moving the items she had removed from the cupboard. Both Florie and I held our breath as we heard the sound of the cottage door bang open and footsteps thud across the room. I reached my arm out and took Florie's hand, squeezing it to comfort her. With my other, I raised my finger to my lips to tell Florie not to make a sound.

"Forgot the bag," came the gravelly voice of Ailig. He didn't sound happy to have had to come back. The footsteps thudded to the back of the room and there was a slight muffled clunk as he picked up the bag with his items inside. There was another few seconds of silence, then he spoke again. "What are you still doing in here anyway, Woman? I thought you were going to get on with digging the foundation?"

Katherine's voice responded, trying to sound carefree. "I was, my love. I was just cleaning up in here a bit first."

"It doesn't look like it. The place looks messier than it did before I left."

Just go, I pleaded in my mind.

Then there was another soft clunk as he dropped the bag again. "If you think you can just lounge about inside all morning, you've another think coming," he said.

"Really, Ailig, I wasn't," she said again.

A shadow fell across the gap in the door as someone walked around the table and stood in front of it. "Has that wench been over here again?" he said. "She and her brat were both out on the field when I left. Now they're not."

"Of course not," Katherine said.

I heard him sniff, then more footsteps come closer to the cupboard where I now assumed Katherine was standing. "I hope not," he said. "I'd hope you have more sense than to disobey me."

Then I heard a sudden scuffle, and Katherine cried out. I jerked slightly, tempted to jump out of the cupboard and help her, but Florie's fingers squeezed mine and I held my breath and listened.

"Please, let go of me, Ailig," came Katherine's choked voice.

"Do you think because you're pregnant you can just piss about all day, doing nothing? Do you think that gives you an excuse to be lazy?" he growled.

"No," Katherine wheezed.

My blood had started to heat up again. I hated Ailig, and at that moment I wanted nothing more than to kill him.

"Do you think it will make me afraid to put you in your place?" he spoke softly now, and there was more shuffling as I imagined Katherine trying to release herself from his grip. "Do you think I won't hit you? That I won't give you a matching bruise on the other side?"

"No," came a barely audible whisper.

"Good. As long as you understand that. And trust me when I say, if the progress you've made on that foundation isn't what I consider satisfactory by the time I get back, you'll find out how much pain you can endure, even in your current delicate condition."

There was another shuffle, and then I heard Katherine coughing. The bag clunked again as it was picked up, then there was a loud clatter which made both Florie and I jump. It took a few moments for me to realise he had emptied the contents of his sack onto the table and was picking through the items, mumbling to himself.

"It'll probably take half of this stuff to cover the materials and labour we need for this project," he grumbled. More clunking as he started throwing items back into the sack. "You know I got this bracelet, which must have been worth double what everything here is. It was silver, had amethysts on it, beautiful." His description made me think of the bracelet that Ualan's son had shown to Florie yesterday.

"What happened to it?" came Katherine's timid voice.

"Ualan," Ailig snarled, still noisily sorting through the items on the table. "When he saw I had it, he claimed it as tribute. He takes a percentage of every man's spoils and he chose that as my contribution."

"That seems very greedy," Katherine said, her voice still a little rough from being partially strangled.

"It bloody well was," Ailig growled angrily. "It was worth far more than he was entitled to and it nearly ended in a fight, but the bastard always gets his way. He probably would have taken my horn too, but I kept that hidden."

Katherine gave no response, but I heard Ailig pick up his sack again. Then his footsteps thudded to the door. "Anyway, I'll see what I can get with this lot and you get your arse out there and get started on that foundation." Then he left, slamming the door behind him.

I looked up at Florie, who had her hands over her ears and wet streaks down her cheeks. Katherine started coughing again, but I didn't dare move until she told us the coast was clear.

After a painful couple of minutes, Katherine finally came back over to the cupboard and opened it. I heaved myself out of the small, cramped space and it took a few moments for my eyes to adjust to the bright light in the room, but once they did, I immediately noticed the red marks around Katherine's throat.

"He's such a bastard," I said.

"I'm alright, but you really must leave now," she said quickly. "That was far too close for comfort." She held out her hand to help Florie, who went to hug her again.

"Hey," Katherine said. "It's alright, I'm fine, see?"

Florie had managed to wipe most of her tears on Katherine's dress, but she looked up now with red eyes and sniffled softly.

I took her hand and said to Katherine, "I'm going to see Faolan today. Maybe there's something he can think of to help."

"Please don't, Anna," Katherine said. "There's nothing anyone can do about this. Anyway, he probably won't even be home. There's a big party tonight at the tavern to celebrate the success of the raids. According to Ailig, everyone's going."

"Well, I'll go right now then," I said, stubbornly. I wasn't willing to accept that no one could help until I'd explored every possible avenue.

Katherine sighed wearily but said, "It was wonderful to see you both this morning."

I gave her another hug. "I really will find a way to help you, Katherine. I hope you believe that."

She hugged me back. "Your determination is what frightens me, Anna. You're going to end up making more trouble for yourself by trying to save me. I really do wish you'd just leave it alone."

"Speaking as someone who just 'left it alone' when we were in trouble?" I said, breaking away from the hug.

"You're still in trouble," she said. "But that's different, anyway. Helping you wasn't a risk to me."

I let out a dry laugh. "Oh yes, I can see that by your face. You're clearly in no danger."

She looked at me seriously now. "Anna, please promise me you won't do anything stupid."

"Oh ye, of little faith," I smiled, trying to make her feel better.

She returned a worried smile and nodded towards the wall next to the door. "Don't forget your bag of oats this time."

I picked up the sack of oats and as I backed out of the door with the sack over my shoulder and holding Florie's hand, I said, "Maybe I'll see you at the party tonight then."

She looked mildly amused. "You're going?"

"Well, I don't need Ailig's permission to go there, do I?" I said, smiling again as I turned to walk back across the pasture.

Florie and I hurried across the field back to our own croft. As we walked, I looked down at my daughter.

"I'm so sorry you had to hear all of that," I said. "You should have stayed where I told you."

"I wanted to see Katherine," she said.

"I know, but that was dangerous."

"I want to help Katherine, too," she went on.

I stopped and stooped down to her level. "You need to stay away from Ailig, do you understand?" I said. "He's dangerous."

"He's horrible," she said. "Katherine should run away."

"It's not that simple, darling," I said.

"She should do what you said and come and stay with us."

I smiled. "Would you like that?"

Florie nodded.

"So would I," I said. "But she can't, Ailig would come after her."

"We could fight him," she said. "We could get some rocks and sticks and —"

"Hey, we can't kill him." Sadly, I added in my head. "We would get into trouble for that. So we need to find another way to help her that doesn't involve killing anyone. Alright?"

She sighed, clearly disappointed that I wasn't on board with her plan. "Uncle Faolan will help though, won't he?"

"I hope so," I said.

After dropping off the sack of oats at the shelter, we headed down to the river track together, then continued the two miles to Faolan's croft. His was in the direction of the village but set further back from the river, higher in the valley. It felt like forever since I'd been there, but the route was still very familiar to me. Before Robert died, we used to go frequently, and I found myself sad when I realised we hadn't been there since. Florie would play with her cousins, and I would chat with Alis, and the visits would be a weekly occurrence. All of that had abruptly stopped after the accident, and though Faolan tried hard to mend the bridges between us, I hadn't been able to forgive him, or even think about him without feeling angry. Until now.

Florie hurried along the path in front of me, clearly anxious to see her cousins after such a long time, and I felt guilty as I watched. The child had always been sensitive enough not to ask to go and see them, but I knew in my heart she missed them a great deal.

I let Florie run ahead and rap on the door, and it opened before I caught up to her. I approached to see an attractive woman in her early thirties with long brown hair, bending down and hugging Florie tightly. Then she looked up and saw me. She let go of Florie but kept her hand rested on the little girl's shoulder, who clung to her aunty's hand with a big grin on her face.

Alis smiled widely at me and stepped forward to give me a big hug. I returned the gesture, hugging her back, and smiled hesitantly at her.

"Anna!" she said enthusiastically, genuinely pleased to see us. "Please do come in. Faolan will be so happy to know you've come. It's been far too long." She started to open the door for me, but I hung back.

"It's wonderful to see you too, Alis. You're right, it has been too long and I apologise for that." I paused for a second, trying not to be rude or sound like I was rejecting her hospitality. "Would it be possible for me to have a private word with Faolan, please? I wouldn't ask, but it's quite urgent."

She gave an understanding smile. "Of course, he's just resting his leg. Do you want to come in, or shall I call him out? I expect you'll have more privacy if he comes out here. Just a minute. I'll fetch him."

"Can he walk?" I asked, suddenly concerned. It hadn't even occurred to me that Faolan might have sustained an injury during his time away, and I suddenly felt guilty for not thinking to ask how he was.

"Oh, he's doing much better now," Alis said, still holding the door. "He can walk and he enjoys going outside. I've been making him stay indoors since he got back because it's easier for me to take care of him, but he can get about when he wants to and he'll be glad to get out into the sunshine for a bit. Sit down, please," she said, pointing to the thick log that rested in the yard. "He's heard you, so he's coming anyway."

She let go of Florie and disappeared back inside. I walked over to the log and sat down, and Florie demurely followed me.

"Why don't you go and see your cousins, Florie?" I said, turning to her. Her face suddenly lit up, and she sat up straighter, looking around.

"Yes, the boys are around the back by the chickens and Isabel is with them. Go ahead, sweetheart," Alis said as she reappeared and stood by the door waiting patiently.

Florie jumped up and took off around the side of the house, just as Faolan came limping out of the cottage, leaning on a single crutch. He smiled as he approached, and I stood up to greet him.

"I'll be right inside if either of you need anything," Alis said cheerfully, and she hurried back in and closed the door gently.

"Sit back down, please," Faolan said, gesturing with his hand. "You're as bad as Alis."

"I'm so sorry, Faolan. I didn't know you'd been injured," I said, sitting down again. I craned my neck to watch him as he made his way slowly around the log. His face looked pale and thin. He'd lost a lot of weight and there was a sheen to his brow which I guessed was caused by the pain and exhaustion of getting around.

"Oh, don't be. It's nothing really." He stopped and lifted his kilt to reveal a bandage which was wrapped from just below his knee to halfway up his thigh. "It was deep, but we don't think it's broken, and it's healing well. I did have an infection, but it's finally under control. If it wasn't for that, I'd be running around with the bairns in the back right now."

"I'm sorry, Faolan," I said again. I felt guilty now for judging him for not stopping by on his way back from the raids.

"It's fine. I'll be walking properly again in no time," he said. "Don't you worry." He had made it around to the log and now slowly lowered himself to sit next to me. I could see it was painful for him, but he kept on smiling. "I'm really happy to see you, Anna," he said, then his face turned more serious. "I heard about your house. I'm so very sorry. As soon as I can get about properly again, I will help you sort that out. I hope you know that."

"Thank you, Faolan, but there's no rush. It's more important that you get strong again for your family."

"What are you talking about?" he said, grinning. "I'm plenty strong." He flexed a bicep for me to see, then leaned in closer and lowered his voice, grinning. "It's all an act, really. I'm just doing this to get a few days' rest and have Alis fuss over me a bit." He winked and sat up again, still grinning.

I smiled back. "It means a lot that you offer to help me like that," I said. Then added, "Especially after what I said to you before."

"Don't think on it," he said, making a brush-off motion with his hand and his expression turned serious again. "I don't expect you to forgive me any time soon. In fact, if you ever do, I will consider myself blessed, but I do hope we can be friends again. My children miss Florie so much and I know she must miss them."

It suddenly occurred to me that for the first time since Robert's accident, I was able to look at Faolan without feeling a sense of debilitating pain and loss. True, his face no longer resembled Robert's as closely. I'd never seen Robert so thin, but that wasn't the reason. For the first time, I genuinely did feel like I could forgive Faolan; one more thing I had to be thankful to Katherine for. "I have to be honest Faolan, I came to talk to you about something more than the longhouse," I said.

He looked inquisitive. "Anything I can do to help, I will, Anna."

"It's Katherine," I said.

He looked perplexed. "Katherine?"

"Yes, Ailig Scarth's wife," I said. This definitely took him by surprise. "I don't know if you know, but she and I have— had been working together the last couple of months while the men were gone. We combined our turnip crop and worked it together to help make the labour easier for us both. Anyway, when Ailig got back, he put an immediate stop to that. But Katherine has become a good friend to me and I'm seriously concerned about her welfare. I just saw her this morning, and she already has a bruised face, and it was the same before he left. He's hitting her and threatening her and he's told her she can't come and see me or Florie anymore and..." I trialed off, realising I was speaking far too quickly and getting upset. "I just told her I would try to find a way to help her. Can you speak to Ualan about it or is there anything you can do? I've told her she needs to leave Ailig, but she has nowhere to go."

Faolan lowered his eyes and shook his head slowly. "I don't understand, Anna. What are you asking me to do?"

"Talk to Ualan, ask him to stop Ailig from hurting Katherine," I said. I knew how I sounded, that what I was asking was pointless, but I had to try.

"And do you think Ualan will do that?" he said gently. "I'm sorry, Anna, but I don't think he will take it seriously. The first thing he'll ask is why I suddenly have an interest in this woman's wellbeing and as soon as he knows it's your neighbour I'm talking about, he'll dismiss the concern completely."

"But there has to be something you can do, Faolan. I promised Katherine I'd find a way to help her. She-she's pregnant. She's already lost one baby because of his relentless beatings, and she's terrified it'll happen again."

He looked sympathetic, but he held up his hands to indicate he was powerless. "I'm so sorry, Anna. If I could help you with this, I would, you know I would, but it's outside my capabilities. If I go to Ualan, the most likely result will be that things get worse for this woman."

"Her name is Katherine," I said, stiffly.

"I'm sorry, Katherine," he said. "But please understand, if I go to Ualan and by some miracle, he does decide to intervene, all he's going to do is talk to Ailig. Then what do you think Ailig will do to Katherine?"

I felt a coldness creep through me as I realised he was right. "Then I'll have to find another way myself," I said, quietly.

"You can't," Faolan gave me a desperate look. "Ualan is on the very edge, Anna. If you go and do something stupid, you could lose the croft."

"Well, maybe I don't care about that anymore," I said, standing up. "Maybe the croft isn't everything and maybe someone around here needs to stand up and do what's right for a change."

Faolan struggled, trying to stand up as well. "Anna," he panted.

I sighed and bent over to grip his arm and pulled him to a stand. He felt fragile, and I realised he was a lot sicker than he was letting on. I picked up his crutch and handed it to him carefully. "Steady on, Faolan," I said, gently.

He was still panting, but he continued, "I agree what Ailig does to his wives is a terrible, terrible thing. But you have enough problems of your own to deal with right now, without taking on someone else's. If it's that awful for her, she'll find a way to get out."

"I've told you, she has no other kin here," I said. "No one to stand up for her. I swear that's why the bastard always brings his wives from abroad, just so he can get away with treating them like dirt, then have no one to answer to when he eventually kills them. And we all know Ualan will always turn a blind eye rather than put himself through any trouble.".

Faolan looked directly at me. The sheen across his forehead had now evolved into a carpet of droplets and his black hair was plastering down against it. "Why do you care so much about this woman?" he asked.

"I just don't want to see him kill another one," I said. This was partially the truth. "Katherine is my friend. She's a good person, and she's helped me and Florie so much. She was here for me when no one else was."

"You've always had my family. You just needed to ask, Anna. I've always told you that," Faolan said.

"So I'm asking now. Help me to help Katherine, please," I begged.

"I'm sorry, Anna. I wish there was something I could do, but I can't. As wrong as it is, it's just the way of things. Katherine is Ailig's wife, she belongs to him. Even if I thought Katherine would be safe, and I asked Ualan to step in, he won't. It's a serious thing to interfere with how another man runs his household. There would be more chance of Katherine getting help from Ualan if she were to approach him herself, rather than someone doing it on her behalf. Though I still think it would be dangerous for her to try. Have you suggested to her to go and talk to him? She could do so in confidence. Ualan would honour her wishes if she wanted to keep the conversation private, but unless he removes her from Ailig permanently, which is very unlikely, it won't solve anything. Ualan can't stop Ailig from beating her up. The best he could do would be to tell Ailig to stop, and if he does that the chances are she will pay dearly for it."

I knew what he said was true, but I just gave a deep sigh and looked away.

"I'm afraid that's the best I can suggest, Anna. I'm sorry."

"It's not your fault," I said. "What you've said is right, I'm just angry." I sighed again and ran my hands through my curls, then called to Florie.

"Let her stay and play a while," he said. "It's been so long since she's seen her cousins."

"I take it you're not going to the celebration in the village tonight?" I said.

He looked surprised, then smiled. "Err, no, I was all set to enjoy a night of drinking and dancing, but my miserable wife tells me I'm not allowed."

"You're absolutely right!" came a call through the window. Faolan smiled and winked at me.

"Alright, can Florie stay with you for the night, then? I have some things to get on with back at the croft."

"Of course she can, but Anna, please promise me you won't do anything foolish," he said.

I didn't answer him and was slightly irked that he was the second person in less than an hour to say that to me. Florie came running, and I stooped down to give her a hug and kiss. "How do you feel about sleeping over at your cousin's tonight so you all can catch up?"

"Are you going to stay too?" She asked quietly.

"No," I said. "But I'll come back for you first thing in the morning. First thing, alright? I won't even collect the eggs without you."

She hesitated a little but gave a slow nod, then embraced me in a tight hug. "I love you, Mam."

"I love you, darling. Have fun."

"Anna, before you go," Faolan said. Then he called into the house for his wife. Alis came out a few seconds later, carrying a medium-sized sack which bulged at the bottom. "I know you lost a lot in the fire," he said. "This isn't much, but it's a few items I thought might be of help to you. They're all extras of things we already had, so it's cost us nothing. We were going to get rid of them anyway, but maybe they might be helpful to you."

I knew he was lying about planning on getting rid of the items to get me to accept his charity, and if things were not as dire, I would have refused the help. But I reached out and took the sack from Alis, smiling softly. "Thank you both. That really is very kind of you."

Alis pulled me into a tight hug. "Don't be afraid to ask if you need anything, Anna, and you know you're always welcome here."

I thanked her again, then said a final goodbye to Florie before walking back down the track towards home. There were things to do, and I was glad she'd be occupied.

Chapter Twenty-One

The walk back to my croft was long and quiet. In one respect, I missed Florie's company, but in another, I was glad to have the time to myself. I needed space to think.

Katherine's battered face remained in my mind's eye, and every time I thought about how Ailig treated her, something inside me burned. Katherine was the kindest, gentlest person I'd even known, and her husband didn't give a damn about her. He didn't deserve her, and it infuriated me that no one else in the clan seemed to take Ailig's behaviour seriously. He needed to be stopped and Katherine needed to be free of him once and for all, otherwise he'd kill her.

After Robert died, I'd spent months consumed with laying blame for his death and torturing myself, thinking about all the things I could have, or should have done which would have changed the outcome of that day. I blamed Faolan, I blamed myself, and I blamed Robert, and that vagrant anger dragged me into a place so dark and isolated that it almost cost both Florie and me our lives.

Katherine had saved us in more ways than one the day she pulled us out of the river. Through sheer persistence and determination, she brought me back to myself and showed me that it was possible to accept the past and forgive. I could not now turn my back on her and leave her to the fate I knew was waiting for her, no matter what she, or Faolan, or anyone else said. It wasn't possible for me to know what was going to happen to Robert, but that was not the case with Katherine, and if she was killed, I feared this time I'd go to a place I could not come back from. The question was no longer about whether I should help her; it was how.

I was glad my feet were so familiar with the route home, because somehow they took me there while my mind drifted far off to another place. I ran through countless scenarios and ideas, mentally assessing each one for flaws, long-term viability, risk, and chance of success. None were perfect across all those criteria, but then I didn't think a plan existed which was. By the time I was a quarter mile from the shelter, I'd settled on one which I thought had a good chance of working. The only problem was it had to be done tonight, and this gave me very little time to prepare and no opportunity to discuss it with Katherine first. Although, as far as the latter point, I decided that was just as well, because I knew she wouldn't go along with it otherwise. The plan was very risky, and my blood ran cold when I thought about the potential consequences if things didn't go well. I picked up my pace, anxious to get back to the shelter and make the preparations I could. If things went as planned, it wouldn't even take very long. I might even be done before it got dark. After all, I had a celebration I needed to show up for tonight.

By the time I made it back to my croft, it was late afternoon and as I walked along the track which followed the river, I looked up the valley towards Katherine's cottage. I could see the small figure of Katherine in the distance, shovelling away at the end of the building alongside the barn. Again, I fumed at Ailig for making her work like that when she was pregnant. I didn't see any sign of him helping out on the croft and guessed he had decided to stay in the village for the rest of the day after conducting his business. He would almost definitely be getting an early start on the celebrations. As much as I wanted to, I didn't dare walk over to see Katherine. He could come back at any time and one close call today was enough for me.

I hurriedly grabbed some kale and turnip leaves, then cooked myself some oats and gobbled up my food quickly. Then I opened the sack which was given to me by Faolan and Alis. Inside they had put several cloths, two linen nightdresses, a tinderbox, two cups, two bowls, two spoons, and two pairs of shoes. The pair for Florie was a little big, but that wasn't a problem. There was a knife, a couple of small blankets, a block of butter, two full lumps of cheese wrapped in cheesecloth, several strips of dried rabbit meat, and a block of hard fat wrapped in a thin rag. I smiled as I went through the items, grateful to Faolan for his generosity. They would be very helpful, and I could now make cheese again. The butter and meat were luxuries I looked forward to tasting, too. I put all the items except the food, back in the sack, then carried the butter, fat, meat and cheese over to the ruins and stored them in the pit larder with the vegetables. I had now taken to resting a heavy rock on top of the wooden board which covered the pit as an added measure to stop the rodents getting into the supplies, and as I heaved the heavy object back into place, I glanced over the stone wall towards Katherine's croft again.

Ailig's new horse was now hitched up outside, and he must have taken Katherine into the cottage with him because I couldn't see anyone in the yard anymore.

I had no idea how long it would be before they headed to the tavern together, but I was fairly confident they would be gone by the time I got back. There was somewhere else I needed to be right now, so I left the ruins, and rather than take the river road to my destination, I hitched up my skirts and prepared for the cross-country trek ahead of me.

Fortunately, due to the lack of rain, the going was fairly easy, and I didn't have to struggle through mud or boggy patches as I ran across the various fields and pastures. In fact, as I went, I thought to myself that the way I was taking was far quicker than it would have been had I taken the more conventional route.

Ualan's longhouse came into view far quicker than I had anticipated, and while the light was getting dimmer as twilight set in, there was still more than I was comfortable with, so I stopped before I got too close and lay down in the pasture. I rested my head on my elbows and maintained my position for several minutes, watching the croft for any activity. I couldn't see any of his labourers working on the fields, and with his croft being so big, his longhouse was beyond the sight of any neighbours or passersby on the river track. It was very still and quiet, and after five or so minutes, I stood up again and began to walk slowly towards the house.

There was a very small trail of smoke rising from the chimney above the central hearth, but that suggested it was being allowed to die down, which was a good sign. I approached in a roundabout way so that I came towards it from the barn side, where there were no windows facing me. I could not afford for anyone to see me here, so I was very cautious as I got closer. I desperately hoped that no one was home, but there was no way to tell from here whether they had all left for the celebrations or not. Had I taken the track, there was a possibility I would have passed Ualan and his family and I would know for sure, but then they would have wondered why I was walking away from the village at this time of night. It would have raised questions that I couldn't afford to be asked now or later, so the way I had come was better.

I tiptoed up to the side of the barn, held my breath, and listened.

Nothing. Not even the sound of the horses.

Still holding my breath, I crept around to the front of the barn and sidled over to the large barn door, before pulling it open slightly and peering inside. Ualan's barn was huge. There were many bales of hay stacked on one side, along with two wheelbarrows, a horse plough, several scythes, hoes, rakes and brooms, three milking stools, and a stack of several large buckets. Along the opposite wall there was a row of five stables, all of them empty. I let my breath go and breathed a sigh of relief. If the horses were all gone, then the family would all be gone. Still being careful though, I slowly moved along the front wall of the longhouse towards the door of the cottage, ducking under the window as I passed it, just to be safe. I held my ear up against the door and listened intently for any sounds coming from inside. My heart was hammering in my chest and I struggled to keep my breathing steady. After hearing nothing for a good thirty seconds, I took another deep breath in and pushed the door to Ualan's house slowly open.

I peeked inside through the crack of the door and all seemed quiet. The fire had clearly been untended for quite some time and had burned down to a pile of embers, which cast a pleasant glow around the main room.

Light still came in through the windows and there was more than enough to see by. I stepped into the house and closed the door quietly behind me.

Ualan's cottage looked much the same as it did last time I was here, but it still made me envious to once again see how big it was compared with my own. His ceilings were high. The main room alone was the size of my entire longhouse, including the barn. Several chairs stood around the centre hearth and there was the large table at the back of the room where Ualan had sat the last time I'd seen him here. There was a box of small wooden and woollen toys in one corner, a separate bench for preparing food, and the wicker partitions which separated the main room from other sections of the cottage.

I looked around quickly, wondering where to start searching for the item I was after. I figured the safest bet would be around Ualan and Agatha's sleeping space, but I had no idea which partition that would be behind. Taking a guess, I crept towards the one situated at the back of the room and poked my head around it.

It was quite dark, but enough light was still filtering in between the cracks of the closed window shutters to see. My blood instantly froze. There was a bed box up against the stone wall; a nice one made of quality lumber boards. The curtain had not been drawn across the box, allowing me the full view of the dimly lit figure who lay motionless inside it. It was an old woman with her eyes closed and at first I wasn't sure if she was asleep or not. I had to watch her carefully for a few moments just to make sure she wasn't dead. She was so still and quiet. But her chest raising up and down ever so slightly under her folded hands told me that she was, in fact, alive, something I wasn't sure if I was relieved about or not. I slowly backed up behind the partition, glad that I had been so quiet even when I thought the house was empty. The old woman must be Agatha's mother, for I knew Ualan's mother lived with his father in a township a few miles away.

I crept up to the next partition and stuck my head around it, this time praying it would be empty. It was. And the shutters were open, so it was better lit than the last room. There were two large bed boxes in this area, and there was a large footlocker at the end of one of them. Deciding it would be best to check here before moving on with my search, I crept into the space and knelt down in front of the box. I opened it quietly and then rummaged through the contents, silently cursing Ualan. His family had so much, and I was sorely tempted to take more than what I'd come for, but I resisted. I couldn't afford to take any unnecessary risks, and even what I was doing right now, being in someone's house, uninvited, carried a heavy penalty if I was caught. The fact that it was Ualan's house made it even more dangerous.

I rifled through the various articles of clothing, a small leather pouch which felt like it was full of coins, and a dirk in a beautiful leather sheath. I was careful not to move any of the items too far out of their original places as I searched, but I couldn't find what I was looking for, so I closed the box carefully, then got up to go to the next partition.

This was the last one, so it had to be Ualan and Agatha's room. Again, I cautiously peeked behind the large wicker panel before stepping in. There was an unlit hearth in the centre of this space, but the shutters were open here too, so it wasn't hard to see. A beautiful woven mat covered the floor and there was a large bed box which could have fit at least four sleepers. This one had doors fixed to it rather than curtains, and some fine carvings had been whittled around the base. The mattress in the bottom was much thicker than I was used to seeing, and it was covered by a thick woollen blanket. I badly wanted to lie on it and see how it felt, but resisted the urge.

I went straight to the huge footlocker by the wall, removed the oil lamp, cup and bowl which were sitting on top of it, taking careful note of exactly how they were arranged, then opened the lid. I gritted my teeth in anger as I looked down at the veritable collection of treasures which lay before me. Beautiful cotton and linen clothes, some in vibrant colours and many of them with intricate embroidery or lace. There were also some of the more elegant looking weapons I had seen a couple of days before, a well-made sporran which felt heavy with coin, two nice brooches and a couple of rings. I shuffled my hands between the clothes, ran my fingers along the bottom of the chest and scrunched the fabric between my fists to check for the item I'd come for.

After a good ten minutes of searching, I felt sure it wasn't here. I silently cursed as this meant it was either in the main room, or the room where the old lady was sleeping. Of course, there was also a possibility that Ualan had already sold or given away what I wanted, but I told myself it was a slim chance since he hadn't been back long enough to get round to that yet. The thought worried me because if I didn't get the specific item I wanted, then I'd have to take another in its place, and it wouldn't fit with my plan as well.

I placed the oil lamp, cup and bowl carefully back on top of the lid, then crept back into the main room with the dying embers and quickly searched the cupboards and shelves. I didn't take as much time doing this because I'd convinced myself the item I wanted would be stowed somewhere more secure, and I'd been in the house for much longer than I felt comfortable with already. There was only one more place I could look, so I snuck back over to the first partition and very carefully peeped around the side of it again.

She still lay there in the semidarkness, her white hair splayed out across the mattress and her wrinkled hands clasped together over her chest, still breathing soundlessly. This bothered me. At least if she was snoring, it would give me more confidence that she was actually asleep, and it would mask any small accidental noises I might make. There was nothing for it though; the room would have to be searched before I could rule out that the item was gone.

I silently prayed that the woman was at least partially deaf as I crept slowly around the partition. There was another foot locker, this one situated at the bottom of the bed, next to her feet. I tiptoed over and knelt down in front of it. I took another quick glance at the old lady as I rested my hands on the lid, then, since she still hadn't moved, I opened the trunk slowly.

The old woman appeared to have less possessions than the rest of the members of the family, and I didn't have to dig around very much before my fingers gripped around the object which felt like the one I'd been searching for. As I pulled it out slowly and opened my hand around it, my heart skipped a beat. This was it, the thing I had come for; the jewelled silver bracelet that Ailig had spoken about. My mouth had gone dry, and I tried to swallow as I carefully turned the weighty object over in my shaking hands.

Now that I was close up to it, I could truly appreciate its magnificence and fully understand why Ailig had been so bitter about letting it go. The craftsmanship was exquisite, and it consisted of several wide plates of silver all hinged together, with every second plate housing an amethyst cabochon. Each stone had intricate engravings surrounding it, and it must have been worth a great deal. I hardly dared to breathe as I carefully slid the bracelet into my pocket, then lowered the lid of the footlocker. As I did, I kept my eyes on the woman's peaceful face and I felt a strong surge of guilt overtake me. I didn't like the idea of stealing from this old lady, who had done me no wrong, and I had not anticipated that the bracelet might have been gifted to someone else so soon. I had no quarrel with any of the other members of Ualan's household, and the fact that I was also invading Agatha's privacy was something which was eating at me as well.

The fact remained, however, that I needed this bracelet more than Ualan did, or any member of his family, come to that, none of whom would ever have to worry about their future or being taken care of. It also made me feel better to know I had no intention of keeping the bracelet forever. Ualan would eventually get it back, so I told myself this was simply a nonconsensual loan. As I slowly stood, I allowed myself a slow release of air, then I slowly backed away from the bed.

I'd made it three steps towards the wicker partition when all of a sudden there came the muffled sound of conversation and I heard the front door bang open and the boisterous voices of two young men enter the main room. My heart leapt into my throat and I froze on the spot. The old woman gave a quick intake of breath, then groaned and rubbed her face with one hand.

I couldn't move, and panic overwhelmed me. I was going to be seen. There was no possible way out of this. Either the woman was going to see me in here, or I'd be seen by the two or more persons who had just entered the cottage. I felt the colour drain from my face as the woman, who was still groaning and rubbing her eyes, sat herself up, then hoisted her legs over the side of the bed. The two voices in the main room were loud, and the owners sounded drunk.

"Well, hurry up and get it then. I want to get back to the tavern," came the first voice. There was a clatter as something fell.

"Bugger! Pick that up, will you?" came a second voice. There was an audible huff, then a clunk. "It's in my chest. Wait there, I'll get it."

I still stood frozen in the middle of the old woman's room. My eyes darted around, looking for something to dive behind, somewhere I could hide, but there was nowhere. There was the window next to her bed, but the shutters were closed and it was small. There was no possible way I could get to it and squeeze myself out before she saw me. She was still hunched over, rubbing her eyes, but in a second or two she would look up and see me. Why did they have to be so loud? What possible excuse could I give for being in here? There was none, and now there would be not just one doddering old woman, but three witnesses to my presence here, so even if I ran, it would be hopeless. I would lose the croft and be flogged, if I were lucky, and my plan would fall apart. Katherine would never escape Ailig and Florie would forever be tarnished by the crime of her mother. I had let everyone down.

A hundred things raced through my mind as the woman lifted her head and opened her eyes.

She stared straight at me and furrowed her brow, irritated. "Will you two keep your voices down!" She croaked, loudly. "Some of us are trying to sleep, you know!"

I stood stock still, staring at her as she stared at me. It took me a full five seconds to register that this woman hadn't seen me. Couldn't see me. The eyes she stared through were two pale blue circles floating under milky ponds. This woman was blind.

"Bollocks!" I heard one of the voices say in a hushed tone. "I forgot about Nanna." Then in a much louder voice, "Sorry, Nanna, I was just getting the dirk father gave me. We'll be out of your hair in a minute!"

The woman huffed and muttered something under her breath about unruly youngsters. Then, with a grunt, she stood up. She picked up a cane which I hadn't noticed was leaning by the head of the bed, then held it out in front of her, tapping the floor as she shuffled forward.

Finally, coming to my senses, I bit down on my lip and sidled myself out of her path and flattened myself against the stone. I had a painful ache in my chest and I realised I had been holding my breath for the last sixty seconds. I didn't dare take a real breath until the woman left the area, and as she shuffled her way around the partition, I breathed out a long sigh of relief, then took several deep shaky breaths. I couldn't believe how lucky I'd been. I'd had to hide from someone twice in one day and both times I'd got away with it. There was no way my good fortune would last much longer, and now I really needed to get out of this cottage as fast as possible.

"Got it!" came the young man's voice again. "Alright, we're off, Nanna. Sorry to have woken you. I just wanted to show the others my blade."

There followed an exaggerated 'mwah' sound as the young man kissed his grandmother, then the sound of the door closing. I could hear the muffled sound of laughter quickly fade as the boys left, and I lifted a shaking hand to my forehead to wipe away the beads of sweat which had formed there.

The old woman was still muttering to herself in the main room and I waited for a few more moments, listening hard, then crept over to the widow. The shutters were closed, but I decided it was worth taking the chance to unlatch them. I opened them wide, as quickly, but as silently as I could, then clambered out and onto the ground, glad to be out of the dim room.

The early twilight was still fairly bright as I turned to push the shutters closed again. I hunched down low next to the house and looked around to make sure the coast was clear before dashing across the pastures, back towards my own croft.

With my heart still racing, I kept up a fast pace until I reached the shelter, and it wasn't until I was halfway across the pasture to Katherine's cottage before I slowed to a fast walk. There was no sign of life around the cottage and the new horse had gone. Unlike Ualan's house, I felt a lot more confident approaching Katherine's, which I was very familiar with and would not have to enter. I was absolutely sure Ailig would be at the tavern until the early hours of the morning, so I barely hesitated as I got closer.

Rather than go inside, I walked around the back of the cottage to where the roosting boxes for the chickens rested. I hoisted one up and moved it, revealing a dampish, dark patch of earth underneath. Using my hands, I dug away at the soil, until I'd made a hole about the width of my fist and several inches deep. I was about to drop the bracelet in the hole when, on second thought, I pulled my skirt to the side and tore a strip from the bottom of my chemise. I wrapped the bracelet up before burying it, then replaced the roosting box exactly as it had been.

Brushing off my hands, I walked over to Katherine's well and pulled up a pail of water. I washed my hands and face thoroughly, paying particular attention to my fingernails, then I raced across the pasture, deciding to take a cross-country shortcut to get to Glenbeag.

The sky had begun to show its darker twilight colours when I finally made it to the tavern. I slowed down as I approached and focused on trying to look nonchalant. Though I knew no one could possibly know what I'd done, I couldn't help feeling like the guilt, which seemed to be oozing from every pore in my body, might be smelled out.

Long before I reached the door, the sound of music filtered through to my ears and the noise of many people enjoying a great deal of merriment permeated the walls. One or two men who stood outside holding mugs of ale grinned and nodded at me as I walked up to the door, and I returned a friendly smile as I passed.

"Late to the celebrations, aren't ye lass?" one of them slurred.

"Well, you know how it is," I said, turning to face them. I forced another grin but still kept walking backwards towards the door. "A woman's work is never done."

The man laughed, then raised his mug. "Get a drink and join us!"

I gave a nervous laugh as I pushed the door open behind me and backed through it.

Once inside, I took a few steps away from the door, manoeuvring myself between the groups of patrons to try and find a good vantage point from which to scan the room. My heart was still hammering and the stress of the evening's nerve-racking exploits had not yet dissipated, so I decided the man's suggestion to go and get a drink was actually not a bad one. Still having not seen Katherine, I picked my way through the sea of stumbling, sweaty bodies, aiming for one of the busy bar maids I could see at the back.

The tavern was completely packed with men, women and children, all chattering loudly and I passed a couple of huge bearded men who stood atop a table, holding their mugs, while enthusiastically recounting one of the skirmishes they were involved in. I didn't catch much of the story as I sidled around the crowd that had gathered to hear the tale, but it must have been epic, considering the amount of arm waving and pretend sword play the men were engaged in. One of them pounded a foot down on the table and held out a knife, then waved it in the air above the mesmerised faces of his audience.

"..and I dunne ken what he were doin' but in the end ah had te slash him right through the belly!" His words were heavily slurred, and he made dramatic sweeping motions with the knife as the people below him roared and cheered heartily.

As I got closer to my target, I could see in one corner of the room there were several musicians. Two were playing flutes, one had a hand drum and one was strumming away on a lute. A few people in that vicinity were dancing, some were singing along, and some couples, who'd clearly still not had enough of each other since being reunited yesterday, were locked in passionate embraces. There were three strong fires burning in the hearths throughout the tavern, and over each there was a spit with a good sized pig being roasted. The smell was wonderful, and if things went well tonight, I thought I may stay long enough to indulge.

When I finally caught up to the barmaid, I gave her a coin and my order, then stood with my back against the wall and scanned the room again for Katherine. After a few minutes, the woman returned and shoved the mug of mead into my hands. I drank it down quickly and then ordered another. I didn't usually make a habit of drinking copious quantities of alcohol, but I needed to relax a bit and I decided I would also attract less attention if I looked like I was doing the same thing as everyone else.

Once I had the second mug of mead, I took a few deep swallows so I would be less likely to spill it, then made my way back through the crowds to continue my search. There were so many people and it was noisy, so I knew it might take me a while. I did see one of the two boys I assumed had come back to Ualan's cabin while I was there. He was passing around a knife between a group of his friends and they took it in turn, unsheathing it, swishing it through the air and inspecting it, suitably impressed.

I spotted Ualan too, who was sat at the biggest table at the far end, looking as boisterous and merry as any of the others. I leered at him as he laughed hard at something one of the men beside him had said, then he took another swig of mead and choked on it when a man behind him, who was still bellowing with laughter, slapped him on the back. I smirked as his drink slopped down his front and he coughed, turning to look at the culprit with a very annoyed expression. As far as celebrations go, it was still early, but there would be plenty of fights throughout the night. Some men would joke that more of them were killed or injured during the after-celebrations than there were during the actual raids. I just hoped I could find Katherine and then leave before that side of things started.

After another few minutes of searching, I finally spotted her standing off in one corner, sipping from a cup. There were a few other women standing around her merrily engaged in conversation, but she didn't appear to be very interested in whatever it was they were talking about. Ailig didn't seem to be with her, and I looked around trying to see where he might be lurking, but then decided it didn't matter. This was a public place and Ailig could not force me to leave, nor would anyone expect me to. He might even let it go if he saw me talking to Katherine. It was, after all, a celebration.

I walked a little closer until I was standing directly in Katherine's field of view, then discreetly tried to catch her eye. At first, she just stared into space vacantly, her face still bruised and swollen and her left eye partially closed, but she suddenly came back to life when she spotted me. She lowered the cup from her mouth and smiled, and I jerked my head slightly, indicating for her to follow me. She looked to either side of her, checking to see if Ailig was watching, then started to walk towards me.

I turned and made my way back to the exit, then walked out of the front door and dawdled a few feet away from the building as I waited for her to catch up. As soon as I saw her emerge, I immediately walked around the back of the building, then across the dirt track which ran behind it and ducked into a narrow alley between two small cottages. I leaned against the wall as I waited for her to come, then beamed when she appeared around the corner.

Even with her bruised face, she was beautiful. She gave me a wide smile as she approached, and as soon as she was in reach, I couldn't stop myself from pulling her into a deep kiss. I was careful not to press hard against her face, or touch her cheek, which I knew must be tender, and though she seemed hesitant for a moment, she kissed me back, wrapping her arms around me and pulling me closer to her. It was the first time I'd been able to kiss her since the night in the barn, and though it had only been a couple of days since then, my heart sang with the delight of it. Her lips were just as soft, her scent just as sweet, and for that moment my worries seemed to melt away. She smiled as she finally drew back, then looked cautiously around again. I couldn't take my own eyes off her, and at that moment, almost didn't care if we were seen.

"You came," she said, still grinning. "I didn't really think you would."

"And miss an opportunity to see you?" I smiled. "I think not."

"I'm so glad you did," she said. Then, looking around, she added, "Where's Florie?"

"Oh, she's staying with her cousins tonight. Today was the first time she's seen them since November, and my visit with Faolan was quick, so I felt bad dragging her away. Anyway, she'll have more fun with them than she would here."

Katherine looked a little confused. "I'm surprised Faolan and his family didn't come tonight. Not many people are missing this."

"Faolan was injured," I said, feeling guilty all over again. "Quite badly. He's not in any shape to do much of anything right now. He acts like it's nothing, but I honestly think he nearly died."

"I'm really sorry to hear that," Katherine said sympathetically.

"I think he's out of danger now, but unfortunately he wasn't able to suggest anything useful as far as our problem with Ailig."

"My problem with Ailig, Anna, not yours. You can't start taking on my problems now, too," she said.

"You sound just like Faolan."

"Good. Faolan sounds sensible," she quipped with a soft smile. I smiled back and shook my head. Katherine sighed. "But we can't stay out here long. Ailig will wonder where I've gone and he'll come looking."

I nodded. "I understand," I said. "I won't keep you long. I just have something I need to tell you."

She looked at me with an expectant smile. "What's that?"

I took a deep breath before I answered. "I've thought of a way to deal with Ailig," I said quickly, now lowering my voice to a whisper.

"What?" she said, a look of shock crossing her face. It was clearly not what she was expecting me to say.

"We're going to frame him," I said.

Her shocked expression disappeared, and she laughed.

"I mean it," I said, grabbing her hand and pulling her deeper into the alley.

Her face turned serious again. "Frame him for what?" she whispered.

"A theft; something stolen from Ualan," I said.

She stared back at me, still looking confused. "How?"

"The hard part is already done," I whispered. "I went to Ualan's house, and I found the bracelet Ailig was talking about; the silver one with the jewels that he didn't want to give to Ualan. I took it." Katherine brought her hands up to her face and her eyes widened with deep concern. "Don't worry," I added quickly. "No one saw me. There was a hairy moment with a blind woman, but I'll tell you more about that later. At any rate, I got the bracelet, and I've buried it under one of the roosting boxes at the back of your cottage."

Katherine was shaking her head now, looking sick. "Dear God, Anna, you risk too much. If you'd been seen, do you know what they would've done to you?"

"Don't worry. I promise no one saw me," I insisted again. "But listen, this is important. In order for Ailig to take the blame, we need to be clever about this. You need to give it three or four weeks; long enough for the bracelet to be noticed as missing and long enough for no one in Ualan's house to be able to identify when it actually disappeared. Then, during a night when Ailig is busy, you need to dig it up, put it on, and come to the tavern when you know Ualan will be there. Make sure he sees you in it. He will come and ask where you got it from and you need to tell him you found it in Ailig's things. The story needs to be that Ailig forbade you from wearing it, but that you couldn't resist, and then beg Ualan not to tell Ailig he saw you with it or you'll be punished. Make sure you sound convincing. You'll need to act frightened."

"I don't think that will be hard, Anna. If we carry out this plan, I wouldn't have to act frightened at all. I would be terrified. What if Ualan thinks I stole the bracelet?"

"He won't," I said. "If you stole it, why would you wear it in front of him? It would be too big of a leap for Ualan to think we planned this to get Ailig in trouble. And when would you get the opportunity to take it, anyway? You're always under Ailig's thumb. Ailig will deny stealing the bracelet, of course, and might blame you. But realistically, who is Ualan going to believe? Ailig never wanted to give up the bracelet in the first place, and there was a big argument when Ualan took it. Ailig has the motive, and he's the town drunk. Who knows what stupid things he might do when he's had a few too many?" I could almost see the wheels turning in her head. The look in her eyes was gradually changing from fearful to hopeful, and I could see she was coming around to the plan. I quickly went on while I knew I was gaining momentum. "So, Ualan will think Ailig stole it back, and Ailig will be punished. And because he stole from Ualan, the tacksman and son of the chief, that punishment will be severe. We're not talking about a public flogging here—"

"He'll be hung or banished," Katherine finished for me. She was now staring off into space again.

I took a deep, satisfied breath as she said it. "Yes. And the croft would be yours. We could live together, Katherine, be a family, all of us. You, me, Florie and the new baby." I waited for her to process the idea.

She came back from her daze and looked at me again, her expression once again concerned. "The risk you took in stealing that bracelet was high, Anna. That was so dangerous."

"Yes. That's why I did it before I talked to you about it," I said, giving her a crafty smile. "Well, that and it needed to be done tonight when I knew most of the township would be at the tavern. It was the best opportunity I could have hoped for, but I also knew if I put the idea to you before that was done, you wouldn't go along with it."

"You're absolutely right," she said. "It could have cost you your life. Did you stop and think what would have happened to Florie if you'd been caught?"

I sighed. "I did. But I wouldn't have gone through with it if I wasn't sure I'd be successful." I decided that perhaps it wouldn't be the best idea to share the story about the blind woman any time soon. "But now that it's done, the most dangerous part of the plan is out of the way, and the next part is easy by comparison," I said.

She looked down and chewed her bottom lip for a few moments.

"Please, Katherine. If we don't at least try, you'll be stuck with that man forever. And even if you say you can handle his constant abuse, I can't. I'll end up killing him myself. I swear I will."

She looked up at me again and the corners of her mouth turned up slightly. She shook her head slowly again, then took my face in her hands. "No one's ever done anything so brave or kind for me before, Anna." She leaned in and planted another light kiss on my slightly parted lips. "So if you can be that brave, then I will too," she said.

I pulled her into another tight hug. "Everything will work out," I said. "You'll see."

Now that we had a real plan to move forward with, it filled both of us with a new sense of hope and excitement.

"You need to tone it down a bit," I said to Katherine as we walked to the end of the alley. We decided not to walk back to the tavern together. Katherine would go first, then I would come after a few minutes. I had originally planned to go straight home, but now that my mood was elevated again, I felt hungry and decided I would go and get some of that roasted pork and celebrate a little myself. "If you keep smiling like that, Ailig will be suspicious," I added. "You need to continue acting sullen and demure. You know? Unhappy."

She laughed, "That's a lot trickier than it was ten minutes ago."

"Mmm. Well, do it anyway," I whispered, grinning myself. Then I stepped back and gestured for her to go. She scooted back around the corner and disappeared, and I leaned against the wall again, enjoying the new feeling of hope. It was only a matter of time now. We'd soon be rid of that bastard and everything would be good again.

I waited about thirty seconds before I walked out of the alley and crossed the dirt track to the back of the tavern. I was still smiling to myself when I suddenly became aware of Ailig's voice floating around the corner. He was shouting at someone about something and my heart dropped when I got close enough to hear the words.

"What the bloody hell do you think you're playing at, sneaking off like that!"

I crept around the corner and along the side wall, stopping at the end so I was still hidden from view. I could hear Katherine's voice, but since she wasn't shouting, her words were harder to decipher.

Ailig's obnoxious, gravelly voice rose up again. "I don't want to hear it! When I tell you to stay somewhere, you stay! When I call for you to come, you come! Immediately! I will not have my wife running about through town on her own, at this time of night, like some kind of harlot! Where did you sneak off to? Tell me!"

I leapt out from behind the wall and saw Ailig, who had hold of the front of Katherine's dress and had a fist pulled back, threatening to strike. Katherine was clutching at his wrist, struggling to free herself, and several patrons stood around holding their drinks, watching the commotion with amusement. It made me fume to see that no one was coming to her aid. "Let her go, Ailig!" I shouted. "It's not her fault. I asked her to come for a walk with me."

Ailig snapped his head in my direction and glowered at me through his blue, hate-filled eyes. He shoved Katherine back, releasing her, then balled up his fists and marched towards me. As he approached, he pointed a finger at me and snarled. "I thought I told you what would happen if I caught you near my wife again."

I held my ground and stared straight back at him, refusing to show any weakness. "It was just a walk, Ailig. I don't know why it should bother you so much."

"It bothers me that my wife forgets her place when she's around you," he spat. "Just because your husband is dead and you're suddenly used to doing as you please all the time, that doesn't mean the same goes for Katherine. She's my wife, and if I say she isn't to see you, then I expect to be obeyed!"

"What are you going to do, Ailig? Hit me too?" I said. I knew he wanted to. His chest rose and fell and he clenched his jaw as the finger which pointed at me hovered closer to my face. Then he folded his finger back into a first and held it there for a few seconds. He leaned into me, lowering his voice. "What I'm going to do is go and see Ualan right now. The fact that this township is still catering to your ridiculous ambition to keep running that croft on your own is a joke. And I highly doubt he'll continue to indulge you any further after I tell him you are constantly ignoring my wishes and harassing my wife." Then he straightened up again and wiped his arm across his brow.

I clenched my teeth together, wishing I could punch him, hurt him, make him just disappear.

He turned his back on me and started walking back to the tavern, calling out to Katherine. "Come on, Woman! Get your arse back inside."

As I saw Katherine's frightened face and watched her hurry along after him, something inside me snapped. "You're nothing but a pathetic coward!" I shouted.

He stopped in his tracks and turned around to face me again. His eyes were blazing, and if he could have got away with killing me there and then,

I knew he would have. "What did you say?" he growled.

"You heard what I said," I shouted again. The crowd around us had gone silent now, and more were filtering out of the tavern to watch. "I called you a pathetic coward, because that's what you are. A sadistic, pathetic coward who can only get hard by tyrannising people who are smaller and weaker than you, knocking seven bells out of your pregnant wife, and trying to dominate every tiny aspect of her life!"

He looked at me with murder in his gaze and then seemed to become aware of the audience who were silently watching. He looked around quickly, then breathing hard, he marched towards me. This time, he didn't stop. As soon as he was up close and before I had the time to prepare myself, he plunged his fist into my stomach, causing me to double up and sink to my knees. Stars flashed across my vision and for several seconds, I was unable to breathe. I retched onto the ground, holding myself up on my hands and knees, and inhaled a choked gasp as soon as the muscles in my chest slackened again. Tears streamed from my eyes and fluid from my nose dripped onto the dirt beneath. He kicked a shower of dry mud at my head, then spat on me.

"Not so mouthy now, are you?" he said, in a satisfied grunt. He crouched down next to me and grabbed my hair in his fist, then lifted my face to look at him. "You see?" he said quietly, so no one else could hear. "It's not just my wife I'm willing to discipline to keep things in order around here. She knows her place, and now perhaps you will too. But feel free to come and see me again if you feel yourself forgetting." He pulled back on my head harder, making me cry out in pain, then snarled into my ear. "But make no mistake. The next time I catch you near my wife, it will be her who pays the price, and what you're feeling now will be nothing in comparison to what I'll do to her. Do you understand?"

The pain radiating from my midsection was crippling and agonising. Sharp pains stabbed through my gut, making it difficult to focus on anything else, and I felt utterly helpless as he held me up by my hair. He pulled harder again. "I said, do you understand?"

"Yes," I wheezed, unable to see anything through my tears. He shoved my head back down into the dirt, then marched away, leaving me still coughing and gasping.

I was afraid to even move, and it took me several minutes before I was able to get to my feet. Two women who'd been close by, ran over to assist me as soon as Ailig had gone, but even as they carefully helped me up, I struggled to stand up straight. Pain continued to shoot through my insides and it hurt even to breathe. One of the women gingerly patted me on the back and I was vaguely aware of her asking me if I wanted to come in and sit down, but I shook my head and brushed them both away. After I wiped my eyes and face and looked up, I noticed most of the audience had ambled away, but Ualan stood by the tavern door, watching me with his arms crossed. I let out a shallow sigh, then went to shuffle down the track towards home.

"Anna!" Ualan called out behind me. "I need to speak with you."

I turned around slowly to face him again, and he walked over and stopped in front of me. I carefully straightened up, wincing with the pain, but my eyes and nose still streamed uncontrollably and I knew I must have looked a state.

He shook his head as he looked me up and down. "What is wrong with you, Anna?"

"Well, I was just punched by a man who is twice my weight," I croaked. I knew I sounded petulant, but I didn't care.

"You deliberately antagonised him, Anna. Why?"

"Because he's a drunk and a bully and someone around here needed to stand up to him."

Ualan sighed. "You know, most of your problems you bring upon yourself, Anna. If Robert were here, you wouldn't have said that."

"If Robert were here, I wouldn't have had to. Robert wouldn't have stood by like all the rest of you and just watched while Ailig abused his wife."

"Robert would have minded his own business, and he would have reminded you to do the same," Ualan snapped. "It doesn't seem to matter what I do to try and help you, it seems like you're set on sabotaging yourself."

"Help me?" I said, choking back a laugh. "What have you done to help me?"

"I've been patient and given you a fair chance to keep your croft."

"No, you wanted to be seen as giving me a fair chance. You haven't gone an inch out of your way to actually help me to do it. Robert's been gone eight months, and you've never once offered any kind of practical help. You sit over there in your ivory tower, with more riches and wealth than you could possibly spend, and have no care for the people below you who are suffering and struggling. Instead, you expect me to be grateful that you have been magnanimous enough not to instantly strip me and my seven-year-old daughter of the only home we have, while you sit back and watch us struggle to cope with an impossible situation. Yes, you really are a true example of what a good and fair leader should be, and forgive me for not giving you the unwavering gratitude you so clearly deserve!" I knew I was digging a deeper grave for myself, but at this point, I didn't care. I was so sick of the useless men around me who walked around with totally unjustified grand opinions of themselves.

Ualan kept his expression under control, but I could see the muscles in his jaw working. "If Ailig hadn't just hit you, Anna, I think I would right now. I am only holding back because I think you've had a hard enough evening as it is. The scene you created tonight deserves punishment, but considering your situation and because I am aware of the stress you are under, I am going to let that slide this time. I have, however, reconsidered my stance on your croft. I understand that the crops there are yours, but know that after harvest at the end of September, I am transferring your lease to Frang, whether you make the quota or not." He paused for a second, as if waiting for me to argue, but I remained quiet. He went on, "I do not believe you can survive on your own, Anna. Ever since Robert's death, you have become more and more wild and unreasonable. I think I have been very patient with you, but your inability to get on with your neighbours, sustain yourself and your child or behave with proper decorum at community events makes me see I am right in making this decision. You and your daughter will do better under the care of another man, preferably a family member, and I would recommend you ask Robert's brother if you can join them. As long as you behave respectfully, he has a duty to take you and your daughter in."

I took a deep breath and gave him a slight nod. The gravity of what he'd said had yet to sink in, but all I wanted at this moment was to go home. I wished I had Florie to cuddle, but then I was glad she wasn't present for what had just happened.

Ualan nodded and then walked back to the tavern, seemingly satisfied by his own handling of the situation. I swallowed hard, then turned away from the track and decided to take the shortest and most direct route across the countryside back to my croft. The pain in my gut stabbed with every step I took, but I tried to tell myself that the walk would be good for me.

As I painfully and slowly shuffled my way across the first of many pastures, and my heart rate slowed back down, I was able to reflect on what had just happened with more clarity. It was a mistake coming here tonight. I should have waited for a different opportunity to talk to Katherine about the plan. My triumph in successfully stealing the bracelet had clouded my judgement, and instead of playing things safe, I had further endangered us both. Why did I have to have such a big mouth and when was I going to learn when to keep it shut? Ualan was right; I was my own worst enemy, and I did bring most of my problems upon myself. The pain in my stomach, which seemed to have ebbed a little when I was talking to Ualan, was now coming back with a vengeance. I needed to get to the shelter soon, but each time I tried to quicken my pace, my vision was invaded by a dark halo. I felt a cold sweat break out across my forehead, accompanied by a strong surge of nausea, and I started to wonder if I'd make it home at all. As darkness swallowed my vision again, I couldn't stop from dropping to my hands and knees and vomiting up the mead I'd drank earlier in the night.

Chapter Twenty-Two

KATHERINE

I lay in bed listening to the noise of loud snoring beside me, a sound I detested with every fibre of my being. I hated that I had to lie here and put up with it, and I hated that it meant the son of a bitch was alive. For at this moment, more so than I ever had before, I wished he were dead.

Still drunk, Ailig was lying on the bed on his stomach, with his head turned to the side, his mouth hanging open and a trail of saliva running from the corner of his mouth to a large wet patch on the straw mattress. His breath was stale and his hair was greasy and plastered to his forehead. I eyed him for a few moments with a deep, burning hatred. He was still fully dressed, having collapsed into bed as soon as we arrived home two hours ago. That was the one good thing about when Ailig was blind drunk; I was almost guaranteed a night off from his unwanted attentions.

I had not been able to go to sleep, though. I had lain awake feeling sick with worry for Anna, who put herself in such a dangerous position in order to stand up for me. I wished so much that she hadn't done it. She should have just remained hidden. If she'd done that, everything would have been fine. Now she was injured, and I didn't even know how badly, or if she'd even made it home last night. She'd lost her croft, the thing she'd worked so hard to try and hold on to, and Ailig had made a point of gloating about it all night, boasting to everyone who would listen, about how he knew how to keep a female under control.

Everything Anna had said to him last night was true. Ailig was a coward, and he was pathetic, and she had certainly struck a nerve when she announced it in front of everyone. While I had felt a small sense of satisfaction when she stood up to him like that, it was also terrifying. I'd never dared to do that myself, and it had cost her very dearly to do it. As I thought back on it, a new wave of sickness rose through my core, and the sound of the heavy 'thunk,' and the way Anna had collapsed and turned pale, replayed in my mind. God, he had hit her so hard.

I hadn't dared to ask Ailig if I could go and check on Anna, and I knew even if I had, he would have revelled in telling me no and watching me suffer. I had made the decision not to mention it for the rest of the night, then go and check on her early in the morning when he was still asleep. Although it still didn't get completely dark at this time of the year, the twilight hue of the sky had brightened a little, which told me it was now around the hour of five. From experience, I knew Ailig would not be up for a long while yet, and nothing short of an avalanche would wake him up when he was like this. Now would be the best time to go and make sure she had made it home, and that she was alright.

I got up out of bed and I wasn't gentle about shoving his arm off me as I did so. He didn't even move as his elbow thudded back down on the empty spot where I'd been forced to lie. I looked down at him again, wishing I could do something to him while he was vulnerable. It was no less than he deserved, but I took solace in the thought that his days of making other people's lives miserable were now numbered. I couldn't wait for the moment when I could watch him be dragged in front of Ualan and then try to insist he was innocent. Perhaps he didn't steal the bracelet, but he certainly wasn't innocent, and he deserved everything that was headed his way. If I felt any doubt or guilt about Anna's plan, it had been thoroughly washed away last night when Ailig nearly killed her.

I had been hit by Ailig many times, but the force he put behind that punch had shocked even me. He'd held nothing back, and I knew it was his intention to seriously injure, if not kill her. He had whispered something to her when she was down on the ground, and though I didn't hear what he said, I could guess. Anna had embarrassed him, and I knew he would eventually kill her if that's what he thought it would take to restore his reputation.

I looked at him again and cleared my throat, a final test to see if he was still fully asleep. His snoring continued, so I walked to the cupboard and took out my medicine bag. Anna would definitely need something for the pain and I hoped to God that's all she would need. I quietly let myself out of the cottage, then raced across the pasture, past her house and continued along to the shelter. There was no noise coming from the building as I approached, but then it was early and I tried to tell myself that even if Anna wasn't hurt, she likely wouldn't be up at this hour, anyway. With my heart hammering and while praying that she was there and safe, I popped my head around the corner to look inside.

A hearth had been erected near the entrance of the space and the chain hung down from one of the rafters on which the cauldron was hung. At the back of the shelter there was a bed, and the shape of a body lay upon it. My heart skipped a beat as my immediate fear was that the body was too still and wasn't breathing. I crept inside the shelter, breathing hard as I approached the bed, and then crouched down.

Anna was lying there, curled up, breathing shallowly, her face crumpled in an expression of pain, even as she slept. She had dark circles under her eyes, and her skin was pale and clammy. I had no idea how she'd made it all the way home on her own, but I was relieved to see she was alive and breathing. Florie was not beside her, but then I remembered Anna had said she was spending the night with her cousins. Of all nights for Anna to get hurt, she had to pick the one when Florie wasn't there to help her.

It was impossible to tell how much damage had been done by Ailig's blow, but I didn't want to wake her. At this stage, rest was the best thing for her. I lay a hand carefully on her forehead and she gave a slight sigh. She didn't have a fever, but she was cold and clammy, so I put my medicine bag down, then pulled the blanket up to her neck. She would definitely need something for the pain, so I decided to light the fire and put together a remedy which I could leave for her to have when she woke up.

I ran over to the woodshed to get more peat and some kindling, and then searched around for the tinderbox. If I'd been thinking more clearly before I came over, I would have grabbed mine, but then I didn't have very far to look. There were several piles of things lined up along the back wall and I soon found the little box. Once I got the fire going well enough to sustain itself, I went back over to her and sat down and opened my bag. I took a bowl from the small stack of dishes she had, then quickly pulled out the herbs and powders I needed and set to work grinding them up together. I drew some water from the well and poured it into the cauldron, then added the mixture I'd made. The tea wouldn't taste nice but it would take the edge off and there would be enough to last her the full day.

I'd finished what I'd come to do, but I wanted to sit with Anna for a while longer. Ailig would still be asleep and I didn't feel like running home to listen to him snoring, and the chores could wait. If I finished them too early, he would just give me more work, and because he'd be nursing a sore head for the rest of the day, he probably wouldn't go to the village which meant I wouldn't be getting a break from his company.

I looked down at Anna and gently ran my fingers through her soft chestnut curls. Her freckles were barely visible. She was so pale, and I seriously worried about what damage Ailig had done. I bent over her face and lay a light kiss on her forehead, then tucked the blanket around her chin again. This caused her to stir and her eyes fluttered open slowly. The grimace on her face slowly softened as she looked at me and she managed a weak smile.

"I must be either dreaming or dead," she said. "My guess would be dreaming, because it still hurts."

I gave a gentle laugh and stroked her face with the back of my fingers. "No, you're awake," I said. "I came over to check how you are."

Her face suddenly contorted again, and she tried to sit up. "Ailig?"

I pushed her back down gently. "Stop, you'll hurt yourself. We can sit you up in a minute. I have some tea for you too which will help with the pain. Don't worry about Ailig. He drank himself into a complete stupor last night and we only got home a couple of hours ago. He'll be out for ages, and even once he's awake, he won't be venturing very far. I doubt he'll leave the cottage today."

"Did he hurt you?" Anna asked, grabbing my hand. "Because of what I said?"

I shook my head. "No. I think he spent all his rage on you yesterday."

Anna closed her eyes and let her head fall back again. "Thank God," she said. "I was worried I'd pushed him too far, and he'd take it out on you."

"Don't worry about me. It's you who we have to worry about," I said. "I honestly thought he might kill you." I squeezed her hand, then lifted it to my lips and kissed her.

"Well, he made a good effort, but it will take more than that," Anna croaked. "I'll admit, I do feel like hell, though."

"I'll get you some tea," I said. "It'll help." I fetched a cup and filled it from the cauldron, then brought it over to her and set it down on the ground next to the bed. "Let's see if we can get you sitting," I said, and I put my arm behind her head and lifted her into a sitting position slowly. She closed her eyes and grimaced, but was able to help shuffle herself back until she was leaning against the wall. I picked up the hot drink and put it in her hands. "It doesn't taste wonderful, but you need to keep drinking this all day," I said. "When is Florie getting back?"

She looked anxious again. "Oh crumbs. I was supposed to go and get her first thing this morning. I promised her."

"Well, I'm afraid you're not going anywhere," I said. "You said last night she was with your brother-in-law? I'm sure they'll bring her over here if you don't show up. I would go and get her for you, but I don't dare leave the croft for that long in case Ailig wakes up."

"Maybe I could try walking," Anna said, putting her arms down and trying to push herself up.

"Don't you dare," I said, grabbing her hand again. "You need to stay where you are and rest. At the very least, you will have some significant bruising, not just externally. Time is the only thing which will help you to recover and the drink I made will help you manage the pain, but you cannot try going on long walks. If there is any internal damage, then you shouldn't move, and since you're awake, I should check you to make sure."

Anna closed her eyes again and shook her head. "I can't be bedridden for days. There's too much that needs doing. I have to take care of Florie, the sheep, I can't just—"

"Florie is more than capable of taking over with most of the chores and she'll be happy to take care of you. I'll help where I can as well, so don't fret about all of that."

"No," she said suddenly. "You mustn't. Ailig won't let you, and I don't want you putting yourself at risk for me. It's too dangerous."

"Rubbish. Ailig can't watch me every hour of every day, and I'll be careful."

"No, you didn't hear what he said, Katherine. He told me he'd hurt you next time he saw me near you. I can survive a punch to the gut, but I don't know what I'd do if he hurt you or your baby, or worse. And he would, Katherine. He hates me. I don't know why, but I could see it in his eyes last night. He wanted to kill me. He's dangerous, and you can't do anything to jeopardise yourself or the plan."

"You mean like pick a fight with him in front of half the town?" I said, raising an eyebrow.

She became sullen and looked down, pouting.

"Anna, you really need to learn to accept help when it's offered. He doesn't have to see. When I go to milk the sheep, I'll milk yours too. It's no extra effort to make a double batch of cheese or butter. Ailig doesn't check the traps, so I can get you a little bit of meat without him knowing. He won't miss the odd potato, which are lovely by the way, so you have to try them. Anything I can get for you, I'll leave in a sack by the river where we buried Sim. At midday, send Florie down to collect it, then put the sack back before you turn in for the night. We can do that every day and I'll make sure he doesn't see. If he's watching, I'll take the sack at a later time."

Anna lifted her head and looked back up at me again. There were still dark rings around her eyes, but they glistened with gratitude. "What would I do without you, Katherine?" she said.

"Well, you wouldn't be suffering like this right now, that's for sure," I said, holding the cup out to her. "Now drink this, then you need to lie down again so I can check your stomach."

Anna obediently drank the liquid, then shuddered as she put the cup back on the ground. "Oh, that is disgusting," she said.

"Don't be such a baby," I said as I unfastened the lace on her bodice. I couldn't help thinking back to the first time I had done this and allowed myself a small smile at the memory of it. She must have been thinking the same because I could feel her eyes on me, and when I glanced up, they were focused and intense.

"Do you ever think about that night?" she whispered.

I looked back down at the tops of her breasts as I pulled the ribbon towards myself. "All the time," I said quietly. It was true. I had thought about it every day. I hooked my finger over the strips which crisscrossed across her chest and pulled them slack. "Hold your arms up," I told her. She took a shallow breath and winced as she raised both her arms above her head. Then I carefully pulled the bodice off. "I need to check your stomach before I loosen your stay," I said. She nodded, then I leaned forward and wrapped my arms behind her, searching for the ribbons which kept the back of her skirt tied. My face was right up against hers and I didn't hurry to find the bow, enjoying the sensation of being so close to her.

I felt her cheek brush against mine and she took a slow breath in, next to my ear. I struggled to keep my breathing steady when I felt her lips press slowly against my jaw, and I couldn't stop myself from lifting my chin and giving her full access to my neck. Her soft lips brushed against my throat, and my hands had all but forgotten their task as I pressed them gently against her lower back, then slid them up behind her shoulders. I closed my eyes as her kisses fell lightly along the side of my neck and her hand found its way to the other side of my face. Tingles radiated through my body from every point her lips touched, and I couldn't stop myself from letting out a soft sigh, then bending my head to kiss her bare shoulder.

Her skin was smooth and cool and I could taste a slightly salty flavour as I opened my mouth wider and sucked her flesh gently. She let out a soft moan herself, and I felt her teeth graze me under my ear.

"We can't do this right now," I whispered, fumbling to find the ribbon again.

"Why not?" she said. "It's helping. It's making me forget about the pain."

I smiled as my fingers found the ribbon and pulled it loose, then I leaned back and looked at her. "That would be my miraculous medicine," I said, then reached down to undo the front ribbon of her skirt.

"Not a chance," she said, returning the smile. "It wouldn't take effect that quickly. So I think you should keep up with this until it does."

"I'd love to, but I need you to lie back now," I said.

She sighed but shuffled herself forward until she was away from the wall and had room to lie flat again. I put my hand behind her head to take her weight as she lowered herself down. The movement was clearly painful, and she closed her eyes and took a few sharp breaths inwards. Once she was flat on her back again, I pulled her skirt off, over her legs, and she now lay in her chemise and her stay.

"I need to feel your tummy now," I said. "I have to press a little so I can tell if there is any distention. But if it gets too painful, you need to tell me, understand?"

She nodded, and I could see a slight sheen of sweat had broken out over her forehead. I left her chemise in place to preserve her modesty and lay my hands gently on her belly. "Ready?" I asked. She nodded again.

Nervously, I pressed my fingers slowly against her tummy through the thin fabric, moving them around slowly. She winced once or twice but didn't complain, and as my hands made their passes, I started to breathe a little easier. Even as I moved my fingers higher, her abdomen felt soft, the way it should. This at least meant there were no internal ruptures, but it didn't rule out damage to some of her organs. In some cases, trauma to the lower abdominal organs took several days to become obvious, and only time would tell how serious the injury was. What I had felt so far was hopeful, however, and I held onto that.

When I'd finished, I removed my hands and sat back.

"Well, will I live?" Anna asked, smiling.

"There's no hardness in your tummy, so that's a very good sign," I said. "It's up to you if you want to keep your stay on or take it off, but I would recommend you stay where you are and get more sleep. It's still very early and you can probably get a few hours in before Florie comes back. Sleep is the best possible thing for you right now."

She sighed, "I still feel guilty about not going to get her like I promised."

"Believe me, when she sees you, she'll understand," I said, crawling closer and sitting down next to her. "To be honest, I'm surprised you even made it home from the tavern. Before I got here, I was terrified you may not have." She held her hand out to me and I took it, rubbing the back of her hand with my thumb.

"I cut across the pastures, but it still took me ages. I think I might have lost consciousness at one point, but I made it in the end." She smiled at me as she said it, but I struggled to smile back. Ailig could have killed her, and she was genuinely lucky she was still alive and had no obvious internal bleeding. I continued to stroke the back of her hand, absently.

"Can you stay for a little while?" she asked.

"If you want me to, I will."

"I wish you could stay forever," she said wistfully. "But I'll settle for a few minutes." She pulled on my hand. "Lie here with me."

I moved myself onto the bed next to her, then lay down beside her, placing my arm over her chest and pulling her towards me. She turned on her side to face me, then reached up to stroke the side of my face. "I miss you so much when you're gone, you know."

I took her hand and then kissed her fingers. "I miss you too, and Florie. It's not the same without you both. But you have to promise me you won't do anything else stupid. The plan you have is good and I believe it will work, but you need to take care of yourself and stay out of trouble until we can follow it through. There's no point in getting rid of Ailig, if you don't survive to see it happen."

"I'm sorry," she said. "I know you're right. I just got so angry at how he was treating you. You deserve so much more, you deserve to be loved."

I smiled and kissed her fingers again. "I don't think I'm wanting for love."

"I know I haven't known you very long, Katherine," she said. "But I want you to know I've never loved anyone like I love you. I can't explain it, but I feel like part of me wasn't alive until we met."

My body flooded with warmth as I listened to her. Ailig was the worst of men and certainly not a model by which to judge others of his sex, but even with that, after my first night with him I had known that even if he'd died and I met another man who was loving and tender, even one like Robert, I would never have been satisfied. Perhaps I could have found some measure of contentment, but I knew I could never love or want a man the way I loved and wanted Anna. I knew there was no man on earth who could make me feel the way Anna had made me feel that night in the barn, nor make me feel as I did now, just looking at her.

Everything about her awakened my senses. The feel of her skin, her lips, the shape of her body, the sound of her voice, the parts of her I hadn't yet seen or touched but longed for the day I would. I struggled to explain the feeling, even to myself, but I knew what I felt for Anna was something I was expected by everyone else to feel for my husband, and whether it was wrong or right, those feelings couldn't be changed.

I didn't know if I had found in Anna something I would never find in another woman, but it didn't matter because she was all I would ever want. I had always tried to mask those feelings, never wanting to pressure her into loving me back in that way, but to hear her tell me she had never felt the same way about anyone else was like having my soul finally set free. If it was wrong, then we would be wrong together in our own secret world and I'd be happy there with her. I couldn't put my thoughts into words at that moment, but one day, I would find the right ones to let her know how much she really meant to me. I leaned in closer, put my hand on the side of her cheek, and pressed my lips into hers. I felt them part slightly and the tip of her tongue danced gently over the inside of my lips for a second. I wanted more of her there and then, but resisted the urge and just kissed her gently, acutely aware of her fragile state. I crept my own tongue forward a little, wanting to explore more of her mouth, and as her tongue met mine, I felt the metallic tingles radiate through me. We kissed deeply, probing each other further and breathing harder. My fingers trailed back through her hair and pulled her head forward, harder into me. I was lost in time as we kissed each other, and I gave a stifled a moan as she moved her lips down to my throat and sucked fervently.

I felt paralysed until she released me, then I whispered, "How do you do that to me?"

"I'm sorry, I think I got a bit carried away," she said with a sheepish smile. She brushed her fingers against my throat, then rubbed the damp patch of skin where she had latched on. "I hope that mark goes away."

I took her hand. "Don't worry. Ailig never notices anything. But I do have to be getting back soon and you really need to sleep."

"I know, I'm sorry. I just can't seem to get enough of you," she sighed. Then she wrapped her arm around my waist again and closed her eyes.

I held her tightly and kissed her forehead, then whispered, "I hope you never feel like you've had enough of me."

I lay there for a while watching her face, which was still pale, but was far softer than when I'd first arrived. At least she didn't seem to be in as much pain, and if she could sleep easier now, then I'd helped in some way. I didn't dare close my eyes myself, as much as I wanted to, and as soon as Anna's breathing changed, signalling she'd fallen asleep, I made myself get up. I was exhausted, but I couldn't risk falling asleep with her in my arms. I carefully moved her arm back to her side, covered her fully with the blanket and added more peat to the fire. If she was lucky, Florie would be back before it burned down completely and it would make breakfast easier to prepare. I walked quietly out of the shelter and then back to my own cottage where, before I even got to the door, I could hear Ailig still snoring. I wanted nothing more than to go to sleep, but the thought of climbing back into bed next to him was deplorable. Instead, I went into the barn and threw down some hay next to the spot where I'd spent the evening with Anna. The filly gave me a few nervous nickers as I lay myself down, and even the hard ground was not enough to keep me awake any longer. I closed my eyes and drifted off into a deep sleep.

Chapter Twenty-Three

ANNA

It felt like it was late morning by the time a small hand shook me awake.

"Mam. Mammy? Are you alright?" came the soft childish voice of my daughter. I opened my eyes slowly and looked up at Florie's worried face, and standing behind her was an equally worried looking Alis. The dull pain in my gut immediately turned into a sharp jab as I sat myself up and winced. The medicine I'd taken earlier must have worn off by now, and I was glad Katherine had left a day's supply of it in the cauldron. I had vague, blurry memories of earlier in the morning when Katherine had shown up. She had made me a remedy for the pain, and I recalled falling asleep again with her next to me.

"What happened, Anna?" Alis said, crouching down behind Florie. "We expected you hours ago. Faolan is worried sick, and you look dreadful."

"I'm sorry," I said, forcing a sheepish smile. "I didn't realise how late it was." I turned to Florie and patted her shoulder. "I'm so sorry, sweetheart. I know I said I would come for you early."

"We were worried about you," Florie said, wrapping her arms around me. I fought the urge to wince in pain and looked at Alis over Florie's shoulder. She didn't look convinced by my story and mouthed the words 'what happened?' again. I closed my eyes and shook my head subtly, not wanting to discuss it in front of Florie.

"Florie, why don't you go and grab us some eggs and I'll stay for a while and make us all some breakfast. I think your mammy is feeling a bit poorly."

Florie pulled away from the hug and looked at me, full of concern. "Is that right? Are you poorly, Mammy?"

I nodded. "Yes. I have a poorly tummy, darling, but it's getting better. I'll be fine. I just need to rest for a while."

She nodded, then got up and scampered off.

Seizing the moment, Alis quickly came forward and sat in front of me. "What happened?" she said. "I'm not joking. You look horrendous."

"I had a bit of a run in with Ailig," I said, hoarsely. Talking even hurt. "He punched me in the stomach. Can you pass me a cup of that liquid in the cauldron, please?"

Alis's mouth dropped open. "He did what?"

"It's my own fault, I antagonised him. I was just so sick of watching him treat Katherine so badly."

"But he can't do that!" she said, picking up my cup and going over to the cauldron. "Did you tell Ualan?" She dipped the cup into the bottom of the cauldron and brought it back up, then sniffed it and wrinkled her nose distastefully.

I gave a weak laugh. "Ualan saw it happen. He more or less told me I deserved it and then told me he was going to hand my lease over to Frang at the end of September."

I didn't think Alis's jaw could drop any lower, but somehow she managed it. "What!? What in God's name did you say? I can't believe Ualan would do that!" She walked back over and handed me the cup.

I shrugged. "You know how Ualan is. He thinks he's so level-headed and fair, but he completely lacks a backbone. I had a go at him too, which is what put the final nail in my coffin, I think. But it's done, Alis. It doesn't matter anymore." I held my breath and gulped down the liquid, which was still quite warm. No matter how bad it tasted, it was preferable to the pain in my abdomen.

Alis shook her head slowly. "Anna, I'm so sorry. I'll talk to Faolan when I get back. Maybe he can go and see Ualan when he's better, after Ualan has calmed down. I wouldn't take it as the final word just yet. You know how men are. They always want to make an example of us in public, but behind the scenes there are always ways to remedy the situation."

"Don't worry about it," I said, wearily. I hiccuped and shuddered, willing myself not to vomit up what I had just drank. "I don't think I can keep going on pandering to people like Ualan and Ailig anymore, anyway."

"Well, think about it. Either way, I know Faolan will go and speak with Ualan on your behalf. All is not lost yet, so don't lose hope. A lot can happen between now and October."

I sincerely hope so, I thought. But to Alis, I just nodded.

"Who lit the fire and made the medicine?" Ailis asked, nodding towards the dying embers.

"Katherine, Ailig's wife," I said.

"The one you were defending? The reason why Ailig punched you?"

I nodded.

"Well, I'm glad to see she came over to help you after that," Ailis sighed.

"At great risk to herself," I said. "Ailig would kill her if he knew she helped me. I'm quite sure he meant to kill me."

"Ailig is a drunken bully. I don't envy that poor woman being married to him, but Anna, it really isn't your concern and you should stay out of other people's marital affairs. For your own sake."

I frowned up at her. "So I've been told," I muttered.

The light patter of feet announced Florie's return, and she came hurrying in and laid half a dozen eggs on the floor in front of me then put down the block of peat she'd been carrying under her arm.

"Thank you, darling," I said, shuffling myself up against the wall. I leaned back carefully and let my eyes close while Florie and Alis got started on resurrecting the fire and making breakfast.

I wasn't able to eat very much, and after the meal was over Alis said, "I think you should both come back to our house with me. I brought the horse and we can take it slow, Anna."

I shook my head. "I appreciate the offer very much, Alis. Thank you, but I'll be fine. Besides, you already have one invalid to look after. I'll rest up today, I'll walk down to the river, and Florie can have a swim and I'll just take it easy."

She tilted her head at me with an exasperated look. "You're worse than Faolan," she said. Then added, "Fine, but I'll be back in the morning to check on you and if you're not improved, then I'm taking you back with me. You can't live like this when you're not well." She gestured to the space around us as she spoke.

"Hey, don't knock it," I said, smiling. "It's comfier and cosier than you think."

Alis rolled her eyes, then gave Florie a hug, and they exchanged their goodbyes. "Take care of your mammy, alright?" Alis said.

"I will," Florie replied, then waved to Alis as she left.

Chapter Twenty-Four

KATHERINE

Over the next several days, I kept a watchful eye towards Anna's croft. On the first day, I saw very little of her or Florie, though I had seen another woman riding away during the late morning, and her horse was there again the following day. I assumed it was her brother-in-law's wife, and it gave me some comfort to know Anna had someone checking in on her, though I would rather have been the person to do that.

Every day, I dropped off a sack with a few food items in, and every day Florie dutifully collected it and then returned the sack to the same spot in the evening. It was never returned empty, though. The first day, I pricked my finger on the thorny little flower which had been dropped into the bottom, and by the end of the week I had a collection of pretty little thistles which I kept tied up with a piece of string in the barn.

Ailig went back to being his usual self, spending a disproportionate amount of his time at the tavern in the village. He'd already traded in a significant portion of the loot he'd brought back from the raids. A lot had gone on whiskey and gin, but true to his word, he had acquired the building materials for the new stable and had even spent a couple of afternoons helping to erect it. I figured this was mostly because he'd taken an uncanny shine to the new horse, which he named Belle, and the project to give her satisfactory shelter was one he took a personal interest in. I wished he would put the same enthusiasm into the other chores which needed doing around the croft, but the help with the new stable was better than nothing.

After I finished digging the foundation, it took us a few days to build the three sides of the dry stone wall. Then he enlisted help to fit the beams and rafters of the roof. A few days later, the thatching was completed by the local thatcher and his sons. Within a week we had a basic structure in which we could fit both horses, but because Ailbeart was behaving quite rambunctiously around Belle, Ailig decided to keep him in the barn separately, for the time being.

When Ailig had first brought the filly home, we had let both horses out to pasture together. But it proved a significant chore to get them back into the stable, due to Ailbeart's preoccupation with chasing and following Belle everywhere. So we now only let one animal out at a time. Ailig had threatened to geld Ailbeart, but I knew he wouldn't. If a foal was produced, it would be a valuable asset.

It took well over a week, and it was the beginning of August before I began to see Anna out and about on her croft more regularly. There had been several nights of rain and I wondered how the two of them were coping with that. In all likelihood, the shelter would stay dry, but there wasn't as much protection from the wind as there could be. As far as I could tell, though, she seemed to be recovering well.

During one particular early evening, I was out in the turnip field pulling up a few good sized vegetables for the stew, and I saw Anna walk to her side of the field to do the same. I stood and watched her, not daring to wave or say anything, but instead just enjoyed the sight of her moving about and looking healthy again. She squatted down and pulled up a few turnips and put them in a small basket she was carrying, then stood up and looked at me.

Our eyes met for the first time in several days, and she smiled at me. She looked so much better. The dark discolouration around her eyes the last time I'd seen her was gone, and though she looked considerably thinner than she did before she sustained the injury, her face was a healthy colour and she moved with an air of renewed vitality. I smiled back, feeling a warmth creep through me and for a few minutes we both just stood there staring back at one another. We were too far away to speak, but that didn't hinder our communication. It wouldn't be long before the plan would go into action and that thought breathed new life into us both.

We didn't break eye contact until I noticed Anna glance over my shoulder at something, then hurriedly back away towards her shelter. She gave me a hesitant smile and waved goodbye, and I returned a subtle wave back, then turned around to see what had caught her attention. I didn't think it would be Ailig, who I'd last seen in the cottage, drinking, but when I looked, I was surprised to see Frang riding up to our house on his horse.

I groaned. I'd completely forgotten Ailig had mentioned yesterday that Frang would be joining us for supper tonight. Both men liked to gamble, and they had arranged to play Pharo tonight, which meant I would probably be kept up until the early hours of the morning refilling their drinks and having to listen to their constant bragging.

I sighed and picked up the basket of turnips, adding a few extra, now that I remembered we were having company. I was careful as I rose, since I'd been slightly more unsteady on my feet recently with my bump having grown a fair bit bigger. I was definitely more aware of it when I had to bend down these last few days, and sleeping on my stomach was becoming uncomfortable. I headed back to the cottage, just in time to run into Frang, who had just finished hitching up his horse. He gave me an unpleasant smile and ran his tongue over his front teeth as he eyed my face.

I'd assumed the bruising had disappeared by now, but there must have been some remaining traces of it, because he said, "I'm glad to see Ailig has wasted no time putting you back in your place since he's been back."

I glared back at him, but kept my mouth shut as he laughed and walked past me into the house.

As I followed in behind him, Ailig got up from his chair in front of the hearth, which he hadn't bothered to light, and the two men gripped each other's arms and shared a boisterous greeting.

Ignoring them, I went to the table and began chopping up the kale and potatoes which I'd collected earlier. I dumped the turnips into the bucket of water I had left out to clean the dirt off them, then walked back to the hearth and dumped the other chopped vegetables in the cauldron.

"Woman," Ailig summoned me. "Where are your manners? Our guest does not yet have a drink."

I went back to the table and picked up the jug of mead and then an empty mug from the shelf. I filled the mug to the brim and carried it over to Frang, who had now sat himself in front of the hearth, next to Ailig.

Frang gave me a smug grin as he took it from me, but Ailig said, "And what about your husband? Do you not see my horn is half empty? Hurry up, Woman!"

I hurried back to the table, picked up the jug and emptied the rest of the contents into the horn he held out to me. Then the two men settled down and continued their conversation.

I finished chopping the turnips and put them in the cauldron, then went back outside and brought in another pail of water from the well. After filling the cauldron and then refilling the jug with mead from the barrel outside, I set to work on lighting the fire. The two men had not yet begun their card game, and instead, Ailig was telling Frang all about his heroic feats during the raids. I wondered to myself how many times I'd have to listen to the same horrific stories, and as I managed to bring some small flames to life, Ailig had started on the tale of how he came to possess the horn. I rolled my eyes, as this latest version now incorporated some entirely new details, which were even more dramatic and improbable than the first time I'd heard it. Rather than having to fight off a single man for the horn, it was now three. And in addition to the small scar on his torso which he had sustained during the fight, he now showed Frang the back of his arm.

"...and as he lay there dying on the ground, in a pool of his own blood, he still clung onto the horn. Then, when ah ripped it from his fingers, the bastard pulled out a blade he had hidden under his kilt and slashed me right here." He ran his finger up the long scar which travelled from his elbow, along the underside of his arm, almost to his armpit.

Frang leaned forward and admired the scar with adequate awe, and it was on the tip of my tongue to ask how Ailig had managed to get cut in exactly the same place by the man he'd taken the horse from.

Considering how many times his stories changed, I decided he probably took that horn from some old man and the scars he was showing off were most likely a result of falling off his horse when he was drunk. I blew into the flames to get the fire going stronger, then brushed my hands off and stood up. There were plenty of other jobs to be getting on with around the croft, but having had experience with Ailig, I knew if I tried to go off and do them, he would stop me. He would demand that I stay in the cottage and make myself available for topping up their drinks and serving them the food when it was ready. I had my suspicions that Ailig also wanted me there so I'd be forced to listen to all of his idiotic stories, but by now I was getting practised at tuning them out. I poured myself a small mug of mead and sat down at the table with my knitting, only catching small snippets of their conversation between my own daydreams.

"Ay, it's a fine horn, worth a fair bit of coin, I'd say," said Frang. Ailig had passed the empty horn over to him and he was turning it over in his hands, admiring it.

"That it is," Ailig responded, letting out a loud belch. "You don't get quality craftsmanship like that in this township."

"No, sadly not," said Frang, taking another swig of his mead. "That's why I used to love raids, back when I was young and fit enough to go on 'em." He handed the horn back to Ailig and lent back in his chair and sighed, as if reminiscing over fond memories of happier times. "I once came back with a dagger you've not seen the likes of before, and I've never seen the likes of since."

"Is that so?" said Ailig, leaning forward. I put my knitting down on the table and brought the jug of mead over to refill the horn and Frang's mug. The men held out their drinking vessels, but other than that, didn't acknowledge my presence and continued with their conversation.

"Ay, it was a beauty. Worth a small fortune as well. I took it from a bastard in the McLeord clan during a night raid. Snuck into his house in the darkness, killed him before he even got his naked arse untangled from his blankets, and found the dagger hidden beneath a trapdoor under his bed. I made his wife tell me about it. Told her I'd kill her unless I left the house with something worth my while."

Ailig laughed at this. "Stupid bitch."

"Ay, well, she told me after some persuasion," Frang grinned as he took another swig of his drink. "And it's a good job she did, or I never would have found it, or even known it was there. It was a clever hiding place."

"And did you let her go after?" Ailig asked.

Frang snorted, "What do you think?" The two of them laughed again, then he went on. "Anyway, I got the dagger, kept it secret because, you know, had Ealar seen it he would have taken it for himself."

I wasn't sure who Ealar was, but I guessed he was probably the tacksman at the time.

Ailig's grin was quickly replaced by a sneer. "Bastard!" he said. "Ualan did that to me. I won a beautiful bracelet, and he claimed it as tribute. As if he doesn't already have enough."

"Ay, well, next time don't go showing it off. The tacksman will always take the best of your booty. Better to keep it secret, then hock it to one of those travelling merchants who passes through every so often. That's what I did."

I sat back down at the table, listening to all of this, surprised by what I was hearing. I wondered what Ualan would do if he knew this sort of thing was going on behind his back. As if he knew what I was thinking, Ailig turned to look at me.

"You better not breathe a word of this to anyone, Woman. I can promise you if you do, you won't live to regret it."

"Oh, you don't have to worry about Katherine," Frang said, looking directly at me. "She's a good girl, aren't you, lass? She's clever enough to know when to keep her mouth shut." His lips curled up into another nasty smile, the same expression he'd worn as he watched Anna's cottage burn down. I refused to give him the satisfaction of a reaction and picked up my knitting while the two men turned back to each other to continue their conversation.

"Sometimes I wish I'd held onto that dagger. If I'd known that was going to be my last raid, then I would've done," Frang said, his voice suddenly sounding angry.

"Because of your leg?" Ailig said.

"Ay, because of my leg." His voice had a hard edge now, the topic being one he was clearly still very sensitive about. "That bitch who lives on the croft next to yours, her father-in-law was responsible for that."

"I didn't know that," Ailig said.

"Ay, there's not many people around who remember it anymore. About thirty years ago, there was a disagreement over that croft. It should have been mine, but Robert's father, Tiobaid, wanted it. We couldn't come to an agreement, so it was decided we would settle it in a duel. It was to be a fight with no weapons, bare hands only, but no other rules. That was something Tiobaid insisted on. We were both young at the time, and I was the better fighter, but Tiobaid was bigger. I went into the fight strong, and I took the bastard down several times, but he wouldn't stay down and he wouldn't give up, so we kept at it. In the end, I fought him to the ground, and I managed to get him into a chokehold. But the bastard picked up a rock, which was lying on the ground next to me, then slammed it down on my kneecap. He hit me with the rock again and again, and I couldn't stand up after that, so Tiobaid was declared the winner and he got the croft. It took me weeks to get back on my feet and I was never able to walk right again." Frang leaned forwards and rubbed the knee of his bad leg, lifting his kilt back to show Ailig. I craned my neck slightly, trying to get a glimpse of the damage, and even from where I was seated, I could see a significant amount of scaring. His knee looked misshapen and, seeing it now, it was a wonder that Frang could walk at all.

"That's a bugger," Ailig said, shaking his head.

"The bastard won that croft by cheating and I've been waiting to get it back ever since." Frang dropped his kilt down again and leaned back in his chair, taking another drink. "But in a few months, I'll have it," he said, smacking his lips and smiling again. "And I probably have you to thank for that," he said, raising his mug towards Ailig.

Ailig clanked his horn against Frang's mug, slopping mead onto the floor. "Ay. Though I should have hit her a bit harder. If I had, the bitch might be dead and you would have the place already."

"Ay, it was unfortunate she lived through that, but what's a couple more months after waiting thirty years?"

"I suppose," Ailig grumbled. "I'll be glad to see the back of her. She's nothing but a meddling busybody, and I'm glad she's getting what's coming to her. Always nosing about round here, not minding her own business. I don't know why Ualan didn't just kick her out straight away. It was ridiculous to even give her a chance to keep the croft. She's a woman on her own with a brat to look after, left to run wild with no man to keep her in check. Everyone knows she'd never be able to cope on her own."

I had to bite down on the inside of my cheek, and I gripped my knitting needles harder as I listened to them both.

"Well, Ualan always wants to be the good guy, doesn't he?" Frang said.

Ailig scoffed. "He's weak. Things would be different if I were in charge, let me tell you. Even in battle, he was useless. Hardly won any treasures for himself, you know. Kept his pretty little hands clean and told us not to kill the women or children. He rarely put himself in harm's way but still claims the best of everyone's takings after we get the victory."

"Well, that's the privilege of being in the cadet branch, isn't it? His father being the clan chief? They're all like that."

Ailig snorted and nodded, staring into the fire with a deep frown. "He's a greedy bastard. It will be months, if not years, before we go on another raid, and I'll probably never get another bracelet like the one he took from me." Then he looked at Frang again. "It nearly ended in a fight, you know. He threatened me. Told me if I didn't hand it over I'd have to give him the same value in produce, in addition to my quota." He sniffed and then spat into the fire. "Though I shouldn't be complaining to you about it, I suppose, considering you can't even go on the raids anymore."

Frang sighed and nodded. "That's true. But then, there are other ways to get your hands on treasures, without going on raids." A corner of his lip raised in a sneaky smirk and my ears pricked. "I could tell you some stories," he added.

Alig tucked his horn between his knees, then folded his arms and leaned forward, intrigued. I stared down at my knitting, listening hard but being careful not to draw attention to myself. "Go on then," Ailig said, an inquisitive expression on his face.

Frang looked at Ailig, then rubbed his jaw, hesitating. "Probably not wise," he said, finally. "Let's get on with the game here and perhaps my fortunes will improve tonight."

Ailig picked up his horn again, looking a bit disappointed, but took another swig and said, "Alright, I've been looking forward to taking your coin."

The two of them dealt out the cards and had me top up their drinks again. I couldn't help thinking about what Frang had said about Robert's father. No wonder he'd hated Robert and held a grudge against the entire family. Though I was sure even if Tiobaid hadn't crippled Frang's leg, Frang would still dislike Anna just as much. He was that sort of man. He and Ailig were as bad as each other and it was sickening listening to the two of them talk about their heinous deeds with such pride. Though from what Frang had said, I felt I didn't know the half of it and I would have loved to learn more. Information like that could be incredibly useful, and he'd been so close to letting it spill. It was clear he was very tempted to brag about it and perhaps he might open up more as the night wore on and he became more drunk. However, they were gambling, and if things didn't go well for him, he may develop a temper and that wouldn't help. I sat and mused about this for a bit until I decided if I wanted to get anything useful out of these men, I was going to have to be more proactive.

Neither man was paying attention to me and probably wouldn't until it was time for their drinks to be refilled, so I casually walked over to the cupboard and opened it. I worked quickly, not wanting to be rummaging around for too long, and pulled out my medicine bag, then took it back to the table and sat down with my back strategically facing them both.

They were staring down at the cards they held in their hands, so I felt fairly confident as I started pulling out various ingredients. I discreetly tipped a small heap of powder into the jug of mead, then swirled it around with a small wooden spoon until it disappeared. I was in a hurry and hadn't taken as much care over the quantities as I usually would have, and for the purposes of tonight, erred on the generous side. Hopefully, I hadn't overdone it. I poured a small amount of the liquid from the jug into my own empty mug and tasted it. I couldn't detect the powder at all, but I knew if I added the laudanum, it would give the mead a bitter edge. They may already be drunk enough not to notice it, but it would be a risk.

To heck with it, I thought, and tipped in a generous helping from the little bottle.

I mixed that in too, then tested the taste again. There was definitely a bitterness to it now, so I casually got up and went to the shelf and took down the pot in which the honey was kept. With my back still to the men, I used a spoon to quickly scrape the contents of the small pot into the jug, then mixed it up again. The honey wasn't dissolving as quickly as I hoped, but I knew it would, eventually. I prayed it would be another ten minutes before they both demanded another round, as that would give the drink time to mellow out a bit.

I tasted another sample quickly and was pleasantly surprised. The mead was slightly sweeter than usual, but not overly so, and the bitterness was a little harder to detect. There was a distinct aftertaste, but hopefully neither of them would notice, or care enough at this stage to say anything. Pleased with myself, I quietly packed up my medicine bag and nonchalantly walked back to the cupboard and put it away. If the two of them finished the jug, they would be loose-lipped and carefree enough to be bragging about their innermost secrets and desires for the rest of the night. Neither of the men took any notice as I returned to the table and sat down, patiently waiting to be summoned again.

Within five minutes, the order came, and I got up and walked over with the jug. Ailig didn't even look at me as he thrust his arm out, holding his precious horn. I poured the mead I had drugged inside it, then walked around to Frang, who treated me in much the same fashion. As I poured Frang's drink, I held my breath while Ailig lifted his horn to his mouth and took several deep gulps. As I finished topping up Frang, Ailig lowered the horn, and I watched his reaction carefully from the corner of my eye as I walked back to the table. Ailig frowned a little and licked his lips, looking down into the golden liquid in his horn. I sat down nervously, picking my knitting back up but still watching the two men and preparing myself to answer any complaints about the taste.

Fang then took a drink but didn't appear to notice the difference, and as Ailig placed the horn back between his knees and fanned out the cards in his hands, I allowed myself a sigh of relief. It seemed like neither of them were going to mention anything, so now it would just be a matter of time for the drugs to take effect. They were both getting a very strong dose of a similar medication I had made for Anna and myself when we'd got the bee stings. Not only would they both suffer from debilitating headaches tomorrow due to the amount of alcohol they were consuming, but they would have little memory of anything which was said or done tonight, which would be ideal if I got them to talk about anything sensitive.

With each additional sip they took, I smiled inwardly, especially when their card game started going to hell too.

"Stop looking, you bastard," Ailig slurred as he dropped two or three cards on the floor and fumbled to pick them up. Frang was leaning over in his chair, trying to see what the cards were, and nearly fell off it in the process. I took the opportunity to walk over and help pick up the cards for Ailig and top up their drinks while I was at it.

"Who's winning?" I asked sweetly.

"I am," Frang slurred, giving me a slack grin.

"Only because you keep cheating," Ailig sniffed. He was swaying a little on his chair now and squinting down at his cards, moving them back and forth as he tried to focus on what they were.

"Well, you're both such good players. I'm sure it will work out quite even in the end," I said, patting them both on their shoulders.

"How would you know, Woman?" Ailig grumbled, "You don't even know how to play."

That wasn't true. I was actually very good at Pharo, my grandmother having taught me when I was a child, but Ailig had never considered asking me to join in with a game, and even if he had, it wouldn't have been worth my life to beat him at it. "That's true, my darling," I said. "Please forgive my ignorance."

He grunted and shrugged my hand off his shoulder.

"That's the problem with women, these days," Frang said. "They all think they're so clever and capable. But women need men to keep them in line," he said. Then he pointed at me. "Your neighbour is living proof of that."

I couldn't refrain from glowering back at him. "Well, perhaps if she hadn't been hit with so much bad luck," I said, "then she wouldn't be struggling so much." I looked directly at him as I spoke. "I mean, there was that fire, and her sheep drowning—"

Frang gave me a nasty smirk and tutted, cutting me off. "Yes, very unfortunate accidents, but then if she had been more careful, I'm sure they could have been avoided. It's no coincidence that all these issues didn't arise until after Robert died. Just goes to show she can't manage on her own."

Ailig interjected, now. "You're absolutely right, Frang. You see how she makes excuses for that woman? She's been nothing but a bad influence on my wife from the first day they met. I remember it because on that day I sent her down to the brewery to collect an order of whiskey. It took her nearly three hours to come back because she told me she had to stop and save that stupid wench and her little brat from drowning in the river. Then I suppose they sat around and had a good chat about it while I waited for her like an idiot. I had to teach her a strong lesson that day, didn't I, Woman?" He sneered at me and I remembered the blow to the face I'd received for that. He'd split my lip on that occasion and punched me in the ribs. I'd been suspicious that I was pregnant at the time and had spent the next several days worrying I would lose another baby.

"Yes, I remember you telling me about that incident. That blasted woman is like a midge you can't squash," Frang said. Then he turned to me again. "You should have let her drown that day. It would have saved us all a lot of bother."

I held my tongue and though I was boiling with rage inwardly, I managed a sardonic smile and said, "Well, it's a good thing you're so clever and managed to find a way around your problem, in spite of that."

Ailig laughed. "One doesn't have to be clever when women are involved. Left to their own devices, they are all bound to fall into immorality and failure."

"I hate to admit it, but you're right, my darling," I sighed, picking up the jug of mead and bringing it back to the men. "I wish it weren't so, but I will have to resign myself to the fact that all females are doomed to live as simpletons. More mead, my husband?"

Ailig narrowed his eyes at me, trying to decide if I was serious or not, but held out his horn. I smiled innocently as I topped it up to the brim again, then walked around to Frang and repeated the process. I decided to wait another fifteen or twenty minutes before pushing for any further information. Both men were on their way to where I wanted them. The fact that Ailig had not lost his temper over some of my comments, or picked up on my sarcasm, meant the drug was working. But I needed to be careful not to push my luck until they were ready.

I sat and knitted for a while, then sniggered quietly to myself as the two of them started arguing about the rules of the game.

"You don't have enough coin to raise the bet that high," Ailig complained.

"Not here with me, but I have it at home, and if I lose, I will give it to you tomorrow," Frang said, hardly able to form his words properly now.

"What guarantee do I have?" Ailig growled.

"Well, I'll leave you my horse as collateral. How about that?"

Ailig seemed tempted by this, and sipped at his mead while he thought about it. "I don't think I have the coin to cover the bet," he grumbled slowly.

"We don't need to bet with coin. Throw your horn in."

Ailig looked so affronted by the suggestion that I had to choke back a laugh. "Never," he snapped, clutching it closer to his chest.

"Well, you must have other treasures you can use," Frang slurred.

The stakes were getting worryingly high in this game and I was certain it was due to the narcotics. Ailig sucked on the inside of his cheek, then snapped his fingers and looked at me. "Pass me my bag, Woman," he said. He didn't specify the one he meant, but I assumed it to be the one which held the remainder of his loot from the raid. I obediently got up, found it, and brought it to him. He put in on his lap and discreetly rummaged through it, taking obvious pains not to let Frang see what he had in there. Eventually, he pulled out a small brass candlestick and placed it on the floor in front of him. Then he closed the bag and thrust it back at me.

Frang leaned forward in his chair, squinting at the item which he must have decided was satisfactory, because he then sat back and returned to examining his cards.

Using the opportunity, I said, "That's a beautiful candle stick. Where did you get that one from?"

"The raid," Ailig grunted, rearranging the cards in his hands.

"Well, it's beautiful. You must win, darling, so we can keep it. Have you ever seen one like it, Frang?"

Frang shrugged, trying not to look impressed. "It's unremarkable, but it has fair value. I've seen nicer."

"I'll bet you've managed to get all sorts of nice treasures in your time," I tried.

He curled his lips into a smile, as if enjoying an inside joke. "Indeed," he said quietly.

"Ailig has an eye for finding beautiful treasures," I said, putting my hand on Ailig's shoulder again and rubbing it. "He's brought home some amazing pieces. You wouldn't believe how lovely." Ailig smiled slightly, clearly enjoying the praise. Then I looked over at Frang again. "What's the nicest treasure you've ever acquired?"

Frang lowered his cards to his lap and then looked at me, then at Ailig, who looked back at him expectantly.

"I have a jewelled dirk. I'd wager it's worth more than everything in your sack there, put together."

"Oh, I think that's a wager worth accepting," I said, still rubbing Ailig's shoulder. "But Ailig would have to see it to determine whether you're right or not."

Frang sniffed. "Well, he can't, I'm afraid. I keep it well hidden."

I took a chance and scoffed loudly. "You have a valuable treasure which you keep hidden, don't sell, and never show anyone? Sorry sir, but I doubt the truth of your story."

"It pains me to say it, but the woman is right, Frang," said Ailig. The comment nearly made me choke with shock. "If you have such a treasure, then why are you afraid to show it?"

Frang scowled. "Because I don't want the previous owner to know I have it, and people around here talk too much."

"Well, you said yourself Katherine can keep a secret, and you know I wouldn't say anything," Ailig said. That was two shocks to my system in less than thirty seconds. The drug really must have made him feel mellow, because I couldn't remember the last time he'd said my name. It was always 'Woman' if he called me anything at all, and I wondered if I shouldn't make a habit of drugging him every night.

Frang didn't seem impressed that Ailig had taken my side, so I made myself demure and I walked over to the shelf and collected two bowls and spoons, then put a few scoops of the stew into each and passed them to both of the men.

Frang took the bowl and stared at the fire for a few seconds, then shrugged one shoulder. "The dagger used to belong to Artur. It was a family heirloom of his," he said, blowing on the spoon and taking a mouthful of the stew. "The bastard brought it to the tavern one night, shortly after a raid; the first one I missed since my leg was hurt. He was boasting about all the loot he'd pillaged, but brought the blade along as well, just to show off a bit more. It was like having salt rubbed in the wound, and he was going on and on about how wealthy his ancestors used to be, and it just got under my skin. That same night, he got really drunk and passed out in the corner. He'd dropped the blade next to him and it was just lying there, so I took it." He gave a snide grin. "He deserved to lose it, the bastard. Didn't appreciate what he had enough to take care of it. But he was sorry when he woke up later and found it was gone. There was a big meeting about it, and Ealar, who was tacksman at the time, warned that whoever took it had better return it or there would be trouble. Of course, there was no way for him to know who it was, and I had hidden it really well, so I didn't own up."

Frang had finished most of his stew and scraped up the last spoonful. Then he took a drink from his mug and grinned to himself again. "That happened nearly thirty years ago, and I've kept it ever since. Most people won't even remember it happened. Artur has probably forgotten himself."

I seriously doubted that. I imagined Artur thought about the dagger often and was still tortured, not knowing who had taken it that night. I kept that thought to myself, and as I collected the empty bowls from the men, I let Ailig do the rest of the talking.

"You sly dog," Ailig chuckled, dribbling his last mouthful of stew down his chin. He wiped a sleeve across his face and added, "Well, I never really liked Artur either, or his son. Perhaps I could learn a few things from you. Though I couldn't see Ualan bringing my bracelet to the tavern and waving it about. I dare say I'll ever get an opportunity to get that back."

"Well, sometimes one must make one's own opportunities," Frang said, looking smug. "You can't get want you want unless you're willing to get your hands a bit dirty. And some things work and other things take more persistence." Then he looked at me. "Like with your neighbour, for instance. I might have accidentally opened the barn one night during a storm and persuaded her sheep to go for a long walk."

My blood froze as he held my gaze, and his lips formed into a spiteful sneer.

"Of course, that particular endeavour was fruitless. They didn't go down to the river and drown as I'd hoped, but then it was probably wishful thinking. I'd thought since the stupid creatures had already done it once themselves, they might be persuaded to do it again."

As Ailig idiotically sniggered along with Frang, I was burning to tell him it was just as well Frang's plan had failed, because our sheep made up half of the flock he had tried to drown that night. Frang continued to stare smugly at me, waiting for my reaction, but I just turned away from him and took the dirty bowls back to the table. So he went on. "But there were other things I tried which saw much more success, and now the bitch's days are numbered."

Ailig snorted another laugh. "Remind me never to get on your bad side."

"That's right. Cripple or not; no one wrongs me and gets away with it." I had my back to him, but I could feel his eyes still on me.

"I'd still like to see the dirk one day, though," Ailig said, as I sat back down at the table and picked up my knitting.

Frang grinned and lifted his cards up to look at them again. "Maybe if you beat me tonight," he said.

The two men continued to try and play the game, but it became harder and harder for them both to concentrate on what they were doing, and eventually neither of them could put a coherent sentence together. I tried to hold back a bit on the mead, worried I might actually end up poisoning them, but they insisted on finishing what was left in the jug.

At one point, they both went outside to piss, and when they didn't come back, I stuck my head out of the door to check on them. In the dim twilight, I could see both of them slumped on the ground, not moving. I took a few steps outside and listened, and then went back into the house, feeling relieved when I discerned two separate snoring noises. They would both wake up completely disoriented and with no memory of tonight's specific occurrences. So I went back to the hearth and put Ailig's candlestick back in his sack, and then split the coins into two equal piles, one next to each chair. I re-stacked the playing cards, which were scattered on the floor, and put them neatly back on the shelf. One had been partially burned on the corner, having been dropped too close to the fire. No doubt it would be used to cheat with in future.

Once the cottage looked presentable again, I undressed and got into the bed, ecstatic to have it to myself tonight. I lay back and grinned as I went over the interesting tidbits of knowledge I had acquired. I wasn't sure yet what I would do with the information, but if anything, it would be protection for me if Frang blustered about shopping me to Ailig about Daniel, or to anyone else about the kiss he had seen me share with Anna. I had my own leverage now, and even if I never had to use it, I was filled with a great sense of satisfaction from my success in acquiring it.

Chapter Twenty-Five

ANNA

After the assault at the tavern, it took me a good couple of weeks before I was able to get about normally again. The medicine which Katherine left for me helped with the pain for the first day, but after that it was generally an agonising week.

As good as my intentions were, I didn't make it down to the river that first day. Instead, I spent most of it sleeping. Florie was very understanding, and I felt guilty when she didn't complain. Though by the end of the week, I could see her tolerance for the situation was wearing thin, and she was getting bored.

After four days confined to the shelter, I finally decided to get up and make an attempt at walking. I got as far as our little garden patch before I had to sit down and let Florie pick the vegetables for the evening meal. It was progress though, and as the next few days passed, I gradually recovered my mobility, and the pain slowly eased. It took tens days before I could resume all my usual chores and carry things such as pails of water and firewood.

Ailis had come over for the first three mornings as she promised she would, and though she kept insisting Florie and I should come and stay with her, I politely refused. Part of that was my pride. I felt Florie and I could manage on our own, but I'd be lying to myself if I didn't admit the biggest reason was Katherine. I hadn't been able to get close to her or speak to her since that very first morning when she had come over to help me, but being able to see her in the distance when she worked around her croft was a huge comfort. I didn't want to be far away where I couldn't have sight of her every day and know she was alright. In addition, I looked forward to the little sack which Florie went to pick up from the river bank each day. It was the closest I could come to communicating with Katherine, and I had taken to putting a thistle in the bottom before Florie would return it.

Florie did not take well to being totally cut off from Katherine and lamented about it constantly. She had asked a few times if she could go down to the bank and wait for Katherine to drop off the sack so she could at least see her for a short moment, but I refused to allow it. I knew it made Florie resent me to some extent, but I consoled myself in the knowledge that the situation was temporary. While I trusted my daughter with my life, she was just a child and I wasn't willing to put Katherine's safety at risk, or her own, by bringing Florie in on our plot. She didn't need to know, and as much as she got angry at me for not allowing her to go near Katherine, I hoped everything would be forgiven once the plan was followed through.

Katherine went out of her way to put useful things in the sack, and she was very generous with her selections. She gave us cheese, bannock, turnips and, on one occasion, a rabbit which she had even gone to the trouble of skinning and gutting for us. There were always a couple of potatoes, which were delicious and very filling in a stew, and after discovering how good they were, we kept some aside and planted them in hopes of starting our own crop.

"I feel like we should be growing these instead of turnips," I said to Florie one evening when we were eating our stew. She shrugged, not showing much enthusiasm. "Don't you like them better than turnips?" I said, trying to get her to engage in the conversation.

"What do you want me to say? In a few weeks we won't have a croft to grow anything on, so what does it matter if I like them better or not?"

I sighed. I'd had to tell Florie a little about the night at the tavern and it had come out about Ualan's decision as to the croft. I knew she had a right to know, but a big part of me regretted telling her because it hadn't gone down very well at all and Florie's mood had taken a significant dive since that day.

"No matter what, we have each other and we'll be alright," I said to her. We'd already had this conversation half a dozen times, but I didn't know what else to say to make her feel better. "Aunty Alis said Uncle Faolan will talk to Ualan and try to change his mind. There's still hope. And worst-case scenario, we might have to go and live with your cousins. That's not so bad, is it?"

"And what happens to Katherine?" Florie said, giving me an accusatory look. "She'll have Frang living on one side, and Ailig with her over there, and no friends nearby."

I was taken aback by this. I hadn't realised how much Florie actually cared about Katherine.

"Well," I said, hesitating. I really didn't know how to respond to the question. I couldn't share the solution we'd come up with, and I didn't want to draw any further attention to how deeply I was invested in helping Katherine out of her situation. I had done enough damage in that respect at the tavern that night. If the plan was to work, there could be no suspicion that Katherine and I were plotting together, or had any aligning goals.

"Katherine is a grown woman, Florie. She has to look after herself and make her own decisions. What happens to her is not for you to worry about and is out of both of our control." I had to repress a cringe as I said this, recalling how many times it had been said to me and how much it annoyed me every time it was. "We'll always be friends, though. That will never change," I added. I reached out to pat her on the shoulder, but as soon as I said the words, I knew I'd made a mistake. Florie gave me a look of utter disgust and pulled away from my outstretched hand.

"How can you say that?" she said. "You say we'll always be friends, but it's like you don't even care about her. She didn't tell us we had to look after ourselves when we needed help. She helped us." She was breathing hard now and trying to fight back the tears which were welling up in her eyes. "And you won't even let me see her or talk to her, so how can we stay friends?"

I rubbed my eyes in frustration. This was not going the way I'd hoped at all. "Ailig won't let us, Florie. We have to give it some time, alright? I'm not going to stop you from seeing her forever, but right now, things are sensitive and it's dangerous. Ailig hurt me, and he wouldn't be afraid to hurt you. You need to be patient and heed what I'm saying."

Florie crossed her arms and turned her back to me as a trail of tears splashed down her freckled face. "I hate Ailig," she said. "And I hate Frang, and I hate Ualan. It's not fair. I don't want to leave and go and live with Uncle Faolan. I want to stay in our home and visit with Katherine and go back to how things were before Ailig came back."

I got up and walked over to her and sat down with my arm around her. "I know, darling. I want all of those things too, I really do. And I'm going to do everything I can to make things better. We just have to be careful and patient right now."

She didn't push my arm away this time and instead gave me a hug.

"You know, I was thinking," I said, quietly. "I'm much better now and we haven't been to the river in ages. How about we take a picnic there tomorrow?"

Florie looked up at me with puffy red eyes and nodded. It seemed to me that the final stage of the plan couldn't come soon enough.

It was a beautiful August day when we packed our little lunch for our picnic at the river. I wrapped up four hard-boiled eggs, some pieces of bannock, some turnip leaves, a boiled potato, a chunk of cheese, and some of the dried meat Alis and Faolan had given us. Then we headed down into the valley in the late morning.

Florie wanted to have the picnic in the place where we'd buried Sim, so we spread a woollen blanket out on the ground right next to the little patch of thistles which marked his grave. The flowers had taken to the spot very well, and I admired the cluster of little purple blooms as I sat myself down on the blanket.

The water was slow moving and crystal clear, and I leaned back on my hands and watched as Florie wasted no time paddling in it. She splashed some water towards me and beckoned me to join her. I resisted for a while until I got so wet from the splashes that I might as well have been in the water with her. Threatening that she was in for it once I got hold of her, I removed my bodice and skirt and started picking my way down the bank, lifting my chemise as the water pooled around my feet.

"Hurry up," Florie said with a cheeky smile, and she hurried over to me, stamping her feet in the water in an effort to splash me some more.

"Well, I don't see you jumping in yet," I said, pretending to be annoyed at being splashed. Then I lunged forward to grab her. She shrieked and lurched away from me, but ended up toppling over and plunging into the water behind her. I couldn't help laughing as she resurfaced, looking surprised and irritated.

"That's cheating!" she gasped. "There's a drop off right there! I can't touch the bottom!"

"Oh, well, that was unlucky," I said, still sniggering. She swam along the bank for a few feet and then clambered out, before putting her hands on her hips and marching back over to me. I could tell by her face that there was a vengeful volume of water about to be splashed my way, but all of a sudden she stopped and stared up the valley.

At first I thought it was a ruse to distract me and I grinned, about to tell her I wasn't going to fall for that, but a movement in the corner of my eye had me turn to look in the same direction.

In the distance I could see Katherine running down the hill towards us, and my immediate reaction was panic. Was she being chased by Ailig? Had something bad happened? I looked beyond her, up to her cottage, but couldn't see anyone behind her. Then, as she got closer and her facial features became easier to make out, I could see she looked happy. Her red hair flew out behind her and shone in the sun, and she was waving and calling out as she ran. Florie lunged out of the river and set off towards Katherine, but still in a state of bemusement, I could only offer a hesitant wave back in her direction. I started walking towards her. Florie was way ahead of me now and Katherine couched down with her arms open to meet her with a big hug. I stepped up to a jog, trying to catch up, and once Florie had released Katherine, she grinned at me and pushed her hair out of her face.

"Anna, I'm so glad to see you looking better," she said, eyeing me up and down. I felt a blush spread across my cheeks as I realised I was standing in the middle of the pasture in my undergarments.

"Uh, thank you," I said, giving a nervous smile. I still wasn't sure what was going on. "You too," I added, noting her face was almost back to normal. The bruise had taken a long time to fade but now there was nothing to be seen except a slight yellowish colour on her left cheek, just under her eye. I looked nervously over her shoulder, up to her cottage, and she grinned again.

"Ailig left this morning on a hunting trip with a few other men," she said, unable to contain her glee. "He said they'll be gone for at least two days, so he won't be back until tomorrow afternoon at the earliest."

I was hardly able to believe it. "Are you sure?" I said.

She nodded blithely, biting her bottom lip. "He said it himself."

Slowly, I allowed myself to crack a smile.

"Does that mean you can visit with us today?" Florie asked hopefully.

"All day," Katherine grinned, bending down and squeezing Florie's shoulders. "We have lots of time to make up for, don't we?"

"We certainly do," I laughed. "Florie has been complaining about not being able to see you for the last fortnight, haven't you?"

Florrie nodded quickly. "I've missed you so much!" she said, grabbing Katherine's hand.

"Oh, you have no idea how much I've missed both of you," she smiled.

Florie clung onto Katherine's hand like grim death as we walked back down the valley to the spot where we'd laid out our picnic.

"Oh, look at this," Katherine said. "You must have known."

"Just a little impromptu day off," I said. "We needed it, didn't we Florie?"

"Yes, and the water is lovely and warm. Are you going to swim, Katherine?" Florie said.

"Oh, certainly," Katherine said, loosening the ribbon on her bodice. I found myself staring at her as she did it and had to clear my throat and look away when she noticed. She grinned at me and lifted the hem of my chemise slightly. "It looks like you've already been in." She grinned.

"Err, no. This would be Florie's doing," I said. "I was about to when we spotted you coming."

"Well, we'll have to get her back for that then," she said. She gave me a playful wink, then pulled her bodice over her head and started undoing the ribbons of her skirt.

Florie was back in the water, splashing around again and I was still in a slight state of unease at the situation when Katherine got up and prepared to go in after her. It seemed too good to be true, but then maybe I was overthinking it. In reality, it was unlikely that Ailig now spent his time plotting up ways to try and trick me and Katherine into getting caught spending time together. He probably really had gone hunting, but I still couldn't shake the worry I felt that he might just show up again at any time.

Katherine's hand came into view and drew me out of my thoughts. I looked up at her and saw she was standing over me, offering me her hand with a mischievous expression. I slowly reached out and took it, the feeling of her skin against mine instantly melting away my concerns and sending my heart racing.

"Come on," she said, tugging me towards the water.

I staggered after her and we spent the rest of the morning splashing about and laughing, and for a while it felt like the last few weeks hadn't happened and things were back to how they were before. Florie was light-hearted and giggling as she tried to splash Katherine and then get away before she could be splashed back, and then there were competitions such as who could hold their breath the longest and who could swim to the other side of the river first. I was pleased that I was able to win both games, despite having been out of action for nearly two weeks. It took it out of me though, and by midday I was exhausted and staggered out of the river and flopped down onto the grass, breathing hard. I still had some way to go before I regained my former stamina, and for a while I sat and watched Katherine and Florie play while I recovered.

Eventually both of them exited the water and Katherine came and sat down next to me, dripping a puddle of water around her. Her hair hung down either side of her face and her thick eyelashes were stuck together in attractive little clumps above her bright green eyes. She grinned at me while trying to catch her breath and wiped the water from her face.

"Are you alright?" she said.

"Oh, yes, I'm fine," I said, trying not to make it look too obvious that I was desperate to kiss her. "I just needed a rest, that's all." I glanced over my shoulder, back up the hill nervously, then looked at her again. She rested her hand on mine and gave an empathetic smile.

"Don't worry, he's not there."

"I'm sorry, I can't help it," I said. "How have you been, anyway?" Florie had pulled up some reeds from the side of the bank and was now swishing them at the water, but I lowered my voice anyway in an effort not to be overheard.

"Things have been... interesting," she said.

"Interesting?"

"Yes, I learned some interesting things. A few days ago Ailig invited Frang over for cards."

I grimaced. "Yes, I remember seeing him arrive. I felt for you, being stuck in the cottage with those two."

"Yes, but it wasn't as awful as you might think," she said. "I made sure of that." She had assumed a crafty grin now, and I listened intently. "I put a little something into their drinks, and well... they talked a lot." I waited for her to go on. "For instance, I found out that it was Frang who opened the barn door that night and let the sheep out."

My jaw went slack. "He what?"

"Not only that, but he chased them out of the barn and tried to get them to go down to the river. He had hoped some of them would drown, like before."

"Bastard!" I shouted. Florie looked over, frowning, and I quickly lowered my voice again. "I can't believe it. I blamed you for that. I should have known. I'm so sorry Katherine."

She shook her head. "That doesn't matter now, but it shows how much meddling he's been doing."

"Did he admit to the fire, too?" I growled.

"Not specifically, but he definitely inferred it," Katherine said. "But it won't help us because we can't prove those things."

I sighed, angrily. "Of course. It's probably why he was blustering about it. He knows we can't do anything."

"Well, that's not all he was blustering about," she added, "but I'll fill you in on the rest later. What I really came over to talk to you about was when we should put this plan into action. I know you said we should probably wait three or four weeks, but it's been just over two and Ailig is gone tonight. I was thinking it would be a good opportunity to go to the tavern this evening with the bracelet."

I felt a cold flutter ripple through my body. She was right. It would be a good opportunity, but the thought of actually following through suddenly became much more real, and my heart pounded with anxiety.

Picking up on my hesitation, Katherine spoke again. "Look, I don't know when there will be a better opportunity. Ailig is almost always at home or at the tavern, so I don't know when we'll get another chance like this. If Ailig was to see me with the bracelet before Ualan did, the whole plan would go to hell, and I don't know what he'd do. Even if Ualan hasn't noticed the bracelet is missing yet, he'll still recognise it when he sees it."

I tried to steady my heart rate and convince myself that what she was saying was sound. I knew it was, but now that the day was suddenly upon us and I hadn't had time to get used to the idea, I was a bag of nerves. "When are you going to go?" I asked her, fighting to keep my voice calm.

"This evening after supper," she said.

I nodded slowly. "And you're sure he's not coming back tonight?"

"He said he wouldn't be back until tomorrow."

"What about Ualan?" I asked. "Are you sure he'll be there at the tavern tonight?"

She shrugged. "He almost always is. It's a fair bet he will be. I know he didn't go with the hunting party. I specifically asked Ailig who was going with him and he didn't mention Ualan. Anyway, even if Ualan himself isn't there, one of his sons will be and they'll recognise the bracelet too, right?"

"I guess so," I mumbled.

"What's the matter?" Katherine asked. "This was your plan, but you don't seem very enthusiastic. Is something bothering you?"

I looked up at her quickly. "Of course something is bothering me," I hissed. "The woman I— love, has just told me she's going to take a huge risk tonight, and I'm nervous, that's all."

She leaned back and smiled, and I looked down again. Then I felt her fingers squeeze my hand.

"Hey, it's going to be alright. The plan is a good one. I know it's happening faster than we thought, but I think that's the only reason you're scared."

I sighed, "You're probably right. I'm sorry."

"I love that you said you love me, though."

We enjoyed the picnic for lunch, but the rest of the day seemed to drift by in a haze. I felt stuck in a frozen state, and I knew I wouldn't rest easy until after the deed was done. I wanted so much to go with Katherine, but I didn't even bother to suggest it because I knew it would be foolish. This was something she would have to do on her own, and I would have to tolerate not knowing how it was going until after the fact. I was dreading the evening, but I tried not to let my concerns bring the others down and made an effort to engage in the conversations and make the most of the unexpected day with Katherine.

After we'd all finished at the river, we trooped back to the shelter, and Florie and Katherine prepared the dinner together, laughing and joking amongst themselves while I hung back. I couldn't help constantly looking outside and walking over to the entrance to peek out. I wasn't sure whether I was checking how late in the afternoon it was, or if I was making sure no one was coming, but after the sixth or seventh time, Katherine came over to me and took my hand and made me come back to the bed and sit down. I noticed Florie was watching me while she dished the stew into three bowls, casting me with a disapproving look. I looked down at my hands for a few seconds before a bowl was pushed into them.

"Thank you," I said quietly. Then looking up to see both of them still watching me, Katherine looking concerned and Florie looking annoyed, I quickly cleared my throat and added, "This looks really good." I picked up the spoon and stirred it around, trying to convince them both I intended to eat it.

Florie sat down next to the fire and began to eat her stew, and Katherine, clearly trying to take the attention away from me, sat down next to her and made a fuss about how delicious the food was and started asking Florie what magic she had used to make it so good. I sipped my stew slowly, mostly for show, because I wasn't hungry, and listened to them both chatter. After dinner, I resisted going to look outside again, but I knew the evening was upon us and Katherine would have to go soon.

After finishing her supper, Katherine came and sat down next to me. "Please try to relax," she said quietly. "I know it's scary, but worrying like this doesn't help."

"I know, and I'm sorry," I said. "I'm trying not to worry, but I can't seem to snap out of it. I just have this feeling that something is going to go wrong, that's all. I know it's stupid and I'm being overly anxious, but I just can't shake it."

Katherine put her arm around my shoulders and tilted her head against mine. The familiar smell of her hair helped to calm my nerves a little, and I leaned my head against hers.

"If you really feel that way, then say the word, Anna, and I won't do it tonight," she said.

I hesitated, suddenly not sure if I liked having the responsibility of deciding whether it would be done tonight, thrust upon me. It was on the tip of my tongue to tell her to abort, but something stopped me. What she'd said earlier echoed in my mind. This was the best chance we had at executing part two of the plan, and it might be weeks before we'd have another opportunity like this. In that time, God knows what Ailig might do to Katherine and I couldn't keep living under the shelter, watching her every day and not being able to talk to her or touch her. Katherine was right. I was just nervous because I hadn't expected it to happen tonight, and I just needed time to adjust to the change in schedule.

I sighed and shook my head. "No, you're right. There's no good reason why it shouldn't be done tonight." I forced a smile and looked at her, and she smiled back.

"Are you sure?" she said, sweeping aside a few rogue strands of hair from my face.

I nodded. "Yes. Let's just get it over with."

"Alright," she said, standing up. I got to my feet too and followed her to the entrance.

Florie came up behind us at the same time. "Do you have to go now?" she asked Katherine, the disappointment in her voice painfully obvious.

Katherine bent down to her, stroking her hair. "I do, but what about if I come back in the morning and we all have breakfast together?"

Florie smiled and nodded.

Katherine gave her a hug and kissed the top of her head. "Look after your mam, alright?"

Florie nodded again, then walked back over to the bed.

"Stay there, Florie," I said. "I just need to speak to Katherine for a second." I stepped out of the shelter and pulled Katherine off to the side for a moment, out of Florie's view. "Promise me you'll be careful," I said.

Katherine gripped me by the shoulders and smiled encouragingly. "It's not hard, what I have to do, you know? You made this plan pretty foolproof."

"I just don't know what I'd do if anything happened to you. I can't imagine my life without you in it now."

She squeezed my shoulders reassuringly. "Likewise. Which is why we have to go through with this. You did your part. Now you have to trust me to do mine. After tonight, we won't have to worry about Ailig anymore. We can stop all this sneaking around and waiting to steal moments when his back is turned. Focus on that and I'll be back before you know it."

Her positive outlook never ceased to amaze me. "I love you so much," I said.

She grinned and kissed me, drawing it out for a long moment. "I love you too," she whispered, after our lips parted again.

"When it's done, promise you'll come straight back here and tell me. I won't be able to sleep otherwise."

"I promise." She started walking backwards away from me, smiling. "I'll see you in a couple of hours." Then she turned and jogged off across the pasture to her own croft.

I took a long, shaky breath in as I watched her go, then whispered under my breath. "Good luck."

Chapter Twenty-Six

KATHERINE

I headed back to my cottage with butterflies in my stomach, caused by a mixture of excitement and nerves. This was it; the moment Anna and I had been waiting for since the day at the tavern. It had been less than three weeks ago, but it still felt like an age. Knowing it was coming was what kept me sane over the last few days, and if everything went as we hoped tonight, then I would be free of Ailig forever, and Anna and Florie could move into the cottage with me. If she lost her croft, it wouldn't matter anymore, and though we would have to put up with Frang as a close neighbour, I had leverage I could now use if he tried to cause any trouble.

Taking a deep breath in, I walked around to the back of my cottage and moved the roosting boxes to the side until I uncovered a darker patch of soil which looked like it had been recently disturbed. I used a small rock to move the dirt, which was still fairly loose, and finally uncovered a heavy little white bundle. I unwound the rag and the weighty object fell free, landing in my lap.

I picked up the bracelet and examined it, rubbing my fingers over the jewels on each second link. The silver glinted in the last of the setting sunlight and the smooth oval-shaped amethysts were outstanding in their engraved settings. It looked exceptionally valuable. My heart pounded as I realised if Anna had been caught stealing this, there would have been dire consequences for her. I slid the bracelet over my wrist, rotating my hand to force it through the tight fit, then I held out my arm and admired the exquisite piece of jewellery. My heart was still hammering, and I had to take a few deep breaths to settle myself. When I got to the tavern, I needed to look normal, not like I had just committed a serious offence. It took a few minutes, but I gradually calmed myself down and prepared to leave.

Ailig had taken Belle with him on his hunting trip, so I walked over to the barn to prep Ailbeart. I felt quite pretty with the bracelet on and I tried to enjoy wearing it for the short time I could. I'd never have another chance to wear something like it, that was certain. When I got into the barn, I was greeted by a soft nicker from Ailbeart and I stroked his nose as I lifted his bridle from the hook and fitted it over his head.

"Shall we go for a ride?" I said to him as I opened the stall to lead him out. His saddle would be easier to put on once I had him outside where there was more room. But before I could get him all the way through the door, I jerked to a stop and froze. Ailig stood before me, a few paces away, holding Belle by the reins.

My throat constricted, and I caught my breath as he glared at me in the dim twilight, his blue eyes piercing me from under his dark eyebrows.

"Going somewhere?" he asked, softly. One corner of his mouth was drawn up into a noxious smirk, as if he was pleased to have caught me doing something I shouldn't have been. His eyes, however, were glued on my face, and it didn't appear that he'd noticed the bracelet yet. For a moment, I was petrified. My hand twitched as I considered quickly trying to cover the bracelet, but I didn't want to draw attention to it either. I realised I wasn't helping myself by looking so guilty, so I forced a pleasant smile, glad of the twilight which I hoped had concealed the colour draining from my face.

"Just going for a ride," I said airily and took a step back. My shoulder knocked Ailbeart's nose, and he tossed his head and nickered again behind me. Using the opportunity, I spun around, putting my back to Ailig and brought my left arm, which bore the bracelet, in front of me and out of his view. With my right hand, I reached up to comfort Ailbeart. Ailig still stood silently behind me, and I could feel his eyes burning into the back of my head.

"I thought you weren't going to be back until tomorrow," I said, trying to sound as casual as I could.

"I know you did," his voice came from behind me, soft and dangerous. "But I thought I might come back and surprise you. See what you get up to while I'm away."

I pressed my arm tighter against my chest, trying to think how I could discreetly remove the bracelet without him noticing.

"Well, I'm sorry to disappoint you, my dear," I said. "As you can see, it's nothing interesting."

I heard him step up closer behind me, then his hand came down on my shoulder and squeezed. "Oh, I don't know about that," he said. "You seemed quite excited about your ride. Where were you going, exactly?"

I forced a laugh, but it didn't come out as carefree as I'd wanted. I twisted my neck and looked at him over my shoulder, then lowered my arm back down to my side. "Nowhere interesting, just to the glen. You're welcome to join me if you like."

He gave a single soft laugh and squeezed my shoulder tighter, making me wince. "Horseshit," he sneered into my ear, then yanked me around to face him. I braced myself for a blow, but kept my hand down and looked him in the eye. "You never go off riding," he said. "You must think I'm a simpleton. So tell me who you were going to meet. Who have you been whoring around with behind my back?" He gripped the top of my right arm and yanked me closer to him.

"What?" I choked, completely surprised.

"I know you were going to meet someone, you reek of guilt! Now tell me his name!" he shouted.

"Ailig, I swear, there's no other man," I gasped.

He gritted his teeth and grabbed the top of my left arm, then yanked me forward, away from the horse. Ailbeart gave a sharp squeal in fright, then reared slightly. The rein which was still in my hand was ripped from my fingers as Ailig dragged me away from the horse. He forced me up against the wall of the barn and then wrapped his fingers around my throat, squeezing hard enough to make me see stars.

"Ailig, please," I choked, gasping for air. I automatically brought my hands up and tried to loosen the grip he had around my neck, and then I felt him go rigid. His hands released their grip on my throat, and he grabbed my wrist and held it up. There was a deathly silence as Ailig examined the bracelet. Then his eyes darted back to mine. "What the hell is this?" he growled. Despite his anger, he looked quite shocked.

"Your bracelet," I said quickly, rubbing my throat with my other hand. I had no idea how to explain how I had it or what I intended to do with it, and tried to think of a plausible story quickly.

"Where did you get it from?" he said. His voice had gone low and gravely again.

"I-I got it back for you," I said. "I know how much it meant to you. It was going to be a surprise." He stared at me, disbelieving. "I just wanted to wear it for a while until you got back."

"How did you get it?" he said, not letting go of my wrist, which had gone white under the pressure of his grip.

"I stole it from Ualan's house. He doesn't know, and he probably won't notice it's missing for ages."

He stared at the bracelet again, then wrapped his fingers around it with his other hand. He pulled and twisted it painfully until it came off. I held my breath, hoping he would believe the story.

As he looked at it again in his hand, his lips curled into a disdainful smile and he nodded. "Very crafty of you, Woman. Impressive." Then he put the bracelet into his sporran. "But if you think I'm going to believe you planned on giving my bracelet back to me, then you really must take me for a fool."

If my back wasn't still pressed up against the side of the barn, I think I would have run. I didn't know what he was thinking now, but I knew it was likely I wasn't going to make it through the night without getting some kind of beating. I was confident he wouldn't tell Ualan, because I knew how much he wanted the bracelet back, but if I couldn't convince him I wasn't riding off to meet some secret lover, then my chances of making it through the night in one piece, were slim.

"I think you had other plans for it," Ailig went on. "I think you were off just now to sell it or trade it, but I'm not sure for what purpose. To help the little wench next door, perhaps? Or to keep the money for yourself?" He tilted his head and raised his eyebrows, as if wanting me to identify which guess was the correct one.

I shook my head. "No, I wasn't going to do that."

"Oh, you were. It's too much of a coincidence that you put this thing on to go for a ride. You were taking it somewhere and you're going to tell me the truth, even if I have to tear it out of you." He held up his fist in front of my face and leaned in so his face was only an inch from mine.

"Please, Ailig," I begged, turning my head away from him. "Please, don't. You'll hurt the baby."

"Then that will be your doing!" he shouted. "Tell me now, where were you taking the bracelet? If you don't tell me, the first blow will be to your face, and if you won't tell me after that, the next will be your belly. Knowing what I do now, I'm not even sure it's mine, so I'm willing to risk it."

I knew he meant what he said, and what's more, I knew he'd be happy to have an excuse to hit me. "Alright, I was going to sell it," I said quickly. "I was going to keep the money in case I ever needed it."

He lowered his fist and looked satisfied. "I knew it," he whispered. "I knew you were a conniving little whore. You think you can just walk away? No one walks away from me. You're mine, Woman. For the rest of your life, which won't be very long unless you start behaving like a proper wife!"

I fought back the tears, but my vision blurred as they welled up and I pressed myself into the stone wall behind me. He stepped back slowly, rubbing his hand over his sporran where the bracelet lay. I knew the only reason he hadn't punched me was because he was pleased about getting it back and satisfied in having shattered my plans for it. He got as much pleasure from torturing me psychologically as he did physically, and I fumed at myself for giving him the satisfaction of seeing me cry.

"Now," he said. "You put that horse back in his stall, then put Belle away. Then you will come to bed with me." Then he leaned in close and lowered his voice again. "And you better not keep me waiting, or I'll change my mind about not giving you a hiding."

As Ailig disappeared back into the cottage, I sank down to my knees and let the tears come. I cursed myself for rushing into this. Why didn't I wait? I should have known he was up to something. Anna was right to be worried. She'd risked everything to buy me this chance, and I'd just thrown it away with one stupid decision. How could I face Anna, now that I'd failed? How could I expect her to forgive me? As I sat and silently cried and felt sorry for myself, I was also acutely aware that Ailig was waiting for me.

It wasn't enough to torture me like this, but he would revel in kicking me while I was down. I knew what was turning him on right now was the fact that I was upset and detested him, and he could force himself upon me anyway. He thrived on it, which made me angry, and that in turn would only excite him more. I hated that he'd beaten me again. The stupid, drunken oaf had managed to outsmart me, and it was my fault for being so damn blind and cocky.

I burned with rage as I pulled myself to my feet and took hold of Ailbeart's reins again. I led him back into his stall and removed his bridle, then closed the gate as I tried to think of what to do. I forced myself to work quickly as I led Belle to the new stable and set about removing her saddle and bridle, because even though I dreaded the thought of him touching me, it would happen whether I liked it or not. But the beating he had threatened was not a foregone conclusion. If I could avoid that, I would.

As I pushed the filly into her stall and locked it up, the beginnings of an idea had formed in my mind. All was not lost. There was time to fix this. Besides me and Katherine, Ailig was the only person who knew about the bracelet. If I could find a way to get it back and get it to Ualan, it would still come down to Ailig's word against mine.

It was the only option left to me.

With a new plan to focus on, I was able to gather myself together and enter the cottage, prepared to do what was necessary to lead Ailig into a false sense of victory. I was careful not to let my new found confidence show on my face and adopted a suitably miserable and dejected posture as I walked inside. Ailig was sitting by the hearth, his horn filled with mead.

"I see you didn't bother to light the fire, and there's no food in the pot," he said. "But then I suppose since you were planning on spending your night gallivanting through the glen, it wasn't necessary. Isn't that right?"

I looked down at the floor. "I had a cold supper earlier," I said meekly. "I didn't see the point in cooking a whole stew just for me. But now that you're back, I'll light the fire and put dinner on. Unless you need me for anything else right now?"

He took a swig from his horn and narrowed his eyes at me. "I'm having a drink right now, so you can get on with that until I'm finished," he said.

I nodded and quickly grabbed some kindling and the tinderbox to get the fire started. Once I had it going, I ran outside and pulled a pail of water from the well, came back and poured it into the cauldron, and then grabbed a few turnips and potatoes from the pit larder. Ailig had now taken the bracelet back out of his sporran and was turning it over in his hands, admiring it.

I walked over to the cupboard and took out my medicine bag, then brought it back to the table with me. I rummaged around inside it and pulled out a few innocuous herbs for flavouring, but at the same time I also selected a large dried valerian root. I was tempted to pull out the little bottle of laudanum, but how to get that out without him noticing and questioning it was going to be a challenge. I chopped up the valerian root into small pieces, then roughly chopped the vegetables and herbs. I scraped the pile onto a plate, then quickly tossed the lot into the cauldron with the water. The valerian root would have a drowsy effect on whoever ate the stew, especially with the amount I had put in, but on its own, it wouldn't be enough to incapacitate him. For that, I'd need the laudanum, and I wasn't even sure if I had enough left in the bottle.

I'd used a lot of it the other night when I'd drugged him and Frang, probably more than I needed to, thinking back on it. The effect had been exactly as I'd hoped. The two men had woken up on the ground the following day with very little memory of what had happened the previous night. Neither of the men could even recall if they had played a single game of cards and ended up assuming they hadn't when they discovered the money still on the floor by the hearth, evenly divided. Ailig had been miserable with a thick head for most of that day, and he'd blamed Frang for leading him on to drink too much. He was terribly grumpy but felt too unwell to make my life significantly difficult, and I enjoyed the feeling of having unloaded a small measure of recompense on both of them.

Frang had likewise suffered. I had secretly hoped he'd fall from his horse and break his neck when he headed off home in the morning, but as always, the devil seemed to take care of his own.

Tonight, though, I needed to repeat what I had done then, but this time it would be harder. Ailig was already on the edge. There was no one else in the cottage to distract his attention from what I was doing, and he was not drunk enough not to notice if I drugged his mead. I would have to get the laudanum into the stew, and he would have to eat enough of it for it to disable him to the extent he couldn't stop me from leaving. Not to mention, all of that would have to be done early enough to give me time to get to the tavern before people started going home.

After dumping the primary ingredients into the cauldron, I walked back over to the table. I glanced over my shoulder to make sure Ailig was still admiring the bracelet, then pulled the small bottle of laudanum from the medicine bag and slid it into the pocket of my skirt. I brought the jug of mead around to Ailig, who was still turning the bracelet over in his hands. The light from the fire bounced off the purple amethysts, and for a moment he seemed entranced. I was tempted to empty the laudanum into the stew right then, but after a moment he seemed to snap out of it and he looked up at me.

"You didn't tell me how you managed to get your hands on this," he said as he lifted his horn for me to fill. "Or when," he added.

I shrugged as I filled the vessel back up to the top. "I climbed in through the window of Ualan's house, that night you and Frang were drunk. You had been talking to Frang about wanting to get it back, and he suggested that you steal it. He made it sound easy, so I thought I'd try."

"I don't remember talking about that with him," he said, frowning.

"Well, you both had a lot to drink," I said.

He sniffed. "I suppose I did that night. Bloody Frang. I'm glad we didn't play cards in the end. God knows what I might have bet." Then he stared at me again. "So you snuck around in Ualan's house in the middle of the night?"

"Yes."

"No one helped you?"

"No."

"That seems very brave for you." Then something seemed to occur to him. "Did you come across any other valuables while you were searching for this?"

"Some," I said, cautiously. "But I didn't want to push my luck. I only took the bracelet."

"Is that so?" he said quietly, rubbing his jaw. I cleared my throat and quickly walked back to the table to put down the jug, which was getting heavy in my hand. I picked up a long wooden spoon and then went back to the cauldron and stirred the vegetables around in the water, not looking at him. The stew was heating up, but it would be almost an hour before it was ready. It would give me longer to find a way to incorporate the laudanum, but it was also an hour in which a lot could go badly. I chanced a quick glance at Ailig, who was still watching me with a thoughtful frown.

"What are you going to do with the bracelet?" I asked, trying to coax the conversation in a different direction.

"That's none of your damn business," he said coldly. "What were you going to do with it?"

"I told you, I was thinking about selling it," I said.

"To whom?" he said, putting emphasis on both words, as though he were speaking to an idiot.

For once, I desperately wished he would hurry up and get drunk. I badly needed his reasoning and logic to deteriorate so he would stop asking me difficult questions. I didn't know how much longer I could skirt around them before it ended in me being clobbered. "I was... going to take it to Daniel," I said, after a slight hesitation.

"Daniel?" Ailig repeated, sounding incredulous.

"Yes, I've heard talk that he sometimes buys things like that. He wasn't expecting me, I was just going to go and show it to him and see what I could get for it."

"Then you're a fool and it's just as well that I stopped you, Woman. If Ualan had announced that the bracelet was missing, that slimy bastard would have shopped you. You would have lost the bracelet and your life."

"I'm sorry," I said quickly, relieved that he'd bought the story. "Of course you're right. I don't know what I was thinking."

"You're a stupid woman. You don't think," he spat.

"It won't happen again. And I'll make it up to you," I said, giving him my best apologetically, pleading look.

He snorted and took a deep pull of mead from his horn, then belched. "When will the stew be ready?" he said.

"I'm sorry, it'll be a while yet," I said. "It's only just warm."

"I'm hungry. I'll have it as it is," he grumbled.

"Um, the vegetables won't be soft yet. If you just wait for—"

He stamped his foot down on the floor and bellowed, "Dammit, Woman! Don't argue with me, and do as you're told!"

I nodded quickly and went to the shelf to get a bowl and spoon. My hands shook as I picked up the items and I panicked, trying to think of what to do. This was not going according to plan at all. The laudanum was not in the stew yet and there was no way I could do that with him sitting right there in front of the cauldron. I felt a cold despair creep over me as I turned to walk back, and I could see Ailig glaring at me. At that moment, something within me went numb, and I stumbled and dropped the bowl, kicking it with my foot so that it rolled under the table.

"I'm sorry, I'll get it," I said, and hurriedly got down on my hands and knees to reach under the table. In that instant, I wasn't sure if I had dropped the bowl by accident, or if something in my subconscious overrode my panic and made a decision, but at that point I knew there was no going back. With my back to Ailig, I reached into my pocket and removed the small bottle of laudanum. I quickly uncorked it and picked up the bowl, then tipped the remainder of the bottle into it.

Leaving the empty bottle under the table, I slowly backed out and stood up carefully with the bowl, then walked steadily back to the cauldron. Ailig was still seated, casting daggers at me, but I held the bowl high enough that he wouldn't be able to see the small amount of liquid that was now already inside it. I ladled out a portion of the stew and poured it carefully into the bowl, then repeated the process until it was full. The lumps of chopped turnip and potato, dried root and bits of leaves from the herbs, all bobbed about, looking unappetising in the clear liquid. I hoped the flavours of the herbs would have diffused enough into the water to mask the bitterness of the drug. If he refused to eat it, I'd be sunk.

Ailig took the bowl and spoon from me, while still casting me with a dirty look, then began to slurp it. He screwed up his face at the first taste but swallowed the mouthful he had and then said, "This tastes like shit."

"I have a little bit of salt in my supply of herbs," I offered.

"No amount of salt is going to fix this muck," he snarled, taking another spoonful. He crunched down on a piece of almost raw potato and ate in silence. "Why don't you eat some? I don't see why I should be the only person to be poisoned by your cooking."

I almost laughed at the irony, but held a demure expression. "I think I'll wait until it's cooked properly," I said. "Besides, I had an early supper so I'm not hungry yet."

He snorted, but kept spooning the watery contents of his bowl into his mouth. I cautiously walked over to the table and sat down, then used my foot to slowly push the empty laudanum bottle closer to the wall, where it would be even harder to notice. I hadn't had time to pay attention to how much laudanum had gone into his bowl. It wasn't much, and there was less in the bottle than I'd hoped, but because it went into just his bowl, he was getting the maximum concentration of it. Between that drug and the valerian, it might be enough to knock him out if he finished the serving. If nothing else, though, it would make him drowsy and he wouldn't be able to think clearly for much longer. Even groggy, he would be dangerous, so either way, I'd have to wait until he was asleep to get the bracelet out of his sporran.

Suddenly, he started coughing hard and banged on his chest with his fist. He spat back into the bowl, then stuck his finger in his mouth and pulled out a stem from one of the herbs I'd put in. "Good God, Woman," he said, stifling another cough and hocking at the back of his throat. "Do you not cut things up?" He tossed the bowl with the remainder of its contents onto the floor, too fast for me to see how much of it he'd eaten. A small amount of liquid splashed across the dirt floor and a few chunks of vegetable bounced off in various directions. "I think I'd rather starve than eat any more of that crap." He wiped his sleeve across his mouth and shuddered. "Now, I remember why I eat at the tavern most of the time."

I got up and started to pick up the bowl, spoon, and bits of food he'd chucked on the floor. I guessed he'd finished more than half of the bowl. It wasn't ideal, but only time would tell how effective it would be.

I took the mess back to the table and picked up the jug of mead. If he kept drinking alcohol, it would help. I carried it over and topped up his horn again, but I was disappointed to see he had slowed down with his drinking and it was still two-thirds full. As I put the jug back, Ailig sat back in his chair and eyed me up and down. I knew the look and quickly tried to think of a way to distract him from the next thing I knew he'd demand of me.

"I'll just refill the jug," I said, lifting it and making for the door.

"It's full enough," he barked. I stopped and slowly returned the jug to its place on the table. "Sit," he said, indicating the chair next to his in front of the hearth. His eyes followed me as I walked as slowly as I thought I could get away with and lowered myself onto the seat.

The fire was warm against my legs and I stared into the dancing flames for a few seconds. If Ailig hadn't shown up tonight, Ualan would have his bracelet back by now, and Ailig's fate would have been all but sealed. I gave him a sideways glance and noticed he was still watching me.

He squeezed the bridge of his nose between his thumb and finger and shook his head. "You know, I can't stop thinking about your little adventure," he muttered. "What doesn't sit right with me is how you took the risk to creep into Ualan's house and search for that bracelet, but didn't take anything else of value which you might have come across."

"I thought it would be pushing my luck to take anything else," I muttered.

"I don't believe it," he said, rubbing his head again and squinting at me. "You took one of the most valuable items in his house. Possibly the most valuable item. You were pushing your luck as it was. What difference would it have made to take a few other things?"

"I'm telling you, I didn't," I insisted.

"And I said I don't bloody believe it," he snapped. "If you have anything else, you better tell me right now, because so help me, Woman, I will turn this place upside down, and when I find what else you've hidden from me, you'll get a hiding which will make all the others seem like playful tickles!" He stood up suddenly, drank the mead which was left in his horn, then dropped it on the floor.

I stood up too and backed away from him. "Ailig, I swear it. You can search the entire cottage, barn, stable, everywhere, but you won't find anything because the bracelet is all I took. I don't know how else I can prove that to you." He started advancing on me and I tried to think of what else I could say to convince him. "I didn't take anything else because I felt it would be wrong!" I added quickly. "I didn't feel bad about the bracelet because it was yours. Ualan took it from you, so I was just taking it back."

He stopped in front of me, breathing hard and swaying slightly. A sheen of sweat had broken out over his brow and he blinked several times and squinted at me. "A thief with morals," he snarled.

"Why don't we go to bed," I said. He looked like he was about to pass out, and I hoped if he lay down it would encourage him to nod off. "You don't look well. Come and lie down, and I'll rub your feet." I tried to walk towards the bed, but he sidestepped me and blocked my route.

"Probably your disgusting stew which has poisoned me," he sneered. "But why don't you lie down. I'm in the mood for more than a foot rub, Woman."

I cracked a nervous smile and sidled my way around the other side of the hearth, putting the fire and the cauldron between us. He watched me as I walked, still breathing heavily and now sweating profusely. He looked very unsteady on his feet and I felt fairly confident if I ran, he would not be in any shape to follow. The bracelet was still in his sporran, though, and I needed to get it before I left.

Using my best sultry voice, I said, "Why don't you take your clothes off first and lie down. Let me take the lead for once." I hoped the idea might be appealing to him, but his top lip curled up into a contemptuous sneer.

"Since when do you tell me what to do?" he said, lunging towards me. His movement was much faster and more coordinated than I had anticipated, and it took me by surprise. I realised, in that moment, I had seriously misjudged how capable he was, and before I could back out of his reach, he grabbed me. I struggled against him, but his grip was solid and he forced me down onto the floor, then straddled himself over my hips.

"Please, stop!" I tried to fight him off with my hands and clawed at his face as he fumbled to grab my wrists.

"Keep still!" he growled. I struggled harder, refusing to submit to him. Then his fist came down and impacted the side of my head with a thick, heavy thud. There was a loud ringing in my ears and everything went black. I felt my arms fall to my sides, and I was vaguely aware of him pulling open my bodice and my body being jerked as he loosened my skirts and yanked down on them.

The blow had forced my head to the side. I could taste blood in my mouth, and my neck burned where the muscles had been overstretched. The blurry flames of the fire danced hotly a few feet in front of my face, and as my vision slowly cleared, I could see something else lying on the floor, just within the reach of my outstretched arm.

The glow of the fire was reflected beautifully on its polished surface, and as I felt my skirt yanked off and his hands start to ride up the bottom of my chemise, I stretched my fingers out and fastened them around its smoothness. I could hear him grunting as he cleared all obstacles which were in the way of his intent, and I turned my head slowly and stared up at his sweaty face, which was red with irrepressible lust. His teeth were gritted together, and spittle dripped from his lower lip. He was like an animal.

Time seemed to slow down as I let what was happening to the rest of my body sink away into a void of nothingness, and I directed all of my focus on the side of his temple. I tightened my grip around the ivory coloured bone, and in a single motion, put everything I had into my arm and swept it round in an arc until the horn met with the side of his head with a sickening crack. His hands instantly fell to his sides, and I shoved him backwards as he toppled off me. I had hit him with the edge of the drinking side, and the gash it left in his temple instantly began to bleed profusely. I dropped the horn and staggered to my feet, my ears still ringing. Then I doubled over and vomited on the floor next to him.

When the heaving ceased, I straightened up and stared dizzily down at him. He lay on his back, moaning and cursing, and his hands rose up to his head slowly.

"You'll never touch me again, you bastard!" I tried to make my voice strong, but my head throbbed. I felt nauseated, and the room spun. I had not knocked him out, and he was already rolling onto his side, trying to get up. If I was still in the room when he got to his feet, I knew he'd kill me.

He slowly pushed himself up onto his hands and knees, blood dripping from his head onto the floor, and his bare, hairy arse pointed at me where he'd pulled his kilt up. At that moment, I was filled with a murderous hatred for the man, and I did the only thing I could think of to slow him further and give myself time to get away. I gripped the edge of the chair beside me for stability, pulled my leg back and swung it forward, up between his legs, with all the force I could put behind it. Dizzy as I was, my foot met its mark, and I felt the soft flesh of his scrotum compress with velocity between his groin and the top of my foot. The pressure felt hugely satisfying and in one instant he went rigid and collapsed back onto the floor, drawing his knees up and choking. The veins in his neck protruded, and he rolled back onto his side, clutching himself between his legs, paralysed and unable to speak or even breathe.

I didn't wait around to see how long it would take him to recover. I staggered to the door, pushed it open, and stumbled into the dim twilight.

Chapter Twenty-Seven

ANNA

"I said, what's the matter, Mam?" Florie asked, sitting down next to me on the bed.

I snapped out of my daze and looked up at her. The glow of the fire in the hearth gave extra light to the shelter and painted a pleasant orange glow across my daughter's concerned face. The sky had become overcast during the course of the early evening and there was now an ominous darkness outside.

"What?" I said to Florie.

She sighed wearily, and I wondered if that was how I looked when Florie didn't listen to me.

"I said," she repeated patiently, "what is wrong? You look completely out of sorts. Did you not have a nice day?"

I took a deep breath and rubbed my hands over my face, trying to wash away the sickening feeling of foreboding which had settled around me like a thick fog. "Of course I had a good day," I said, forcing a smile.

"Then what's wrong? You've been off all night. Longer than that, actually. You were acting miserable even when Katherine was here."

"I'm fine," I said, obstinately. "Just worried, I suppose, in case Ailig finds out we spent the day together. I don't want Katherine to get in trouble." It was the best excuse I could give, and it was partially true.

Florie reached out with her small hand and patted me on the leg reassuringly. "You don't have to worry about that. How will he find out? No one is going to tell him, are they?"

I had to genuinely smile at my nearly eight-year-old, who was now so frequently taking on the role of comforting and looking after me. Sometimes it bothered me how she'd had to grow up so abruptly since Robert died, but at other times, like this one, it made me proud that she was becoming so confident and capable.

"You're right, sweetheart," I said. "You know me, though. I like to worry."

She gave me another pat and then got up to bank the fire.

"While you're up, can you put another chunk of peat on, please?" I said.

She looked back at me questioningly. "Why? It's warm. We don't really need it through the night, do we?"

"I'm not ready to go to sleep yet, and it's a bit darker than usual out there, so I'd prefer to have the light for now," I said. In reality, I had no intention of sleeping tonight until Katherine came over and told me things had gone according to plan, so I was prepared to stay up quite late.

I'd spent some of the early evening, hanging around outside, next to the ruins, watching to see when she would leave, but when Florie started to get exasperated, I went back into the shelter to spend time with her. I had no idea when Katherine had left, or when she might be back, but she'd promised she'd come after the job was done. The waiting was driving me mad, however, and though I knew it was pointless, I was strongly tempted to sneak over to Katherine's cottage, just to check and make sure she hadn't already gone home and forgotten to tell me she'd made it back.

Florie didn't argue and dutifully placed the extra fuel on the fire, then came and sat down with me again.

"Do you fancy a game of backgammon?" I asked her, thinking it might take my mind off things for a while. Florie yawned but nodded, and I collected the game from the back wall where it was stored, and we set up the board.

The sky darkened further with heavy grey clouds, and a light pattering of rain began to come down outside. We played several rounds, and I made sure to let Florie win most of them. Usually I struggled to do that, even with my own daughter, but my usual competitive urges had been overshadowed by nervous apprehension. The game seemed to play itself, and I struggled to feign enthusiasm at Florie's victories or mock frustration at my losses, and my mood was clearly affecting my daughter, who soon got bored and announced she was tired and going to sleep.

I wasn't sure what time it was, but the sky was quite dark, which made me think it was one or two hours before midnight. Florie was lying motionless in the bed with her eyes closed, and I walked to the front of the shelter and stared outside. It annoyed me that I couldn't see Katherine's cottage from here and would need to walk back to the ruins to get a clear view. I gave another glance back at Florie to make sure she definitely was asleep, then stepped outside. I was thirsty, and a mug of mead would help to calm my nerves, so I decided to walk over to the barrel next to the woodshed to get some. Then perhaps I might see if there was any light coming from Katherine's cottage, or maybe I might just walk over there and check to see if she was back yet.

Making the best excuses I could think of to justify leaving the shelter, I grabbed a mug and set out towards the woodshed, which was situated near to the ruined longhouse. I walked quickly, wanting to avoid getting too wet. The rain wasn't heavy yet, but from the looks of the sky and the faint sound of thunder in the distance, there was a lot more on its way. When I got there, I lifted the lid of the mead barrel and filled up my mug. I drank about half as I replaced the barrel lid and then turned to look across the pasture towards Katherine's cottage. As I squinted through the dim light and haze of precipitation, my heart skipped a beat. I could see what looked like a figure, halfway between my longhouse and Katherine's, staggering in my direction. I lowered the mug and kept staring, my heart rate rising as I recognised the shape of Katherine.

Dropping the mug, I dashed out over the pasture towards her, unsure if she'd noticed me or not. When I reached her, she just about collapsed into my arms. Even in the low light, I could see she had been badly hurt. There was blood around her mouth and the side of her head was swollen and red under her damp hair. She was in her chemise, which was crumpled and filthy and splattered with a few spots of blood, and her stay had been pulled apart at the front.

"My God, Katherine, what happened?" I said, hooking her arm around my neck and propping her up.

"We have to get away," she gasped. She was breathing hard. "He'll kill me!"

"Ualan?" I said, shocked. She was still pushing forward, towards my croft, so I moved along with her, supporting as much of her weight as I could.

"Ailig," she gasped. "He came home. He found the bracelet." She was trying to catch her breath between each short phrase. "He's coming, Anna. He'll kill me. We have to get away."

I looked behind us and could not see anyone following, but I still picked up the pace and hurried Katherine back to the shelter.

Once I got her inside by the fire, the extent of the damage was far more obvious. Her lip was cut, and the water from the rain had created several tiny, bright red streams which travelled down her chin and neck and onto her chest. Her right eye had haemorrhaged. She was as pale as death, and the swelling on the right side of her head was extensive. As I sat her down, she leaned forward and retched, bringing up a mouthful of bile.

"Oh, God, Katherine," I said, rubbing her back and panicking. "What do you need me to do? How can I help?" If I had a horse, I would ride us into town, but she was in no condition to walk that far.

"I'm so sorry, Anna," she said, after she'd finished coughing and heaving. Her voice was strangled and coarse, and tears ran down her cheeks. "I was so stupid."

"No," I said quickly, taking her face in my hands and kissing her head. My own eyes were welling up and I couldn't afford to break down. I needed to know what was happening.

"Where is Ailig?" I said. Florie was sitting up in her bed now, rubbing her eyes.

"He's at the cottage," Katherine said shakily. "I hurt him when he tried too... But he's coming. We need to leave, now."

I looked over to Florie, whose face was now stricken with fear as she saw Katherine.

"Florie, get up now," I said quickly, beckoning her over. She hurried over and crouched down next to Katherine, her lip quivering.

"Florie," I said again, grabbing her face and making her look at me. "I need you to be brave. Katherine is hurt. She can't run, but you can. I need you to run to Faolan's house and get him. Do you understand? Faster than you've even run before. Can you do that?" Florie let out a choked sob, and the tears splashed down her face.

"It's a long way, Mammy," she said, gripping my wrists in her small hands.

I pulled her into a hug and squeezed her tightly. "I know, darling. I know it's very far, and it's raining. But Faolan has a horse and he can get back here much faster. But you need to run, sweetheart. Alright? You need to get there as fast as you can. And listen; this is very important. Tell Faolan he needs to bring help - Ailig is trying to hurt us. And you stay with your aunty Alis. Don't you come back here with him. Do you understand?" She sobbed again and shook her head, more tears trailing down her cheeks. "Florie, you must!" I said again quickly.

"He'll hurt you," she sobbed. "I want to stay and help."

I took her face in my hands again. "Florie, I promise, I won't let Ailig hurt me or Katherine. I'll take care of us both. I swear I will. You can help by getting Faolan. Remember Daddy? No one could help him and we lost him. But this time you are here, and you can run for help. Will you do that for Katherine?"

Florie, still shaking with sobs, looked at Katherine, then nodded.

"Good," I said, wiping the tears from her eyes. "Good girl." I grabbed her shoes and deftly tied them to her feet, then grabbed her cloak from the back of the room and pulled it over her shoulders. I hugged her tightly again and kissed her cheek repeatedly. "You must go now. It's faster if you cut over the pastures." She nodded again, a new expression of determination crossing her face. "I love you," I said as she backed out of the shelter, into the rain.

"I love you, Mammy," she said, then turned and ran off.

I bent back down to Katherine and brushed the hair out of her face. She had her eyes half closed, and her head hung down.

"Katherine," I said, lifting her chin. "Talk to me, please."

She shook her head slowly. "I'm so sorry, Anna. I ruined everything."

"Don't say that," I said. "Everything will be alright."

"He's coming," she whispered.

"I know."

"He'll kill me this time."

"No, he won't. I won't let him touch you," I said, firmly. Though my heart was thumping, and I had no idea how I would follow through with that promise. "Come and sit on the bed, you can lean against the wall." I pulled her to her feet and sat her down on the makeshift mattress at the back of the shelter, then covered her with my blanket. It wasn't particularly cold. The air was heavy and humid, but she was damp and in shock. "You said you hurt him? How badly?" I asked. I needed to know what I would be dealing with once he arrived, and I guessed she must have delivered some significant damage or he would have been right behind her when I'd found her.

"Not badly enough," she said. Weak as her voice was, there was an edge of bitterness to it. "I hit him over the head with his horn and kicked him in the sack. It won't keep him down for long."

"Alright, that's something," I said, standing up. I hurried over to the other wall and picked up one of the logs which had been put aside for the fire, silently thanking God that I'd asked Florie to put the peat on the fire earlier and not the wood.

The log was slightly thicker than my wrist and I brandished it tightly and passed a few practise swings through the air. I hoped that Katherine was wrong, that Ailig would have just given up and gone to bed after the blow to his head, because even if he was injured, I didn't think much of my chances in hand to hand combat with him.

Even if Florie ran the entire two miles to Faolan's house, it would be at least forty minutes before he would get back here, and if Ailig was set on coming after Katherine, the chances were he would arrive long before Faolan did. I didn't really believe Florie would fetch Faolan in time, and a large part of the reason why I had sent her to her uncle's was to get her out of harm's way.

Katherine stood herself up slowly, letting the blanket fall away back to the floor. "Give me one of those too," she said, pointing at the club I was holding. She looked menacing with her bright red eye, but her face was still deathly pale. "We stand a better chance if we're both armed."

I hesitated, wanting to tell her to sit back down and rest, but she was right. Even if she couldn't wield it very effectively, two people with clubs were better than one. I picked up a slightly smaller log and brought it over to her.

"If he comes, I'll try to talk him down," I said. "We only fight as a last resort."

"He won't be talked down," she said resolutely. "You didn't see him. He had murder in his eyes."

"Did he take the bracelet?" I asked.

"He caught me wearing it when I was about to leave. He just showed up, said he came back to check on me. I had to tell him I'd stolen it from Ualan. I tried to drug him so I could get it back and follow through with the plan, but he didn't get enough of the laudanum to knock him out. He got nasty, and I resisted him. I should have just let him. I know it was a mistake to fight back. I just couldn't bear to let him touch me this time."

"You did what you had to do," I said, leaning against the wall next to her. "Don't apologise for it. It wasn't your fault."

Then I walked over to the entrance of the shelter, still brandishing my club, and cautiously looked outside towards the ruins. The rain had picked up now and was coming down hard, and the sporadic thunder claps were getting louder. Lightning streaked down from the sky in the distance, lighting up the open yard between the shelter and the longhouse.

"I still don't see him," I said. "Maybe he did just pass out back at your cottage."

"That would be too easy," Katherine said, using her club to prop herself up.

"If I could get to your stables, I could bring Ailbeart and we could get away on him. Ride to Faolan's house." I said, looking back at her. "I could also look inside the cottage and see if Ailig is conscious. If he's passed out, I could try and get the bracelet back. Does he have it on him?"

"No," she said quickly. "I mean, yes, it's on him. But don't go. It's too dangerous. Please, just stay here and wait for Faolan."

I leaned out, large droplets of rain splashed onto my nose and the front of my face. "If he was going to come after you, I think he would have by now," I said, feeling more confident. "How about I just look in through the window to see if he's still there?" I looked back at Katherine again to see her shaking her head, about to plead with me not to go, when an arm thrust out from around the corner and yanked the club out of my hands.

I staggered back into the shelter in shock as Ailig stepped from behind the wall and came into view at the side of the entrance. He was saturated, and the side of his face glistened bright red with blood which dripped off the bottom of his chin and onto his soaked white shirt. He sneered as he tapped the club he had just relieved me of, up and down into the palm of his opposing hand. He tutted at me and shook his head as he walked into the shelter.

Even as I backed away, I could see he still wasn't altogether steady on his feet. He swayed slightly and his wet hair lay flat against his head, dripping down his face. The laudanum would have dampened any pain he might otherwise have been in, but it would also make his reactions slow. He was breathing deeply as he advanced, his eyes flashing from me to Katherine.

"How did I know you'd come running here?" said he quietly, directing his question at Katherine. "You are just so pathetically predictable," he continued, still swatting the club into his hand threateningly. Katherine held her club up in front of her, trying to ward off Ailig, and he stopped for a moment and gave a condescending laugh. "I'm happy to see you still have some fight left in you, Woman. It always makes things more fun."

The way Ailig looked at Katherine was the same way I imagined he looked at every one of the women he'd raped during the raids. He enjoyed terrifying her and it was clear it excited him. I looked over to the small pile of logs where there was only one left which would have been suitable as a mildly effective weapon.

Ailig followed my gaze and then looked back at me. A dangerous smile pulled at his lips and he stopped tapping his club and stood still. "Go on then," he said. "Go and take one. I won't stop you."

I stood frozen to the spot, unsure what game he was playing. Then he walked over to the pile, picked up the branch I was looking at, and tossed it across the room to my feet. "See? I'll give you a fair chance. Otherwise it's too easy," he said. He looked at Katherine again. "Are you watching? First, I'm going to teach your meddling friend a lesson, because the last one I dealt out was clearly not enough. Then I'll get back to you."

"Don't you touch her," Katherine hissed.

His smile disappeared, and he held the club up and pointed it at her. "What have I told you about trying to tell me what to do?" he snapped.

I bent down slowly and picked up the log he had thrown towards me. It wasn't very heavy and wouldn't stand up to the thicker one he was holding, but then he wouldn't have given it to me if he thought I could do any real damage with it.

My movement caught his eye, and he turned back to me again and grinned. "That's more like it," he said. "But you should hold it higher, like this." He lifted his club up, demonstrating, then took a step towards me.

Under the influence of the laudanum or not, the muscles in his arms bulged, and I knew from his confidence that he had done this plenty of times before. This was what he did. Revelled in giving his victims hope that they might have a chance, back them into a corner, force them into a confrontation on his terms, then watch the hope fade from their faces as he killed them. I knew that's what he planned to do to me, and it would give him all the more pleasure to do it in front of Katherine. A coldness crept through my body as I realised I could not beat him this way. If I tried to fight him here, with this pathetic stick, he'd win.

I'd never been so sure of anything in my whole life.

I stared back at him for what felt like an age, and he grinned, looking at me from under the damp fringe of his dark hair. I was sure he could see the shake in my arms and legs as he adjusted his grip on the club.

"Alright," I whispered, and raised the stick up above my head. "Is this right?"

His grin widened. "That's right. Tell me when you're ready." He twisted his hands around the base of the log he held, preparing himself.

I took two deep breaths and fixed him with a hard stare.

"I'm ready," I said, then flung the branch over my head directly at him.

Chapter Twenty-Eight

As soon as the branch left my fingers, I turned and ran out of the shelter. I heard him curse, and from the corner of my eye I saw him try to duck out of the way of the projectile, but the satisfactory thud and following grunt let me know I had hit him.

The rain lashed against my face as I raced around the side of the shelter and headed down the hill and into the valley. After a few seconds, I chanced a look over my shoulder, praying I had ticked him off enough to follow me. I'd counted on him giving chase and if he didn't, I would have to go back. I couldn't leave Katherine there, alone with him. His voice bellowed out and I could see him about fifty yards behind, staggering after me.

"I'll kill you, you goddamn whore!" His words were faint, the sound dampened by the rain and a loud crack of thunder followed them. I pumped my legs as hard as they would go and squinted through the water which was running into my eyes.

I could see the river had risen already, and the surface of the water shuddered and rushed under the shower which pelted it from above. I kept going until I reached the long reeds at the edge and then scanned up and down to find the place where Sim was buried, where the patch of thistles was planted. Ailig was further up the hill, but noticing I had stopped, he slowed down and strode towards me gripping the club.

I looked back along the bank again and spotted the grave, then ran along to it. Then I turned to face Ailig, who was still fast approaching. I backed myself through the long reeds; the water swelling up around my ankles and flowing steadily between them. With each step he took towards me, I shuffled backwards until the water was up to my knees and I felt the familiar steep drop off, just under my heels.

Ailig came up, stopping a few meters in front of me, breathing hard and baring his teeth. He was momentarily illuminated, and another crack of thunder rippled across the sky. As the current swept between my legs, I held my ground and faced him.

"Nowhere else to go," he shouted above the rain. He swapped the club back and forth between his hands. "I was going to make it quick, but now I'm really going to take my time and enjoy it." He took another two steps closer, closing the gap between us. I glanced behind me at the water, which was rapidly flowing downstream. A haze covered the surface where the rain lashed down and as I turned back to Ailig, he stepped closer again. He was now only a few feet away.

"Now, you'll see what happens to women who just won't stay out of trouble. And if you try to run again, I'll go back up there and play with Katherine instead." A bright flash lit up his malevolent leer and a loud crack of thunder instantly followed.

"I'm not going to run," I shouted, piercing him with the bravest stare I could manage.

"Very brave," he said with a twisted grin. He stepped forward again, but when his foot submerged into the water, he stopped and hesitated for a moment, glancing down. The smirk left his face and his eyes betrayed a momentary flash of fear. He looked back at me again and resumed his sneer. "I expect you think being brave will save you," he said, "but I've killed dozens of women, and many of those fought bravely. Some ran, like you, but they all met the same end, eventually." He lifted the club and pointed it at me again. It hovered only a foot from my chest. "And I've been looking forward to yours," he added.

I lifted my chin defiantly, trying not to reveal my fear. He was bigger, stronger and faster than me, but if he would just come a little closer, I could make those things count for nothing.

Over Ailig's shoulder, I could see the outline of a figure making its way down the hill through the rain. My pulse quickened again as I realised Katherine had followed us. I could not afford to have his attention drawn away from me. If he went after her now, my plan would fall apart.

"Because I called you a coward?" I taunted, glaring at him. "You're going to kill me because I called you out in front of everyone?"

Katherine was closer now, and I could see she was dragging along the log I'd given to her earlier. My words had the desired effect, and his face split into an angry snarl.

"I'm going to kill you because you're a meddling whore who can't keep out of other people's business." He lurched forward, swinging the club at my chest, but he was still two inches out of reach. I leaned away from him as much as I could, but didn't try to step back. I needed him to come closer, but he was up to his calves in the water now and another flash of panic crossed his face as he swung his arms out, trying to regain his balance after he missed his swing at me.

"I meant what I said that day. You are a coward," I shouted, trying again. I cast him a look of bitter disdain. "And everyone else in the clan knows it, too. You stand there and point your club at me, trying to frighten me with your empty threats! But you couldn't kill me before, and you lack the backbone to do it now!"

He leered and made to move towards me, but again, stopped and looked down as the water rushed up around his knees. If he swung at me now, he might just hit me, but he still wasn't as close as I wanted him.

Katherine had made her way right behind Ailig, but I didn't look directly at her for fear of giving her away. I kept my eyes glued on Ailig's and broke into a derisive laugh. "Look at you. You're pathetic!" I shouted. "The great warrior Ailig, afraid of a few inches of water!"

He was struggling to mask his fear now, but the fury in his face was unmistakable. His chest heaved and I could see there was a war waging inside him between his fear and his rage. "Don't push me, Woman. So help me, I'll—" He stopped, mid-threat, as his foremost leg sunk further down and he broke eye contact with me again. His gaze was pointed downwards at the water rushing between his legs, and I could see the terror inside him taking over. He swung the log at me again, but the attempt was graceless and lacked the passion of before, the tip of the log only just grazing the front of my dress. Standing directly behind him, Katherine had now raised her own weapon above her and held it hovering over the back of Ailig's head.

I shook my head at him and grinned tauntingly, but under the water, I was teetering on the very edge of the drop-off and struggling to maintain my balance. "I think that's exactly what you need, Ailig!" I shouted. Then I looked directly at Katherine and added, "One big push!"

Too late it dawned on Ailig that something else was going on. Following my gaze, he turned to look behind him, but at that moment, Katherine brought the club down hard. The log met with his skull with a heavy 'thunk' and he staggered towards me, dropping his club, his eyes rolling back. Before he had the chance to recover, I lunged forward and grabbed the front of his shirt, then yanked on him, pulling him towards me. I took a deep breath as he fell over the ledge with me, into the deep, cold, rushing water.

Ailig was still for a few seconds as we sunk into the dark torrent, and I clung onto him and wrapped my arms as tightly as I could around his waist. Then I felt his panic set in and he struggled, thrashing his arms and legs as he tried to claw his way to the surface. His terror was his worst enemy here, though, and his movements were ineffective and uncoordinated.

I held fast, wrapping my legs around his to inhibit him further. His heavy woollen kilt also pulled him down and created significant drag, and we were swept along together through the cold darkness. He writhed and tried to push me away from him, but his movements were panicked and indecisive, as if part of him wanted to be free of me, but another still wanted to cling on to something. I could hear his screams under the water as he expelled precious oxygen, but it did nothing to weaken my resolve to see this through.

I wanted him to feel the same hopeless terror that he had inflicted on so many others, and I pictured Katherine's battered face as I squeezed my arms around him harder and focused on controlling my own heart rate. I needed to make my lungful of air outlast his, because I refused to let go until I was sure it would be too late for him. My still bruised stomach hurt with the effort and my chest ached as the urge to go back to the surface intensified, but it wasn't until I felt his body go limp and then spasm, that I released my grip and kicked up to the surface.

I gasped and spluttered as I broke through and kicked my way to the bank, which was still sweeping past me at a rapid rate. I could see the familiar bend in the river coming up in the distance and I swam hard towards it, reaching for the partially submerged grass and reeds. The river was not as high as it had been the last time I was in this position. I could feel the bottom with my feet now, and this time I wasn't struggling to pull another body from the water, so my hands easily gripped a clump of reeds as they swept by.

Clinging to the foliage, with the water flowing around me, I dragged myself up the mild incline of the muddy bank and crawled a few feet clear of the water. I collapsed onto the grass, still trying to catch my breath, and rolled onto my back, letting the rain fall down on my face.

After a few minutes, I heard the anxious calls of my name come from further upstream and as I sat myself up, I could see Katherine making her way towards me.

"I'm here!" I called out, waving my arm above my head. The rain was lightening up again and the occasional cracks of thunder were lacking their former intensity. As she came closer, I smiled at the look of relief on her face and she flopped down on the grass next to me.

"You're alright," she gasped. She wore a look that was new to me, something between disbelief and cautious optimism.

"Of course I am." I gave her an encouraging smile and brushed a few wet strands of hair out of her face. The blood had washed away from her mouth, but her eye would take some time to heal, and the side of her face was still swollen. I consoled myself in the thought that this would be the last time I'd have to see her like this.

"Ailig?" she said, looking concerned.

I shook my head. "Halfway to the loch by now." She still looked afraid. I took her hand in mine, realising I must have been much colder than I felt because her fingers felt warm in mine. "He's gone, Katherine. He'll never hurt you again. I made sure of it."

The rain on her face masked her tears, but I could tell she was crying. She closed her eyes and sighed, then leant her forehead on my shoulder. I wrapped my arms around her and held her close, pressing my lips against the exposed skin of her shoulder.

Chapter Twenty-Nine

KATHERINE

The door banged open suddenly, and Florie came running into the cottage as I stoked the fire under the cauldron. It needed to be kept hot in order to heat the massive portion of stew, which came almost up to the brim of the pot. It had not yet started to give off any tantalising smells, but as long as the fire stayed strong, it wouldn't be too much longer. I had put two rabbits into it, generous helpings of kale, potatoes, turnips, cabbage and several handfuls of various herbs I'd collected earlier in the day. I'd probably got carried away with the amount I was cooking, but then there were a lot of people to feed.

"Ualan's coming!" Florie gasped. She was breathing hard, and I guessed she must have run over from Anna's longhouse.

"What? Now?" I said, putting the poker down and trying to calm the knots which had tied themselves in my tummy. The door opened again and Anna came in behind Florie, looking anxious.

"Don't worry," she said. "We've been over this dozens of times. It'll go just fine. Just say what we talked about."

I nodded and took a long, calming breath. "How far away is he?" I asked her.

"He'll be here in a couple of minutes," Anna said. "Just stay calm and I'll be outside if you need me, but I know you'll be fine. Come on, Florie." Anna grabbed Florie by the wrist and, giving me another wink, she pulled the reluctant child back outside with her. I could hear Florie complaining and Anna shushing her before the door closed behind them and I prepared myself for Ualan's visit.

I went over the story Anna and I had practised over the last two days and avoided second-guessing it any more. Anna was right, it would be fine. But this was the last stage of a journey which had been stressful and dangerous, and while I wanted it out of the way, I had also been dreading going through it.

The night Ailig had gone into the river, Faolan had arrived at Anna's croft nearly twenty minutes after I had found Anna alive, having pulled herself from the water. We'd gone back to the shelter, and he'd arrived shortly thereafter with two of his sons, but by then the need for help was gone, and we had ended up explaining what had happened. Anna did most of the talking, which I was glad about, and told Faolan that Ailig had come home early from his hunting trip and lost his temper after getting drunk. After he hit me, I'd ran to Anna for help. When it came to the river, Anna adjusted the story slightly, saying we had both run from him and swam across, trying to get to safety, but he had followed and been swept away. Concerned that we might be accused of murdering Ailig, Faolan said he would tell Ualan that he arrived just in time to see Ailig wading into the river after us.

"I'll even tell Ualan, I shouted at Ailig to stop, but he wouldn't listen," Faolan had said to us on the night. Anna had been so grateful and Faolan had insisted it was a small lie, but the least he could do to help. "If I'd got there faster, then the whole incident might have been avoided," he'd said. Though both of us were secretly elated that things had worked out the way they did.

We knew Faolan had later shared a brief version of this story with Ualan, and he'd reported back to us that Ualan planned to take a party of men to find the body in the lock. We had no idea if they would be successful, but after two days of searching, Faolan brought news that the body had been recovered this morning. This meant Ualan would most likely have found the bracelet in his sporran and would have questions about it and possibly also about the wounds to the side and back of Ailig's head.

Over the last two and a half days, Anna and I had discussed at length the possibility of this happening and came up with a story to cover both eventualities. Now, I just had to deliver the explanations calmly, without looking guilty. We had decided to stick as closely to the truth as possible if we were questioned about the head wounds. With the gash on the side of his head, I was going to say I had hit him with the horn in an attempt to defend myself after he'd struck me. The wound on the back of his head, if indeed there even was an obvious one, could be put down to hitting himself on a rock or a branch as he was swept downstream, and we decided I would simply deny any knowledge of how he might have sustained that one. But it was the bracelet that I was really nervous about. That explanation was going to be harder to get Ualan to believe. I was running over it one more time in my head when a loud knock came at the door.

"Come in," I called out, then had to clear my throat because my mouth had gone dry.

Ualan stepped inside, ducking slightly to get under the door frame. He looked a little uncomfortable and had his thumbs tucked into the waistband of his breeches.

"Hello, Katherine," he said.

"Hello, Ualan."

He stood in silence for a few moments, drumming his fingers against his hips and looking like he was struggling over where to start. I walked over to the table and gestured for him to sit, which he quickly did.

"Um, I just came over to offer you my sincerest condolences," he said as he sat down. "I can imagine how difficult the last few days must have been for you."

"Thank you, Ualan," I said. I did my best to look appropriately heartbroken over my husband's demise, but was careful not to overdo it, as it was fairly common knowledge that the grief of his loss would pass quickly.

"I expect you heard we found his body this morning?" he asked, looking up at me.

"Faolan told me," I said. Then, because it seemed like a question I should be asking, "Can I see him?"

Ualan shuffled uncomfortably in his chair and interlocked his fingers, then stared down at them. "I wouldn't recommend it," he said. "His condition is... deteriorated. The fish and eels... you know, they—" he sighed and pursed his lips, not wanting to finish.

I nodded. "I understand," I said.

"I have asked my wife and daughter to clean and wrap his body. If you want to be involved with that, of course I wouldn't stop you, but I thought you might find it difficult, considering the circumstances." He gave me a questioning look, and I noticed he seemed to have trouble looking me directly in the eye. I couldn't see my eyes, but according to Florie, my right one looked quite frightening. I nodded again.

He went on. "I have also instructed a few of the young men to dig a plot at the burial site so we can put him in the ground tomorrow, if you are happy to do the service then?"

"Yes, that's fine," I said, quietly.

"Do you have anything in particular you might want to send with him?" he asked.

I shook my head.

"Alright."

There was a long moment of silence as I waited for what I knew he was burning to ask.

"His clothing is in reasonable condition, so will be returned to you, but when we removed them, something was discovered in his sporran which I had hoped you might be able to help explain."

I gave him a well practised, quizzical look, and in response his hand disappeared under the table for a few moments, then came back up holding the bracelet which he placed between us.

"Oh," I said, concentrating everything I had on keeping my pulse steady and raising my hand to my mouth in my best enactment of a shocked expression. "Frang must have got it for him."

The comment had the exact effect Anna and I had hoped for.

Ualan looked genuinely surprised, clearly expecting an altogether different explanation. "Frang?" he said.

"Yes. Frang came over a few weeks ago to play cards with Ailig, shortly after you all got back from the raids. They were drinking a lot and talking, as they do. I didn't want to listen in, but they're so loud when they get drunk, I couldn't help it. Ailig was complaining bitterly about you having taken the bracelet." I looked at him apologetically.

"What did they say?" he said, leaning forward now.

"Frang asked Ailig how much he'd be willing to pay to get it back. I thought it was just harmless bluster, and they were drunk, so I didn't take too much notice. But Ailig said he'd trade all the rest of his loot for it, if that's what it took. Then Frang said he could get it for him." I looked at the bracelet lying on the table. "I guess he did."

Ualan shook his head. "That just sounds unbelievable," he said.

I shrugged. "It's just what I heard."

Ualan stared at the bracelet, mulling the story over, and I waited a few more seconds before I delivered the final damning comment.

"Frang said some other things I didn't take seriously at the time. But maybe if he took your bracelet, then the rest of what he said was true too."

Ualan's eyes darted back up at mine. "What else did he say?"

"He said he'd taken things before, that it was easy. One item he was particularly proud of was a dagger belonging to Artur. He said he had a special hiding place under his bed; a trapdoor where he kept his treasures. That's what I remember him saying, but whether it's true or not..." I shrugged again and looked back up at Ualan, whose face had darkened. He took a deep breath and nodded slowly, then stood up. "I'm so sorry, Ualan. I just thought they were blustering. I didn't think for a second it meant anything, otherwise I would have come to you."

He put up his hands to quieten me. "It's alright, Katherine. I appreciate you sharing this with me now. Have you mentioned this to anyone else?"

I shook my head. "Of course not. Ailig would have killed me if he thought I was repeating the things he'd said in drink."

"Good," Ualan said. "Please keep it to yourself for now. Can you do that?"

"Of course, Ualan." I nodded, also standing up.

He slid the bracelet off the table and pocketed it, then gave me an appreciative nod and walked back to the door. He paused as he put his hand on the latch. "I see Faolan and his boys are working on Anna's roof today?"

I looked over to the cauldron, which was full enough to feed an army, and nodded, smiling. "Yes, he's been very kind," I said. "We're having a gathering tonight and I made far too much food, so you're welcome to join us if you wish."

Ualan scratched the back of his neck. "I'm afraid I've got some things I have to deal with this evening," he said, his other hand going into the pocket he'd put the bracelet into. "But I'll send a few extra hands over to help with the roof, if that would be welcome?"

I had to suppress the smile which was forming on my lips as I nodded. "That would be very much appreciated. Thank you, Ualan."

He gave a small smile back and nodded again before walking out.

Epilogue

ANNA

It had been three weeks since Ailig had lost his life at the river. His burial had been an inauspicious event, attended by only a handful of people. As Tacksman, Ualan had to attend, and Katherine went along as the dutiful widow and later told me she had made an effort to look convincingly solemn, but failed in her efforts to shed even a single tear.

Her face had healed, and the small bump in her abdomen had grown significantly in the last month. Many well-meaning folk from the village made a point of patting her belly and offering encouraging words such as, "Well, take comfort that part of your husband will live on in his son." To which Katherine usually responded with something like, "Thank you, but I have a feeling this one is a girl."

"Though, even if this is a boy, we'll make sure he'll be nothing like his father," she'd said to me.

I'd pressed my hands against her belly and smiled, saying, "You're absolutely right, we will."

Faolan and his sons, along with several other men from the village, had helped to restore the roof of our longhouse. Ualan had even shown up on one of the days to personally pitch in with the work. He only stayed for a couple of hours, but the gesture had meant a lot. On that occasion, he'd made a comment to me, mentioning what a beautiful day it was and how he hoped next year's crop would be as good as this year's looked like it would be. That was the closest he came to telling me he'd had a change of heart about my lease, and when I hugged him, his face had turned bright red and he'd muttered something about needing to bring some more hay for the thatching, before hurrying off.

When the roof was finally repaired, small donations of items came in drips and drabs. Someone weaved a new mat for the floor. I was given another blanket by Agatha, and Katherine traded in some of Ailig's loot to have the horse plough mended.

Katherine came to live with us in our longhouse, much to my delight, and told Florie she would rather stay with us than live in the home she'd shared with Ailig.

After Katherine's performance, which I was sorry to have missed, the dagger was found in Frang's cottage and then returned to its owner after nearly thirty years. Whether it was found behind a trapdoor under his bed or elsewhere, we never knew, but it was found, along with several other valuable items of interest. The seriousness of his crimes required the assembly of a clan committee, over which the chief himself presided. The specifics of what was said during the hearing was kept confidential between the few senior clan members who comprised the panel of judges, and the common clan folk knew better than to pry, but the result was announced publicly.

We didn't know if Frang had accepted his fate, or vehemently professed his innocence, but he was sentenced to immediate exile, and his exportation to the Americas was swiftly arranged. Ualan made a point of announcing that his sentence had been lightened due to his age, and for the sake of his family, and would otherwise have been death by hanging. His wife, grown children and grandchildren were all given the option to leave all their assets and go with him, but even his wife declined the invitation, and he was sent away on his own.

It was the beginning of September and Katherine and I sat on the hillside, looking down into the valley as the sun was setting. Florie was in the cottage, having insisted she was going to make dinner by herself, now that she was eight, and Katherine and I had been instructed to stay out of the way. Katherine sat between my legs, with my arms wrapped around her and her hands on top of mine as they rested on her belly.

"Was that a kick?" I asked excitedly. Over the last week, she'd kept randomly squealing throughout the day and grabbing my hand to press it against the ever-growing bump, insisting the baby was moving and asking if I could feel it. I hadn't been able to until just now, and I grinned excitedly as I rested my chin on her shoulder.

"Hurray! You finally felt one!" she said, patting the back of my hand.

"Have you thought of any names yet?" I asked, enjoying the smell of her hair, which kept feathering against my face with the evening breeze.

"Well, I've thought of a couple of ideas, but I wanted to run them past you first," she said.

"Alright, what are they?" I asked, kissing her neck softly.

"Well, I was thinking Robert, maybe, if it's a boy?" she said.

"Beautiful name," I said, smiling. "And if it's a girl?"

"Rose."

I turned the name over a few times in my head. "I like it," I said. "It's beautiful, strong, resilient—"

"Kind of like you?" Katherine said, turning her head to kiss me back.

I smiled and kissed the corner of her lips. "Like us," I said.

Hope You Enjoyed It

Thank you for purchasing
Like the Down of a Thistle

I hope you enjoyed reading, and if you did, please
consider leaving a review.

It helps enormously.

Even a couple of sentences make a difference.

Thank you,
Love,
Sarah x